A FIRE IN THE BLOOD

"Listen to me," Jared said, seizing both her hands, "I don't care a damn about being a gentleman. I want to be your lover."

Desperately trying to pull her hands away, Diana gasped, "Please—I don't want . . ."

"Don't you?" Jared caught her in his arms, and, though she tried to twist away, his lips found hers in a kiss that released the pent-up desire that he'd been suppressing since her flight from the Royal Arms in Lichfield. For a moment her lips were unresponsive, and then, with a little sound that was half sob, half sigh, she slipped her arms around his neck and returned his kiss eagerly . . .

Lois Stewart

THE BARTERED BRIDE

ZEBRA BOOKS
KENSINGTON PUBLISHING CORP.

For Tony and the kids—
Thanks

ZEBRA BOOKS are published by

Kensington Publishing Corp.
850 Third Avenue
New York, NY 10022

First Printing: September, 1995

Printed in the United States of America

One

"Diana, do you really wish to dance anymore? It's such a frightful squeeze here tonight. We very nearly lost each other coming down the line in the last set!"

Diana, Lady Windham, glanced from her escort, Aubrey Dalton, to the mass of humanity in the ballroom situated beneath the vast dome of the Pantheon. Aubrey had just succeeded in extricating her from a crush of dancers to a less crowded spot near the entrance of the room.

It was not only a crowded, but a faintly disreputable scene. Most of the people wore some variation of fancy dress, ranging from simple dominoes to more exotic costumes, and had obviously come to the Pantheon, like Diana and Aubrey, to participate in a gala masquerade ball. Just as obviously, many of the gentlemen were in attendance, not to dance, but to fondle willing females, of whom there seemed to be a generous number present.

Diana winced as a vulgar-looking female nearby squealed in raucous enjoyment at the advances of a dashing Harlequin who had already removed her mask and whose hands were now burrowing underneath the folds of her garish domino.

"No, Aubrey, I *don't* wish to dance—or rather, attempt to dance—any more tonight," Diana said, fanning herself vigorously. Even though it was midwinter, the temperature of the ballroom had risen oppressively. A blaze of light from a myriad of candles in the elaborate chandeliers beat down on the overcrowded and perspiring occupants of the room. "Let's find Miles and go home."

"Oh. I'd hoped . . . Diana, can't we go somewhere for a quiet chat? It's been so long since we had an opportunity to talk privately. And the Pantheon has such a maze of rooms, surely we'll be able to find at least one that's unoccupied."

Diana sighed. She was tired and bored and much too warm, and yet she felt obliged to respond to the wistfulness in Aubrey's voice. "Just for a few minutes, then, and after that I really must go home to bed. I'm exhausted. Papa insisted that we come all the way from Oxfordshire to London in one day."

"I won't keep you too long," Aubrey promised. He tucked her hand under his arm and guided her through the congested corridors surrounding the ballroom, pausing to glance into a room here, a room there, until he found a small card room that was empty of players.

Breathing a sigh of relief to be out of contact with her fellow masqueraders, Diana took off her mask and pushed back the hood of her loose domino of heavy green satin. She felt a blessed current of cooler air on the nape of her neck. Smiling up at Aubrey, who had also removed his mask and pushed back the hood of his domino, she said, "Like most people, I find it hard to resist my brother Miles when he exerts his considerable charm. I should never have allowed him to persuade me to attend a masquerade ball at the Pantheon. The place is beginning to have a very common tone. Perhaps raffish is the better word."

Aubrey nodded. "I believe the management isn't doing very well. There are rumors about the sale of the lease. But don't blame poor Miles for inviting you here. The old fellow simply wanted to indulge you in a gala evening on your first visit to London in more than a year. He wanted to share your company. He's scarcely seen you for months. *I've* scarcely seen you. You've been immured almost like a cloistered nun at Abbottsleigh since—"

"Since my husband died."

Aubrey swallowed hard. He was a tall, slender man in his late twenties, fair-haired and gray-eyed, whose good looks had always depended more on a beguiling smile and charm of manner than on regularity of features. Diana had known him since he became a classmate of her brother Miles at Eton.

"You had no need to go into such deep mourning for that husband of yours," he said roughly. "You didn't care a pin for him. He was forty years older than you, and practically doddering. Everyone knows you only married him to haul your family out of the River Tick."

Diana lifted her chin. "My marriage to Roger—Lord Windham—wasn't a love match, certainly. It could hardly have been, considering the difference in our ages. However, Roger was a kind, honorable man, and I was deeply grateful to him for clearing Miles' debts."

"And your father's." Biting his lip, Aubrey seemed chagrined by his impulsive remark.

"Yes, and Papa's," Diana replied evenly.

Flushing, Aubrey said, "I'm sorry, Diana. I've no right to intrude into your personal affairs. It's just that—"

"It's just that you've been such a close friend to me and Miles for so many years." Diana flashed Aubrey a forgiving smile. "I understand why you're concerned."

Aubrey stepped up to her, placing his hands on her shoulders. His eyes kindling, he exclaimed, "A close friend? Good God, I've been much more to you than that, and well you know it. I was your lover. I wanted to marry you, though heaven knows I couldn't fault your father for discouraging my suit. I was a younger son with no prospects."

Diana made a slight effort to pull away. "That was all so long ago, Aubrey. You shouldn't brood about it."

"I'm not brooding. Because now I'm a much better catch. Remember my old uncle, the Nabob? He died last year. Left me a nice number of shares in the East India Company. Also there's a possibility that a vacancy will occur soon in the Company Court of Directors, and I'll be a candidate. I think I have a good chance, with my uncle's connections. Then there's my income from my position at the Treasury. I could support you now, at least in a modest style. We wouldn't starve. I haven't stopped loving you, Diana. I want you more than ever."

Aubrey's hands dropped to her waist, and he drew her close to him. He bent his head, pressing eager lips to her mouth. In a moment he recoiled as Diana braced her hands against his chest and tried to push him away from her.

"Diana . . . what is it?" he faltered as he stepped back from her. "You loved me once. I know you did. Your feelings can't have changed entirely." His mouth hardened. "I know what it is. Someone else caught your fancy while you were married to your ancient husband. Certainly you've had little opportunity to meet any eligibles this past year while you've been living in mourning in Oxfordshire."

"There isn't anyone else, Aubrey. And no, my feelings for you haven't changed. I'm very fond of you. It's just that it's too soon to think about getting married again. I haven't been a widow for even a year."

"Oh, I understand that you want to observe the *convenances*," Aubrey said quickly. "But if you're still fond of me, that's all that matters. Darling, I'm not asking you to set a date, or to make a public announcement. We could have a private engagement. No one would have to know about us."

Diana shook her head. "I'm sorry. I can't make you any promises. I told you, I'm not ready to consider another marriage." Possibly I never will be ready, she thought, but I can hardly tell Aubrey that.

She'd never been able to bring herself to tell anyone about the shambles of her marriage. Oh, Roger, Lord Windham, had indeed been the kind, honorable man she'd described to Aubrey. But Windham had also been an aging man who'd taken an eighteen-year-old bride to his bed in a desperate effort to revive his flagging sexual energies. For three years Diana had endured his fumbling, impotent attempts to make himself a whole man again. Now he was dead, and Diana sometimes felt sickened at the very thought of submitting her shrinking flesh to the touch of another male.

Catching Diana in his arms again, Aubrey exclaimed, "I'm willing to wait for as long as you want me to, if only you'll give me a little encouragement. Kiss me, Diana, and tell me I won't have to wait forever."

Averting her face, Diana said in a strangled voice, "Aubrey, how can I make myself any clearer? I don't want to kiss you, I don't want to become engaged to you. Please, just let me go."

His face flaming with mingled embarrassment and anger, Aubrey abruptly released her. "Of course. You surely can't think I'd force myself on you." He put on his mask and jerked his hood in place. "I'm sorry if my company has been unwelcome to you. Doubtless you'll wish to be alone for a spell. I'll wait for you in the foyer." His back stiff with offended dignity, he stalked to the door.

Diana watched him go with helpless regret. Was there something very wrong with her, that she equated Aubrey's boyish kisses with her husband's joyless, pathetic attempts to entice her to his bed?

"Beautiful ladies shouldn't be without an escort. May I offer my services?"

Diana tensed as the strange man entered the card room. "Thank you, I'd prefer to be alone," she began, and paused in mid-sentence. The tall stranger was the most magnificent-looking man she had ever seen. He wore an exotic Eastern costume, consisting of loose trousers in a brilliant red silk topped by a loose coat of crimson brocade embroidered in gold thread. His head was enveloped in a high, wrapped turban of gold cloth adorned with flashing jewels. Gold earrings and glittering neck chains set off his lightly tanned face with its straight severe features and startlingly blue eyes behind the bejeweled gold mask.

"Do you really mean that?" said the stranger, advancing into the room and taking off his mask. His voice had the faintest of accents, which Diana couldn't place. "Why would you wish to be alone on such a romantic evening?" He smiled, displaying perfect white teeth. "What would be the harm in our spending a few minutes together tonight? No need to commit ourselves. No names. No past. No future. Just the present. Two ships passing each other in the night."

Diana opened her mouth to order the impudent stranger to leave her. Then, as if mesmerized, seized by some wild instinct the like of which had never before disturbed her ordered existence, she heard herself saying in a bemused voice, "Perhaps you're right. What would be the harm?" She gazed at him, taking in every detail of his barbarically colorful costume. "You're dressed like a prince, sir. Are you a prince? And do you come from a foreign land?"

He laughed. "No, I'm not a prince. Perhaps you could say that I come from a foreign land. I'm from India, here to make my fortune."

"Or perhaps to make a conquest?" What am I saying, she thought in sudden panic. I'm flirting with the man.

"Would a conquest be possible?" He stepped closer, putting out a finger to touch the red-gold cluster of curls on the crown of her head. "Your hair is like spun silk," he murmured. His finger dipped lower to trace gentle patterns on her cheeks. "Your skin feels like velvet. And your eyes—they're like emerald pools. I'm drowning in them. And your lips—can they possibly taste as enticingly luscious as they look?"

Slowly he bent his head, his arms slipping around her waist as his mouth brushed hers in a feathery kiss that changed almost instantly from quicksilver to fire. A shiver of molten delight raced through Diana's body. She leaned into his embrace, feeling the hard taut body beneath the stiff brocade of his *chapkan.* A low moan of sheer physical pleasure rose from his chest, and the pressure of his mouth grew voracious.

When at last he raised his head, looking down at her out of eyes that glowed with a lambent blue flame, he said huskily, "I was wrong. I want more than a few minutes with you. More than the present. I want the future. Who are you, my beautiful one? Tell me your name. When can I see you again? When can I kiss you again?"

His voice broke the spell. Frantically Diana pushed against him, breaking the embrace. She fled to the door, fearful that if she lingered even a minute longer in the same room with the stranger prince she would be lost to the power of his sensuality.

Two

Jared Amberly lingered in the card room for a few moments. He knew it was useless to pursue the titian-haired beauty with the hauntingly sad eyes. He'd been too aggressive. He'd frightened her off. Shrugging, he adjusted the gold mask over his eyes and walked slowly into the passage and down the stairs, avoiding amorous couples and inebriated clowns and cavaliers. He stepped out under the portico of the main entrance to the Pantheon on Oxford Street, breathing in a welcome gust of cold fresh air, and walked halfway down the street to his waiting town carriage. The coachman, his face pinched-looking from the chill of the night, hastened from his box to open the door.

Jared relaxed against the squabs as the carriage traveled from Oxford Street into the heart of Mayfair, stopping at length in front of a house on Chesterfield Street in the vicinity of Berkeley Square. After he stepped down from the carriage, Jared paused to look up at his house with a distinct pride of ownership. It was a handsome Georgian house, no rival to the great Palladian expanse of Chesterfield House looming behind it, but still it was a substantial residence befitting a successful businessman and financier.

An alert-looking footman in a smart livery answered his knock immediately. Jared nodded to the servant and walked up the graceful curving staircase to his bedchamber on the floor above. As he opened the door a small woman rose from a chair near the fireplace, where banked coals shed a comfortable warmth into the room.

"Did you have a pleasant evening, Sahib?" asked the woman in Bengali.

"A most pleasant evening, Rana," replied Jared in the same language. He flashed her an affectionate smile. "It's very late. There was no need for you to wait up for me."

"I like to wait for you. Come, sit down, and let me help you with your turban."

Jared took a chair and sat quietly as Rana removed the jeweled ornaments from the turban and unwound the eight-foot length of gold cloth from his curling black hair. He watched her as she carefully folded the shimmering material. She was a pretty woman, her abundant dark hair worn in a simple knot at the nape of her neck, her slender figure enhanced by her graceful embroidered *sari*. She looked ageless. Indeed, Jared didn't know how old she actually was. She had been in his life as long as he could remember. She had been his mother's *ayah* in Calcutta.

After Rana had put away the turban material in the wardrobe she returned to Jared's side, deftly slipping the gold necklaces from around his neck. Then she knelt in front of him and began removing his embroidered red slippers with the pointed toes. He drew back his feet. "I can take off my own shoes."

"I know," she replied serenely, "but I like to help you dress and undress. After all, I've been doing it since you were a baby."

He laughed. "So you have." Jared rose, stripping off his voluminous *chapkan* and the thin linen shirt beneath it. Handing the garments to Rana, he said, "There. You can put these away and then I want you to go to bed and get some rest. I can certainly put myself to bed."

He was well aware that his proper English household, complete with butler and assorted maids and footmen, looked askance at his intimate domestic arrangements. He had no valet, nor had he brought with him from Calcutta any of his male personal servants. Rana was in charge of his clothing and his personal hygiene. Without a doubt Jared's English staff entertained a strong suspicion that Rana was his mistress as well as his servant. He didn't care what they thought. Rana was his lifeline, his one link to whatever security and love remained from his childhood.

She lingered after she had taken care of his clothing. "What did you do tonight at your grand ball?" she asked with a wistful curiosity. "Did you dance with some beautiful ladies? Did all the guests admire your costume? They should have, you know. You looked as splendid as a *nizam,* or even a *maharajah!*"

"No, I didn't dance. I didn't bring a partner, and I didn't much like the appearance of the ladies who seemed willing to oblige me. Mostly I just wandered around, an interested on-looker." Jared's thoughts turned to his unsuccessful encounter with the green-eyed enchantress in the card room. Ruefully he decided that there was no reason to mention that! He went on, "As for my costume, no one actually commented." Jared cocked his head at Rana's disappointed expression. "I did receive a goodly number of appreciative stares, however!"

Rana said in a dissatisfied voice, "It doesn't sound to me as though you enjoyed yourself very much tonight, Sahib. I'd hoped. . . . You work so hard. Much too hard. What's the point of all that work if you don't get some return for it? You should find ways to relax, make friends, have a woman in your life to love you, give you a child."

Jared sobered. "I didn't come to England to enjoy myself, Rana."

She gave him a direct look. "Oh? Why did you come here? You've never told me."

Speaking slowly, even reluctantly, Jared said, "I came to prove something to myself."

"Oh?" Rana said again. "And have you done that?"

He shook his head. "Not yet."

"When you do achieve your 'proof' I hope you'll be happy. You aren't happy now. I don't think you've ever been happy." Rana sighed. "Goodnight, Sahib." She made three low bows, bending her head and body very low, touching her forehead with her fingers.

Jared lifted his hand. "Goodnight." He shrugged into the loose robe that Rana had left draped over the bed and threw himself into a chair beside the fireplace. He stared broodingly into the flames. Rana's loving concern and her probing questions had revived festering memories. . . .

Jared walked through the garden of his father's town house on the esplanade of Chowringhee Road and mounted the stone steps leading to the second story. It was suffocatingly hot, even though it was well past midday. The rainy season would not start for at least another two weeks, he reflected, as he mopped his brow with a damp handkerchief. *Tatties*—fine strips of bamboo threaded together—hung in the spaces between the lofty pillars of the piazza, and *kus-kus*—mats saturated with water—had been applied to the great door, but Jared knew that neither expedient would do very much to reduce the scorching temperature.

The *durwan* opened the door with a low bow. "Your revered father wishes to see you, Sahib," said the doorkeeper. "He waits for you in his library."

"Thank you, Nand." Removing his hat, and fanning himself with it as he walked along, Jared went down the long corridor to a room at the end. After a perfunctory knock he pushed open the door of the library. His father sat stretched out, half-reclining, in a low chair, a glass in his hand. Blinds at the windows shadowed the room. A servant pulled at the cord of a large *punkah* overhead, the swinging fringes of the fan producing the illusion of a cooling breeze.

"Good afternoon, Father. You wished to see me?"

"Yes. Sit down, Jared. Have some wine." Richard Amberly nodded a curt dismissal to the servant operating the fan.

Jared poured a glass of Madeira and took a chair opposite his father.

Richard Amberly peered at him over the rim of his glass. "You didn't come back to the house from the cemetery. A number of people commented on your absence from the luncheon."

"I don't fancy the custom of consuming baked meats after a funeral. It smacks a little of barbarism, don't you think?"

"It indicates respect," said his father sharply. "In this case, respect for your dead brother."

"Half brother. Andrew was my half brother, as your lady wife never ceased to remind me, just as she never ceased to remind me that I was born on the wrong side of the blanket."

Richard Amberly's expression changed. "I didn't know—I was convinced that you weren't nursing a grudge any longer. Not since . . ."

"Not since your wife died, you mean?"

Richard Amberly winced at the brutally frank remark. "Try to be fair. Augusta didn't really understand local customs," he said stiffly. "When we were married she was fresh out from England. She didn't realize that . . ."

Jared finished the sentence. "She didn't realize that it was quite customary in Anglo-Indian society for English fathers to recognize their bastard children, even their half-caste bastard children, even to treat them as members of the family, to give them a decent education. She didn't realize, so she banished me from her sight, and yours. For years you had only one son, a proper English son. A legitimate son."

"I—" Richard Amberly closed his mouth, as if he found it impossible to think of an adequate reply.

Jared stared bleakly at his father. Richard Amberly was a man in his early sixties, fair-haired, florid, stocky. The blond hair was now thickly interspersed with gray, and the ruddy complexion had deepened to the telltale red tinge, streaked with spider veins, of the heavy drinker.

Jared didn't resemble his father. He had inherited only Richard's intensely blue English eyes. Jared's dark hair and aquiline features came from his Eurasian mother, Lucia Pereira, the half-caste daughter of a Portuguese tavern keeper in the "Black Town" of Calcutta.

Lucia hadn't been married to Richard Amberly, but in Jared's early childhood it hadn't mattered to him that he was illegitimate. At the time of his son's birth Richard was a highly successful commercial resident at Patna, one of the chief subordinate factories of the East India Company in Bengal. Lucia presided over his household as his acknowledged mistress, treated respectfully by his friends and acquaintances. Jared was the spoiled darling of the establishment.

Then, when Jared was three years old, Richard had retired from the Company, as a result of Governor-General Cornwallis's reforms that proscribed residents from engaging in private trade. Wealthy from his years with the Company, in which he had started as a lowly writer at the age of fifteen, Richard hadn't returned to England to enjoy his fortune, as so many of his fellow officials had done, to form the new social class of "Nabobs," but instead had set himself up as a merchant trader and banker in Calcutta. It was the beginning of Lucia's downfall and that of her son.

Richard caught the eye—or, more probably, it was the other way around—of Augusta Whitney, newly arrived in Bengal with her father, an officer in one of the regular English regiments stationed in India. Soon Richard and Augusta were married. Lucia, maintaining her dignity, went quietly off to her own establishment in Black Town. Augusta, with the insular disdain for "natives" that was beginning to be a feature of the English mentality in India, had adamantly refused to allow Richard to recognize Jared in any way, especially after the birth of her own son, Andrew.

Jared lived in obscurity with his mother in Black Town until Lucia died prematurely when he was nine years old. Then, at Richard's insistence, he came to live in the great house in Chowringhee Road, but in the servants' quarters, under the care of his mother's ayah, Rana, unacknowledged, sent to an inferior grammar school with the bastard Eurasian sons of common British soldiers.

Augusta's death in one of the outbreaks of putrid fever that periodically decimated the English population of Bengal had set Jared free, after a fashion. No longer bound by his wife's strictures, Richard sent his Eurasian son to England, enrolling him at Eton. After four years at the prestigious school, and another two years at Oxford, Jared returned to Calcutta to take up a position as clerk in his father's firm. Demonstrating a flair for business and for moneymaking, Jared soon became Richard's chief assistant. But his success was flawed. At the back of his mind was the truth that, no matter how talented or how trusted, he would always be an alien in his father's banking establishment. When Richard died, Jared's legitimate, wholly English half brother Andrew would become the head of Amberly and Son.

Now Andrew was dead of the same putrid fever that had killed his mother so many years before. This morning Jared had attended the funeral, outwardly properly subdued and grieving, inwardly feeling not a flicker of remorse. Andrew had made it abundantly clear over the years how little regard he had for the son of Richard's Eurasian mistress. Andrew had snubbed and ignored his older half brother socially, and his example had been followed by the English society in Calcutta.

Richard put down his glass on the table next to his chair. His face lined with a weary sorrow, he said, "If I could change the past . . ." his voice trailed off. He studied Jared. "It's the present now. Andrew's death changes a good many things."

"Yes." Jared returned his father's direct look. He had been wondering what would happen now to Richard's property, but he had been too proud even to think of asking. The fact remained that, so far as he knew, he was Richard's only descendant, illegitimate or otherwise.

But Richard made no reference immediately to the family business. Instead, he fell silent, averting his eyes from Jared, refilling his glass with Madeira, taking a sip of the wine, glancing aimlessly about the room. Finally he said, clearing his throat, "I was very fond of your mother."

Jared gave his father a quick, affronted look. "Then, sir, I wish you had informed her of your sentiments. It would have made her last years much happier." It occurred to Jared, with a faint tinge of surprise, that he had been speaking his mind to Richard for literally the first time in his life. The sensation felt strange, but at the same time liberating, after so many stoic years of biting back his words, of concealing his feelings, of refusing to admit to anyone how much he had been hurt by the ostracism of family and society.

"I did tell Lucia, many times, how much I loved her, in the beginning," said Richard unexpectedly. Like Jared, he had never been one to express his feelings openly.

"In the beginning," repeated Jared. "You think that made up for—?"

Richard interrupted Jared. The words poured out of him, as if they had been released by the sudden failure of a dam. "I told Lucia I loved her, but she wouldn't come to me at first, not unless I agreed to marry her. She was religious, you see. She didn't want to be my leman." Richard's eyes half closed. His voice dropped to a murmur. "She was so beautiful. I couldn't stand not having her. So we were married."

Jared became suddenly still.

"The ceremony was secret," Richard rushed on. It was almost as though he feared to pause lest he lose the courage to continue his revelations. "I told Lucia not to tell anyone, not even her father. She understood. I was no common soldier, no insignificant clerk, either of whom could have married a native wife without fear of scandal. I was an important official in the Company. I thought I might even become a member of the Council one day. I had to preserve my reputation. Lucia was satisfied, knowing in her heart that she was really my wife."

Jared's heart was pounding. His breath was coming in short, hard bursts. He said between clenched teeth, "Then you met Augusta and decided you wanted a proper English wife. So you pushed Lucia aside and committed a bigamous marriage. My mother died of a broken heart, you know. After you sent us to Black Town, I can't remember a day that she didn't cry."

His face twisted, Richard said, "I wronged Lucia. I wronged all of you. You, Jared, perhaps most of all. Augusta and Andrew, too, though they never knew it. But now I want to make up for what I did. I intend to make a new will, leaving you the bank and everything I own, acknowledging you as my legitimate son. You'll find your mother's marriage lines among my papers when I die. Yes," he nodded, at Jared's quick, questioning stare, "I'm dying. My body has simply worn out. I've lived too long in this cursed climate." He lifted his hand, making an odd, groping gesture toward Jared. "Can you forgive me? If I could do anything more for you, I would."

The bitter bile rose in Jared's throat. He was morally certain that Richard would never have revealed the truth about his elder son's birth if Jared's half brother hadn't died. Bereaved and ill, Richard simply didn't want to die alone without the support of a member of his family. Probably also he felt the need to unburden his soul from a guilt of many years standing. Jared drew a long, difficult breath. "Yes, Father, I forgive you."

A tremulous smile curved Richard's lips. "Thank you, my son."

Jared's answering smile was perfunctory. He hadn't forgiven Richard, of course. Nothing could make up for the years of rejection. But his life would be easier and smoother until Richard died if his father believed that he had fully accepted Richard's amends.

Jared shifted in his chair. The dying coals in the grate sent shadows flickering around the stylishly furnished bedchamber in Chesterfield Street. His memories of Calcutta merged into those of England.

He had been in London for almost a year. During that time he had made a niche for himself in the banking community, and he had increased his already substantial fortune with shrewd investments on the Exchange.

After his father's death three years before, he had made the Amberly bank the foremost financial institution in Calcutta, and in the process he fulfilled the vow he had made to himself and forced the Anglo-Indian society of the city to welcome him into their ranks by the sheer power of his wealth and influence.

Now he had another goal, dating from his schoolboy experiences in England. He was twenty-eight years old, but he could remember those experiences as clearly as if it were yesterday. At Eton one of his classmates was Miles Amberly, Earl of Brentford, son of one of the premier peers of England, the Duke of Edgehill. Richard Amberly had been a member of the same family, a descendant of a distant cadet branch. Miles Amberly had not only refused to acknowledge Jared's claim to the family connection, he had made Jared's life miserable for four years at Eton, deriding him for being a "nigger," ragging him unmercifully.

Miles Amberly's petty persecution reached a climax in Jared's last year at Eton. His face wreathed in a saccharine smile, Miles had declared genially, "See, here, Amberly, let's have a truce, shall we? You're a member of the family, after all. M'father's hosting a gala affair at our town house in Berkeley Square to mark the opening of Parliament. Would you care to attend?"

Jared had very much cared to attend. His heart strumming with excitement, dressed in expensive new evening clothes— Richard hadn't stinted his bastard son's pocket money—he had climbed up the steps leading to the ballroom of the elegant mansion in Berkeley Square. It was his first venture into the London *ton*. He would never for the rest of his life forget what happened next.

At the head of the steps the footman called out his name. Standing just inside the ballroom at his father's side, Miles Amberly, a gloating, malicious smile wreathing his lips, turned his head to murmur into the Duke of Edgehill's ear.

An expression of acute displeasure, almost of disgust, crossed His Grace's face. He stepped out of the receiving line and stopped in front of Jared. "You were not invited here, sir. I am not accustomed to receiving into my house by-blows of mixed blood who claim to have some sort of dubious connection to my family. I must ask you to leave."

The duke possessed a carrying voice. The people near the door ceased their conversations and craned their necks to stare at Jared. The guests waiting on the stairs behind him to greet their host listened with a greedy fascination. His face a frozen mask, Jared made a jerky bow to the duke and turned to go back down the stairway.

His mouth set in a grim line, Jared stared into the fire. He had already triumphed over his past in Calcutta. Now he intended to prove to London in general and the Amberly family in particular that he was a force to be reckoned with.

Three

As Diana reached the door of her father's sitting room, a footman was emerging from the room with a tray. She peered inside. "May I come in, Papa?"

"Of course." The Duke of Edgehill leaned back in his chair, smiling at her affectionately. "As you can see, I've just finished my luncheon."

Taking a chair near him, Diana said, "I was a little concerned about you when you didn't come down for lunch. Are you feeling ill?"

"No, no. Oh, a trifle lazy, perhaps. I'm not a young man anymore, you know. I daresay I'm entitled to be a bit lazy."

Diana gave the duke a searching look. He seemed tired, and his color wasn't good. It was true, he was no longer young, but at sixty-four he couldn't be considered ancient. His tall figure was still trim, his handsome face had few lines, his thick dark hair was only lightly salted with gray. During the past year, however, his health had deteriorated. The local doctor in Oxfordshire had diagnosed a heart problem. The duke had accompanied Diana to the city on this occasion to consult his usual London physician.

With a catch in her voice, Diana said, "Papa, did you tell me everything Dr. Phelps told you yesterday?"

The duke chuckled. "Don't be a pea-goose, my girl, always fretting about my health. Yes, I told you everything Dr. Phelps said, which wasn't much. I have a mild heart condition, and I must be careful to eat properly and get sufficient rest and above all, not overdo. So you can stop worrying about me." He cocked his head at Diana. "Did you enjoy your evening at the Pantheon? Was Miles an attentive escort?"

"Most attentive. As was Aubrey Dalton."

Frowning, the duke said, "Dalton went to the masquerade with you? Is the fellow still wearing the willow for you, do you think?"

"Aubrey's a very old friend, Papa. You'll recall that he and Miles entered Eton the same year. They've been inseparable ever since."

"Oh, I don't begrudge Dalton's friendship with Miles. But as an old friend of yours . . . This is an 'old friend' who was once very much in love with you. Is he renewing his suit? If so, I must remind you that Dalton is still not an eligible *parti*. As far as I know, his older brother is still alive. He's a younger son with few prospects. How would he support you in a style according to your rank?"

"Your point is moot, Papa," Diana said quietly. "I have no plans to marry again."

"Oh." The duke's face clouded. His daughter's marriage was not a subject he cared to discuss. He changed the subject. Gazing appreciatively at Diana's dark-green velvet pelisse and her cottage bonnet of matching green chip trimmed with ribbons, he said, "You're wearing colors again, I'm happy to see. You've dressed in mourning long enough. Where are you off to this afternoon?"

Diana hesitated. With a faintly apologetic glance at her father, she said at last, "I thought of going to Christie's. I'd like to see the Canalettos one last time."

The duke's lips tightened. This midwinter excursion to London had been prompted not only by his desire to consult his London physician, but also by the necessity to sell some prized paintings at Christie's Auction Rooms to relieve yet another crisis in the family finances. He looked away. "I'm sorry, Diana. I know how much you prize the Canalettos."

"Don't distress yourself, Papa. We must have some ready cash."

The duke sighed. "I know. We can't refuse to honor Miles's vowels. You might like to know that I've spoken to him about his gambling. He's promised to mend his ways. Again. But sometimes I think he can't help himself. I've watched him play. He doesn't really seem to enjoy wagering, as I was used to do. In my case, I was able to stop gambling when . . ." He paused, looking mildly embarrassed.

To save his pride, Diana didn't press him to finish his sentence. Her imperious father, who had rarely in his life felt constrained to do anything he didn't care to do, had voluntarily ceased gambling when she married the Earl of Windham.

Clearing his throat, the duke went on, "I'm not sure Miles can stop gambling. With him, playing for high stakes is more like—more like a compulsion than a pastime." He shook his head. "Oh, well. Miles is a good lad. He'll come around. By the way, he had great plans to entertain you while you were in town. He was very disappointed to learn that you were returning to Abbottsleigh so soon. Can't you stay on a few more days?"

"We discussed this, remember? Old Roberts is getting beyond his duties, and you won't turn him out to pasture. Admittedly, that would break his heart. But until you can bring yourself to appoint a new estate agent, someone has to supervise Roberts's work, and we've agreed that you should stay in London until the warmer weather."

Turning pensive, the duke said, "Let's wait a while longer to replace Roberts. He's been at Abbottsleigh for so many years, since my father's time. I'm sure he can continue to perform his duties with your help." He smiled at his daughter. "By rights you should have been a boy. My older son. I think you care more for Abbottsleigh and the Amberly heritage than all the rest of us." As if ashamed of his lapse into sentiment, he added hastily, "Go along with you. You'll be late for the auction at Christie's."

As Diana rode with her abigail from Berkeley Square across Piccadilly and down St. James's Street in the direction of Pall Mall, she mused about her father's comment that she cared more for the Amberly heritage than did the other members of the family. She realized with a sudden insight that the duke was probably right. Since her childhood, Abbottsleigh had been the abiding passion of her life. She had reveled in the glorious saga of Amberly family history reaching back through their centuries in England to the Conquest, and even beyond. One of her ancestresses had been the proud daughter of a Saxon thane, constrained to marry her Norman conqueror. In Diana's case, nothing could have prevailed on her to marry the Earl of Windham except the stark necessity to preserve the financial stability of the Amberly inheritance.

The auction room at Christie's was already comfortably filled, although the sales had not begun. Prospective customers crowded together on the narrow benches or roamed about the room, inspecting the paintings on the walls. Diana walked straight to the two pictures occupying prominent places behind the auctioneer's podium.

Her eyes misted as she gazed from one Canaletto masterpiece to the other. In one, the Italian master of perspective and luminous light had painted Abbottsleigh, a glorious blend of Tudor and Stuart and Georgian architectures sprawled on a wooded eminence. In the other picture, the artist had painted the Thames as it wound its way to the sea under a succession of London bridges.

When the auctioneer approached the podium Diana reluctantly left the Canalettos and took a seat on one of the benches. The first few pictures that the gallery servants displayed on the easel next to the podium were minor works and occasioned scant interest among the customers, many of whom talked and joked with their neighbors during the bidding. The hum of conversation faded into an expectant silence when the servant deposited the Canaletto painting of Abbottsleigh on the easel.

As the bidding proceeded, Diana clenched her hands together so tightly that her nails bit into her flesh. She not only grieved for the loss of the Canalettos, but she also felt a great apprehension that the sale of the paintings would not bring in the sum she hoped for and needed.

The auctioneer intoned the first bid, a substantial one. Diana began to relax. Successively higher bids came thick and fast. Finally the auctioneer banged his gavel on the podium. "The Canaletto goes to the gentleman in the rear for the sum of one thousand guineas." Diana breathed a sigh of relief. Even if the

Thames painting sold for much less, she had already realized the sum she needed. She craned her neck in an attempt to catch a glimpse of the purchaser of the picture, but the crowd behind her obscured her vision.

Shortly afterwards, the Thames Canaletto fetched a good price, not as high as the offer for the Abbottsleigh painting, but still very welcome. No longer interested in the auction, Diana rose, and, trailed by her abigail, made her way to the rear of the room. As she emerged into the foyer she heard quick steps behind her. A faintly accented voice said, "I'm not mistaken? It's really you?"

Her heart suddenly pounding, Diana turned to face the speaker. He looked different today, without his silks and embroidered brocades and flashing jewels. In fact, he was wearing conventional—and very well-tailored—city attire of coat and pantaloons and highly polished Hessians. But the blue eyes were the same, and the handsome, faintly tanned features, and the curling dark hair and the smiling sensual lips.

Keeping her voice carefully blank, Diana said, "Yes, you're quite mistaken, sir. We are not acquainted."

The stranger raised a quizzical eyebrow. "Not by name, you mean? We can easily remedy that. Allow me to introduce myself. I'm—"

Diana lifted her hand. "You force me to be blunt. I don't care to know your name. I'm not accustomed to admitting strange gentlemen into my circle of acquaintances without a proper introduction. Good day, sir." Inclining her head slightly, she turned on her heel and left the foyer. She walked hastily to the carriage waiting for her outside the auction rooms in Pall Mall.

As the carriage started up, Diana caught out of the corner of her eye her abigail's surreptitious, frankly curious glance, and she felt her cheeks growing warm. She was well aware of her mixed motives in repulsing the stranger's overtures. Oh, of course it would have been unthinkable to respond to the advances of a man to whom she had never been introduced. But she hadn't been merely virtuous, observing the rules of deportment governing the behavior of a lady of quality. The truth was that she'd been a coward, fleeing from the sexual magnetism of the first man who'd been able to arouse her physically since the days before her marriage. The truth was that she didn't trust herself.

"Catalani is in marvelous voice tonight, don't you agree?" The Earl of Brentford's low-voiced remark sounded properly appreciative, but Diana knew her brother very well. Opera wasn't among his many loves. She looked away from the stage and followed his gaze to the pit of the great horseshoe-shaped auditorium. As she had suspected, Miles had his eye on a painted young female in a surpassingly vulgar gown of bright purple satin.

"I daresay the young lady in the purple dress has many accomplishments," Diana murmured. "Perhaps she can even sing. Well, she must be musical. Why else would she come to the opera?"

Miles had the grace to look sheepish. "Sorry, old girl. Just looking, you know." He grinned at his sister. "Speaking of gowns, you're looking very top of the trees tonight, but haven't I seen that pale green *soie de Londres* dress before? You should buy yourself some new clothes, now that you're out of mourning."

"New clothes are expensive, Miles. And I won't need a new wardrobe in Oxfordshire."

Miles's laughing expression turned bleak. He muttered, "God, Diana, it's not like you to turn the screws. I'm sorry you had to sell the Canalettos. I know it was my fault. But I've promised Papa I'll do better. You didn't have to remind me."

Diana felt a twinge of remorse. Her remark about the expense of new clothes *had* carried a sting. The loss of the Canalettos was still too fresh. But she hadn't meant to wound Miles, not seriously. In spite of his faults, she was very fond of her scapegrace brother. She smiled at him. "It's not your good intentions I question, brother mine. It's your infernally bad luck. Don't you ever win?"

He burst into a laugh. "By Jove, you certainly can't deny that I try hard enough!"

Diana studied him affectionately. He was twenty-eight years

old, with a boyish charm that made him look younger. He resembled his father with his dark hair and gray eyes and fine-boned elegance of feature, and, like the duke, he had an easy grace that usually enabled him to escape the consequences of his peccadillos.

"May I share your box?" said a voice behind them.

Miles waved Aubrey Dalton to a seat beside Diana. "I'd given you up, Aubrey. The second act is almost over."

"I hope you don't object to Miles's invitation to join you tonight," Aubrey said under cover of the concluding moments of the second act of *The Marriage of Figaro*.

"Why would I object?"

Grimacing, Aubrey said, "I was afraid you wouldn't wish to see me. You were so out of sympathy with me last night at the Pantheon, and I don't blame you. Diana, can you forgive me? I shouldn't have pressed you. When you feel you're ready to accept another proposal of marriage, I'm sure you'll tell me. I'll be waiting."

Diana sighed. Once, it seemed so long ago, she'd been girlishly flattered by the attentions of "an older man," her brother's handsome and dashing friend. Briefly she'd even fancied herself in love with Aubrey. Now she simply felt empty, older. Aubrey's romantic overtures of courtship failed to stir her. She said quietly, "I hope we'll always be friends, Aubrey." He looked his disappointment and dissatisfaction.

The Duke of Edgehill looked over his newspaper at his children. Contrary to his usual custom, he had come down to the family breakfast in honor of Diana's departure to Oxfordshire. "I hope you both realize that we're living in momentous times," he said severely. "The old king is mad, and the Regency Bill has passed both Houses, and yesterday the Prince of Wales was sworn in as Regent at Carlton House."

Diana and Miles exchanged smiles. "Yes, Papa, I think Miles and I appreciate the importance of this news," said Diana solemnly. "What do you think will happen now?"

The duke's mock severe expression faded. "I have no idea.

The Prince of Wales has never struck me as a great political mind. Let's hope that the kingdom survives." He turned a worried gaze at his daughter. "What's more important at the moment is the weather. My valet informs me that it turned much colder during the night. Perhaps you should delay your journey to Abbottsleigh until the weather moderates."

Miles, who had driven to Amberly House from his rooms at the Albany to say goodbye to his sister, having risen at what was for him an ungodly hour, nodded his agreement. "February weather can be unpredictable. Do stay on for at least another day, Diana," he coaxed. "We'll go see Mrs. Siddons in *Macbeth*. It may be your last opportunity to see her act, you know. The *on dit* is that she's thinking of retiring."

"Don't tempt me, Miles. I have a great deal of work waiting for me at home." In point of fact, there was nothing really pressing demanding her attention at Abbottsleigh, nothing, at any rate, that couldn't be postponed for a few days, but she had no wish to stay on in London. She was always happiest in the country, she had few acquaintances in the city, having lost contact with her friends from the period before her marriage, and now there was the problem of Aubrey and the renewal of his suit.

"Don't you worry about my comfort on the journey to Oxfordshire," she said, smiling at her brother. "I don't mind the cold—a few hot bricks at my feet will take care of that—or even a little snow."

Miles accompanied her to the carriage. After he had tucked the lap robe around her he stood for a moment at the door. "Don't stay away so long this time, Diana. Come back to London for at least a part of the Season. I miss you."

As the carriage moved off, Diana found herself thinking about her brother with a rueful amusement. She didn't doubt Miles's real affection for her, but apparently it hadn't occurred to him that, if he missed her so much, he had only to visit Abbottsleigh to see her. But then Miles, proud though he was to be an Amberly, was essentially a city person. He quickly became bored at his ancestral home.

As they drove along Tyburn Turnpike toward Bayswater, Diana's abigail, Rose, pulled her pelisse around her more tightly and said, shivering, "Indeed, 'tis bitter cold today, my lady."

"Nonsense, Rose. It's not too cold for countrybred folk like us. We're a hardy lot," Diana replied bracingly. But she was grateful for the hot brick that warmed her toes.

She had been able to make an early start from Berkeley Square this morning, and she had entertained thoughts of traveling the entire eighty-odd miles to Abbottsleigh in one day, as she and her father had done on their journey to London shortly before. After the first few stages, however, she began to have a change of heart. By the time they reached Uxbridge, the temperature had plummeted. The hot bricks she and Rose renewed at each stop cooled quickly, and the sunless sky gradually darkened from gray to a dull leaden color.

Snow began falling at Uxbridge, a dusting of lightly falling flakes that became steadily heavier as they crossed from Middlesex into Buckinghamshire. Peering out the window at the thickly falling snow, which was rapidly reaching blizzard proportions, Diana said to Rose, "I think we'd be wiser to stop for the night at Beaconsfield, or possibly High Wycombe. At this rate the coachman soon won't be able to see more than a few feet in front of the carriage."

They never reached Beaconsfield, a principal coaching stop some twenty-five miles from London. A few miles farther on the coach lurched to a halt, listing sharply to the left. Thrown against Rose, Diana was trying to pull herself upright when the righthand door opened. Her coachman inquired anxiously, "Be ye hurt, my lady?"

"No. Are you all right, Rose? Yes? Thank goodness. What happened, Seth?"

"We struck an icy patch, my lady. Skidded right off the road, we did. I'm afeared we splintered a wheel."

"I see. What should we do, then?" asked Diana, trying to keep herself from sliding back against Rose on the steeply inclined seat.

"Here, my lady. Take my hand. Ye can't stay in the carriage." After the coachman had helped Diana and Rose from the vehicle, he motioned to the postilion, who was unharnessing the lead horse. "I'm sending the feller on ahead to the nearest town, a tiny place by the name o' Litchfield, as I recall. It ain't a reg'lar posting stop, but I reckon they'll have some kind o' carriage that the postilion can hire. Me and the footman, we'll stay here wi' ye, my lady."

Diana stood on the roadway, peering after the departing postilion, who became invisible in the swirling snow after he had gone only a short distance. The temperature was still dropping. A biting wind drove snow particles against her face with the sting of tiny icicles.

"I hope the postilion doesn't lose his way. Surely he can't see clearly where he's going," she muttered to the coachman.

"Never fear, my lady. He'll get to the village safely." The coachman's voice sounded less convinced than his words.

The minutes dragged miserably by. Diana turned her back to the cruel wind. Her hands and feet were beginning to feel numb. She wondered how long it would be before help came. If it came.

"My lady, look."

Diana turned her head. In the distance she could make out a pair of lights moving slowly toward them. Soon a carriage emerged from the driving snow and stopped. In a moment a tall figure alighted from the carriage and walked toward them. His hat was pushed down over his eyes, shielding his face from the storm and obscuring his features, and an ankle-length many-caped greatcoat disguised his figure, but Diana recognized the faintly accented voice immediately.

"Can I be of help?"

Suppressing a momentary urge to deny her predicament and send the stranger on his way, Diana said, "Yes, thank you. As you can see, we've had an accident. Perhaps you would be so kind as to take me and my abigail to the next village? My coachman and my footman could follow along behind with our horses." From his sudden quick glance she realized that he had also recognized her.

"Certainly. Allow me." He extended his hand. In a few moments Diana sat in a comfortable, light traveling carriage, sheltered at last from the buffeting wind. The stranger solicitously spread a rug over her numbed legs and offered another to Rose. "I'd gladly give you my hot bricks, but I fear they're stone cold now," he apologized. "Now then, may I tell your coachman to transfer your luggage to the boot of my carriage?"

"Yes, please." Diana looked at him with real gratitude. In her discomfort she'd forgotten about her portmanteau. She had already resigned herself to spending the night in the next village while a wheelwright repaired her carriage. Thanks to the stranger's thoughtfulness she wouldn't be obliged to sleep in the clothes she was wearing.

After the stranger settled into a seat beside Diana the carriage moved off slowly. The snow was still coming down heavily, and Diana knew that the postilion would have difficulty seeing his way even with the aid of the carriage lamps. She felt a pang of sympathy for him and for the stranger's coachman and her own two servants, exposed to the wind and cold and snow.

Her companion glanced out the window. "I see no sign that the snow is slackening off," he observed. "Granted, I'm no expert on English weather! As I told you the other evening, I'm from India. However, I've spent several winters in England, and I don't ever recall such a heavy snowfall."

Diana bit her lip. The man's manner was perfectly polite, without a trace of familiarity, but he had made it quite clear that he rejected the myth that they had never met before.

"Yes, I think the storm is unusually severe," Diana said noncommittally. He had rendered her a service, yes, but she would not allow him to encroach on her acquaintance on the strength of it.

A moment later her heart sank when he said, "My postilion's informed me that there's an inn of sorts in the next village. I think I'd be tempting fate to continue my journey in such weather. I've decided to stay the night in—what was the name of the village?—oh, yes, in Litchfield." He added politely, "I presume you'll be doing the same, ma'am? Because of the damage to your carriage?"

Diana stole a look at him. His dark features were impassive, but she didn't doubt that he was feeling quite smug. Probably he thought he would have little difficulty in furthering their acquaintance in the intimacy of a country inn. "Yes, I'll be staying the night in Litchfield, sir," she said coolly. "I trust the landlord can make both of us comfortable."

Silence settled over the carriage. Apparently the stranger was satisfied that he'd made his point, and didn't attempt any further conversation. Diana had no intention of giving him another opening. She avoided her abigail's eyes. She was sure Rose had recognized their rescuer as the man who had accosted Diana at Christie's Auction Rooms.

The carriage slowed to a crawl. In a few moments it turned into a dimly lighted enclosure. Diana's coachman opened the door of the carriage. His face pinched with the cold, he said between chattering teeth, "Litchfield, my lady. The Royal Arms, such as it is. And it's a mercy this gentleman came upon us. We'd have waited 'til doomsday for help if he hadn't come along. The landlord o' this establishment has no carriages fer hire."

The proprietor of the Royal Arms, unshaven and carelessly dressed, appeared overwhelmed by the unexpected influx of genteel customers. "I've got two spare bedchambers, ma'am," he told Diana. "I can put ye and the gentleman inter the one, and yer servants inter t'other." He gazed dubiously at Rose. "Yer abigail wouldn't object ter sharing a bed wi' my daughter?"

"The gentleman and I are traveling separately," Diana said sharply. "We require two bedchambers. My abigail will occupy my room."

"Indeed, ma'am. Please ter come wi' me."

Ignoring the stranger, who had entered the foyer immediately after her, Diana swept up the stairs after the landlord. As he was leaving the bedchamber, she said, "I would like some hot food as soon as possible, please, served in a private dining parlor, if you have such a thing."

Although the bedchamber was spartanly furnished, Diana was glad to observe that it seemed reasonably clean. A brisk fire in the fireplace spread a heavenly warmth. "The sheets have been freshly changed," reported Rose after an inspection of the bed, "and the mattress seems well enough, my lady."

After combing her hair and washing her hands Diana descended to the private dining parlor in a decidedly more congenial frame of mind. The landlord himself, bowing and scraping, arrived to present the menu. "We've nothing fancy, ma'am," he apologized, "but if ye'd care ter have a bit o' ham, or a bite o' roast chicken, why, we'd be pleased ter oblige ye."

Though not up to her father's fastidious standards, the food, Diana decided, was perfectly satisfactory. Seated at a small table drawn up in front of the fireplace she made a leisurely meal of ham and chicken and cheese and a crusty loaf. As she was pouring herself a second cup of tea, a knock sounded at the door.

"Come." Diana looked up, expecting to see the inn servant who had served the meal. She froze at the sight of the stranger standing in the doorway, a pair of glasses in one hand and a bottle of wine in the other.

"Perhaps you weren't aware that this is a private dining parlor, sir," she said coldly.

He walked toward her and set bottle and glasses down on the table. Ignoring her remark, he said, "I hoped I might persuade you to share a glass of wine with me. Our landlord had this one bottle of excellent port in his cellar, which he informed me he was saving for a special occasion. What better occasion than now?"

Diana put up her chin. "I thought I had made it quite clear that I didn't know you, and didn't care to know you. I must ask you to leave."

He lifted an eyebrow. "Aren't you being rather missish? The snow is still falling heavily. If the storm continues I daresay the roads will be impassable tomorrow, perhaps for several days. You and I are trapped here until the roads are cleared. Under the circumstances don't you think we should abandon this charade that we've never met before? This inn is a very small place, you know. Unless you shut yourself up in your bedchamber we can't avoid each other."

He poured the wine and picked up one of the glasses, holding it out to her.

Diana hesitated. What was the harm in drinking a glass of

wine with him? It didn't commit her to anything. No one whose opinion she valued would know about it. And the prospect of an enforced stay in the inn, with no one to talk to except Rose, without even a newspaper to occupy her mind, was daunting.

Pressing his advantage, he said coaxingly, "I'm only proposing a temporary acquaintance, not a permanent friendship. A brief interlude to while away the hours until the storm is over. You can be as anonymous as you like. I won't even ask your name."

Slowly Diana extended her hand and took the glass. "I'm Miss Smith," she said with a tinge of defiance.

He chuckled. "I know. I asked the landlord how you were registered, of course. You knew I'd ask him, didn't you?" Drawing a chair up to the table, he sat down opposite her. He took a sip of wine and gave her an inquiring look. "However, must I really call you Miss Smith? You do have a Christian name? May I use it? Mine is Jared, by the way."

She hesitated again. Was she sliding deeper into the abyss? Etiquette dictated that she shouldn't allow the use of her Christian name to any new acquaintance, male or female. Then the idiocy of the thought struck her. Etiquette also dictated that she shouldn't even be talking to this man. Common sense told her she could be just as anonymous under her Christian name. Clearing her throat, she said, "I'm Diana."

"Diana," he repeated. "A lovely name. It suits you. Is it your real name?" At her quick frown he said, "I'm sorry. I promised I wouldn't pry." He took another sip of wine. "Tell me something about yourself. No really personal details, naturally," he added hastily.

"Well . . . there isn't much to tell. I live in the country. I manage my father's household. I like to ride. I'm interested in farming. I read a good deal. I enjoy going to the theater when I'm in town. Actually, I expect you would say that I lead a rather boring existence."

"You, boring? Never! Nothing about you could be boring."

The deep blue eyes looked deeply into hers, and Diana had a moment of panic. Had she made a mistake, agreeing to this anonymous, informal *tête-à-tête?* Jared was the most magnetically attractive man she had ever met. She was intensely conscious of every aspect of his appearance, from his austerely handsome face to the smoothly muscled shoulders beneath his meticulously tailored coat to the grace of his long slender hands, with their carefully tended nails.

"It's your turn," she said, a trifle breathlessly.

He shrugged. "Well, now, I really *am* boring. I'm a stockbroker and banker. What could be more boring than that?"

"You said you come from India. Tell me about India."

"Well . . ." He looked oddly reluctant, almost as if he didn't care to remember the place where he was born. Then, shrugging, he started to speak. Diana listened, fascinated, as Jared told her about a tiger hunt in the interior of Bengal, about the visit of a local nawab to Calcutta, mounted on the back of a bedizened elephant, about the blistering heat of the Indian dry season.

He also told her about the lavish life style of the well-to-do Anglo-Indian. "My father had an army of servants, each performing only one special function," he said with a rueful grimace. "Father literally never had to lift a finger to do anything for himself. There was a *banian,* or steward, who ruled the household. Palanquin bearers, always preceded by a *chobdar* carrying a silver pole. A *kitmatgar,* whose only duty was to stand behind my father at dinner. A *hookah-burdar,* in charge of his pipes. Grooms, grass cutters, horsebreakers, dogkeepers, water carriers, doorkeepers, watchmen, sweepers."

"Good heavens," Diana exclaimed. "What munificence! And here I've been trying to convince Papa that we employ too many superfluous footmen at—" She broke off.

Jared cocked his head at her. "Yes? At—?"

Recovering herself, Diana said, "At home, of course."

Jared chuckled. "You very nearly gave yourself away, Diana."

"A miss is as good as a mile," she retorted.

"True." He poured more wine and handed her a glass. "Here's to another slip of your tongue."

She made a face at him. Raising her glass to her lips, she looked at him over the rim. "Do you miss India? Do you plan to go back there? Or do you prefer England?"

"No." Jared bit off the curt monosyllable almost with venom. His face had turned somber.

Looking at him curiously, Diana said, "No, what? I asked you three questions."

Making an obvious effort, Jared shook off his dark mood. "I'm sorry. What I should have said was that I hadn't made up my mind about my future plans. If my bank continues to prosper, I may stay in England." He abruptly changed the subject. Glancing at her bare left hand—Diana had removed her gloves to eat her supper—he said in a rough voice, "You're wearing a wedding ring."

"I'm a widow." Diana felt a twinge of surprise at her quick reply. For some reason that she didn't care to probe, it seemed important to inform Jared about her marital status.

Jared looked at her intently. "You're a widow? Recent? Grieving?"

"My husband died a year ago." To her horror, Diana heard herself saying, "No, I'm not grieving. I'm glad he's dead."

Jared said gently, "Why is that, Diana?"

The floodgates burst. "He—I hated him. He was old. I married him for family reasons. He pawed me. . . . He tried to prove he was a whole man, but . . . I couldn't bear to have him touch me." The hot tears welled up in her eyes.

Jared took her hand in a warm clasp. "Have you ever told this to anyone, Diana?"

"No." Her father and her brother knew that her marriage had been unsatisfactory, but she had never been able to reveal to them any of the furtive, shameful details. "How could I tell anyone about—about . . ." The tears were coming in a torrent now.

Jared rose abruptly and pulled her out of her chair. He folded her closely in his arms, resting his face against her hair. "It's all right, Diana. It's all right to cry. Crying helps to heal the hurt," he murmured.

The tears still flowed, but Diana gradually relaxed into Jared's embrace, resting her head against his chest. For the first time in her life, it felt natural and right to be encircled by a man's arms.

Jared continued to murmur his words of comfort. "You'll soon feel easier, Diana, now that you've shared these terrible memories, instead of burying them deep inside you where they kept festering away, renewing the pain." His arms tightened. "You'll marry again one day, you know, this time to a man who will satisfy you and love you as you deserve to be loved, because you're much too beautiful, much too desirable, to stay a widow all your life."

As she slowly comprehended what Jared was saying, Diana stiffened.

Jared lifted his head. His eyes narrowed. "What is it? What did I say—?"

Breaking away from him, she ran to the door, frantically wrenching it open. She could hear his voice calling after her as she raced up the stairs. She burst into her bedchamber, slamming the door shut behind her. Her abigail, sitting half slumbering by the hearth, jumped to her feet.

"My lady, what's wrong? Are ye ill?"

Diana shook her head. She threw herself on the bed, burying her face in a pillow. She was in an agony of humiliation. How could she have revealed her deepest hurts, her feelings of degradation and despair, to a stranger?

Four

Jared lifted his eyelids and promptly lowered them again. The light streaming in through the window hurt his eyes. He suddenly realized he had a blinding headache. The evening before, the landlord of the Royal Arms had discovered several bottles of a very inferior madeira in his cellar. Jared had disposed of all of them.

Smothering a curse, he sat up and swung his legs over the side of the bed. His head felt as if a thousand Maratha warriors were battling inside it. He put out a groping hand to the table beside the bed. He thought he remembered—yes, there it was, a nearly empty bottle of Madeira. After downing the wine in several gulps he waited a few moments until the hair of the dog that bit him began its restorative work.

Unlike most of the Anglo-Indian community in Calcutta, including his own father, he had never been a heavy drinker. He disliked the feeling of not being in control of himself. It was Diana's fault that he'd gotten so foxed, he thought morosely.

He hadn't set eyes on her since the night before last, when she'd rushed out of the private dining parlor. She'd spent all of yesterday shut up in her bedchamber. Her abigail had brought up her meals from the kitchens. At one point he sent her a note by one of the inn servants, asking her if or how he'd offended her. There was no reply. Once he knocked at her door. The abigail informed him frostily that her ladyship was resting.

Actually, he knew perfectly well why Diana was avoiding him. He'd approached too close to her, he had been the recipient of confidences that she had never shared with anyone else, and now she was angry and embarrassed that she had bared her soul to him.

He stood up, grimacing as the sudden movement sent an excruciating pain to his head. He'd fallen asleep in his shirt and pantaloons. Ripping off his soiled and rumpled shirt he quickly shaved and washed and dressed. Perhaps, after another night of reflection, Diana had mellowed toward him. He would seek her out again after breakfast.

The landlord greeted him jovially as he strolled into the taproom. "Good morning, sir. Or I should rightly say, this afternoon. It's past noon. Would ye fancy a bit of ham and some buttered eggs and a tankard of ale? Very good, sir."

When the landlord brought Jared's breakfast he continued his cheerful chatter. "Would ye believe, sir, that the snow's mostly gone? I was afeared, two nights ago, when ye and the young lady arrived, that we'd be snowbound fer several days."

Jared looked up from his ham in quick interest. Yesterday, in a surprising reversal in the weather, the temperature had risen rapidly, and by late afternoon the snow had begun to melt. "Do you think the roads will be clear enough for driving by tomorrow?"

"Oh, yes, sir. Ye could travel today, fer that matter. The young lady, that Miss Smith, she's already gone. Her postilion rode ter Beaconsfield early this morn, and brought back a hired post chaise and four fer the lady and her abigail, and they set off right away. The lady's coachman and footman stayed behind, o'course, but I reckon they'll be off, too, so soon as the wheelwright gits here."

Jared put down his fork. Suddenly the ham had lost its savor. Diana was gone. Oh, he could pursue her, inquiring about her at each post stop. Or he might question her coachman about her real identity and place of residence, but he had no doubt Diana's servant would be as closemouthed as she was. In any case, he disliked the idea of playing the spy. And even if he did discover who Diana really was, what would be the use? She had made it quite plain that she wanted nothing to do with him.

No, he had to face up to it. He'd lost her. He'd had his opportunity to breach the wall of anonymity between them, and he'd failed. A feeling of utter desolation overwhelmed him. In the years since his mother died he'd never formed an emotional bond with anyone except Rana. He'd never wanted to be close to anyone. Until now. In their few brief meetings Diana had stirred him as no other woman ever had. He'd yearned to be close to her, not just physically, but in every other way. Her life had been damaged, as his had been damaged. Together they might have helped each other to heal. Now he would never see her again.

"I'm very glad indeed ter welcome ye ter the Bull and George, sir. We'll make ye as comfortable as we know how."

"I'm sure I'll have no complaints," Jared said gravely, suppressing a twinge of amusement. The proprietor of the Bull and George, though too polite to ask an intrusive question, was obviously bursting with curiosity about the presence of his guest in this remote Oxfordshire village in the middle of winter.

"How long will ye be staying wi' us, if I might be so bold, sir?"

"I haven't decided. Several days, possibly."

The village of Westbridge was situated in the undulating countryside of the foothills of the Cotswolds near the border of Gloucestershire. After leaving the Royal Arms in Litchfield yesterday Jared had traveled the sixty-odd miles to Westbridge, and now that he had arrived he was almost as dubious about his presence here as was the landlord of the Bull and George.

Probably his decision to visit the ancestral family estates had been a mere quixotic impulse, Jared decided as he consumed a hearty supper in the private parlor of the Bull and George. Or, more likely, he'd been impelled by simple curiosity, a desire to see the place where the Amberlys had originated. Certainly he had no real tie to Abbottsleigh, the principal Amberly estate. His father had been only a distant connection of the family. Still, as long as he'd come this far . . .

When the maidservant came to remove the supper dishes, Jared observed, "I enjoy visiting country houses. I understand there's a large estate in the area. Abbottsleigh, I believe it's called."

"Oh, indeed, sir." The girl beamed. "Abbottsleigh's a very grand place. It's the seat of the Duke of Edgehill. His Grace is the Lord Lieutenant of the county, and the greatest landowner for miles around. Would ye be thinking of going ter see Abbottsleigh, sir?"

"I would, yes. The duke has visiting days, I presume?"

"Yes, sir. Mondays and Thursdays. O'course, not many folk come ter visit at this time o' year."

"Good. I dislike crowds." Jared added casually, "Is the duke in residence now?"

"No, sir. His Grace and her ladyship went to London a few days back."

Jared felt relieved. He had no desire to encounter the duke. One day, after he had achieved an even greater position in the London financial community, he intended to confront the Duke of Edgehill to settle old scores. But that time wasn't yet. He had deliberately chosen to visit Abbottsleigh in February because he had assumed the duke would be in London at that time for the sitting of Parliament.

The next morning Jared drove out to Abbottsleigh, located several miles from the village. The road led along a high stone wall, which seemed to extend endlessly. The park must be enormous, Jared thought, impressed in spite of himself. At the massive iron double gates, a man dashed out of the keeper's lodge to open the gates and wave the carriage on. A wide drive wound through an extensive park, well-wooded, with some very fine oaks and beech and ash. Jared remembered that the landlord of the Bull and George had told him that the Edgehill estate bordered the vast royal forest preserve of Wychwood.

The road began to climb, emerging from the parkland into a large circular courtyard facing a long building whose central entrance was a forbidding-looking medieval gatehouse flanked by two tall towers. As Jared stepped down from the carriage a watchful footman in powdered wig and gold-laced livery came out of the gatehouse. "Sir?" he inquired respectfully.

"This is a visiting day, I believe. I would like to tour the house."

"Indeed, sir. Please come with me."

Jared followed the footman through the arch of the gatehouse into an interior court surrounded on the other three sides by a range of more modern buildings. He missed a step when he observed a young woman in riding habit crossing the quadrangle. Giving him a casual glance, she stopped in her tracks. "You!" she exclaimed. "How dare——" She stopped short, biting her lip. "You may go, Roberts," she told the footman. "I'll see to the gentleman." She nodded to Jared. "This way, please."

His mind a blank, Jared walked in uncomprehending silence with Diana as she led him across the quadrangle and into a room in the building opposite the gatehouse.

She closed the door, in what was obviously a reception or waiting room, with a decided slam. Her face flushed, she said angrily, "You followed me. And I daresay you call yourself a gentleman!"

Jared stared at her in honest bewilderment. "I didn't follow you. I had no idea you would be here. What *are* you doing here, anyway?"

She drew an indignant breath. "I live here, of course! Don't pretend you didn't know that!"

"I didn't know it. Are you employed here? Are you a relative of the family?"

"Of course I'm a member of the family," Diana snapped. "You know very well who I am. I'm Lady Windham. The duke's daughter."

Jared felt breathless, as if a heavy blow had knocked the air out of his lungs. "You're the Duke of Edgehill's daughter?" he faltered. "You're an Amberly, too?"

Her eyes narrowing, Diana said, "What do you mean? Are you claiming to be an Amberly?"

Recovering himself, Jared said coolly, "My name is Jared Amberly. My father was Richard Amberly. His grandfather was Josiah Amberly, a son of the fourth Duke of Edgehill."

"But that . . ." Diana paused, frowning. After a moment she said, "The fourth duke had a large family. One of his younger sons—I think his name was Josiah—made an unfortunate marriage and became estranged from his father and his brothers. He later went into trade in the colonies, I believe. We weren't aware there were any descendants."

"I think I must be the sole descendant. My father was an only child, and I recall his once telling me that his own father was also an only child." He gave Diana a direct look. "I didn't come here in pursuit of you. You'd indicated quite plainly that you didn't wish to continue our acquaintance. I accepted your decision. I came here out of curiosity. I simply wanted to see the place where my great-great-grandfather once lived."

Diana's angry expression faded. "But why didn't you tell me who you were? Oh—" she broke off in confusion.

Jared said dryly, "As you'll recall, you forbade me to mention my surname."

"I couldn't allow you to introduce yourself," Diana burst out. "You were a complete stranger. I thought you were making improper advances to me."

Breaking into a grin, Jared said, "Advances, yes. Improper, no. I had the purest of intentions, Diana. I just wanted to know you."

"But we hadn't been properly introduced . . ." Diana paused. A slow smile curved her lips. "Jared, shall we declare a truce? Each of us will admit to his or her fault. You were overly bold, and I was overly missish. Our sins cancel each other out. Agreed?"

"Agreed." Jared gave Diana a wary look.

"Then welcome to Abbottsleigh, Cousin Jared. Would you care to have a personally conducted tour of the house?"

"Yes, thank you," Jared managed to say. He felt stunned. He had fully expected to be shown the door.

"Come along, then."

For the next hour Diana dragged Jared the length and breadth of the vast mansion. "Abbottsleigh began as a late medieval fortified manor," she told him. "The gatehouse at the entrance is the last vestige of the manor. When the first duke, as he became, caught the favor of Henry VII he decided he needed a house more in keeping with his rank. The central block is pure

Tudor. Later dukes in the Stuart and Georgian periods made additions. I've been told the house is an architectural nightmare."

She showed him the Great Hall, with its enormous fireplace that could accommodate several roasting oxen and its walls hung with suits of armor and battle-axes and shields and swords. "We still use the hall for balls and other great events, but can you imagine dining here every day with all your retinue? It's impossible to heat the place. The drafts are horrendous. My mother was always cold. She refused to set foot in the hall if she could possibly help it."

But however much she criticized the comfort of the Great Hall, or commented on the other imperfections of the house, Diana's face wore an expression of affectionate pride as she spoke of her home. She paused in front of an unusually large-sized suit of armor. "The eleventh Earl of Brentford wore this armor on the field of Bosworth. It's said he saved Henry Tudor's life in the course of the battle. At any rate, shortly afterwards, King Henry created him Duke of Edgehill."

Watching Diana's vivid face, alive with interest as she talked, Jared observed, "You're very proud of your family history, aren't you, Diana?"

"*Our* history," she reminded him. "Of course I'm proud. The Amberly family has been serving king and country since before the Conquest. On the Saxon side, one of our ancestors was a trusted counselor of King Alfred in the kingdom of Wessex. In Normandy, the first recorded Amberly arrived in the entourage of Duke Rollo in the tenth century."

Diana paused, smiling self-consciously. "Papa always laughs at me. He says I'm a real braggart where the Amberly family history is concerned." Changing the subject, she said, "Will you stay to dinner, Jared?"

Taken aback, Jared said, "Why—yes, thank you. I'd like that."

Lifting a finger to a hovering footman, Diana told the man, "Tell the butler that my cousin, Mr. Amberly, will be dining with me." To Jared she said, "Are you lodging at the Bull and George in the village?" At his nod she turned back to the footman. "Mr. Amberly will also be spending several days at Abbottsleigh. Send to the inn in the village for his luggage."

After the servant had left, Jared said, "Do you think that was quite wise, Diana?"

She raised an eyebrow. "You're displeased? You don't wish to stay here? I understood that you wanted to become acquainted with the estate."

He looked at her from under drawn brows. "Diana, don't play games with me. From the first moment we met, you've been fearful of scandal. You wouldn't tell me your name, you wouldn't let me tell you mine, because you thought someone might consider you fast for associating with a man to whom you hadn't been properly introduced. What will people say, what will your family say, if you invite that same strange man to be your guest?"

"They won't say anything. Why should they?" Diana retorted. "You're not a strange man, you're my cousin. I not only have a right, I have a duty, to extend hospitality to a relative."

Smiling, Jared said, "That being the case, I accept your invitation with pleasure, *Cousin* Diana." Inwardly, however, Jared had his reservations. Diana had welcomed him as a member of the family, but actually they were very distant cousins. Making a rapid calculation, he concluded that they were third cousins, beyond the forbidden degree of consanguinity, as far as marriage was concerned, if he recalled his youthful catechism lessons correctly. And surely she must know that his feelings toward her were far from cousinly. Had she considered at all that he might construe her invitation to become a guest at Abbottsleigh as a prelude to a more intimate relationship?

He continued to mull over the situation, trying to divine what was in Diana's mind, as he dressed for dinner in a baronial-sized bedchamber furnished with dark, magnificently heavy pieces that he guessed must date to several generations back. Tying his cravat, he wondered what the servants thought of this visit by a hitherto unknown Amberly cousin. They probably were well acquainted with the names of Diana's relations. However, the servants he had already met had treated him with an impersonal courtesy, and if they felt curious about him they hid their feelings well.

Jared shrugged, refusing to think about the matter any further. It was enough, just to be here with Diana. He went down to dinner.

Diana gave him a considering glance as he walked into the drawing room. "Weston, at a guess," she remarked with a teasing smile. "I'll wager no Indian tailor made your clothes."

"Weston it was. I inquired around, and it seems that Weston is the best tailor in London." Jared felt obscurely pleased that Diana approved of his appearance.

Diana, also, had taken pains with her toilet. She wore a gown of dark green velvet trimmed with gold cord, and her amber curls were confined in gold netting.

If she had any qualms about her invitation to him to stay at Abbottsleigh, she didn't display them. She seemed to have made a complete about-face. It was as if, having once accepted Jared into her friendship, she saw no reason to observe any precautions. During dinner, which was served in a small family dining parlor rather than in the vast state dining room, she chatted easily. She seemed particularly interested in his profession. "I gather you and your father were successful bankers in Calcutta," she observed. "Why did you decide to come to England?"

Jared hesitated. He couldn't very well tell her that his main reason for settling in England was to become so preeminent financially that the Amberly family would be forced to recognize their once-despised relative as their equal. In any event, now that he had met Diana, that reason didn't seem as important to him. Certainly he had no animus against her. She had had no part in the humiliation meted out to him by her father and her brother.

"I'd accomplished everything I wanted to accomplish in Calcutta," he told her, "and at this point in history, London is the place to be for a banker. England is fighting alone against Napoleon and the entire continent of Europe, and the government needs to borrow vast sums of money to carry on the war. So for the canny investor, the market in government securities and bullion can be immensely profitable. There's also money to be made in discounting continental bills, especially if a banker is willing to shave his commissions."

Diana looked thoughtful. "Last year, during the summer and autumn, many people, including my father, expected the Percival government to fall. If the Whigs had come to power, Papa believed, they would have stopped prosecuting the war. Would that have had any effect on your banking business?"

Grinning, Jared said, "I might have slipped perilously close to bankruptcy, of course. Fortunately, the Percival cabinet survived and pushed through a fresh army budget, and I'm still very much in business. And if the rumors I hear are correct, and the government goes off the gold standard, trading in bullion will be even more profitable."

"And the Jared Amberly banking establishment will be even more successful."

"Precisely."

Later, over coffee in the drawing room, after the soft-footed servants had left them alone, Jared gave Diana a quizzical look, saying, "You didn't flinch even once while I was talking about my financial activities."

"Oh? Why should I flinch?"

"Why, because I'm in trade. The aristocracy doesn't soil its hands with trade, so I understand."

Diana laughed. "Oh, these days the ban against trade is being observed more in the breach than in the observance, at least in the case of younger sons, who must make their own way in the world. They're going into trade, or the professions, or they're marrying wealthy heiresses, which is much the same thing, don't you think?" She sighed. "Sometimes I wish *I* could go into trade and make a great deal of money. Then I wouldn't have had to sell the Canalettos . . ."

She paused, looking startled, as Jared, making an involuntary movement, spilled his coffee and mopped at his breeches with a handkerchief. After a moment she said in a tone of discovery, "You were at Christie's the day the Canalettos were sold. You bought them, didn't you, Jared?"

"Yes." He looked at her, tight-lipped. "I wanted to own some sort of family memento. Diana, I meant you no harm. I didn't know who you were then. If I'd known, I wouldn't have—"

She cut him off. Sounding rather brittle, she said, "Don't apologize. You had a perfect right to buy the paintings. They were being offered for sale, after all." She added wistfully, "They're so beautiful. I've always preferred them to the Gainsboroughs and Van Dykes in the long gallery. I'm glad they found a home with a member of the family." She paused, a frown creasing her brow. For a moment Jared feared that their fragile new relationship had been damaged by his purchase of the Canalettos.

She stared at him, her eyes widening. "Speaking of you as a member of the family—it's just occurred to me that, if your father really was the fourth duke's great-grandson, you yourself may very well be the next heir to the Edgehill title, after my brother Miles."

"What—?"

"I think so," she nodded. "I know the family genealogical charts by heart. Our branch of the Amberly family has thinned out in the last few generations, at least in the male line. We had thought that the next heir after my brother Miles was my father's distant cousin, George Amberly, who descends from the fourth Duke's son Matthew. But unless I'm completely mistaken, Matthew was younger than your great-great-grandfather Josiah. So that puts you into position behind my brother, for what it's worth. Not very much, probably. Miles will surely marry and have children."

"I assure you I won't hold my breath until I succeed to the Edgehill title," Jared said dryly.

"But you do have documentation? Birth certificates, marriage lines?"

"Oh, yes," Jared replied, even more dryly. "My father had all the papers proving his descent from the fourth duke. He was very proud of the connection."

"Good." Diana smiled. "Mind, I trust you'll never have occasion to use them. I'm prejudiced in favor of my brother. I hope to see his son succeed him as Duke of Edgehill." Changing the subject, she said, "Can you stay on through tomorrow, Jared? I'd like to show you over the estate."

By the end of the following day Jared was much more familiar with his roots. Diana first took him to the site of a ruined abbey on the banks of the little river that meandered placidly along the border of the parkland on its way to join the Windrush.

"The king granted the abbey lands to the second duke at the time of the Dissolution," she told him. "The grant doubled the size of the Amberly property." Gazing over the ruins, which consisted mainly of foundation stones and an occasional lonely arch, she went on, "Over the years the local farmers carted away most of the stones in the buildings to repair their own homes and fences. Papa put a stop to the vandalism when he succeeded, but there wasn't much left by that time. I've always liked to come here, though. It's so peaceful. Sometimes I feel guilty that the Amberlys increased their wealth by turning all those pious, humble monks out of their community."

Standing quietly, conscious of the sighing of the wind in the trees and the murmuring ripple of the river, Jared could almost hear the shuffling of sandaled feet on the cloister walks. "I daresay the monks, wherever they may be, have long since forgiven the family for evicting them," he told Diana with a smile. "The Amberlys have taken good care of the land."

"Yes, I find that comforting."

The sheer size of the Amberly holdings amazed Jared. He was, of course, familiar with the great estates of the petty princes and the *zamindar*—tax collecting—families of Bengal, but he was unprepared to find an estate as large as Abbottsleigh in a much smaller country like England. As he and Diana rode through villages and woodlands and past prosperous farms, he realized that the Duke of Edgehill must own a large part of the entire county of Oxfordshire.

"Oh, yes, the estate is large enough, but it could be much more productive," Diana had replied discontentedly when he commented on the size of Abbottsleigh. "Our agent, Roberts, is an old man, and a very old-fashioned and stubborn one. He won't press our tenants to use the more efficient Small's swing plough, for example, even though it has proved its value for some years now in other parts of the country. Nor will he encourage the growing of turnips, which is the single crop that will most help us to improve our livestock."

"Why does your father keep the man on, then?" inquired Jared. "Or possibly you have a situation like the one that is all too common in Bengal, where, once you acquire a servant, it becomes almost impossible to dismiss him."

"Oh, we haven't quite come to that. It's just that old Roberts has been the Abbottsleigh estate agent for so many years—well over forty—that Papa is loath to turn him off," Diana replied, sighing. "Papa has a great loyalty to the people who serve him, and they to him. Then, too, in general Papa dislikes change. He likes affairs to go on as they always have. So I've appointed myself unofficial agent. I try to persuade Roberts, gently and diplomatically, to make the changes in management that I consider necessary." She made a little face. "With varying degrees of success. You'll notice we still aren't growing turnips!"

That evening after dinner, as they sat over coffee in the drawing room, Jared remarked, "I've really enjoyed my visit to Abbottsleigh. I thank you for showing me your home. However, much as I dislike the thought, I must return to London tomorrow. Banks don't run themselves, you know."

"I'm sorry you're leaving so soon. I've enjoyed your visit, too."

"When will you return to London, Diana? Your father and your brother are there. Don't you sometimes feel lonely?"

"Oh, no. We're quite active socially in this remote corner of Oxfordshire. I have friendly neighbors who frequently invite me to their parties," Diana said lightly. "What's more to the point, I like living at Abbottsleigh, and I'm not very fond of London. And, as I told you, I must supervise our estate agent and bully him into administering the estate as I think proper."

"But is it necessary for you to stay at Abbottsleigh indefinitely? When the Season starts, for example, won't your father require you to act as his hostess?"

"Oh, I'm well past my salad days, remember? Taking part in

the Season doesn't interest me anymore. Besides, I'm needed here. Spring planting will soon be upon us."

Jared stared at Diana in frustration. Before he could stop himself he said, "Are you really immuring yourself here in the country out of a sense of duty, or is there some other reason?"

Her expression turned glacial. "What do you mean?"

Cornered, Jared blurted, "I think you want to avoid being in the company of people who might hurt you, especially men. Men who might remind you of your husband."

Diana's cheeks turned a bright red. "You've no right to . . ."

"I've no right to speak about your marital problems? But you've already told me how unhappy you were in your marriage, Diana."

"I was overset—If you were a gentleman, you wouldn't remind me of what I said . . ."

Setting down his coffee cup, Jared left his chair and sat down beside Diana on the settee. He seized both her hands, saying, "Listen to me. I don't care a damn about being a gentleman. I want to be your lover."

Desperately trying to pull her hands away from his grasp, Diana gasped, "Please—I don't want . . ."

"Don't you?" Jared caught her in his arms, and, though she tried to twist her face away, his lips found hers in a kiss that released the pent-up desire that he'd been suppressing since her flight from the Royal Arms in Litchfield. For a moment her lips were unresponsive, and then, with a little sound that was half sob, half sigh, she slipped her arms around his neck and returned his kiss eagerly.

Lifting his head at last, he said unsteadily, "Did that mean what I think it meant?"

The lovely color rising again in her face, she looked into his eyes, murmuring, "It meant that I like to kiss you, Jared. That's all."

He put out a gentle finger to brush her cheek. "I don't believe you. I think you felt what I felt. Tenderness. Passion. Love. Diana, my heart's darling, I love you, I want to marry you, I want to be with you always."

An expression of panic crossed her face. "No. Please don't say any more. I can't marry you."

Placing his hands on her shoulder, he shook her lightly. "Why? Because you didn't love your husband? Because you couldn't bear to have him touch you? You like my touch, you've said so. And I think you care for me, just a little. Not as much as I care for you maybe, because I adore you, you're a fire in my blood, but a little."

"I—I can't promise . . ."

"I'm not asking you for a promise. I just want you to think about giving me a promise." He kissed her again, a clinging, tender kiss that deepened into a hungry passion. "Will you do that, Diana? When I leave you to return to London, will you think about loving me?"

Looking dazed in the aftermath of the kiss, Diana whispered, "Yes, Jared. I'll think about it."

Five

Rana poured Jared a second cup of tea and moved the plate of toast nearer to his hand. Now that he lived in England, Jared still clung to the Indian custom of eating a light breakfast. Today, however, the plate of toast had been left untouched as he sat reading and rereading a letter that had arrived in the morning post.

Without taking his eyes from the letter, Jared murmured a "thank you" and waved his hand, saying, "Sit down and drink a cup of tea with me, Rana."

It was a request he had repeated at almost every meal since they had settled into the Chesterfield Street house, to which Rana now returned her invariable answer. "It wouldn't be seemly for me to eat or drink with you, Sahib. What would the other servants think?"

"Hang the other servants. This is my house, and I'm the master here."

She smiled, shaking her head. Opening the newspaper, which had also remained untouched beside his plate, she skimmed through the news columns. "The English general in Portugal has forced the French army to retreat to Spain, it seems."

"Yes, the newspapers reported yesterday that Marshal Massena was making for Salamanca," Jared replied, still without looking up from his letter.

"That must be a very important letter to cause you to neglect your newspaper," Rana teased. "You are always so interested in the news from the—the . . ."

"The Peninsula." Jared looked up with a quick grin. "I'm

interested in how the war is being conducted there because the English government needs to expend large sums of money to maintain its troops, who must be paid in specie. As a banker who also deals in gold—well, you see my point."

"Oh, yes." Cocking her head at the sheets of paper in Jared's hand, Rana observed, "I hope your letter was worth what it cost you to receive it. I had to pay eight pence for each page of the letter. I told the carrier it was a shocking charge."

"You always tell the carrier that. As I've tried to explain to you, postage in this country is billed on the basis of the number of miles a letter travels. For example, this letter came from Oxfordshire, a distance of about eighty miles."

"The postal service in Bengal is much more efficient," Rana sniffed.

"Oh, come now, you simply miss having a *hurcarrah* waiting in the servants' quarters, ready to carry a message anywhere, at any hour of the day or night."

"Well, the *hurcarrah* was very convenient, you can't deny that." Rana's eyes shifted back to the letter. "Your correspondent has a very graceful handwriting, almost like a lady's. In fact, you have received several letters of late in that same handwriting."

Jared burst into a laugh. "You're prying, Rana, you can't deny *that!*"

"If I have offended the sahib, I am very sorry," said Rana with an expression of wounded dignity. "Perhaps you would wish me to leave and allow you to read your letter and eat your breakfast in peace."

"Oh, come off your high rope." Jared's affectionate smile belied the curtness of his words. "Of course I don't want you to leave. Yes, my dear prying Rana, this letter is from a lady. And yes, I've been corresponding with her for—let me think— since February. Almost two months. I haven't told you about her before because . . ." Jared flicked Rana a sheepish glance. "Well, to tell you the truth, I wasn't sure anything would ever come of the letters."

Her pretty face glowing, Rana said eagerly, "And now you are sure? Tell me about her, Sahib. Who is she?"

"Do you remember the masquerade ball I attended at the Pantheon several months ago? I met Diana there. That is, I talked to her, but she didn't wish to know me. She wouldn't even give me her name. I came away from the ball thinking I would never see her again."

"I knew it," Rana declared. "I knew something had happened at that ball. You had a look about you. A look of sadness, of disappointment. And so, you've met the lady again, and this time you do know her name." Rana's face lighted up. "I see how it was. You met her again on that journey you made to—what was that place?—oh, yes, to Oxfordshire, where you went to see the place where your great-great-grandfather was born. Isn't that right?"

Nodding, Jared replied, "Yes, that's right. Diana turned out to be my cousin, Rana. A very distant cousin. She's also a widow, who had decided never to marry again."

"A widow," Rana repeated, looking thoughtful. "You know, Sahib, some of the English customs are superior to ours. In Bengal a Hindu widow of high degree like your Diana must end her life when her husband dies by throwing herself on her husband's burning funeral pyre."

"*Suttee* is a dreadful practice," said Jared roughly. "It should be abolished. I blame the Company for not doing more to discourage it."

"Yes, I agree." Rana's dark eyes met Jared's in a long look. "And now your lovely widow—she *is* lovely?—has changed her mind about marrying again?"

"I think so. No, I hope so." Jared's face registered an agonizing uncertainty. "At any rate, she writes that she's coming to London. She may be here already, staying in her father's house. I don't think she would have left Oxfordshire if she hadn't decided to accept my proposal of marriage."

A tender smile curved Rana's lips. "Finally you will have the happiness that has always escaped you, Sahib. I am sure of it."

I wish I could be as sure, as confident, as Rana is about my future with Diana, Jared thought a little later, as he accepted his hat and cane from an attentive footman and strode out his door to the carriage waiting to take him to his offices near the

Bank of England and the Royal Exchange. As he began the long drive along Oxford Street and into Holborn, he could think of nothing but Diana, and with each passing moment his uncertainty increased.

She'd written to him often during the past weeks. Her letters were warm and friendly and interesting, full of details about her daily routine at Abbottsleigh, but they didn't begin to match the emotional heights in his own letters. For the first time since the death of his mother when he was nine years old, Jared had stripped away the stoic reserve he'd assumed to conceal from the world his hurts and fears and uncertainties. In his letters he'd opened his heart completely to Diana. He told her she was the first woman he had ever loved. He told her that if she didn't marry him the rest of his life would be a desolate wasteland. He told her that he'd never before dared to become close to a woman because he couldn't bring himself to trust another human being. He told her . . .

Lord, what hadn't he told her? Jared thought morosely as the carriage proceeded from Cheapside into Poultry. He was a grown man, almost thirty years old, and his letters to Diana had probably sounded to her like the outpourings of a lovesick juvenile swain in the throes of calf love. She had never told him she returned his love, and in the letter he'd received that morning she had made no promise to marry him. What she had said, condensed from two pages of cheerful, friendly, newsy prose, was: "I've decided to come to London. I hope to see you there." Hardly a commitment. Not even the whisper of a promise.

The carriage stopped in front of his offices in Lombard Street. Jared had deliberately established his premises here. He was very conscious that Lombard Street had been the banking center of London since merchants from Lombardy had settled here in the twelfth century, and the location gave him both prestige and exposure.

Seated at a desk near the entrance of the bank, Kamal, his head clerk, looked up from his ledgers as Jared entered. "Good morning, sir," he said in English. "You'll be happy to hear that the price of gold is up another three shillings on the Continental exchanges."

Kamal always spoke English during business hours. Jared had never been sorry that he'd brought the quick-thinking, multilingual young Eurasian from Calcutta to head his office staff. Kamal had quickly established a firm authority over the English clerks who at first had looked askance at his dark skin and faint accent.

Looking thoughtful, Jared paused in front of Kamal's desk. "That's very good news about the foreign exchanges. We'd best be taking immediate advantage of the situation."

"Indeed, sir." No more needed to be said. Kamal perfectly understood that he was to set in train a shipment of bullion to the Kentish coast, where Jared, like a number of other enterprising London bankers and merchants, had contacts with sea captains who were willing to engage in the risky—and highly illegal—smuggling of gold to the Continent.

Jared dropped into a chair behind his desk in his private office, his mind not on the profits to be gained in illicit dealing in gold, but on Diana. She hadn't said she would marry him. She hadn't said she wouldn't, either. But at least she was in London, or soon would be. Before very long, he would know, one way or the other, if she would marry him.

Diana poured her father's tea and handed him his cup. They were sitting in the cozy morning room that had once been the retreat of Diana's mother. Diana had arrived from Oxfordshire earlier in the day.

"I'm so glad you decided to come to London," the duke remarked. "Frankly, I was despairing of you. You kept saying in your letters that you had no interest in taking part in the Season, and yet here you are, almost a full month before the Season gets under way. What made you change your mind?"

"Oh, I was becoming a little bored in the countryside, but most especially I missed you, Papa." Diana smiled cheerfully at her father, but she had to suppress a nagging fear as she looked closely at him. He was thinner and paler than he had been in February, and he was noticeably less energetic.

"Have you been seeing Doctor Phelps, Papa?"

"The man practically lives at Amberly House," the duke snorted. "You'd think I was his only patient. Well, I daresay I *am* his only ducal patient. Doubtless I give him a certain *cachet*. As to what he gives to me in exchange—well, he keeps telling me to watch my diet and to drink less Madeira, which advice should be self-evident to anyone who has passed the sixty mark!"

"But how are you feeling, Papa?"

"In prime twig, my dear. In prime twig. I've dropped almost a stone, and I think you must agree that I look decidedly more trim."

Diana abandoned the subject of her father's health, which he obviously didn't care to discuss. "What has Miles been up to since I returned to Abbottsleigh?"

The duke looked away. "I see very little of Miles. He does have separate lodgings, you know." After a pause, he added reluctantly, "If you must have it, I think he may be gambling heavily again. He came to me last month for an advance on his quarterly allowance."

"But —"

"I know. Miles receives a handsome allowance, ample to take care of all his needs except for excessive gambling debts. I'll speak to him, Diana." Clearing his throat, he said, "That's enough about your brother. We must make some plans to amuse you, now that you're here. We'll have a dinner party, of course. We might invite the Prime Minister. He was inquiring about you just the other day. After that, possibly a ball."

"You needn't make great plans to entertain me, Papa. I'm no green girl, remember? I had my come-out years ago."

"What nonsense is this?" inquired a cheerful voice. Miles entered the morning room, exquisitely turned out as befitting a tulip of fashion. Diana didn't recognize the discreetly elegant coat, and she felt an irritated urge, quickly suppressed, to ask Miles if he'd recently added to his tailor's bill.

"Of course you must be entertained, sister mine," Miles went on. "Matter of fact, it's high time you entered the Marriage Mart again. There's old Aubrey, of course. I know, I know, Papa," he added hastily as his father frowned. "You don't fancy

Aubrey as a son-in-law. Well, I met a fellow the other evening at White's who just might be a prime candidate for Diana's hand. Good family. Prospect of a title, if a sickly older brother should kick the bucket. Recently invalided out of the Guards after taking a bullet in the Peninsula but in reasonable health. A tidy fortune, too."

Diana gave her brother a disdainful look. "Coming it on too strong, Miles. If I decide to acquire a second husband, I'll find one for myself, thank you."

The duke gave Diana an inquiring look. "If? Did I hear you say if? The last time you and I discussed the matter, you assured me you had no intention of marrying again. Ever."

Diana bit her lip. "I still have no immediate plans for marriage, Papa."

"Immediate?" Miles pounced on the word. His eyes sparkling with mischief, he went on. "You've given yourself away, my girl. At the very least, you've at last found a gentleman who's captured your interest. Now, who could he be? Almost certainly, someone in your circle at Abbottsleigh. You haven't been anywhere else for a year. Let me think. There's young Sheldon, for one, but you never fancied him. Lord Olney? No, you always said he had only one thing on his mind, riding to hounds, and he bored you to tears. Then there's—"

Frowning in vexation, Diana cut him off. "I'll thank you, Miles, not to speculate about my personal affairs. Yes, what is it?" she asked the footman who had appeared in the doorway.

The footman extended to her a tray containing a *carte de visite*. "I realize it's not the usual calling hour, my lady," he apologized, "but the gentleman seemed right insistent. Are ye at home?"

As she examined the card, Diana could feel the color rising in her cheeks. She hesitated—and then called herself to task for the hesitation. "Bring the gentleman here," she told the footman.

"Who is your caller, my dear?" asked the duke with a slight show of curiosity. "I wasn't aware that anyone among your acquaintances knew you were in residence."

Diana had known this moment would come, but she would

have preferred that it not come this soon. True, she was here in London because she had decided to accept Jared Amberly's proposal of marriage. However, the idea of marrying Jared was still so new to her that she longed to keep the relationship secret from her family for at least a little while. Also, her father had never fully approved of any of the suitors who had pursued her since her come-out, on the grounds that none of them met the high standards he demanded for his daughter. She didn't doubt that the duke would look askance at a man, who, though a distant cousin, was also a colonial engaged in trade.

"Papa," she said quickly, "I have a pleasant surprise for you and Miles. I've discovered a relative we didn't know existed."

"And who might that be?" the duke said in surprise.

"Well, the relationship is actually a very distant one. Do you recall the fourth duke's son Josiah—?"

She broke off as the footman announced, "Mr. Jared Amberly." Her heart missed a beat at her first glimpse of Jared. His dark, smoldering good looks, the blue intensity of his eyes, were exactly as she remembered them. During the past few weeks she had sometimes wondered if her memory hadn't exaggerated his sheer physical appeal.

He paused for a moment on the threshold of the room as he realized that Diana wasn't alone. Then, his lips tightening slightly, he walked toward her. Bowing, he said, "Good afternoon, Diana. I'm pleased to see you again."

"And I you." Diana had to force herself to speak formally. She wanted to exclaim, "Darling, darling, I'm so happy to be with you. I've missed you so much. I can't wait for you to kiss me." Instead she said, "Allow me to present you to my father, the Duke of Edgehill, and my brother, Lord Brentford. Papa, Miles, this is our long-lost cousin, Jared Amberly."

The duke had risen at Jared's entrance. His tone was aloof as he inquired, "And how is it that you claim to be related to us, Mr. Amberly?"

Aghast at the note of hostility in her father's voice, Diana said hastily, "As I told you, Papa, the relationship is very distant. Jared's great-great-grandfather was the fourth duke's son Josiah.

You remember, the man who made that unfortunate marriage and went off to the colonies and was never heard from again."

"I see."

"No, you don't see, Papa," Miles cut in. He had been standing quietly beside his father since Jared's arrival, skewering his sister's guest with an intent stare. "I wasn't sure about this fellow's identity, just at first. It's been over ten years, after all, since I last saw him, and he's changed somewhat. But he's the same half-caste Indian who claimed to be related to the Amberly family when he attended Eton with me. Don't you remember, Papa? You had him removed from the premises when he attempted to attend the grand ball you hosted during my last year at Eton."

"Ah. Yes, I do remember." The duke's expression was glacial as he looked at Jared. "I must ask you to leave, my man. I am most displeased, not only because you again tried to gain entrance to a house where you knew you were not welcome, but also because you inveigled my daughter into believing she could become friendly with a person like yourself."

His face an expressionless mask, save for a muscle that twitched in his cheek, Jared stared into Diana's eyes. "Diana?" he muttered, with a queer groping movement of his hand. She could only stare back at him, in a state of utter shock, dazed and silent, unable to speak or to comprehend. He bowed jerkily. "I beg your pardon for intruding." He turned on his heel and walked out of the room.

Moments after Jared left, Diana recovered from the strange mental paralysis into which Miles's remarks had plunged her. "Papa, Miles, how could you treat a guest in our house like that? How could you say those dreadful things to Jared? A man who is actually a member of our family, however distant."

Miles said roughly, "Diana, this man is no more a member of our family than the scullery maid. You've been taken in by the half-caste bastard of a fellow who claimed some sort of obscure family connection to us and who went out to India many years ago and debauched himself with the native women."

Diana faltered, "What do you mean, half-caste? You've used that term before. And bastard? Jared tells me he inherited his father's banking business, which would hardly have happened if he had been illegitimate . . ."

Cutting in, the duke said, "Miles is right, you've allowed yourself to be taken in, my dear. Actually, you shouldn't have believed a word this fellow told you. It's all coming back to me now. I had the man investigated after the episode in which he tried to gain entry into my house. Strictly speaking, he's not a half-caste. Is there such a thing as a quarter-caste? It was his mother who was the half-caste. She was the daughter of a disreputable tavern owner in the native quarter of Calcutta, as I recall. She lived openly as his mistress with a man named—let me think—a man named Richard Amberly, who went out to India to seek his fortune and who claimed to be a descendant of an earlier Duke of Edgehill. This fellow Jared is their son. As for inheriting a bank from his father, the idea is ridiculous. Richard Amberly was an employee of the East India Company, probably not a very successful employee, or he would have returned to England when he retired to enjoy his profits like the rest of the Nabobs. No, no, my dear, there's probably not a word of truth in anything this man told you."

Frowning, Miles asked, "In the fiend's name, Diana, how did you chance to meet this fellow, anyway?"

In a state of shock over her father's revelations, Diana blurted out the truth. "I—I met Jared at the Pantheon ball I attended with you and Aubrey in February."

Miles frowned. "How could that be? *I* never introduced him to you, nor, I'm sure, did Aubrey."

"I—if you must know, Aubrey and I had words, and he left me in a huff. Jared—er—introduced himself."

"And you allowed such impertinence?" Miles swelled with indignation. "And doubtless you've been corresponding with him since you returned to Oxfordshire?"

"Yes, I have." Diana was beginning to recover her composure. "I presumed I didn't need my brother's permission to correspond with a friend."

"One moment, my dear," interjected the duke. His face, normally so serenely impassive, had turned cold. "You may be of age, you may have achieved a certain independence by virtue of your marriage, but your brother and I have an indisputable right to interfere with your actions when it seems to us that you're dishonoring your family. Such is apparently the situation here. Am I correct in my surmise that you were actually considering marriage to this Jared Amberly?"

"Yes." Diana almost choked on the word as she looked at her father's hostile face.

"But—good God, Diana," spluttered Miles, "how could you entertain such a notion for even a moment?"

"Be quiet, Miles. I'll take care of this matter," said the duke with a cold finality. "Diana, listen to me. Under no circumstances could you ever marry this Jared Amberly. He's a nobody, a man of mixed blood who was also born on the wrong side of the blanket. If you were to marry him you would perpetrate such a disgrace on the family that I would be forced to disown you. Marry him, and I would never see you again. You would never again be welcome at Abbottsleigh."

"Bring me another bottle of port, Rana."

"But Sahib—you have already drunk half a bottle," faltered Rana, her face troubled. She glanced at Jared's plate. He hadn't made even a pretext of eating. "Won't you try the *Burdwan* stew? It's always been your favorite. I prepared it myself."

"I'm not hungry. Do as I bid you, Rana. As you've so often pointed out to me, you're a servant in this household, not the mistress of it."

"Yes, Sahib," Rana whispered. She left the dining room with dragging steps.

Jared's heart contracted. He had never before spoken to Rana so roughly. It was the pain speaking. Not only had he been thrown ignominiously out of the Duke of Edgehill's house for the second time, but Diana had abetted his humiliation. Diana, who he had thought returned his love. Diana, who he had thought was about to accept his proposal of marriage. Diana, who was the only woman, save for his mother and Rana, to whom he had ever given his heart.

Rana, appearing wan and subdued, returned with the bottle

of port and a message. "A lady has come to call on you, Sahib. Do you wish to see her?"

Jared looked up, suddenly alert. "Did the lady give her name?"

"No, Sahib. I could not even see her face clearly. She is wearing a cloak with a hood. I asked her to wait in the drawing room."

"Yes, I'll see her." Jared rose from the table. As he passed Rana, he paused, placing his hand gently on her shoulder. "I'm sorry. I shouldn't have spoken to you like that. You know how important you are to me, don't you, Rana?"

Her eyes welling with tears, Rana caught his hand, putting it to her lips. "Yes, I know, Sahib."

Jared strode into the drawing room. Diana turned away from the mantelpiece as he entered. She pulled back the concealing hood from her head. Her face was pale and drawn.

"Good evening, Jared."

"Good evening. How did you know where I lived?"

"You mentioned during your visit to Abbottsleigh that you had purchased a house in Chesterfield Street, behind the gardens of Chesterfield House, remember?" Diana's voice sounded lifeless. After a moment she said abruptly, "I came to apologize to you."

Standing stiffly erect, Jared said, "Oh? Why is that?"

Twisting her gloved hands nervously together, Diana said, "Papa and Miles were cruel to you this afternoon. I make no excuses for them. What they did was unforgivable."

"Actually, I'm becoming accustomed to the behavior of the duke and Lord Brentford," Jared jibed. "As your brother Miles mentioned, this is the second time I've been tossed out of the sacred precincts of Amberly House."

Diana winced. "I'm sorry. I don't know what else to say." She pulled her hood back over her head. "Thank you for seeing me, Jared. Goodbye."

Jared put out his hand to her arm as she tried to pass him. "Is that all you have to tell me, Diana?"

She looked away. "Yes. I couldn't let you believe that I approved of the way Papa and Miles treated you." Seen up close, she was very pale, and there were dark circles under her eyes.

Jared placed his hands on her shoulders. "Diana, look at me."

"Jared, please . . ."

"Look at me."

Slowly she raised her head and met his eyes. A faint color crept into her pale face.

"Diana, I want the truth. Do you care for me?"

She hesitated. "Yes," she said in an almost inaudible voice. "But Jared, how I feel is beside the point now . . ."

Jared went on ruthlessly, "Did you come to London intending to tell me you would marry me?"

Another pause. "Yes." Her voice was only a sliver of sound.

"Well, then?"

Diana burst out, "Jared, I can't marry you, now that I've found out who you really are. You should have told me you have mixed blood, you should have told me you're illegitimate."

Jared suddenly felt chilled. He removed his hands from her shoulders and stepped back. "Let me understand you. You love me, but you won't marry me because I'm not good enough for you. Is that what you mean?"

Her face twisting in pain, Diana said, "You make it sound so crass. I have obligations to my father, to my family line. I can't indulge my personal wishes if it means going against the standards that have been upheld by the Amberlys for centuries."

"You mean you can't abide the thought of sullying the high and mighty Amberly family tree with a dollop of 'nigger' blood, as your brother so crudely puts it," Jared said, his lip curling. "Well, Diana, I don't doubt that, somewhere, sometime, during those centuries you speak of, not a few Amberlys have been guilty of a mesalliance, but I won't labor the point. You don't wish to marry me, and I have no desire to marry a woman who looks upon me as inferior. The feeling, then, is mutual. Please allow me to escort you to your carriage."

Diana's face had turned expressionless. "That won't be necessary. Goodbye, Jared."

He stepped aside and bowed. "As you wish. Goodbye, Diana."

As soon as Diana had left the room, Jared snatched up a China figurine from a low table and hurled it against the floor. The act of vandalism relieved some of the damage to his lacerated pride. He hunched his shoulders. He'd allowed himself to be distracted from his reason for coming to England by Diana's beguiling beauty. Now she was no more to him than her father or her brother. He could proceed with his intention to make the Amberly family rue the day that they had discarded him on the scrapheap of humanity.

Six

Walking quickly out the door of Jared's town house, Diana kept her calm until she reached the carriage waiting in Chesterfield Street in front of the house. But as soon as the footman closed the door of the carriage on her the hot tears began to flow down her cheeks.

She knew hearts couldn't really break, despite what the poets said. And hearts couldn't bleed either, except from a bullet wound or something equally drastic. And yet she felt this piercing pain in the vicinity of her heart. In the space of a few hours she'd lost her love and her happiness.

Huddled in misery against the side of the carriage, Diana remembered the surging joy and the delirious excitement of her journey to London, during which every passing mile had brought her closer to the man she loved and intended to marry. Oh, she'd remained clearheaded enough to know that her father would have reservations, perhaps strong objections, about a marriage to Jared, a man of no social pretensions, engaged in trade, and with only a tenuous connection to the family.

A bitter taste of failure in her mouth, Diana recalled how she had determined to resist any opposition the duke might make. After enduring one sacrificial marriage for the sake of the family, she had decided she was now free to choose her own husband. If that husband didn't meet her father's rigorous standards of rank and family connections, so be it. She would rather be happy in Jared's arms.

But not at any cost. Proud though she was of her Amberly heritage, she had been joyfully prepared to overlook his lack of social position. In fact, Jared had far greater disabilities as a bridegroom. He hadn't been truthful with her. He hadn't told her he had native blood and that his mother came from the dregs of society. He hadn't told her he was illegitimate. Had the omission been deliberate? Had he hoped to bind her into an engagement, or even marriage itself, before she discovered the truth of his background?

Jared must have known, from his previous experience with her father, who had refused even to admit him as a guest to the family house, that the Duke of Edgehill would never countenance a marriage to his daughter. Had he expected her to defy the standards of her family and her class to marry him? Had he realized that such a marriage would have cut her off from her family, that in all likelihood she would have been ostracized by everyone she knew? Because the only acceptable reason for marrying outside the tight circle of upper English society was money, vast sums of money. And it was doubtful that even a great fortune would compensate for a tainted ancestry and illegitimacy, certainly not in her father's eyes. And not in hers, God help her. Jared might consider her a snob and a coward, but she couldn't go against the strictures of centuries of family pride.

As the carriage swung into Berkeley Square, Diana took a handkerchief from her reticule and hastily wiped away the vestiges of her tears. It was over and done with. She had made her decision, and it had cost her the only man she had ever loved. Now she must live with the consequences of that decision. She was quite composed as she walked up the steps of Amberly House and entered the foyer.

"Good evening, my lady," said the footman who admitted her. "His lordship is waiting for you in the drawing room."

"My brother is here?" said Diana in surprise.

Miles came into the foyer at the sound of their voices. "Diana, where in heaven's name have you been? I—" he broke off, glancing at the footman. "I'm glad you're back. Papa had some sort of attack about an hour ago. Yeats sent for me. Thank God Papa employs an intelligent butler. Yeats also called the doctor immediately. Doctor Phelps is with Papa now."

"Oh, God. How bad is it, Miles?"

He shook his head. "I don't know. Yeats says he complained of severe pains in his chest. We can only wait to speak to the doctor."

Diana hurried up the stairs to the second floor and paused outside the closed door of the duke's bedchamber. Miles followed her. Together they waited in tense silence until the doctor emerged into the corridor.

"Doctor Phelps—?" breathed Diana.

The doctor, managing to sound kindly and respectful and professional, all at once, said, "His Grace had a moderately severe heart attack, my lady, but I'm happy to tell you that he's resting comfortably now."

"My father will recover, then?" said Miles sharply.

The doctor pursed his lips. "I believe so, my lord. For the time being, at least."

"The time being?" Diana exclaimed in alarm.

Doctor Phelps looked mildly surprised. "Of course you're aware, my lady, that His Grace is not a well man."

"No, I'm not aware. I had understood, from your examination in February, that Papa had a mild heart condition."

"Ah." The doctor hesitated. "I'm not sure if I . . ." He paused again. "Obviously His Grace wished to spare his family, but perhaps it's best that you and Lord Brentford know about your father's condition. His Grace's heart condition is serious. He survived this attack, and he may well survive another, but sometime, in the not too far distant future, in my best judgment, his heart will give out, to put the matter in layman's terms."

"Oh, God." Diana choked back her tears. After a moment she said, "How long?"

"Some months. A year. Possibly longer, if His Grace doesn't put too much strain and stress on his heart."

Diana swallowed hard. "Thank you for being so frank with us. Can we see Papa now?"

"Yes, of course. But only for a few minutes. And don't say or do anything that might cause him distress or worry. With your permission, my lady, I'll take my leave now. I'll return tomorrow to see the patient."

As Diana and Miles entered the duke's bedchamber, his valet, who had been sitting beside the bed, rose with a respectful bow and retreated to a corner of the room.

Diana stood quietly by the bedside, gazing down at her father's face. His skin was waxy, and his strong features looked more pronounced than ever, as if the flesh had retreated beneath his bones. His eyes flickered open, focusing vaguely for a moment. Then he smiled. "There you are, my darling girl. And Miles. Don't look so blue-deviled, the two of you. I'm going to be right as a trivet."

"Of course you will, Papa," said Diana with a false cheerfulness. "But now you must get lots of rest."

"Oh, I shall, depend on it. Well, you know what a lazy fellow I am!" An entreating note crept into the duke's voice. "You'll stay on in London? You're not thinking of returning to Oxfordshire right away?"

Diana managed a smile. "Certainly not. You have all those plans to entertain me, remember?"

"Grandiose plans," the duke murmured. "Balls. Routs. Dinners." His eyes were becoming heavy. "It's so good to have you here, darling."

"I'm happy to be here, Papa. But now Miles and I are going to leave you for a bit. You must get some rest."

Diana kissed her father's cheek, pressed his hand and left the bedchamber. Miles joined her in the corridor. "I never thought to see Papa in this state. He's weak as a kitten," said Miles bleakly.

"I know. He's always been larger than life. Indestructible. When he walked into a room he gave the impression that he was the premier duke of the realm, even though Edgehill was by no means the first dukedom to be created."

Miles nodded. Suddenly he said, "Diana, where did you go tonight? The servants told me you went out alone, without even your abigail to accompany you."

"Why, I—" Diana bit her lip.

"You went to see that fellow Jared Amberly, didn't you? Don't bother to deny it. I can see it in your face."

Diana gave Miles a level look. "Yes, I went to see Jared. We had unfinished business between us."

"My God, Diana! After everything that Papa and I said to you about the man, you're continuing to see him?" Miles's eyes sparkled with anger. "You realize, don't you, that you may have been responsible for Papa's attack? The butler told me that Papa inquired after you, and seemed overset when he was told that you'd gone out without telling anyone where you were going. Shortly after that he collapsed."

Diana's heart constricted. Was she really responsible for her father's latest bout of illness? The duke had been highly incensed to discover her relationship to a man he despised. When he learned, not long afterward, that she had left the house in the evening hours, unattended by any of the servants, he probably had suspected that she had gone to see Jared. Were her affairs sufficiently distressing to him in his weakened state of health to cause his heart attack? She didn't know. She would never know.

"Diana, I'm sorry," said Miles impulsively. "I shouldn't have said what I did. Of course you would never do anything knowingly to harm Papa. It's just that he was so concerned about you and that half-caste Jared Amberly."

"He needn't be concerned in the future. I've made it quite clear to Jared that we can't see each other again."

On the following afternoon Diana sat in the library of Amberly House, conferring with the duke's secretary about cancelling his current engagements. She had already paid several visits to her father during the day, and had been relieved to find him significantly improved. "My little setback was all my own fault," he had told her jauntily. "Dr. Phelps had ordered me to drink no more than one glass of Madeira a day, and yesterday I had three! Let that be a lesson to you, my dear. Never pay out good money to a sawbones and then refuse to take his advice."

Her father's good spirits had almost persuaded Diana that the doctor's prognosis was overly grim. At any rate, and at the very least, he was feeling much better.

Shuffling through a pile of invitations, Diana said to the secretary, "It's agreed, then, that you'll send regrets to everyone whose invitations Papa had accepted for the next week. No, perhaps you should make that the next ten days."

"Yes, my lady." The secretary coughed. "What about His Grace's speech in the Lords? He had scheduled that for—let me be sure of the date—for Friday week. Nine days from now. He was to speak on the Bullion Report. He has been most concerned that Parliament may negative the Report. The decision is expected next month."

Frowning, Diana said, "I think it would be best to reschedule the speech, John. Nine days from now, if Papa felt indisposed, he would still insist on making an appearance in the Lords."

The secretary nodded. "I quite agree, my lady. His Grace has such a strong sense of duty."

A knock sounded at the door. Two footmen entered the library, each carrying a large parcel wrapped in heavy linen. "These jist arrived fer ye, my lady," one of the footmen reported.

"What on earth—?" Diana felt a stirring of uneasiness. "Please remove the coverings, Beetson."

She waited in silence until the footmen had carefully unwrapped the parcels.

"By jove," exclaimed the secretary. "Aren't those the—?"

"The Canaletto landscapes of Abbottsleigh and the Thames, yes," replied Diana, keeping her face wooden.

"But I thought . . ." The secretary paused, his face reddening with embarrassment.

"Here's a letter, my lady, or mayhap a note, that was enclosed wi' one o' the pictures." The footman handed Diana a folded piece of paper.

"Dear Lady Windham, I send you these paintings," the note began, in Jared's familiar neat handwriting. "I believe the paintings have great significance for you, since the one depicts your family estate of Abbottsleigh, and the other had occupied a prominent place in the Amberly collection. They no longer have any significance or interest for me, in the light of recent events. That being the case, I am returning the paintings to you. Please regard them as a gift."

A hot wave of anger swept over Diana. "Put the pictures back into their wrappings," she ordered the footmen, "and take them to—" she broke off. After a moment she said, "Take them to my dressing room."

"Yes, my lady."

After the servants had left the room, Diana said to the secretary, "I would prefer that you didn't mention the Canalettos to my father, John. Papa believes the paintings were sold at auction. In his present state of health there's no need to burden him with the fact that he was misinformed about the matter."

"Indeed, my lady. Quite so." The secretary tried valiantly to look discreet and understanding, though obviously he didn't understand the situation at all and was intensely curious about it.

Diana was still trying to control her anger as she left the library and went up to her rooms, where the footmen had just deposited the Canalettos in her dressing room. She stared at the swathed paintings in renewed resentment. Clearly Jared had sent them to her in order to indicate the disdainful indifference he now felt for her and her proud Amberly heritage.

Her first impulse had been to return the paintings to him without a message of any kind. But that gesture would have marked her as petty and adolescent as Jared himself, and, moreover, would probably have revealed to him how hurtful his action had been. No, it was better simply to ignore the matter. She would keep the Canalettos in her dressing room until she returned to Abbottsleigh. Eventually she might be able to convince her father that their financial situation had improved sufficiently so that she had been able to buy the paintings back. Until then she would not risk distressing him with the information that their prized paintings had been in the possession of Jared Amberly.

Jared looked up from his desk as Kamal entered the inner office.

"I've dispatched the paintings to Lady Windham, as you requested, sir," said the head clerk.

Jared's fingers tightened on the pen he was holding. Last night, in his anger and disillusionment, the return of the Canalettos to Diana had seemed a fitting gesture, marking a definitive end to their relationship and indicating how little her refusal to marry him had meant to him. Now he wasn't so sure. Diana might interpret that gesture as a mere petty act of retaliation. She might even guess at the bitter pain that had prompted it.

"Lady Windham should already be in receipt of the paintings," Kamal added. He sounded incurious, neutral, qualities Jared prized in him. Jared would not have tolerated any intrusion by an underling into his personal life, always with the exception of Rana. Kamal spoke as matter-of-factly as if he had just completed an ordinary business transaction, although, since he was privy to all of Jared's financial accounts, he undoubtedly knew to the penny what his employer had paid for the paintings at Christie's.

"A gentleman has called to see you, sir." Now Kamal's expression was less impassive. A flicker of what might even be called excitement showed in his dark eyes. "I believe you will wish to see him."

"Oh? Who is this gentleman?"

"He's a Colonel Pomeroy, sir. A member of the Prince of Wales's household."

"Ah. By all means, send the gentleman in."

Jared rose as his visitor entered the office. Colonel Pomeroy was a tall, imposing personage, dressed today in mufti, though it required no effort to visualize him in scarlet regimentals.

Motioning the colonel to a chair, Jared said, "How may I be of service to you, sir?"

The colonel gave Jared a long, considering look. "Mr. Amberly, His Royal Highness has been paying you and your bank a good deal of attention of late," he began, seemingly at a tangent.

"Really? I'm honored, sir."

The colonel inclined his head. "The Regent is convinced that you have become, in a very short period of time, one of the most successful men in the London banking scene. I'll come to the point at once, Mr. Amberly. His Royal Highness wishes to know if you would be willing to extend to him a substantial loan."

Jared's eyes narrowed. "How substantial?"

"The Regent requires fifty thousand pounds at once. Construction on his new home at Windsor, which I believe will be known as Royal Lodge, will begin soon, and he also has plans to make alterations at the Pavilion in Brighton."

"Fifty thousand pounds is a very large sum, Colonel."

"It is. Which is precisely why we are applying to a banker who is known to have large interests."

Smiling, Jared said, "Impeccable logic, sir." He thought for a few moments longer. "I should be delighted to oblige His Royal Highness."

"Splendid. I trust the arrangements can be made soon? Then I'll bid you good day, Mr. Amberly."

Jared walked his visitor to the door with a cool courtesy that concealed an inner feeling of exultation. He had done it. When it became known that he had sufficient assets to extend a large loan to the Regent himself, nothing could stop him from becoming one of the most powerful operators in the London financial world. Oh, granted, producing a sum as large as fifty thousand pounds might crimp him a bit temporarily. He was also well aware that he couldn't expect the return of the loan in the near future. It was well known in the city that the Regent's debts were astronomical. Half a million pounds was the sum bruited about. Moreover, it was equally well-known that His Highness's interest payments were often in arrears. No matter. The interest on the loan would be forthcoming eventually. He could afford to wait for his money.

Kamal smiled in triumph when he heard the news. "We'll soon be the biggest banking house in London, sir."

"Don't forget a banker by the name of Rothschild," Jared replied dryly. "He's making a name for himself, too."

Rana was less impressed by the news of the loan to the Regent. When Jared reported to her playfully that he was now doing business with the Prince Regent—"He's the King of England's son, Rana, and now he's actually taking his father's place in the government"—Rana had said serenely, "That's very nice,

Sahib, I'm sure. But then, I've never doubted you would be very successful."

Rana showed much more emotion when Jared informed her she was to be his companion at a theatrical performance at the Royal Opera House at Covent Garden.

"No, Sahib, that is out of the question. I am your servant. It would not be seemly for me to appear in public with you."

"Rana, listen to me. You asked me once why I came to London. I'll tell you now. I want to be so successful, so well-known, so looked up to, that I can redress a great wrong that was done to me years ago. Do you understand?"

"Yes, Sahib, I think so," Rana faltered.

"Good. Well, then, I can think of no better way of calling attention to myself than by appearing at the theater in the company of the most beautiful woman I know. You brought my mother's trunks to England, did you not?"

"Yes."

"I know she had a store of lovely costumes and a casket of jewels that she didn't have the heart to wear after my father deserted her. Choose whatever takes your fancy. You and I are going to the theater."

Diana looked up from her cup of tea when a footman appeared in the doorway of the morning room with a tray bearing a pile of cards. She sighed as she looked at the cards. People had been calling at Amberly House in swarms since the news of the duke's illness. She was under no obligation to receive the callers physically, of course, but she would certainly have to return the cards.

"Mr. Dalton is here, my lady. Will you see him?"

Diana sighed again. She suspected that Aubrey had called to renew his suit, however indirectly, but she couldn't refuse to see such an old friend. "Ask Mr. Dalton to come in."

Aubrey bounded into the morning room, his blonde good looks set off, as usual, by meticulous grooming and expert tailoring. "Lord, Diana, I've been so concerned about you since

Miles told me of the duke's illness. I know how close you are to your father. How is he today?"

"Much better, thank God. It's only two days since his heart attack, and already he's clamoring to be out of bed."

"What good news, by Jove." Aubrey's tone was cordial, but it was clear he had other concerns on his mind. "Diana, I couldn't believe my ears when Miles told me about this Jared Amberly. Remember the fellow well. He and Miles were both in my form at Eton. Did the man really have the gall to cast out lures to you?"

"I would prefer not to discuss my personal affairs with you, Aubrey," Diana said repressively. "Miles had no right to confide in you. He was very indiscreet."

"Good God, 'indiscreet' isn't the word to describe Miles. Don't you realize that he feels guilty? He considers that he and I are responsible for your meeting with this fellow Amberly, which he tells me took place at the Pantheon masquerade ball. The meeting wouldn't have occurred if we'd been more conscientious escorts. Although, in all truth, I'm more responsible than Miles. I should never have left you alone in that card room, where any loose fish might see fit to accost you."

"That's enough, Aubrey. I told you I didn't care to discuss Jared Amberly."

For a moment Aubrey stared at her, his lips clenched together, as if on guard against an incautious remark. Then he burst out, "Why don't you wish to talk about him? Is it because he struck a little too close to the bone? Miles said you had actually considered marrying the fellow. Did you allow that half-caste to kiss you, Diana? And did you enjoy those kisses, more than you ever enjoyed mine?"

"Aubrey!" Diana glared at him in outrage. "I think you had better go."

Aubrey hung his head, obviously fighting for control. At length he mumbled, "I'm sorry. I don't know what came over me. It's just that . . . I'm so head-over-heels in love with you that I can't bear to think of you with another man, and that man a half-caste ruffian who dared to raise his eyes to you." He took a deep breath to steady himself. "I'd promise never to mention the fellow's name to you again, except that I have some information I think you should know about him."

"Aubrey —"

"No, please listen to me. When you're dealing with dubious characters it's best to know all you can about them. So when Miles told me this Amberly had claimed to be a banker, I decided to look into the matter. In my position at the Treasury, naturally, I have access to a great deal of information about the financial community. I was surprised by what I learned.

"Amberly really is a banker. At least he didn't lie to you there. In a fairly short time he's become a power in Lombard Street. Now that the Prime Minister has determined to prosecute the war, government borrowings have skyrocketed. Some say the government will need to borrow as much as twenty million pounds this year, and as of this date, I can tell you, a very large part of these new securities have moved through the hands of Amberly and another comparative newcomer, a German Jewish banker and trader by the name of Rothschild. Amberly is a very rich man, Diana. It frightens me to think how he might have acquired his fortune—theft, or embezzlement, or blackmail, who can say? Because when Miles and I knew him he was a nobody, a worse than nobody, the raggle-taggle by-blow of an obscure ex-East India official in Calcutta."

"I see. Thank you, Aubrey. Can we talk about something else now?"

"Good God, yes." Aubrey smiled in relief. "For starters, will you allow me to escort you to Covent Garden tonight? Kemble is doing *Coriolanus*. I recall you once said you wanted to see him play the part."

"Oh—no, thank you. I don't think I should be attending the theater while Papa is so ill."

"But you've just told me the duke is recovering. I'm sure he wouldn't wish you to stay immured behind the walls of Amberly House, simply because he's obliged to keep to his bed temporarily. Please reconsider, Diana."

Diana knew Aubrey was right. Only this morning her father had chided her for hovering about his bedchamber. "The servants take very good care of me, my dear, and Doctor Phelps calls several times a day. I'm in good hands. You mustn't spend all your time fussing over me. I want you to relax, enjoy yourself."

"Very well, Aubrey. I should like to see Mr. Kemble in *Coriolanus*."

Later that evening, seated beside Aubrey in a box at the Royal Opera House, Diana had to admit she was glad she had accepted the invitation. Attendance at the play would take her mind off her father's illness and help her to suppress the aching feeling of loss that she would never see or talk to or touch Jared Amberly again. She was conscious of looking her best, too, in a gown of creamy satin embroidered in seed pearls, with a wreath of white roses in her amber curls.

She turned to Aubrey at the end of the first act, her face glowing, as she said, "I'm so glad we came. Mr. Kemble is in splendid form."

Uncharacteristically, Aubrey was paying her scant attention. His gaze was fixed on a box in the third tier of the great auditorium, where a man and a woman had just taken their seats.

"By Jove, who do you suppose that could be?" Aubrey muttered. "Some sort of Eastern royalty, do you think?"

Diana followed Aubrey's gaze. The dark-haired, dark-skinned woman was strikingly beautiful. She wore a garment in gleaming cloth of gold, seemingly wrapped around her waist and thrown over her shoulder and around her head, worn over a red silk bodice heavily embroidered in gold. A heavy gold necklace set with rubies and diamonds circled her neck, matching her earrings and numerous bracelets. She was not a young girl, but a mature woman. The man sitting next to her leaned closer to speak to her, and Diana caught her breath.

"What is it? Do you know the lady?" Aubrey inquired. His gaze sharpened. "My God, is that—? Yes, I swear it is. I haven't seen the man in ten years or more, but I recognize him. That's Jared Amberly, isn't it?"

"Yes," Diana murmured. Each time she saw Jared she found herself remembering with a fresh shock of surprise how barbarically handsome he was. He looked across the auditorium in her direction just then, and she saw him stiffen slightly. After a moment's hesitation he rose, bowing to her, his face expressionless. Feeling the color mount to her cheeks, she inclined her head.

"The gall of the man to greet you publicly," Aubrey fumed. "You shouldn't have acknowledged him, Diana. It may give him ideas. And what barefaced effrontery to seat his leman in the choicest location in the Royal Opera House. That's who the woman is, you know. I'm sure of it. The *on dit* around the Royal Exchange is that Amberly brought his native mistress from India to live with him."

Seven

Diana sat at the desk in the morning room, beginning a letter to the duke's estate agent at Abbottsleigh. "Dear Mr. Roberts: I've had occasion to read a report by the Board of Agriculture about the practice of using a winnowing machine as a part of the peg-drum thrasher, in which grain can be cleaned and thrashed in one operation. I think it might be advantageous for us to try this new combination machine on the home farm . . ."

Her pen ceased moving as her thoughts drifted to the performance of *Coriolanus* at Covent Garden the evening before. She felt the same surge of anger she had experienced then, when Aubrey had explained that the lovely native woman sitting beside Jared in the third tier box was the mistress he had brought with him from India.

That Jared had a mistress was none of her affair, she told herself. However, she would have expected him to display better taste. Most gentlemen who kept women didn't flaunt them at the Royal Opera House, nor did they maintain their paramours in their places of chief residence.

Diana chewed the end of her pen. She knew quite well she was deceiving herself. Jared's behavior wasn't a matter of indifference to her, nor was it purely a matter of taste. She was both angry and hurt to learn that Jared had mounted a mistress. She was even more angry and hurt to realize that during the weeks he was writing his impassioned letters to her, urging her to marry him, he had all the while been sleeping with his native inamorata in the fine new town house he had described to her.

"There you are, Diana." Miles walked into the morning

room, pausing beside her to drop a kiss on her forehead and to glance at the letter she had started. "In the fiend's name, my girl, is it necessary for you to do old Roberts's work for him?"

"He needs to be nudged now and then, that's all."

Miles threw himself into a chair. "I've just been to see Papa. He was sitting up in an easy chair, looking quite the thing. Do you know, I can't believe that Doctor Phelps's prognosis was correct. Papa certainly doesn't give the appearance of a dying man. If you ask me, he'll live to be a hundred."

Shaking her head, Diana said, "I'd like to think that, but I suspect Papa's rapid recovery is purely illusory. He's fighting the disease with every ounce of his strength. He'll never give in to weakness and disability. In the end, though . . . in the end, gallantry and courage simply won't be enough."

Miles gave her a somber look. "Deep down, I know you're right." He hesitated. "I expect that's why I didn't plague Papa with any talk about money during my visit. The fact is, Diana, I'm in desperate need of five hundred yellow boys. Can you help me? After all, you must have realized a nice sum from the sale of the Canalettos."

Diana could feel her expression growing cold. "Papa told me that you just applied to him for an advance on your quarterly allowance."

Flushing, Miles replied, "I needed the money to pay a pressing debt on quarter day. Well, yes, it was a gambling debt. Debts of honor have to be paid, I don't need to tell you that, and I didn't want to go to the cent-per-centers again. Then last night I had a cursed run of luck at the faro tables at Brooks's. I lost another five hundred. Diana, I know what you're thinking. I know I promised to curb my gambling. I give you my sacred word, this is the last time I'll ask you for money to recoup my losses."

"It's hard for me to believe that, Miles. You've promised so many times to stop gambling."

"I know, but this time I mean it. I'm going to change my ways. You see, I've decided to get married."

Forgetting her displeasure, Diana exclaimed in delight, "Really, Miles? I was beginning to fear I'd never see you properly leg-shackled. Who is the young lady?"

Looking self-conscious, Miles said, "Mind, there's nothing official. I haven't offered for Miss Lyon. Miss Charlotte Lyon, that is."

Diana knit her brows. "I don't believe I know her. Who are her family?"

"Oh, she's a few years younger than you. You wouldn't have met her. Her father is Baron Lyon of Radnor. He has a large estate in Lancashire. You'll call on her, won't you? She lives in Cavendish Square."

"Yes, of course. Miles, I'm very happy for you."

"I, too. Mustn't count our chickens prematurely, though. She may not take me, eh?" Rising, Miles said, "I'll be off. Lunch with Aubrey at Boodles's. Er—about the five hundred . . . I really need it, if I'm to do the pretty with Miss Lyon."

"Very well. I'll see that you get the five hundred. But this is the last time, absolutely. You *must* stay within your allowance."

"I will, never fear. I told you I was a changed man, remember?"

After her brother's departure, as Diana walked up the stairs to have lunch with the duke in his bedchamber, she speculated on Miles's latest resolve to quit the gaming tables. Would he succeed in keeping his pledge this time? She remembered her father's concern that Miles might not be able to control his gambling, in the same way that some men seemed unable to control their drinking. But perhaps a wife and a family would be a steadying influence. There was such a thing, after all, as a reformed rake.

As Diana entered her father's bedchamber a pair of footmen were placing covered dishes on a table drawn up next to the window.

The duke smiled a welcome and rose from his easy chair to walk to the table. "You're in good time, my dear, as usual. Let's see what Cook has provided for us." His color was good today, and, though he walked slowly, he was perfectly steady on his feet. Diana allowed herself a smidgen of hope that Doctor Phelps had, after all, been overly pessimistic.

"Well, now, this broth is quite tasty," said the duke, taking a spoonful. "I'm dubious about the chicken, though. Not too appetizing looking. Boiled, at that. Cook knows I prefer beef."

"Doctor Phelps has prescribed a bland diet, Papa."

"So he has. And I've promised to obey doctor's orders, and I'm a man of my word." The duke sighed. He pointed at his glass. "That, however, is the outside of enough. Barley water is *not* a gentleman's drink!"

Diana smiled at him affectionately. Whatever the circumstances, her father would conduct himself like a complete gentleman. Unlike someone else she could name. . . . She shook her head slightly, banishing the specter of Jared Amberly and his seedy love life. "Papa, did Miles talk to you this morning about getting married?"

"No." The duke raised an eyebrow. *"Is* he thinking of getting married? I'd have thought he might have informed me."

"Oh, he hasn't actually made Miss Lyon an offer."

Frowning, the duke said, "Lyon? I don't recall. . . . You don't mean Lyon of Radnor's daughter?"

"Yes. If that's the same Lord Lyon who lives in Lancashire. Why, what is it, Papa?" Diana added as she observed the sudden tightening of her father's mouth.

"It's not the match I'd have chosen for Miles," the duke muttered. "This Baron Lyon's father was a country squire who became a rich mill owner in Lancashire. Bought himself a large estate, succeeded in obtaining a peerage. The son is even richer, I hear." He gave himself a little shake. "Ah, well. I believe this second Lord Lyon has only the one child, a daughter. She'll inherit a tidy fortune one day. If the girl is personable, and Miles has a fancy for her, I won't object to the match."

"Miles asked me to visit Miss Lyon."

"Do so, by all means. You have a shrewd eye. You'll soon know if the girl is acceptable."

Lord Lyon occupied a large impressive house in Cavendish Square. Diana waited in her carriage while her footman went up to the door to deliver cards for Lady Lyon and Miss Lyon, with instructions to inquire if Lady Lyon was at home. Soon the footman returned with an invitation for Diana to come into the house.

She waited for only a few moments in the handsomely furnished drawing room. Almost before she was settled in her chair two women entered the room. The elder woman greeted Diana with a beaming smile. "My dear Lady Windham, what a great pleasure it is to meet you. May I present my daughter, Charlotte, to you?"

Diana inclined her head. "Lady Lyon, Miss Lyon." She studied the women. Lady Lyon was a rather hard-looking lady in early middle age, whose manner, it seemed to Diana, was overly cordial and effusive to the point of being obsequious. Her daughter—well, Diana could easily see why Miles had decided to become a Benedict. Charlotte Lyon was a beautiful creature with golden curls, soft blue eyes, rose-petal skin, and an enchanting smile.

"Lady Windham, I almost feel as though I know you already," said Charlotte shyly. "Your brother has spoken so much of you."

"Yes, indeed," put in her mother. "Such a charming man, your brother. So affable, so considerate. And so very fond of you, my dear Lady Windham. Why, on his last visit to us, Lord Brentford could speak of little except your coming visit to London, and we have been anxiously awaiting your arrival, hoping we might have the opportunity to make your acquaintance." She put her hand to her head in a rather theatrical gesture. "I'm being remiss. How is your dear father? We were so saddened to hear the duke was ill."

"Father is much better, thank you." Diana made a quick decision. Charlotte Lyon was more than presentable, and the duke would want Diana to acknowledge the connection. "Lady Lyon, I should like to invite you and your husband and Miss Lyon to come to dinner at Amberly House. A very small dinner, since my father is ill and cannot act as your host. Just your family and my brother and I and an old family friend, Mr. Aubrey Dalton. I think it would be a fine opportunity for us to know each other better."

"Oh, I agree," exclaimed Lady Lyon, her rather prominent eyes fairly popping out of her head in delight. "We accept with pleasure."

Diana named a date and left shortly thereafter. Her thoughts on having met Miles's possible bride were mixed. She could not like Lady Lyon, who she suspected of being a social climber, though doubtless it was unfair to judge the lady on such short acquaintance. With Charlotte she could find no fault. In addition to being beautiful, the girl was charming and well-bred, with seemingly a natural gift for making people feel at ease. To Diana, for example, she had remarked at one point, "Lord Brentford tells me you're very interested in farming, Lady Windham. He says you virtually manage your father's estate." Charlotte had added with a deprecating smile, "For my part, I know nothing of farming. I daresay I couldn't tell the difference between a sheep and a goat!"

The dinner party took place a week later. Diana had been curious to meet Lord Lyon, who she decided almost instantly was a masculine version of his wife.

Charlotte's father was a small, rotund man with an air of great self-importance and a tendency to monopolize any conversation. Speaking to Diana, he called attention complacently to the fact that he and the duke were associates in the Lords. "Your father and I, my dear Lady Windham, share our devotion to our duties in this august body, unlike others I could name!"

Lord Lyon spoke at length of the improvements he was making at his estate in Lancashire. "While I hesitate to compare my estate at Crossways to the splendors of Abbottsleigh, I don't doubt that the onlooker could find many points of resemblance."

About his daughter the baron remarked, "Charlotte is a beautiful girl, if I do say so myself. Accomplished, too. Plays the pianoforte as well as any professional musician. I saw to that, providing her with the best masters. She speaks fluent French and Italian, too. You wouldn't believe the swarm of suitors we've had buzzing around her. Some of them fortune hunters, no doubt. Charlotte will be one of the greatest heiresses in England one day. But of course my wife and I couldn't allow her to marry just anybody. She must have a husband who is worthy of her, a man of the very highest status, wouldn't you agree, Lady Windham?"

"Oh, very much so," Diana murmured, trying not to show her distaste. Short of a direct declaration, Lord Lyon could hardly have indicated more clearly his desire to unite his family by marriage to that of the Duke of Edgehill.

She kept a close eye on Miles and Charlotte in the drawing room before dinner, trying to determine the degree of affection between them. They made a handsome pair, Miles with his father's good looks and grace of carriage, Charlotte almost too beautiful in an ethereal gown of blue silk gauze that exactly matched her eyes. Charlotte was demure and smiling and obviously pleased by Miles's attentions, but she also displayed a ladylike reticence. Miles appeared captivated, but then, as Diana knew from experience, he was a very susceptible man as far as females were concerned, although in the past most of those females had been of a regrettably vulgar variety. Diana could only conclude that, if Miles and Charlotte weren't in love, they were well on their way to being so.

After dinner in the drawing room, when the men had returned from their port, Aubrey sought Diana out. "I haven't had a word with you tonight," he said aggrievedly. "That Lord Lyon monopolized you. What do you think of him?"

"He seems perfectly pleasant."

"You know, don't you, that he's after Miles as his future son-in-law? The betting in the clubs was fifty-fifty until recently. Now the odds have shifted a bit, favoring a proposal by Miles to about sixty-forty."

Diana glared at him. "Aubrey! How vulgar!"

He grinned at her. "You're a woman of the world. You know full well that anything at all is fair game in the betting book at White's." His smile faded. "That's enough about Miles's affairs. I have some personal news. Do you remember I told you that a vacancy might occur soon in the Court of Directors of the East India Company? Well, the vacancy is now official. Old Sir Percival Olney died last week. Election of the new director will take place in about two weeks, and I plan to present myself for the position."

"That's very interesting, Aubrey. Are there many candidates for the post?"

"Oh, a whole gaggle of them, no doubt. There's always fierce competition for such a plum. There are about two thousand proprietors in the Company, you understand, but only those with a holding of one thousand pounds of stock can vote in a ballot. Those with holdings of ten thousand pounds or more have four votes each. Now, about fifty proprietors hold stock of over ten thousand pounds. Most of them live in London, *and* most of them were friends of my uncle the Nabob, who left me his stock. So I daresay many of those proprietors would be inclined to vote for me, because of the family connection. At any rate, I intend to call on as many of them as possible in the next weeks to solicit their votes."

"I think your chances sound excellent. I'll be waiting with great interest to learn the outcome."

"Thank you. Of course, if I should be elected to the Court, I think your father might well look more favorably on my suit—"

"Aubrey . . ."

"I know, I know. I promised not to press you." Aubrey sighed. He hesitated. "There's one more thing. I suppose I should tell you . . ."

"What is it?"

"Well, Lombard Street to a Brummagen sixpence it's of no consequence, but I've heard a rumor that Jared Amberly is also seeking a seat on the Court."

"Oh." Diana thought wryly that it was hard to put Jared out of her mind when she was reminded of him at every turn in the conversation. She tried to sound impersonal as she said, "Strictly speaking, Mr. Amberly has a perfect right to try for the post. His father was an official with the East India Company and may very well have bequeathed him shares of stock, even though Jared is an illegitimate son. And you've told me yourself that he's a wealthy and influential banker. Perhaps his wealth might appear to be an important qualification to some electors. After all, the East India Company is in business to make money."

Aubrey reacted angrily. "Lord, Diana, you can't think the proprietors of the East India Company would elect a creature like Jared Amberly to their Court. A half-caste, illegitimate, unknown to everyone until he appeared mysteriously in London with a fistful of money, acquired from who knows what source! For all we know, he may have engaged in piracy on the high seas!"

Aubrey paused, his face darkening. "The devil of it is that money does speak, sometimes. There are many small proprietors who might well be impressed by a snippet of news I heard the other day. It seems that Amberly has succeeded in becoming an important creditor to the Prince Regent himself."

"Indeed," said Diana doubtfully. "I've heard that the Regent is in debt to a great many people, and that often he's a slow payer. But I presume you consider Jared Amberly's loan to His Royal Highness to be quite a feather in his cap?"

"Feather!" Aubrey snorted. "I should say so. The Regent isn't in the habit of borrowing paltry sums, you know."

"Well, I'm sure most of the proprietors aren't venal. You'll see, the electors will place much more confidence in a candidate like you, Aubrey."

Diana's soothing words expressed less confidence than she actually felt. On the surface it might seem improbable that the proprietors of the East India Company would elect a man of Jared's low antecedents to their Court of Directors. But she had an uneasy sense that Jared might be unstoppable in what was beginning to appear to her as a relentless drive for power and riches. If he succeeded in becoming a member of the Court of Directors he would achieve an even more prominent place on the London scene, and he would be that much more difficult for her to avoid. Unless she retreated to Abbottsleigh, of course, and she couldn't leave her father while he was so ill.

Jared stood with Rana in the dining room, inspecting the long table set for twenty-four guests. On the snowy linen the Imari porcelain service glowed in deep colors of blue, rose, and gold. The large centerpiece in silver gilt was in the form of a dessert stand with a foliated central column upon a triangular base. Flanking the centerpiece on either side was a pair of candelabra, one in ormolu, the other in silver gilt. Arranged on the rosewood sideboard cupboard was an impressive array of silver plates. The furnishing of his dining room had cost him a pretty penny, but Jared didn't regret the cost. In a sense, it was a business expenditure.

"Your table looks splendid, Rana," Jared said. "It certainly ought to impress my guests."

"I am happy you are pleased, Sahib. It is good to see you entertaining in a manner that suits your station, as your father was used to do. These guests who are coming to dine with you tonight, are they very important people?"

"Only in a sense. You recall I told you that I wished to become a member of the Court of Directors of the East India Company? Well, my guests tonight—I had to invite their wives, naturally—are men who own small amounts of stock in the Company, and thereby possess votes. I intend to wine and dine as many of these small shareholders as I can reach in the next few weeks. A large number of single votes can add up to an impressive total."

Jared glanced at the far end of the table, where a place remained unset. "Won't you change your mind about acting as my hostess? I want my guests to realize I'm knowledgeable about India, since that's the main source of the company's revenue, so I'm offering them a typical Indian meal—*pilau, cabob, curries, mangoe achar, sony sauce,* and *dumpoked* fowl. I think they would be intrigued to have an Indian hostess as well."

Rana shook her head. "No, Sahib. I am your servant, not your hostess. If I were to sit at your table tonight your guests would conclude that I was your mistress. This is not India, where such a practice is . . ." She stopped in confusion.

"You mean that, at least until fairly recently, Anglo-Indian society didn't necessarily frown upon a man who invited his friends—male, of course—to sit at table with his mistress. As my father 'honored' my mother."

"Yes, Sahib." Rana winced at the bitterness in Jared's voice. After a moment she said, "I am a foreigner, and I do not understand fully the English customs, but I feel certain that my presence among your guests would only shock them."

His expression reluctant, Jared nodded. "I suppose you're right. How did you become so wise, Rana?"

Smiling, she shook her head. "Oh, you give me too much credit, Sahib." Her smile fading, she said hesitantly, "I have not mentioned this before because I feared to offend you . . ." She paused and began again. "That night you insisted I go with you to the theater—which I still think was very unwise—you bowed to a beautiful lady in the box opposite us. I recognized her. She was the lady who came to the house to see you one evening. Can you—would you—tell me if that was the lady you hoped to marry?"

Jared's face hardened. "Yes," he said briefly. "The lady decided not to marry me. Like my father, she objects to public union with someone of Indian blood."

"Sahib . . ." Rana faltered. Her pretty face looked stricken. "Is there nothing you can say to the lady to change her mind?"

Jared patted her shoulder. "No. There are no such words. Even if there were, I wouldn't say them. I don't want a wife who's ashamed of me."

On polling day for the election of a new director to the Court of the East India Company, Miles hosted a luncheon for his sister and Aubrey Dalton at his rooms in the Albany.

"I thought it proper to offer you my hospitality today, old fellow, to indicate my support for you before you go off to the wars—I mean the balloting glasses," Miles remarked jocularly to Aubrey. "A little pre-celebration, so to speak. Mind, I don't guarantee the food here at the Albany will be epicurean. If—when—you win the directorship, you can take me and Diana to dine at the Pulteney. I hear they have a superb new French chef."

"The Pulteney it is," Aubrey replied. He looked pleased with himself. "I don't wish to appear overly confident, but I'm quite hopeful about the election today. I've received solid promises of support from my uncle's old friends."

Diana smiled. "I'm sure you'll be one of the leading candidates, at the very least. It was kind of you to invite us to East India House to view the proceedings."

"And to share the triumph," chortled Miles, raising his glass in a toast.

As the luncheon proceeded Miles raised his glass more and more often. Diana looked at him askance. Ordinarily he wasn't a heavy drinker, not in the middle of the day, at any rate, and rarely in the presence of ladies.

At one point, after pouring himself a glass from a second bottle of Madeira, Miles growled, "If you don't win this election, Aubrey, I jolly well hope you'll come out ahead in the returns over that bounder Jared Amberly."

Flicking Diana an embarrassed glance, Aubrey protested, "I say, old boy, you know we'd agreed not to talk about the fellow in front of your sister."

Miles gulped down half a glass of wine. "Well, perhaps Diana should know what a loose screw Amberly really is, if the full horror hasn't dawned on her. Do you know what Amberly did, Diana? Yesterday I discovered he had the gall to buy several of my notes from a cent-per-center I sometimes do business with. Why did he do that, do you suppose? Does he think to cancel my obligation to him in return for permission to visit Amberly House—and you?"

"I can't imagine," said Diana quietly, although she felt a *frisson* of uneasiness. Did Jared ever act without a definite motive? "It makes no matter, in the event. If he presents the notes for payment, we'll pay them. Don't concern yourself about it."

As Miles was about to continue his tirade, Aubrey created a diversion by consulting his watch. "It's time we left. Many of the proprietors will already have arrived."

As they descended from their carriage near East India House, Aubrey and his party found the street in front of the building swarming with people, making it almost impossible for Aubrey to force his way with Miles and Diana through the stately entrance beneath the six tall Ionic columns. Inside the building the corridors and passageways were also jammed with people, many of them liveried servants. One servant edged his way up to Aubrey, grabbing at his sleeve. "Yer Honor, if ye 'as a vote, kin I beg ye ter cast it fer Mr. George Rountree?"

"No, you may not!" Snatching away his arm, Aubrey glared at the speaker. "As it happens, I'm a candidate for the post of director myself."

"Ah, be ye, sir." With a shrug, the man turned to Diana, giving her a rakish leer. "How's aboot ye, ma'am? Ye're sich a 'andsome creetur, I'll warrant ye'd like ter vote for a fine gentleman like Mr. Rountree."

"You're wasting your time. I have no vote." Diana edged away from the speaker.

"Be off with you, my man," exclaimed Miles. Diana had a moment of alarm. Miles was better than half-seas over from the effect of his drinking at the luncheon, and he sounded belligerent. To her relief, a quarrel was avoided when the stranger stepped back, turning his attention to another gentleman, a possible voter, who had just entered the foyer.

"Dash it, Diana, I'm very sorry to subject you to a scene like this," Aubrey said in a low voice. "I'd been warned, of course, that a crowd of hangers-on, many of them personal servants of the candidates, would be here to solicit support for their men, but I never imagined a mob like this." He gazed indignantly at the mass of humanity in the foyer. "You'd hardly think this was the scene of the election of officers to a great company. It's more like the election of a parish churchwarden! Why, at this rate I'll be hard put to make my way to the balloting glasses!"

"Don't apologize, Aubrey," Diana said. "You're not responsible for these people. Go along and vote. Miles and I will wait here for you, primed to congratulate you on your victory."

"Yes, go ahead, Aubrey," Miles joined in. "I'll take good care of Diana."

The balloting had apparently been going on for some time. As Diana waited with Miles, she observed that the number of people entering the building was gradually decreasing, and judged that most of the voting proprietors had probably arrived. The haranguing by the hangers-on of prospective voters gradually tapered off also, and the crowd of spectators settled down, like Diana and Miles, to await the result of the balloting.

The minutes dragged by, and Diana was beginning to feel overwhelmed by the sheer press of bodies crowding around her. Her feet ached in her thin slippers on the cold marble floor. Gradually she became aware of a low rumble of voices from the other end of the corridor. The crowd around her roused from its lethargy and started to push toward the interior of the building. Aubrey appeared, pushing his way through the mob, his face set and grim.

"I lost," he muttered, when he came up to Diana and Miles. "I lost to Jared Amberly. I'm told he wined and dined every proprietor in London who possessed even one vote. God knows what he promised them in the way of patronage and perquisites."

"Damnation, Aubrey," Miles burst out. "What you're saying is that Amberly bribed his way into office. It's a plain miscarriage of justice. It shouldn't be allowed."

"Hush, Miles," Diana remonstrated. "You're speaking too loudly. And Aubrey has no proof that Jared Amberly bribed anyone."

"I don't need proof. I know the man." Miles tensed as the crowd began to part, pressing back against the walls of the foyer, and Jared walked into sight, followed, and half surrounded, by a large group of people, all of them shouting congratulations and trying to gain his attention.

Cursing under his breath, Miles elbowed his way through the people standing in front of him and headed toward Jared before Diana and Aubrey grasped his intention. He strode in front of Jared, blocking his path.

Glaring at Jared, Miles exclaimed, "Well, you damned hellkite, I daresay you're proud of the way you bubbled the honest proprietors of the East India Company into voting you into office. They certainly wouldn't have done so if they had known who you really are, a half-blood adventurer, the by-blow of some failed company official who apparently lacked the means to return to England when his working days were over. What did you promise the poor benighted souls, Amberly? Do they realize there aren't enough plums in the whole East India Company to pay off your debts to them?"

The crowd noise had died away completely. His face a mask of disdain, Jared's quiet voice carried in a vacuum of silence. "Please step aside, Lord Brentford. As far as I'm aware, you have no connection to the East India Company, and I'm under no obligation to explain my actions to you."

"Perhaps not, but you certainly have an obligation to explain to my friend Aubrey Dalton how you managed to cheat him out of a position he could fill admirably," Miles flashed. His voice was slurred now, and he had a difficult time keeping his balance.

Eyeing him contemptuously, Jared snapped, "If Mr. Dalton chooses to talk to me, that's one thing. I have nothing to say to you. Good day, Lord Brentford."

"Not so fast, Amberly." Miles put out his hand to strike a stinging blow on Jared's face. "There. Will you talk to me now?"

A red mark showing against the dark skin of his cheek, Jared stepped back, his mouth tightening. After a moment he said, "No, I won't talk to you, Brentford. *You* can talk to my second." Giving Miles a hard shove that sent him staggering, Jared strode past him and out the entrance door of East India House, ignoring the curious stares of the people crowding the foyer.

Eight

"Oh, God." Aubrey seized Diana's arm and pulled her through a group of interested onlookers in the foyer of East India House. "We must get Miles out of here."

When they reached Miles in the middle of the foyer he was very nearly incoherent. He looked around wildly, saying, "Where's Amberly? I hadn't finished speaking to the damned loose screw."

"Confound it, Miles, you're foxed," hissed Aubrey. "Come along with me and Diana." He put his arm over Miles's shoulder and propelled him toward the door.

Miles virtually collapsed after Aubrey and a footman helped him into the waiting carriage. He sat slumped in a corner of the carriage, breathing stertorously, occasionally muttering, "Where's Amberly?"

"I told the coachman to take us to the Albany, rather than to Amberly House," Aubrey said to Diana in a low voice. "Miles's valet can take care of him perfectly well. There's no need to acquaint your father's household with—er—the problem."

"Thank you, Aubrey," said Diana in relief. "I hope we can prevent Papa from learning about this. Doctor Phelps warned us about causing Papa any stress." She paused to think, a worried frown creasing her forehead. "Do you think Jared will really challenge Miles to a duel?"

Aubrey shook his head. "How can I say? Amberly *is* the injured party. Miles struck him. But—" Breaking off, Aubrey turned red. "Dash it, Diana, I shouldn't be talking to you like this. A gentleman doesn't discuss such matters with females."

Diana gave Aubrey an impatient look. "Nonsense. For one thing, I already know about the possibility of a duel. I was a witness to Miles's irresponsible behavior, remember? For another, I'm no missish female whose innocent ears must be guarded against indelicate disclosures. Now, then: do you think Jared Amberly really means to fight a duel with Miles?"

Aubrey threw up his hands. "I can only guess. Amberly's no gentleman. What would it benefit him to fight a duel? Certainly neither social acclaim nor recognition, since he's already outside the pale of society. One good thing, it's as likely as not that he's unfamiliar with a pistol, because that's a gentleman's weapon. And if he's the challenger he has no choice of weapons, so he can't elect to use a scimitar or a—a *kris,* or some other outlandish Eastern knife with which Miles is unfamiliar. But perhaps we're worrying over nothing. Amberly may simply have been bluffing when he told Miles to talk to his second. Very probably he has no intention of fighting a duel." Pausing, Aubrey muttered, "I hope to God that's the case, because . . ."

"Because of what?"

"Because if Amberly is any kind of a shot, and challenges Miles to fight, I'd be afraid of the outcome. Miles is the worst shot I've encountered in my life. He can't hit a stable door."

Diana's blood ran cold. It couldn't come to that, a fight to the death between her brother and the man she . . . She said firmly, to chase the demons her thought had aroused, "I'm sure you're right. A duel wouldn't profit Jared Amberly. He's interested only in making money. He won't challenge Miles."

Jared's head clerk entered the inner office. "I thought you would wish to know, sir, that the gold transaction has been satisfactorily completed."

"No problems, I hope. I'm sorry I wasn't able to accompany you this time."

"You had other concerns with the Court of Directors of the East India Company." Kamal shook his head. "There were no problems, except that Captain Appleton reminded me that smuggling is a dangerous profession. I think perhaps the good captain is angling for larger fees."

"Let him ask, then." Jared looked up from the papers on his desk, studying the clerk. "Kamal, what do you know about duelling?"

"Nothing, sir." As was his wont, except when he was discussing business, Kamal displayed no curiosity at the question.

Jared said abruptly, "I want you to act as my second in a duel. Don't worry about your lack of knowledge of duelling. I can explain what you need to know in a few sentences."

The impassive expression faded from Kamal's face. "Sir, I'd remind you that acting as your second is the prerogative of a gentleman. I'm no gentleman."

Jared laughed shortly. "Nor am I, in the opinion of most of London."

"You, not a gentleman, sir?" Kamal's eyes sparked. "You own the Amberly Bank. You have a seat on the Stock Exchange. You're the son and heir of the most prominent banker in Calcutta. Whereas I—but you know who I am. The illegitimate son of an English army sergeant and an Indian girl. Tolerably well educated in a charity school. But when my father returned to England with his regiment he left my mother penniless, and me with nothing to look forward to except the life of a 'kranny,' a subordinate clerk. You saved me from that. You gave me a real position. But you couldn't make me a gentleman."

"Gentleman or no, you're the only man at my disposal, Kamal. I'm not on such terms with any of the proper English 'gentlemen' I've met since I arrived in London that I could ask one of them to serve as my second. You'll start by calling on a certain Lord Brentford, who I believe resides at the Albany. Inform him that I wish to challenge him to a duel because of the public insult he rendered me yesterday at the East India House. Request him to appoint a second to meet with you to make the arrangements for the meeting."

"Yes, sir." Kamal's face was again expressionless. "Will that be all, sir?"

"Not quite. I want you to know that I've made a will. If I

should be mortally wounded in this duel, you'll find that I've made provisions for you and Rana. You won't suffer from my demise."

Lady Lyon leaned forward in her chair in the drawing room of Amberly House and fixed Diana with an arch smile. "We so enjoyed dining with you here the other evening, dear Lady Windham. I vow, I haven't enjoyed myself so much in ages. Don't you agree, Charlotte?"

"Yes, indeed, Mama," Charlotte replied dutifully.

Diana wondered if Charlotte ever felt embarrassed by her mother's overly effusive manner. If so, the girl's own good manners prevented her from expressing her views.

"We were disappointed not to see Lord Brentford last evening at Lady Chiswick's ball," Lady Lyon observed. "Such a distinguished occasion. I do believe everyone of any consequence attended. And I'm almost certain Lord Brentford mentioned to Charlotte he would be present. Isn't that so, my darling?"

"He did say something of the sort, Mama."

Mention of Miles brought pressing worries to the forefront of Diana's thoughts. Miles would have been in no condition to attend a ball last night, of course. He would still have been suffering the effects of the excessive drinking he'd indulged in before the election at East India House.

Diana had been waiting all day on pins and needles for news of a possible duel between Miles and Jared. It was now late afternoon, and she had heard nothing. Not that she had expected any word from Miles. And perhaps Aubrey had again been racked by qualms about the indelicacy of speaking to females about their menfolks' participation in a duel, and had decided not to keep her informed. Or perhaps Jared simply hadn't acted as yet.

And he wouldn't act. She had to believe in that. Angry he might be at Miles, and humiliated, but he was a practical man. He must know that duelling was illegal, and that if he killed his man in a duel he could be charged with murder, and, if convicted, hanged. It didn't matter that the authorities seldom prosecuted duelists, especially aristocratic participants, even in cases with fatal outcomes, and that convicted duelists were rarely executed. The possibility was always there.

Diana aroused herself from her thoughts in some confusion. Apparently she had lost track of the conversation. Lady Lyon looked faintly offended.

"I'm so sorry, Lady Lyon. What did you say? I fear I was woolgathering."

Charlotte intervened smoothly. "Don't apologize, Lady Windham. We know you're very concerned about your father. Your thoughts can never be far from him. And Mama, we really must be going, if we're to ride in the Park this afternoon."

With a sense of relief Diana watched her guests take their leave. Her mind was too full of Miles's predicament to allow her to be a gracious hostess. She was grateful, too, for Charlotte's tact. More and more she was beginning to think that Miles had chosen well.

"Mr. Dalton, my lady," announced the footman.

Diana turned eagerly to the door as Aubrey strode into the drawing room. His face was set in grim lines. Diana looked at him apprehensively. "Aubrey, what is it?"

"The worst, that's all," Aubrey exclaimed. "And, fiends of hell, I know I shouldn't be mentioning a word of this to you, but you're Miles's sister, and you love the man. I love him too, y'know. Known him since we were grubby schoolboys."

Motioning him to a chair, Diana said, "You're not making sense, Aubrey. Are you talking about a possible duel between Miles and Jared Amberly?"

"Not just possible. A certainty." A muscle twitched in Aubrey's cheek. "I was with Miles in his lodgings a few hours ago when a half-caste clerk in Amberly's offices—fellow's a great deal darker than Amberly himself, let me tell you—called on Miles to inform him that Amberly required satisfaction for the insults Miles had offered him at East India House. Suggested pistols as the weapon, and appointed this half-caste as his second." Aubrey smiled bitterly. "It's significant, don't you think, that Amberly couldn't find a proper English gentleman in all of London to act for him?"

Trying to stay calm, Diana said, "Miles needn't accept the challenge."

"So I told him. No one in the *ton* would look askance if he chose not to fight a duel with a ruffian who has no claims to being a gentleman. But Miles would have none of that. He maintains he would dishonor himself if he refused the challenge. He's asked me to be his second."

"Aubrey . . ." Diana clenched her hands together so tightly that the knuckles looked white. "Isn't it true that most duels don't end mortally?"

"No, it ain't true, worse luck. I'd say about half of all duels end fatally."

"But . . . I'm sure I've heard that many duels are formalities, in which one or both of the participants simply fires into the air. Deloping, I think they call it."

"Don't raise your hopes. Miles is determined to at least wing his man." Aubrey smiled grimly. "Fat chance of that. I told you what a terrible shot he is. And Amberly . . . Diana, I feel in my bones that he intends to kill Miles. He probably will. I talked to several regulars at Manton's Galleries this morning. They told me Amberly is a crack shot. Cups his wafer nineteen out of twenty times."

Diana stared at Aubrey in horror. "But—is there nothing we can do? Duelling is such a barbarous, senseless practice. It's also against the law. Can't we inform on Miles and Jared Amberly to the authorities?"

Shaking his head, Aubrey said, "If either of us did that, Miles would never see us again. Can't say I'd blame him. He'd be a laughingstock or a coward, depending on which of us did the informing."

"If this duel takes place, the chances are we'll never see Miles alive again. Aubrey, think. There must be some way to stop it."

"It's not in my power, or anyone's, to stop it. Oh, I did my best, in my capacity as second, to suggest that Amberly's sensibilities might be soothed by some alternative to a duel, say an apology by Miles. But Miles adamantly refused to apologize.

So unless . . . but no . . ." Swallowing hard, Aubrey clamped his lips firmly together.

"What do you mean? Aubrey, you've thought of something. Tell me." Diana studied Aubrey as he maintained his obdurate silence. She caught her breath. "I know. You think Jared might withdraw his challenge if I went to him and begged him to do so."

"No! I never suggested such a thing. I couldn't. You've finished with Amberly. You can't demean yourself by pleading with him for Miles's life. Miles would writhe at the thought. He'd never forgive you."

"I'd never forgive myself if I didn't make the effort. I'm going to see Jared."

"Diana, I forbid . . ."

"You can't forbid me. I'm my own woman."

"Oh, God . . . very well, then. I'll go with you." Aubrey beat a fist into his other hand. "I can't go with you. I'm Miles's second. I can't discuss the duel except with that damned half-caste Amberly appointed to act for him."

"You can drive with me to Chesterfield Street and wait for me in the carriage. It will comfort me to know you're there. We'll go at night. The fewer people who glimpse me entering Jared Amberly's house, the better."

Bundled into a voluminous, old-fashioned cloak, with the hood drawn closely around her face, Diana waited nervously in front of Jared's door after lifting the knocker.

A footman opened the door. "Yes, ma'am?"

"I wish to see Mr. Amberly. Is he at home?"

"I will see, ma'am. Who shall I say is calling?"

"A—a friend. Tell Mr. Amberly my name is Diana."

"Ah. Will you wait, please?"

The footman closed the door firmly in Diana's face. She could feel the hot flush rising in her cheeks. The footman obviously considered her a prime bit of muslin, whose visit might or might not be welcome to his master. She glanced over her shoulder at Aubrey's waiting carriage, half tempted to flee to his comforting presence.

The door opened. The footman said, "Will you come with me, ma'am?"

As Diana followed the footman into the foyer she caught a glimpse of a woman in a brightly colored silken garment at the far end of the corridor to the right of the staircase. It was only a brief glimpse, but Diana knew she wasn't mistaken. This was the woman she had seen on her previous visit to Jared's house, the same lovely dark woman who had sat with Jared in his box at Covent Garden. Guarding her turf against a possible competitor, no doubt, thought Diana ironically.

Keeping a discreet silence, the footman conducted Diana to a room halfway down the corridor, opened the door, and left her standing on the threshold.

"Come in, Diana." Jared rose from his position behind his desk in the library.

Diana entered the room and closed the door. "Good evening, Jared."

He walked around his desk and approached her, stopping several feet away. Instantly she felt her bones begin to melt under the pull of his sheer physical magnetism: curling dark hair, startlingly blue eyes, austere aquiline features, graceful, powerful physique.

"Why have you come, Diana? To seek a reconciliation, perhaps?"

The open mockery of his words steadied Diana's nerves. "I think you know why I'm here, Jared. You've sent a challenge to my brother. I ask you to withdraw it."

"Oh?" Jared raised an eyebrow. "Why should I do that? Lord Brentford insulted me before a goodly part of the financial community of London. He slapped my face. Most people would consider that ample reason to issue a challenge."

"Duelling is a barbarous practice. It's also against the law. If you should kill Miles, you'd be committing a capital offense. You could be hanged."

"The same is true of Lord Brentford, is it not? Incidentally, did he ask you to come here and plead his case?"

"No, he didn't. I came on my own."

"Well, then, I'll tell you what my second has already informed him. I'll withdraw my challenge if Lord Brentford offers me a public apology."

"Miles would never do that. He considers that his honor is involved."

"As do I."

"It's not the same, Jared, you must see that . . ."

A throbbing note of anger crept into Jared's voice. "You mean, of course, that since I'm not a gentleman—not on Lord Brentford's exalted level, that is—no one would look askance if I abandoned this duel."

"I didn't say that."

"No, but that's what you meant, judging by the past history of our relationship."

Diana winced. "I—Jared, please. No amount of satisfaction is worth another person's life. Aubrey Dalton tells me you're a crack shot. Miles . . . ," Diana broke off, biting her lip. If Jared didn't know about Miles's poor marksmanship, she shouldn't tell him.

"You were about to say that Lord Brentford is a miserable shot," said Jared coolly. "I know. I fail to see why that should be a concern of mine. Lord Brentford should have considered his lack of ability before he confronted me with his public accusations of bribery and dishonesty."

As she gazed at Jared's implacable face, Diana's spirit faltered. "You're so hard. Isn't there any way I can persuade you to withdraw your challenge?"

Jared's eyes narrowed. Some sort of inner struggle was reflected in his face. After a moment he said in a voice devoid of emotion, "There is one thing you could do. Spend the night with me, Diana, and tomorrow morning I'll withdraw from the duel."

The bald brutality of the offer temporarily paralyzed Diana's vocal chords. When she was able to speak she exclaimed scathingly, "Your price is too high. Not even to save my brother's life would I stoop to sleeping with a man like you."

He bowed. "There's nothing more to be said, then." He put out his hand. "May I see you to your carriage?"

Recoiling, Diana snapped, "Don't touch me. I'll see myself out."

She rushed from the room, scarcely able to see where she was going because of the scalding tears flooding her eyes. How could she have been so mistaken in Jared Amberly? How could she have believed, for even one second, that he was a warm, caring man who, despite the flaws in his ancestry, was the only man she would ever love until the day she died? She was almost glad that Jared had tossed his demeaning proposition in her face. Now that she knew who he really was and what he was capable of, she could put to rest any lingering regrets that she hadn't turned her back on her family and class in order to marry him.

Rana brought Jared's tea to him before dawn. She watched him as he fastened a plain black stock around his neck, omitting a cravat, and put on a black vest over his black pantaloons. Conventional wisdom dictated that a duelist present as unobtrusive a target as possible to his opponent, Jared thought wryly. However, if Brentford was as poor a shot as rumored, he had nothing to fear from Diana's brother in any respect.

"Kamal is waiting downstairs, Sahib," said Rana quietly.

"Good. Tell him I'll be down shortly."

"Sahib—forgive me if I intrude—but may I ask you to tell me why you are going off with Kamal so early in the morning? Is something amiss? Kamal looks so grim. I feel frightened."

Jared paused in the act of putting on his black coat. He suddenly felt a pang of guilt. He'd thought to spare Rana anxiety, but was it fair to her to go off without an explanation when the next news she received of him might be about his death?

"Rana, I daresay I should have told you. I'm going with Kamal this morning to fight a duel." At her quick intake of breath, he hastened to add, "Don't worry about me. I'm a much better shot than my opponent. I fully expect to return home without a scratch. But if I don't return, I want you to know several things. You and Kamal are fully taken care of in my will. More especially, I want you to know how much I love you, how much I appreciate the tender care and love and loyalty you've given me all these years."

"Sahib . . ." Rana's voice choked with tears. She rushed to him, burrowing her face into his shoulder.

He held her closely, murmuring words of comfort. Then, setting her aside, he shrugged into his coat. "I should be back by eight o'clock, Rana. Please have my breakfast ready."

Jared stirred as the carriage passed over the arched wooden bridge into Putney and turned right up the broad High Street toward the Heath. "We're almost there."

"Yes, Mr. Amberly."

Jared glanced at Kamal's somber profile. "I trust you're not nervous. You haven't been out before?"

"No, sir, neither as a principal nor as a second. I'm not nervous about my duties, which will consist mainly of checking the pistols with my opposite second. But I'll admit that I'm concerned about the outcome of this duel. I know you're a crack shot, sir, but accidents do happen. I'm a selfish man. I've been very happy in my post at Amberly's, and I should dislike to have my employment interrupted."

Jared laughed shortly. "I assure you, Kamal, I would dislike that prospect even more."

The carriage came to a stop on the heights of Putney Heath, a broad tract of land, desolate and empty, consisting mostly of sand, heath, and furze. A strong wind blew, and a faint drizzle was falling. Another carriage had already arrived. Three figures stood beside it: Diana's brother, his second, Aubrey Dalton, and a bulky middle-aged man carrying a black bag, who Jared assumed was the doctor whose presence was required by the protocols of the duel of honor.

Aubrey Dalton left his companions and approached Jared and Kamal. He wore an ankle-length coat, and his face was pinched from the chill of an early April morning. He nodded to Jared and addressed Kamal. "Will you come to our carriage to check the pistols, please?"

Jared removed his own greatcoat and tossed it into his carriage. He waited, flexing his fingers against the chill, until Kamal returned, carrying a pistol that he handed to Jared. "We can begin at any time, sir. Fire within twenty seconds at the command. The distance is twelve paces."

Nodding, Jared left Kamal to walk toward the other group, holding the pistol loosely in his hand, pausing when he judged he was twenty yards from his opponent. Aubrey Dalton positioned his man, then took a stance midway between Miles and Jared. "Gentlemen, you may fire as soon as I drop the handkerchief." Hesitating for a brief second, Aubrey raised the hand holding a white square of fabric.

Jared fired in the split second it took the handkerchief to fall. Miles dropped to the ground without returning the shot, groaning loudly. Jared stood quietly while the doctor hurried to Miles, dropping beside the wounded man to examine him. After a few moments the doctor rose, speaking in a low voice to Aubrey Dalton. Shortly afterwards Aubrey came over to Jared as he stood beside Kamal.

On the morning of the duel, Diana sat by the fire in Miles's sitting room at the Albany, sipping but not really tasting the tea that her brother's valet had brought to her. It was the third cup of tea the valet had served her since her arrival shortly after dawn.

The clock had dragged, but it was still only eight o'clock. Such a short time, but time enough to snuff out a man's life.

She jumped from her chair as the door opened and Aubrey and a stranger carried Miles, his face twisted with pain, into the sitting room.

"Miles!" she half screamed.

"It's all right, Diana," Aubrey assured her. "Miles isn't badly hurt. The doctor and I will just take him into the bedchamber."

Aubrey returned to the sitting room in a few minutes to tell

Diana about the duel, and especially to describe the effects created on the human foot by a bullet impacting at the tip of a boot.

"Miles will be in great pain for days," Aubrey declared angrily. "Amberly shot deliberately. He meant for Miles to suffer.
Even worse, though, he threatened Miles."

A cold chill ran through Diana. "Threatened Miles? What
do you mean?"

Aubrey narrowed his eyes. "Let me think of Amberly's exact
words. . . . He said he intended to make Miles regret the day
he crossed him."

Nine

"You're very far away today, Diana. You're certainly not here with me!"

Diana blinked at her father's teasing words. She and the duke were having lunch together in his bedchamber, which had become their custom during his convalescence, and she had indeed fallen into a brown study during the meal.

"I'm sorry, Papa. I *was* far away, wasn't I? Not paying attention to what you were saying, at any rate. I was thinking about the letter I just received from old Roberts. Stubborn man, he won't hear of trying the new thrashing machine on the home farm."

Which wasn't true, or only partly true. The Abbottsleigh estate agent had politely disagreed with her by letter over the thrashing machine, but the old man's recalcitrance wasn't the real reason for Diana's absent-mindedness. She had been thinking, as she had so often during the past week, about Miles's duel with Jared and its possible consequences.

Aubrey had told her that Jared, not content with his triumph in the duel, had further vowed to revenge himself for Miles's intemperate behavior at the East India House. Diana had begun to suspect that Jared was conducting a vendetta that extended to her entire family. She remembered, with an angry hurt, Jared's proposal that she spend the night with him in exchange for his withdrawal from the duel. He hadn't made that proposal out of passion or a renewed desire to possess her physically; she believed it had been sheer vindictiveness, Jared's way of punishing her for rejecting him. And he had more than one score to settle with Miles, and with her father, too. Miles and the duke had twice humiliated him in public by ordering him out of the house.

With a cold logic, Diana had convinced herself that Jared would try to exact some kind of retribution from the Amberly family. The question was, what form would Jared's revenge take? Not another duel, certainly. Jared was too protective of his own skin, according to Aubrey, to risk prosecution for murder or assault. And there was no way he could cause a public scandal for Miles, since his own social status was nonexistent. Then, what?

She realized she had lost the thread of conversation again as she heard the note of testiness in the duke's voice. "I *said,* my dear, that I was pleased to receive a note from Miles, proposing himself for a visit this afternoon. I presume that means he's recovering from his sprained ankle."

"Oh, yes, I believe his ankle is much better." Diana felt decidedly guilty at the repetition of the falsehood about Miles's injury, but she and Miles had both considered it essential that their father not learn about the disastrous duel.

"The ankle apparently isn't that much better," commented the duke as a footman conducted his son into the room. Miles was still limping badly, even with the help of a cane. "I daresay, Miles, that the real reason why you fell down a flight of stairs and sprained your ankle isn't a proper subject for your sister's ears," said the duke acidly.

"Just so, Papa," Miles replied with a grin, tacitly accepting the duke's innuendo that he had been foxed at the time of his "accident." Miles drew up a chair and settled into it with a sigh of relief. "This feels better. I'm not up to walking much yet." He cocked his head at the duke. "I come with very good news, Papa. I wanted you and Diana to know as soon as possible. I've offered for Miss Charlotte Lyon's hand, and she's accepted."

"And her father?" said the duke, raising an eyebrow.

"Lord Lyon is very pleased with the match."

"As well he should be," sniffed the duke. "What about the settlements?"

"Well, the lawyers will be discussing the details, but Lord Lyon and I came to some preliminary arrangements. Charlotte is to have a proper pin money, and I've suggested Brandon Manor as part of her jointure." Miles glanced questioningly at his father.

The duke nodded. "That seems fair enough. What about Miss Lyon's dowry?"

Miles named a sum that caused a frown to appear on his father's forehead. "You can't have agreed to such a paltry amount," the duke said sharply. "Lyon is one of the richest men in England, and Miss Charlotte is his only heir. What disposition does Lord Lyon propose to make of the remainder of his fortune?"

Looking uncomfortable, Miles said, "Lord Lyon wishes to set up a separate estate for Charlotte in his will, whereby . . ."

"Whereby the bulk of the Lyon fortune would become a trust overseen by Chancery Court," the duke snorted, "to which her lawful husband would have no access. I won't agree to it, Miles."

Diana intervened. "You must remember, Papa, that Charlotte is an only child, her parents' ewe lamb. You can't fault them for wishing to ensure their daughter's future against any possible catastrophe. It's nothing against Miles or his family. It's simply that the Lyons realize that marriages sometimes turn sour. Perhaps, when the lawyers begin their negotiations, a larger dowry can be arranged."

"Yes, that's a possibility," admitted the duke, appearing slightly mollified.

"What's also important, Papa, is Miles's happiness, don't you agree?" Diana smiled at her brother. "You *are* happy, Miles?"

Miles beamed. "Can't you tell? Charlotte is an Incomparable. I'd be happy to marry her if she didn't have a penny to her name." At his father's look of horror, he chuckled. "I thought that would get a rise out of you, Papa." Sobering, he said, "Lord Lyon plans to send an announcement of the betrothal to the newspapers immediately. And I think, Diana, it might be a nice gesture if you and Papa were to host a party in honor of the engagement. Something more than a dinner. A ball, perhaps."

"A ball," Diana repeated thoughtfully. "The Season hasn't really started yet, so London is still a bit thin of company. . . .

But yes, I agree that the Lyons would be pleased if we gave a ball. I'll see to it, Miles."

Afterwards Diana would recall the ball in honor of Miles's engagement as the last happy occasion in her family. However, in the interval before the ball, as she made her preparations and sent out the invitations, she had no suspicion that disaster was about to strike. Except, perhaps, for one thing.

Several days after the betrothal announcement appeared in the newspapers she received a letter in a familiar small, clear hand-writing that raised her pulse rate at the sight of it. "Dear Lady Windham: In view of my last encounter with Lord Brentford, I considered it inappropriate for me to send him congratulations on his engagement. However, since I wished to acknowledge the event in some fashion, I decided to write to you. I wish Lord Brentford very happy, and so I trust he will be, at least for the time being. I remain, your most obedient servant, Jared Amberly."

Feeling suddenly chilled, Diana sat down abruptly and read the letter again. Why had Jared written? Certainly the letter was no mere polite and hypocritical expression of pleasure at Miles's engagement. Jared might, of course, simply have wanted to remind her that he was still there, on the periphery of her life, aware of everything that concerned her. Diana was more inclined to consider the letter as a veiled threat. What else could that final phrase mean? "At least for the time being." Was he planning to disrupt the ball? If so, how? The servants would have orders not to admit him. Or had Jared callously hoped to cause her disquiet with a deliberately obscure message?

Diana rose, crumpling the letter. Worrying about Jared's possible moves would be playing into his hand, giving him immense satisfaction if he found out about it. She tossed the letter into the fireplace and put its contents firmly out of her mind.

In the event, the ball was a complete success. The ballroom was crowded, even though many notables of the *ton* had not yet arrived in London for the Season. The orchestra was spirited, the supper delicious. Diana felt festive in a new gown bought

for the occasion, a confection in pale violet *crêpe lisse*. Though
he couldn't dance, Miles hovered about his fiancée, giving every
appearance of a man deeply in love.

Charlotte was angelically beautiful in a gown of white mull,
worn over a blue satin slip, trimmed in seed pearls and knots
of blue ribbon. In one interval, when Diana had an opportunity
to speak to her future sister-in-law, she said smilingly, "My dear
Charlotte, you look very happy."

Blushing faintly, the girl murmured, "I *am* happy. I—I'm
very fond of Miles." In a burst of confidence, she added,
"Mama says people in our walk of life don't marry for love.
She wouldn't admit it, but she cares more about the fact that I
will be a future duchess than about my married happiness. I
think she's wrong. I wouldn't have accepted Miles's proposal if
I didn't—if I didn't care for him."

"I'm glad," said Diana softly. "I'm glad for both of you."

Affectionately touching Charlotte's shoulder, she went off to
check on her father, who had insisted on leaving the sickroom
to welcome his guests. He sat in a comfortable chair—which
Diana had insisted upon—at the side of the ballroom. To her
anxious eyes, the duke looked very tired.

"Papa, you've hosted this affair long enough. You should go
back to your bedchamber."

"Nonsense. Pray stop worrying about my health, my dear. I
feel very fit. It's not every day that my only son announces his
betrothal, and I intend to honor the occasion."

Well acquainted with her father's granite strength of will,
Diana shrugged and sat down beside him. "The ball is going
very well, I think. I noticed you had a long conversation with
Charlotte earlier in the evening. Your first real contact with her,
I believe. Do you like her?"

"Yes, I believe I do. The girl has very pretty manners. She'll
be a credit to Miles and to us. I only wish she didn't have
parents."

"You don't care for Lord and Lady Lyon?"

"Can't abide the pair of them. They fawn all over me, he
reminding me with that oily smile of our joint service in the
Lords, she twittering away about what a charming chatelaine

Charlotte will be when she becomes Duchess of Edgehill. The fool woman must think I'm doddering on the edge of my grave!"

"Cheer up, Papa. You'll not be living with the elder Lyons, only with Charlotte!"

Aubrey joined father and daughter. "Evening, Duke. Fine party, eh? May I have this dance, Diana?"

When Diana headed for the middle of the floor, where a set was forming, Aubrey said cajolingly, "Do you really want to dance? Can't we go to the card room? I've scarcely seen you all evening."

In the card room, after he had seated Diana at a small table in the corner, Aubrey said with a smile of satisfaction, "I say, this is much better. It was getting to be much too warm in the ballroom. Your ball is a *succès fou,* Diana. Exceptionally well attended. I thought Miles looked very happy. I fancy this marriage will be the making of him. Oh, I know he's been a bit wild in the past. Well, we both were. In Miles's case, he's had a special problem, keeping away from the tables. I think marriage will steady him."

"Yes, I do think Miles may settle down now."

"Leaving you with one less worry. Diana, isn't it time you thought of yourself and your own happiness? No, don't shut me off. Look, I didn't succeed in becoming a director of the Court of the East India Company, but I can still support a wife and my own household. Altogether, from the allowance my family gives me, and the dividends from my stock in the Company and my salary from my post at the Treasury, I have two thousand pounds a year. You must have some money of your own, too. I understand from Miles that, although you surrendered your dower rights, Lord Windham gave you a decent jointure."

Diana sighed. "Aubrey, please understand. If I wanted to marry you, our combined incomes would be ample. But I don't wish to marry. I don't think I'll ever wish to marry. Can't we leave the matter at that, and remain the good friends we've always been?"

"Of course," Aubrey muttered. "I didn't mean to distress you. I'll do whatever you say."

But Diana had a despairing conviction that Aubrey would never abandon his dogged pursuit of her until he had worn down her objections.

Diana had been concerned that his lengthy appearance at the ball might be too much for her father, and his condition the following day confirmed her fears. When she entered his room in late morning she found him still in bed, apparently too tired or too weak to rise for breakfast. He had evidently spilled the tea served to him on a tray, and his valet was trying to mop up the spilled liquid from the bedclothes.

"Oh, go away, Joseph. I wish to speak to my daughter," the duke exclaimed impatiently.

"But Your Grace, the bedclothes . . ."

"You can change the bed linens later. Just go."

After the valet had gone, the duke waved a letter at Diana. "Do you know anything about this?"

With a sinking heart, she recognized the handwriting. The superscription read, "To His Grace the Duke of Edgehill," and the letter contained no salutation. The short message was blunt. "I propose to call on you at Amberly House this afternoon at three o'clock for the purpose of discussing with you the future of the Edgehill estates. Lord Brentford should also be present. If you do not meet with me in private about this matter, I will be obliged to make your concerns public. Jared Amberly."

"What does this effrontery mean, Diana? Do you have any idea? You know the man, after all. I was so flabbergasted when I read this drivel that I knocked over the damned teapot."

"No, Papa. I can't imagine what Mr. Amberly has in mind."

"Well? What shall we do about this letter? My first impulse was, and still is, to ignore it. Damned impudence."

Trying to keep her voice calm, Diana said, "That might not be wise. I suspect that Jared Amberly never does anything without a sufficient reason. We know he dislikes our family, mainly because we've refused to recognize him as a member, so I don't think this letter merely reflects a petty desire to annoy us or worry us. He has something deeper in mind."

"Are you advising me to receive the fellow?"

"Yes," Diana replied reluctantly. "What can we lose? If what he has to say is sheer impudence, as you suggested, you can order the servants to show him to the door."

The duke's color rose. "I don't like threats, and I don't like blackmail, and this letter smacks of both. However, I don't care for scandal, either, and if there's any possibility that this fellow can embarrass the family . . . very well, I'll see the man. I'll also send for Miles."

"I think I should be present, Papa."

"Absolutely not," exclaimed the duke, glaring at his daughter. "This is a matter for the men of the family to settle."

"I'm a member of the family, too."

"No!"

"Papa, listen to me. I'm at least partly to blame for any ill will Jared may feel toward us. I rejected his proposal of marriage, and he bitterly resented that. I think I have a right to hear what he has to say."

Obviously struggling with his feelings, the duke muttered, "I don't like it above half, but . . . all right, you may be present at the interview. You're no green girl, after all. Nothing the fellow might say will likely offend your sensibilities."

The silence in the drawing room was oppressive. Diana stole a look at the clock on the mantelpiece. It was just on three o'clock. She and her father and her brother had been waiting for Jared's visit for more than ten minutes, unspeaking, avoiding each others' eyes. Diana's spirit felt leaden. She sensed that this encounter with Jared would be, if not catastrophic, at the very least highly unpleasant.

Miles had been voluble enough when he first arrived at the house. "The gall of the man," he'd snorted, when the duke acquainted him with Jared's letter. "Papa, you shouldn't dignify Amberly's impudence with any acknowledgment. Order the servants to turn him away at the door. He's just out for another opportunity to make me look like a fool. . . ." At Diana's quick, warning look, Miles had subsided.

"What do you mean, Miles?"

Shaking his head, Miles said, "Nothing, Papa. It was just a manner of speaking. The man doesn't like us."

The duke didn't pursue the matter, and Diana released a sigh of relief. Miles had almost blurted out the story of the disastrous duel.

At one minute after three o'clock, a footman entered the drawing room, announcing, "Mr. Amberly, Your Grace."

Jared strode into the room. His gaze sharpened as he noted Diana's presence, but he said nothing, merely making an inclusive bow to her and her father and brother.

Waiting until the footman had left, the duke said coldly, "State your business as quickly as possible, sir, and leave. You are not welcome here."

"Oh, I'm quite aware of my status in this house, Duke," Jared replied, his lip curling. He remained standing, not because he hadn't been invited to sit down, Diana surmised, but because he considered that a standing position gave him an advantage over a seated audience. He was superbly groomed and dressed today, she observed, and he might have appeared totally self-possessed save for a slight stiffness in his bearing, as if he was poised for a difficult battle.

"You asked me to state my business as quickly as possible, Duke. I will do so. As of today, I have in my possession every outstanding promissory note signed by you or your son, whether to moneylenders or to any bank in the London area."

"Damn you," Miles burst out. He jumped up from his chair and hurled himself at Jared. Diana rushed to throw her restraining arms around him, and his father barked, "Sit down, Miles. I'll take care of this."

Breathing hard, Miles paused for a moment, then mumbled, "Yes, Papa." Disengaging Diana's clinging arms, he returned to his chair.

His face a rigid mask of disdain, the duke turned his attention back to Jared. "If your facts are as represented, what action do you propose to take?"

"I intend to call in your obligations, of course. Lord Brentford's notes to the moneylenders are demand notes. No problem there. Yours to the banks, Duke, were all five-year notes, converted to demand notes when you didn't repay the principal. No problem there, either. Collectively, you owe me—" Jared pulled a slip of paper from an inner coat pocket and studied it. "You owe me fifty thousand, five hundred and thirty-eight pounds. When may I expect payment?"

The duke said in a voice of controlled fury, "Since you've been dealing behind my back with my bankers—who, incidentally, will be informed immediately that I will never do business with them again after this betrayal—you must know that I've paid all interest as it came due. Miles?"

"Nor am I behind in my interest payments, Papa." Miles spoke quietly, but it was obvious that his anger simmered just below the surface.

"Oh, yes, I know that neither of you was in arrears on your interest payments," Jared replied. "In point of fact, the bankers and even the moneylenders were perfectly satisfied to continue holding your notes. They didn't discount your bills to me, you understand. I paid them a healthy premium for the privilege of buying the notes. And now I want payment. Immediately."

Diana spoke for the first time. In a tone of distaste she said, "Obviously you know a great deal about our family financial position, Mr. Amberly. You must be quite aware that my father and my brother can't produce so large a sum on a moment's notice."

Jared gave her a long, level look, completely devoid of emotion. "Indeed, I am aware, Lady Windham. That was the point of my—er—financial maneuvering."

Jolted out of her carefully assumed calm, Diana exclaimed, "What do you mean?"

"It's really quite simple. My interest in this matter isn't the duke's money. I have no pressing need at this time for fifty thousand pounds. What I want is your father's property. Either he pays me immediately the sum he and your brother owe me, or he must bar the entail on the Edgehill estates."

"What?" The exclamation of horror came simultaneously from the duke and Miles.

Jared nodded. "Need I explain the legal principal involved,

Duke? You must be as familiar with the action of common recovery as I am. I buy the Edgehill estates, the purchase price being the return to you of all your notes, marked, 'paid in full.' I then enter suit against you, as the tenant in tail, for the transfer of the land. You inform me that you obtained the land and the title to it from a third party, some propertyless fellow named Jones, or whatever. You vouch this Jones to warranty, and he then conveniently disappears. The court then gives judgment against the defaulting Jones, and awards your lands in fee simple to me. You thereby bar Lord Brentford from inheriting the family estates. Oh, he will become Duke of Edgehill on your death, but he won't inherit anything except an empty title."

"You devil," shouted Miles. His face twisted with fury and chagrin, he turned to his father. "Papa, you won't let this happen? Think about my marriage. The Lyons will almost certainly cry off the engagement if we lose the estate. They expect Charlotte to become mistress of Abbottsleigh as well as Duchess of Edgehill."

Looking suddenly much older and very tired, the duke replied, "I know, Miles. The devil of it is, we have few options. Amberly demands immediate payment, and we can't raise the money immediately. Failing prompt payment, he could put us both in debtors' prison."

"Which I wouldn't hesitate to do, I assure you," said Jared. "Matter of fact, I have here in my pocket an arrest warrant. If I don't receive a satisfactory answer to my request before I leave here, I'll give the warrant to a sheriff's officer, who will arrest you and Lord Brentford and escort you to a sponging house for several days. Just to make sure you appear at your court trial. At that later trial the court will pronounce you debtors, and you will then go to the Marshalsea, or, more probably, to Newgate."

"Papa!" exclaimed Diana in anguish. "Your health—you might die in prison."

"I would hope so," said the duke grimly. "Better by far to die than to be a prisoner."

"Papa, no. . . . Tell me, has Mr. Amberly correctly described this legal process, common recovery, as you understand it?"

"Oh, yes. He knows how to bar an entail as well as any gentleman, I should say."

Ignoring the bitterness in her father's voice, Diana looked at Jared, saying, "Abbottsleigh and the other Amberly entailed properties are worth far more than fifty thousand pounds."

He inclined his head. "True. The transaction would be a real bargain."

"Then won't you acknowledge how unfair you're being? In simple justice, won't you allow us time to raise the money we owe you so that my family won't lose property we've owned for hundreds of years, and which is worth at least double the amount of our debt?"

"You'd find it difficult to raise that kind of money without collateral, you know. And the duke has no real collateral, except possibly for movables. He can't mortgage entailed property. Given enough time, however, on the strength of the Amberly name, you might succeed. I don't propose to grant you any time. I'm a businessman, not a sentimentalist. Certainly not a gentleman, as you and the duke and Lord Brentford have so often informed me. I want that property, and I want it at my price." He smiled faintly at Diana. "You see, I grew rather fond of Abbottsleigh after you gave me a guided tour. I'd like to live there."

"What's this about a guided tour?" the duke said sharply. "Diana, did you receive this man at Abbottsleigh?"

Shooting Jared an angry glance, Diana replied, "Yes, Papa. That was before I realized what kind of a man he is. I didn't tell you about it because I thought it would distress you."

"Distress me! I'm appalled. This must mean you were a great deal more involved with the fellow than you led me to believe."

Jared laughed. "For shame, Diana. You didn't tell your father about the romantic idyll we shared at Abbottsleigh? How we fell in love and very nearly married, until you decided I was unworthy of the honor?"

Feeling her cheeks grow hot from anger and embarrassment, Diana flared, "That's neither here nor there, Jared. What's important is the Amberly heritage. Sending my father and Miles to debtors' prison is unthinkable. Is there nothing short of barring the entail that you would accept in payment of our debt?"

"No." The answer was emphatic, but then Jared paused, frowning. After a long moment he said slowly, "There is one thing, yes. If you promised to marry me, Diana, I would agree to continue holding your brother's and your father's promissory notes on the same terms as they enjoyed with their original lenders."

"Never!" snapped the duke. "I'd rather be in prison, I'd rather be dead, Diana, than see you married to this man."

"As would I," Miles said immediately. But despite the promptness of his words, Diana detected a curious strain of reluctance in his voice. Left to himself, she wondered, would Miles have been so quick to deny the possibility of her marriage to Jared?

In the event, the decision belonged to her. She stared at Jared, her heart slowly congealing into ice. This was the terrible ending to the love she had shared with him, a proposal for a marriage based not on passion and caring but on revenge.

She said levelly, "You have my promise, Jared."

"Diana, no!" The duke's voice trembled. "I won't let you sacrifice yourself for this family, not a second time. I won't let you marry a half-caste, illegitimate nobody to save me and Miles from debtors' prison."

"You're mistaken in several of your premises, Duke," Jared cut in. "Strictly speaking, I'm not a half-caste. My mother was the half-caste. And I'm not illegitimate. I can produce papers proving not only that my father, Richard Amberly, was a direct descendant of the fourth Duke of Edgehill, but that I'm the legitimate son of Richard and one Lucia Pereira of Calcutta."

He paused to flick a taunting smile at Miles. "Remember that, Lord Brentford. Regardless of my maternal ancestry, in law I stand next in line to you as the future Duke of Edgehill. Marry your wealthy heiress quickly and produce a male heir, or you may hear the echo of baby steps toddling behind you. The steps of my children and Diana's."

Clenching his fists, Miles muttered, "Filthy blackguard."

Jared's shoulders tensed slightly, then relaxed. "That's hardly a term I would use to describe a future member of *my* family, Brentford, but you must do as you like, of course."

Turning his attention back to Diana and the duke, Jared said, "I take it, then, that we're agreed on the matter of the betrothal. I would ask you, Duke, to take care of certain arrangements at once. Please send an announcement of the engagement to all the London newspapers no later than tomorrow. Also, since I wish the ceremony to take place as quickly as possible, in a church sufficiently prominent to mark the occasion, I request that you post the banns immediately in a church of your choosing. St. George's, Hanover Square, I presume? Or possibly St. Margaret's, Westminster? I've noticed that those churches seem much favored for fashionable weddings. In any case, whichever church you choose, I want the first of the three banns published this coming Sunday."

Jared paused, glancing interrogatively at his listeners. None of them spoke. The duke sat still as a statue, looking down at the floor, his hands gripping the arms of his chair. Miles glared silently at Jared. Diana gazed at him without speaking.

Jared seemed unfazed by the lack of response. "Well, then," he said briskly, "that covers everything I have to say for the moment. Our solicitors will be meeting to make the more mundane arrangements." He walked across the room, taking Diana's hand and raising it to his lips. "Goodbye, Diana. You've made me a very happy man."

As soon as Jared left the room Miles exploded. "That devil! That cunning, unscrupulous devil! You see what he's trying to do, don't you, Diana? He hopes to make it impossible for you to withdraw from this infamous betrothal in the event that Papa and I succeed in arranging a loan to redeem our promissory notes. He thinks you would hesitate to cause scandal by crying off the engagement after the announcement had appeared in the newspapers and the banns had been published in the church. Well, we'll show him he can't dictate to the Amberlys. We'll get that loan and . . ."

"Miles, be quiet," Diana ordered, her eyes fixed on her father. The duke had turned a pasty white. His hands, released from their iron grip on the arms of the chair, were trembling. "Papa, you're ill. Miles, call a servant. We must get Papa to bed."

"Diana, my darling girl, I can't let you do this," the duke whispered.

"We'll talk about it later, Papa. Now you must go to bed."

As she watched Miles and a footman help the duke out of the room Diana felt utterly helpless. She knew her father's fragile health might deteriorate under the strain of seeing his daughter forced into a marriage he abhorred. She knew, too, that neither his health nor his pride could survive a stay in prison. So she had had only two choices, either of which could kill her father, and she'd chosen what she considered the lesser of two evils.

Diana's heart ached from a mixture of emotions. Fear for her father's health. Guilt. If she had discouraged Jared Amberly at the very beginning, she believed her family wouldn't be facing this crisis. Anger, as bitter, unrelenting, and unforgiving as the anger that had prompted Jared to seek his revenge.

Ten

When Diana entered her father's bedchamber the following morning she was heartened to find him looking stronger. More than that. Combative. "Well, now, my dear, we must come around," he had begun briskly. "We were taken by surprise yesterday by that fellow Amberly. There's no real reason to think we can't raise the money to repay him. The Amberly name still counts for something, I daresay. Send my secretary up to see me after breakfast. We'll make applications for loans today to all the leading bankers in London."

"Papa, it won't do," Diana said gently. "There's no time. If the announcement of my engagement doesn't appear in the newspapers, by tomorrow at the latest, if the banns aren't cried at St. George's on Sunday, Jared Amberly will make his move. The sheriff's officer will conduct you and Miles to a sponging house."

"But—we can't do nothing. We can't give up . . ."

"Papa, listen to me. You don't want me to be unhappy, do you?"

"In God's name, you're not telling me you *want* to marry this creature?"

"No—no. When I said 'unhappy,' I used the word in a comparative sense. I'd be far more unhappy to see you and Miles in debtors' prison than I would be to marry Jared Amberly. I'm only being realistic, Papa. You taught me that."

"Yes, I see." The duke sighed heavily. "You pay a very high price for being an Amberly, Diana." Though deeply depressed, he also seemed reconciled to her decision. Diana felt a sense of relief. If he stopped fretting about her marriage to Jared he would be under far less of a mental strain.

In the meantime, life must go on. She went down to the morning room for her usual daily task with her correspondence. As she sat at her desk she nibbled the end of her pen, trying to concentrate on a letter to the housekeeper at Abbottsleigh. "Dear Mrs. Gunderson: I received the copy of your accounts for last month, and . . ."

The memory of the confrontation yesterday with Jared kept coming between her and her instructions to the housekeeper. "You've made me a very happy man," Jared had said. Why had he spoken like that, those proper, formal, customary words, except to wound her? He'd been gratuitously cruel. If he felt any happiness at all, it was a macabre happiness, the product of revenge. He'd evened his scores with the entire Amberly family. He'd triumphed over them and humiliated them by forcing Diana to marry him. Would he continue, once they were married, to keep turning the knife in the wound?

"Diana, I must talk to you."

Diana looked up with a feeling of dismay as Aubrey stalked into the room. His usually meticulous grooming had been neglected; his cravat was carelessly tied, his blonde locks indifferently arranged.

"Diana, what in the fiend's name possessed you to agree to marry Amberly?"

"How did you—?"

"Miles came to me last night. He was half out of his mind. Diana, if you won't listen to your father and your brother, you'll listen to me. I won't allow you to enter into this monstrosity of a marriage."

Diana stiffened. "You have no right to forbid me to do anything I choose to do."

Aubrey walked over to her, pulled her out of her chair and stood looking down at her, holding her hands in a grip that hurt. "I have every right. The right of common humanity, to prevent goodness and innocence from being allied to the scum of the earth. The right of my love for you, a love that has never failed you, and never will."

Diana jerked her hands from Aubrey's hold and stepped back. "Aubrey, please don't say any more. I've agreed to marry Jared Amberly. Nothing you say or do can stop me."

His eyes blazing, Aubrey exclaimed, "Can I not? I'll tell you what I can do. I can kill him. I'll challenge him to a duel—any trumped-up reason will do. I'm a decent shot, far better than Miles, at any rate. Then you'll be free of this half-caste bastard."

"No!" Diana said sharply. "I won't have Jared's blood on my head, or on your hands."

"He doesn't deserve to live, Diana."

"That's not for you to say. And you forget, I think, that even if Jared were dead the Amberly promissory notes would still be a part of his estate."

"Lord, I'd forgotten about those damnable notes. Whoever possessed them would have a hold over you and your family. I wonder who inherits? Amberly has no family that I ever heard of." Aubrey's mouth twisted in a sneer. "Perhaps he's left his entire fortune to that half-caste mistress of his, and of course she'd probably stop at nothing to punish you for being responsible for the death of her paramour."

"I don't doubt it." Diana's voice sounded calm, but she felt a sharp pain in her heart at the thought of the beautiful dark woman who shared Jared's house, and very probably his heart. "So you see, Aubrey, it wouldn't be of any use to kill Jared in a duel. His estate would still hold my family hostage."

"At least you wouldn't be sharing Amberly's bed," flashed Aubrey. His face crumpled. "Oh, God, Diana, I feel so helpless. Isn't there anything I can do to prevent you from selling yourself a second time? Windham was bad enough. He was old and infirm, and you didn't love him, but at least he was a gentleman. Amberly is a nothing, a worse than nothing, a half-caste bastard straight out of the gutter, with no scruples, no breeding. I can't bear to think of him laying a dirty hand on you."

"Aubrey, stop. What's done is done. And for what it's worth, it seems that Jared isn't a bastard after all. He's the legitimate son of a man who's probably a distant connection of the Amberly family."

"And that makes him a suitable match for you?" Aubrey said incredulously.

"No, of course not. I—" Diana drew a deep breath. "Aubrey, if you really want to help me, you'll accept what I've decided to do. The future won't be easy, and I'll need the support of all my friends. You *are* still my friend, aren't you?"

"My God, need you ask?" Aubrey swallowed hard. "Very well. I won't say any more against this marriage. But every day I'll pray that lightning strikes Amberly dead before he can meet you at the altar!"

Rana poured Jared a second cup of tea. "Kamal is here, Sahib."

Jared smiled at her apprehensive expression. "Not to worry, my dear. Kamal isn't here to act as my second in another duel. Send him up."

Escorted by Rana, the head clerk strode into the dining room. "Good morning, sir. Since you won't be coming into the office this morning, I thought you should see this application for a loan. The gentleman called late yesterday afternoon. Name of Langland. Represented himself as a friend of the Prince Regent. Mr. Langland wants a very large loan, sir. He said he would return today for his answer."

Jared examined the document briefly. He shook his head. "Refuse the loan, Kamal. I know of this Langland. He's no crony of the Regent. A hanger-on at best. He's a bad risk."

After Kamal had bowed himself out, Rana said, "You are not going to your bank today, Sahib?"

"No. I have business elsewhere." Jared hesitated. "I have news for you. I'm to be married."

Rana brightened. "Who is the lady?"

"You know her. That is, you've seen her. She's Lady Windham."

"The lady at the theater? The lady who called here several times?"

"Yes.

"But . . . the lady refused to marry you because you had

Indian blood. And you told me you did not want a wife who was ashamed of you. Have Lady Windham's feelings for you changed? Does she now consider you worthy to be her husband?"

"No." Jared's mouth hardened. "She hasn't changed her opinion of me in the least. She's decided to marry me in order to save her father and her brother from debtors' prison, where I was prepared to send them if they didn't pay the fifty thousand pounds they owed me."

"Oh." Rana's delicate face looked troubled. Her slender fingers crumpled the silk of her sari. "It is not for me to question you, Sahib, I know that, but all the same . . . you have forced this lady to marry you by threatening the welfare of her family. Will either of you achieve any happiness from such a marriage?"

"Doubtless both of us will derive some sort of satisfaction from the relationship," said Jared coolly. "Which is more than many people can say of their marriages."

However, as he drove in his carriage to Berkeley Square, Jared found himself thinking about Rana's question, and his reply to it. Why was he marrying Diana?

He hadn't intended to offer marriage as an option to her and her family. When he'd arrived at Amberly House yesterday, he'd meant only to force the Duke of Edgehill and his son to choose between two unpleasant alternatives: to bar the entail on the Amberly estates, thereby transferring ownership to him; or to languish in debtors' prison. Either alternative would have satisfied his urge to settle the score with the Amberly family by showing them he was a force to be reckoned with. He'd been indifferent as to which course they would choose.

Then, on the spur of the moment, out of the blue, however one cared to describe it, he had found himself offering to postpone payment of the promissory notes in exchange for Diana's promise to marry him. Why?

The answer struck him like a physical blow. Because he still loved Diana, that was why. Because he still wanted her, even though she despised him as a man, even though she considered his touch a contamination. He was no more to her than were the untouchables to the higher castes in his mother's Hindu ancestry.

He'd tried to tell himself that he didn't care, that her rejection had killed his love, but it wasn't true. He'd refused to admit that he ached to have her on any terms, excepting only the annihilation of his pride. Yesterday, from some deep, unconscious part of his mind, he'd discovered a way to possess Diana without surrendering his pride and self-esteem.

Diana and her family believed that revenge for past ill treatment was the motive for his move to gain control of the Amberly estates. Let them think that his marriage to Diana was simply a part of that revenge, that love and longing and desire had nothing to do with it.

The carriage stopped in front of the gracious mansion in Berkeley Square, and Jared walked up the steps and lifted the door knocker. He thought he detected a flicker of curiosity in the eyes of the footman who opened the door. Did the Amberly servants, via some inexplicable domestic grapevine, already know that he was to marry Diana? Or could it be that this same footman had been employed here all those years ago, when the Duke of Edgehill had had him escorted from the house as an impostor?

It didn't matter. Jared said smoothly, "Good morning. Please inform Lady Windham that Mr. Amberly has called to see her."

Diana carefully examined her image in the dressing table mirror while her abigail, Rose, put the finishing touches on her hair. "I'll wear the lace cap," she said when Rose had arranged the last shining amber curl.

Rose sighed. "Ye can't rightly see yer hair wi' that cap atop o' it. And ye have sich pretty hair, my lady."

"We must observe the *convenances,* Rose. All respectable matrons wear caps," Diana retorted. She checked her morning dress of sea-green *gros de Naples* in the cheval glass before leaving her bedchamber. As she walked down the stairs she felt annoyed with herself for being so concerned about her appearance. Why should she care what Jared thought of her looks?

Jared rose from his chair as she entered the drawing room. For a brief instant she had a confusing sense of unreality, as if she were confronting a stranger. Momentarily Jared seemed to be an entirely different person, now that he was her official fiancé. She steeled herself to appear calm. "Good morning, Mr. Amberly."

Jared smiled. He seemed perfectly at ease. "Mister? Don't you think we've gone beyond such formality?"

Diana bit her lip, feeling foolish. "Yes, of course. Won't you sit down, Jared?" She took a chair well away from him. "I didn't expect to see you today. You spoke of meetings between our solicitors."

"Oh, yes. The lawyers will hammer out the essential arrangements. However, I thought you and I should meet to discuss the details of the engagement itself."

Diana felt a spasm of foreboding. "What do you mean?"

He looked politely surprised. "Why, I refer to the various social events that will mark our engagement. I'm most anxious that our marriage will be received favorably by the *ton.*"

Diana stared at Jared's smiling face and had to restrain an impulse to throw the nearest available object at him. "Why are you doing this, Jared? I realize you hate the Amberly family. But why are you insisting on this marriage? You'll not ask me to believe that you're still—er—romantically inclined?"

Jared grimaced. "Perish the thought," he said lightly. "You must have thought me incredibly naive, Diana, when I mooned after you like a lovesick calf. I've learned since I arrived in London that members of the *ton* don't marry 'for love.' No, I suggested this marriage out of family pride, of course, the same quality you yourself so often extol. I wish to bring my cadet branch of the Amberly family into the prominence it deserves. What better way than to ally myself with the daughter of the current Duke of Edgehill? And don't forget, also, that I stand second in line to inherit the dukedom."

"Never," Diana muttered under her breath.

"Never? Oh, come now, Diana, never say never. Meanwhile, I expect you to help me convey the impression that we are a happy, well-matched couple by appearing with me at the major social events of the Season."

"The Season hasn't really started as yet. And I've been refusing most invitations. You forget that I'm scarcely out of mourning for my husband."

"A husband you hated. This is a different game, Diana. I want you to accept every invitation you receive, and to note that I will be accompanying you. I will be your escort every afternoon—or virtually every afternoon—when you drive in the Park. I expect that several of your influential friends will wish to entertain for us as a newly engaged couple. I trust that your father will see fit to mark this important family occasion by hosting an event at least as auspicious as the ball he gave for your brother's betrothal."

Diana gazed at Jared's face, pleasant, polite, but implacable. He was turning the screws of his revenge, and there was nothing she could do about it. "I'll do what I can to carry out your suggestions," she said quietly.

"Good. I knew you would be cooperative. After all, no more than I, do you want this marriage to appear as something less than a spontaneous affair."

"Of course not," Diana said with a biting edge in her voice. "It's inconceivable that anyone would regard us as a less than an ideal couple."

"Exactly." Jared beamed. "Goodbye then for now, Diana. I'll return this afternoon to drive with you in the Park."

Diana watched him go, his darkly handsome face lit by a charming smile, and wished him to the devil.

It was a beautiful late April day, a perfect day for a drive in the Park. The carriage drive was thronged with vehicles and riders, very nearly as many as the numbers that would crowd the Park during the height of the Season.

Diana hadn't been a part of the daily five o'clock Hyde Park promenade for several years, but she recognized, and was recognized by, many of the fashionable people present. As she nodded and smiled in response to greetings she thought she observed an element of strong curiosity in the glances directed at her. No doubt this was understandable. Her face was well-known, even to those outside her immediate circle, because she was the daughter of the Duke of Edgehill, but Jared was an outsider to the *ton*. She knew what these people were thinking. They were wondering if her appearance with this darkly handsome stranger, at the end of her year of mourning for her first husband, had any significance.

She glanced sideways at Jared, who was driving the smart curricle with an easy skill she could appreciate. An excellent driver herself, she often drove a curricle on the roads around Abbottsleigh. Her father and her brother were good drivers also. How had Jared learned to drive so well, in a country where, she was sure, people didn't regard horses with the same passion as did sporting Englishmen?

Her eyes rested on the hands handling the ribbons, noting again how graceful and well-shaped and strong Jared's hands were, how meticulously groomed, as every other part of his person was. Momentarily a tremor ran through her as she envisioned those hands touching her, caressing her . . .

"No!" she exclaimed.

Jared turned his head. "Is something wrong?"

"No. I'm sorry. My mind was wandering." She sought a safer topic. "You drive very well. Did your father teach you?"

"No." The voice was clipped, almost rude. He cleared his throat. "I don't believe my father ever drove, once he arrived in India. Remember all those servants I told you about? He was driven or carried. No, I learned to drive by watching his coachmen. Did the duke send off the announcements to the newspapers?"

The abrupt change of subject caught Diana by surprise. "No, not yet."

"Why is that? I specifically asked that the announcements be sent today. Has he advised the rector at—is it St. George's?—about the banns?"

"No." Diana tried to keep the irritation out of her voice. "You forget, I think, that Papa has been ill. He'll take care of the announcements."

"Today?"

"Yes, today." This time it required a real effort to remain polite. She would notify the newspapers and the church herself.

"What church have you selected for the ceremony?"

"I hadn't really decided. . . . I'm inclined toward a small church near Berkeley Square. St. Anselm's, perhaps."

Jared shook his head. "Oh, no. A small church won't do at all."

Diana clenched her fists, intensely conscious of the presence of the diminutive tiger perched behind the passenger seat. He hadn't uttered a sound, he'd stood still as a statue, but she didn't doubt that he was following his master's conversation with avid interest.

"Jared, could we walk for a bit? I'm used to long walks in the country, and I miss the exercise."

"Certainly." Jared guided his team to the verge of the Ring and tossed the reins to his tiger, who had jumped down from his perch. Climbing down from the driver's seat, Jared offered his hand to Diana.

"I wanted to talk to you out of your tiger's earshot," she said, as she and Jared began walking along the path in the direction of the Serpentine.

"So I gathered. You must forgive me, Diana, for speaking about private matters in front of a servant. In India we have so little privacy that we're quite resigned to the fact that our servants know all about our affairs. What did you wish to talk about?"

"About the church. I consider St. Anselm's quite perfect for a small wedding."

"But we aren't going to have a small wedding. On the contrary. I expect you to invite everyone who is anyone, as the saying goes. That includes the Regent."

"The Regent! Why would he come to your wedding?" Diana's lip curled. "Because he owes you money?"

"Why not? His Royal Highness has a healthy appreciation of money. However, I think he might wish to attend because your father is one of the premier dukes of the realm. Now, then, for my part, I'll shortly be sending you a list of my colleagues in the banking establishment and the Stock Exchange, and also the names of certain proprietors of the East India Company. As their new director of the Court, I think I owe them this courtesy. Good for business, too."

Diana stopped in her tracks. "But that means the church will be half filled with—with tradesmen!"

Jared shrugged. "So? I'm a tradesman, of sorts, don't forget."

"How could I forget it?" Diana snapped. "Papa won't hear of such a wedding. He—" she paused, trying to collect herself. "Jared, I don't wish to have a large wedding. It's not necessary. Many prominent families choose to have small, virtually private ceremonies. In my case, as a widow entering into a second marriage, a smaller ceremony would be more appropriate."

"For you, perhaps. Not for me. It suits me to marry you in a large, publicized ceremony."

Diana glared at him, heedless of any passersby. "Why can't you at least be honest?" she burst out. "This morning I asked you why you were insisting on this marriage, and you said it was because of family pride. That's a lie. You've set out to drive the Amberly name into the ground. This marriage will accomplish your purpose better than anything else, other than throwing my father and my brother into debtor's prison. And you knew that would never happen. I would have forced Papa to bar the entail and lose his estates rather than allow him to go to prison, and you knew it. So why don't you admit that your reason for wanting to cut a splash with this wedding is to make your triumph all the more enjoyable?"

Not a ripple of expression crossed Jared's face. "You are, of course, free to think anything you like," he said politely. "Your attitude, however, is scarcely what one would wish to see in a young woman about to enter into holy wedlock. If I might make a suggestion, I would urge you to try to temper these wild ideas of yours, Diana."

"I hate you," she said simply.

He shrugged. "I can only repeat what I've already said. Shall we continue our stroll? You won't want passersby to jump to the conclusion that we're having a quarrel."

Diana gritted her teeth.

* * *

The next three weeks were like a confused kaleidoscope to Diana. She was very busy, for one thing. No sooner had she sent out a myriad of wedding invitations to everyone of note in the *ton* than she was confronted by Jared's long list of people she had never heard of. Or had mostly never heard of. One of the names was Nathan Rothschild.

She had to shop for, and be fitted for, a gown sufficiently magnificent to withstand the critical gaze of a packed congregation in St. George's, Hanover Square.

She had to return the calls of the people who began showering cards on Amberly House the day that her engagement was announced in the newspapers. Fortunately, she had merely to return the cards, but that took time.

She had to keep a close eye on her father to prevent him from overdoing. He had insisted on resuming his normal routine, which included his postponed speech in the House of Lords about the Bullion Report. Diana heard the speech from a position behind the Bar of the Lords, hanging on every word, not so much because of a filial interest in what he was saying but because she was intensely concerned about the duke's physical condition. He was pale and appreciably frailer than he had been before his illness, and several times while he talked his voice faltered, but he finished his speech, to his daughter's great relief.

"Papa, you were splendid," she complimented him later. "I'm sure your speech will have a great deal of influence."

"I don't share your confidence," the duke snorted. "The Bullion Report will come up for debate in Parliament in several weeks, and I've no doubt it will be negatived. Many of my fellow members, my dear, have no common sense. They can't understand that if a one pound bank note, which is a promise to pay a certain weight in gold, will only buy four-fifths of that amount of gold on the market, then the bank note is no longer worth a pound. It's the same as saying that if a fifth part were to leak out of a pint bottle of wine, it would still be a pint of wine because it was contained in a pint bottle. Utter nonsense and stupidity, Diana!"

Diana laughed at her father's indignant remarks, but she discovered later with some surprise that Jared shared the duke's opinions. On the day after the speech in the Lords, as he and Diana were driving in the Park, a practice which had become almost a daily routine during their engagement, Jared remarked, "I read the account of your father's speech. He understands perfectly the currency problem and its relation to the foreign exchanges."

Diana lifted an eyebrow. "This must be the first time you've ever agreed with my father's views."

Jared looked thoughtful. "So it is. I wouldn't have believed it of him. He's a man who despises trade and the making of money. As a gentleman and aristocrat he would feel soiled to be in my shoes, for instance. And yet his grasp of the real nature of money is astounding." He smiled suddenly. "Fortunately for me, I gather that the duke's ideas aren't shared by most members of Parliament."

"What do you mean?"

"Why, only that the government won't act to restrict the unlimited issuance of bank notes, so the price of gold will go up. For gold traders like myself that represents a—er—golden opportunity."

Diana didn't return Jared's smile over his little pun. She found little to smile at in her frequent encounters with him, which often turned into a disagreement about some aspect of their engagement. Several times she had been forced, against her inclination, which was to be in his company as little as possible, to invite him into the house after the conclusion of a drive in order to have a conversation out of the hearing of his tiger.

One such occasion occurred shortly after the announcement of the betrothal. "Papa's lawyers came to see him yesterday," she said after settling into a chair opposite him in the drawing room.

"Oh, yes?" he said politely. He was always polite and imperturbable. Sometimes she longed to shatter his composure.

"Yes. The lawyers came to report on the marriage settlement they had negotiated with your solicitors."

"I trust the arrangements were satisfactory."

THE BARTERED BRIDE 137

"No, they were not!"

Frowning, he said, "Not generous enough?"

"Too much so. I don't wish to accept such a large allowance for pin money, or such a large jointure."

Studying her for a moment, Jared said softly, "Why is that, Diana? Most brides are happy to be adequately provided for. In your case, if I should die, you would have your right of dower. However, I'm not a landowner, so your income from my real property would be precisely nothing. That's why I decided to offer you the larger amounts for pin money and jointure."

Before she could stop herself, Diana blurted, "I don't wish to be provided for by you. I don't wish to profit from this marriage."

For a moment Diana thought she had pierced the hard shell of his imperturbability. His mouth tensed slightly, and a faint flush rose in his cheeks. After a brief pause, however, he said merely, "Does your father share your views?"

"No," Diana admitted unwillingly.

Her father had, in fact, exclaimed, "Well, at least our lawyers have forced the fellow to pay, and pay handsomely, for the privilege of marrying you, Diana."

Jared shrugged. "Well, then . . ."

Another altercation occurred over his choice of wedding attendant. Jared had asked her who would be attending her, and she had replied, "Mrs. Armstrong, Dolly Madden as she used to be. Dolly and I had our come-outs together, and we've kept in touch, mostly by mail. Who will be your groomsman?"

"I hadn't thought . . . Kamal, I should say."

Diana had been startled. "Isn't he your clerk? The young man who brought over some papers for Papa the other day?"

"My head clerk, yes. Kamal Mukherjee. A highly valued employee."

"But—he is an employee, a tradesman. And he's also . . ."

"A half-caste? Yes, indeed. He has more Indian blood in his veins than I do."

"This Kamal is out of the question, Jared. You must ask one of your friends to be your groom."

"I have no friends, only acquaintances. And they're all bankers or stockbrokers. I'm afraid you can't escape the whiff of trade at your wedding, Diana. You see, I don't know any aristocrats, except your family, of course. Do you think your brother Miles would like to volunteer to be my groom?"

It was checkmate, or rather defeat, to be more accurate. Diana also believed that Jared's choice of his clerk to be his groomsman had been deliberately made to inflict still another humiliation on the Amberly family.

The delicate fabric of civility between them had, finally, nearly shredded a week ago when Jared had announced that he and Diana would reside at his house in Chesterfield Street after the wedding.

"Oh—I thought we'd be living here, at Amberly House."

Jared had flicked her an incredulous glance. "It's surely a husband's duty and prerogative to provide a place of residence for his bride? And can you imagine me living in the same house with the Duke of Edgehill?"

"No, I suppose not," Diana muttered in some confusion. In point of fact, a joint residence by her father and Jared could only result in armed hostility.

"I'm glad you agree. Naturally, if you don't like my present house, it would be a simple matter to buy another. You have only to say the word. Where would you like to live? Grosvenor Square? I understand a house may be available there. Or Park Lane? Bruton Street?"

Diana bit her lip. "I have no preferences about another location. I fancy the Chesterfield House will be satisfactory, judging from what I've seen of it. But—"

"Yes?"

"Who will be the mistress of this establishment?"

"You will, of course. You'll be my wife."

"I understand there is already a woman presiding over your house."

Jared's face became expressionless. "Are you referring to Rana?"

"If that's the name of the woman I've seen in your house. Beautiful, dark, exotically dressed."

"Rana is my—my housekeeper. She was my mother's *ayah,* her maid."

"Will she continue to be a part of your household after we're married?"

"Certainly." Jared's brows grew together. "Where would she go?"

Diana faced him defiantly. "I won't live under the same roof with your mistress. I won't be a third member of a *ménage à trois.*"

"Rana isn't my mistress."

"I don't believe you. You forget that I've seen you together at the theater. Housekeepers don't appear in public with their masters, decked in expensive jewelry."

"This housekeeper does, if I invite her."

Diana threw down the gauntlet. "I won't live with you in the house on Chesterfield Street if this woman is still a part of your household."

Jared said silkily, "May I remind you, Diana, that after we're married you will live where I say, do as I say, and generally conduct yourself like a dutiful wife?"

Diana's heart sank. It was true. After her marriage she would have no personal rights. She would belong to her husband, body and soul. If he chose, he could beat her, starve her, desert her, bring a mistress into her house, and she would have no recourse, except to conduct herself with as much dignity as possible. She said quietly, "I don't need to be reminded of my marital duties, Jared. I'm quite aware of them."

"I'm glad to hear it." The faint expression of levity faded. "To return to the cause of this argument: I repeat, Rana is not my mistress. I have certain standards. I wouldn't dishonor either you or myself by forcing you to share a house with my mistress."

Diana was inclined to believe him. Why would he bother to lie to her? And what could she do about the situation if he *was* lying? But she still felt that she had lost another round in their long, drawn-out battle.

After a number of these confrontations Diana became almost philosophical. She schooled herself to cease chafing against

what she couldn't change. In this marriage Jared had the right
to dictate the terms, and it was simply profitless to waste time
or energy in opposing him.

Today, for example, as she rode with Jared on another of their
interminable drives in the Park, she had had no intention of
arousing dissension between them. She was merely making
small talk when she remarked, "You recall, of course, that we
have an important engagement tomorrow night?"

He frowned. "I won't be free tomorrow night. I must leave
London in the morning on a business matter. I won't be back
until the following day."

Diana flicked him an annoyed look. "I'll remind you that you
told me to accept every invitation I received. Lady Jersey is a
very influential hostess. She's also a neighbor here in Berkeley
Square. She'll take it amiss if you don't appear at an event that
she's described to her friends as being held largely in our
honor."

"I'm sorry. Pray give Lady Jersey my apologies. I can't neglect my business for a social event."

"Then why—?" She had been about to ask why, if he placed
so much importance on the recognition of their betrothal in the
highest social circles, he was willing to risk the disapproval of
a powerful hostess because of a business matter, but what was
the point? He would do exactly what he chose to do, as he
always did.

"Kamal is here, Sahib."

Jared glanced up from his newspaper. "Ask him up, Rana.
Perhaps he'd like a cup of tea before we leave."

As he entered the dining room, Kamal said, "Good morning,
sir. We have good weather for our journey."

"Yes, I'd noticed. A good thing, too. It's a tediously long drive
to Folkestone." Jared waved Kamal to a seat at the table and
resumed reading his newspaper.

After a few minutes he became aware that Kamal and Rana
were conducting a lively conversation in Bengali as she served
the head clerk tea and toast. They were talking about Calcutta

mostly, but Rana also asked Kamal about his living arrangements in London. She even teased him about his very smart, caped greatcoat. Jared felt mildly surprised at the interplay between them. He would not have thought, if he had thought about it at all, that the pair had anything in common, indeed that Rana, so many years older, was completely out of Kamal's orbit. Now, as he listened to their banter, he realized that they were much of an age. Rana had entered his mother's service as a very young girl. She was probably only in her early or middle thirties, Kamal, a few years younger.

Jared put down his cup. "Time to leave, Kamal. We have eight to nine hours of hard driving ahead of us."

The traveling carriage drawn up in front of the house looked much like any other vehicle on the road, but appearances were deceiving. The two footmen in the rear were clerks at his bank, and both were armed, though not visibly so. The two large valises in the boot looked ordinary, too, but they were specially constructed to hold a heavy weight in gold ingots. Jared and Kamal carried pistols in their pockets. Jared wasn't prepared to take any chances with his irregularly scheduled gold shipments.

As the carriage rolled over London Bridge and the start of the journey to the coast, Jared's thoughts returned to Rana and Kamal. He felt vaguely guilty as he reflected that it had never occurred to him to wonder about their personal lives here in London. He had ordered them to accompany him from India because he needed both of them. Were they happy with the change? Rana, for example. Did she ever feel lonely in a house full of English servants?

"Do you like living in England, Kamal?" he asked abruptly. "Would you have preferred to stay in Calcutta?"

Kamal looked surprised. "No, sir. Not unless you had stayed there, too. I wanted to come with you. I thought you understood that. I knew you would be even more successful in London than in Calcutta. I wanted to be part of that success."

"Yes, but—what about friends? You're the only Indian in our offices. Except for me, of course. Do you ever feel, well, left out?"

Kamal shrugged. "Sometimes. It doesn't matter. You know

all about that, sir." He stopped short, biting his lip. The words had slipped out of him.

Jared was silent. Oh, yes, he understood what it meant to be left out. Nevertheless, he felt ashamed of himself. It must have been excruciatingly difficult for Rana and Kamal to be transported to an alien land in which he was their only point of reference, and he had never given their predicament a moment's thought. He had been too absorbed in his own personal hell of ostracism and bitterness.

The long journey ended in late afternoon. Jared took a room at the Royal George Hotel and sent off one of the footmen with a message to a Captain Appleton in the town.

The ship's captain arrived in Jared's private dining parlor after dusk had fallen. He was a hard-bitten, ruddy-faced man in early middle age. "Ye have a shipment fer me, yer honor?"

"The usual. Kamal and I will be at the docks soon after full dark."

"Yes, sir. The shipping charges will be higher this time."

Jared gave the man a long look. "Why is that?"

"Because this business is getting dangerous, that's why," said the captain bluntly. "Last time we was transferring yer shipment on board, we was attacked. One o' my crew was hurt bad. Smuggling is one thing, sir. Brandy and gloves and tobacco and tea and the like. Gold is quite another. People will kill for gold. I needs more money ter serve ye, or ye can find yerself another captain."

"That seems reasonable to me," Jared said calmly. Captain Appleton stared his amazement. "I'm prepared to pay for efficient service, Captain, and you've always served me well. Kamal, see to it."

The ballroom of Amberly House was jammed with people. There was scarcely room to dance in the middle of the floor. Many of the guests didn't try. They milled around the sides of the room, standing when they couldn't find chairs.

"A frightful squeeze, as they say," murmured Jared as he

stood beside Diana and the duke and Miles in the receiving line at the door of the ballroom.

"Yes, everyone has come to stare, no doubt," Diana replied in a low voice. Fortunately she had placed herself between Jared and her father and brother, or Jared's comment would have gone unanswered. The duke and Miles had greeted him on his arrival with the curtest of nods, and had not addressed a word to him since.

"At you and me, do you think?" Jared smiled faintly. "Oh, no, my dear, you're far too modest. Your guests are staring at you." His eyes roamed over her figure in the sea-green gown of aërophone crape. "You look superb."

"Thank you." There was a curiously intent look in the startling blue eyes that made her feel uncomfortable.

Her father said, "I fancy most of our guests are already here, Diana. Indeed, I don't know where we should put them if any more people should arrive. I believe we can leave the receiving line."

"Oh, yes, Papa, you should sit down." Diana felt a qualm as she looked at the duke. His back was ramrod-straight, but he was obviously very near the end of his strength. It was useless to suggest that he leave the ballroom, however. His sense of duty was too strong for that. She settled him into a comfortable chair in a secluded corner.

Lady Lyon, with Charlotte in tow, pounced on her as soon as she left the duke's side. "My dear Diana, what a triumph. Such a distinguished company. I counted four of Almack's hostesses here tonight. Lord Alvanley, too, and Mr. Hughes. And the prime minister. You must be very happy."

"Well, of course Diana is happy, Mama," said Charlotte, looking faintly uncomfortable as usual at her mother's gushing way of speaking. "She's about to be married." Charlotte glanced at Jared, standing nearby in conversation. "Mr. Amberly is so handsome," she said shyly. "You make such a beautiful couple."

"Oh, indeed." Lady Lyon stared at Jared. "A magnificent-looking man." She lowered her voice, saying, "I've heard, you know, that Mr. Amberly is—that is to say, that he isn't wholly English."

"That's right. He has a partly Indian ancestry." Diana gave Lady Lyon a level look.

"Not that it has anything to say to anything, I'm sure," Lady Lyon added hastily. "Such a successful man. My husband tells me that Mr. Amberly possesses one of the largest fortunes in England."

Lady Lyon's vapid comment set Diana to thinking furiously. Jared's presumed illegitimacy and his lack of social position would by themselves have disqualified him as a suitor in her father's eyes, but his mixed blood had been by far the most powerful count against him. Diana had anticipated that society in general would share her father's views, and she had been prepared to be criticized for marrying Jared.

However, she hadn't heard a whisper of condemnation on that score from any of her friends and acquaintances. In fact, Lady Lyon was the first person to mention the subject to her face. There might, of course, be gossip that she hadn't heard. Perhaps, she'd thought, the people in her circle had simply been too mannerly, or too kind, to mention their opinions, and she was grateful to be spared the embarrassment, without questioning their reasons.

Now she wondered, as she gazed around the crowded ballroom. As Lady Lyon had said, everyone in London who counted for anything was here at Amberly House this evening. Was it possible that Jared's vast wealth had sanitized his ancestry in the eyes of the *ton?* Diana's lip curled. Money, it seemed, was even more powerful than she had imagined.

Finally the long evening was over. The last guest had departed down the stairs. The duke, looking ready to drop from exhaustion, had left the ballroom on Miles's arm.

"Goodnight, Jared," said Diana, as the servants began swarming into the room to set it aright.

"Can I speak to you for a moment, Diana?"

"It's so late . . ."

"I won't keep you long."

"Very well, then. Shall we go to the library?"

He shut the door behind them and stood silent for a moment. Then he said, "Day after tomorrow is our wedding day."

"Yes." Diana felt a twinge of impatience. Why state the obvious?

He cleared his throat. "I fancy I won't see you again before the wedding. You'll be far too busy tomorrow with your preparations to welcome a drive in the Park or a meaningless conversation. So I decided to give you this now." He took a flat velvet-covered box from an inner pocket of his coat and handed it to her.

"This" was a magnificent necklace of amethysts and diamonds. Diana's eyes widened. She had never seen anything quite so beautiful in her life.

Jared went on, "You told me your wedding gown was made of a blue-violet material. I thought this necklace would go well with it."

"It—it's perfectly lovely, Jared. Thank you. I fear I don't have anything for you."

He reached out to place his hands on her shoulders. "I don't require a wedding gift, but you could kiss me. After all, I haven't been a particularly demanding suitor, would you say?"

She was suddenly very conscious of the heat in the blue eyes and the strength in the slender hands that held her so closely. She was afraid that, if she kissed him, she would melt against his tautly muscled body. She pulled away from him, saying breathlessly, "You have no right to demand anything until . . ."

The blue eyes turned cold. "Until our wedding night? Correct, Diana. Be very sure I'll present my 'demands' then. Goodnight."

Eleven

The abigail, Rose, arranged the amber curls on the crown of Diana's head, leaving a few tendrils to curve artfully around her face, and placed a short tulle veil over her hair. She was about to put a small tiara over the veil when Diana exclaimed, "No, Rose, I won't wear the tiara."

"But you wore it at your first—" Rose stopped short, turning a fiery red.

Diana ignored the abigail's embarrassment. "Keep the veil in place with a circlet of artificial violets, the one I wore to Mrs. Austen's ball last week." This wedding ceremony might be as distasteful to her as that first ceremony, but she wanted no reminder of the first to intrude into the second.

"Now for the necklace, my lady," said Rose a few moments later. She fastened the amethyst and diamond necklace around Diana's throat and stepped back from the dressing table. "Oh," she murmured. "You look so beautiful."

Diana gazed at her reflection in the mirror and had to agree without false modesty. She knew she had never looked so well. The gleam of the blue-purple stones interspersed with the flashing diamonds did not overpower the gown of delicate violet silk gauze worn over a slip of deeper blue-violet, but rather complemented it.

A tap sounded at the door and Rose admitted the duke. He dismissed the abigail with a slight nod of his head. Diana rose to face him.

"It's time, my dear." The duke looked tired and old this morning.

"Yes, Papa."

He said impulsively, "Diana, it's not too late. You have the right to cry off from this monstrous marriage up until the very moment that mountebank places a ring on your finger."

"No, Papa, I can't. You know I can't. I'm committed."

He stared at her in angry impotence. "Oh, God, Diana, the world—our world—is falling apart. I'm your father, I'm supposed to take care of you, and I can't save you from this marriage to a half-breed money-grubber. I feel like such a failure."

Diana gave him a quick hug. "A failure? Never. You're the most successful man I know." In an effort to raise his spirits she said jokingly, "If it's any comfort to you, there are people who actually feel I've achieved a great coup in snaring a wealthy man like Jared Amberly."

It was the wrong thing to say. The duke scowled. "I'm well aware of such obscenities. You won't believe this, but at the ball the other night Argyll remarked to me that, while of course one would wish to have a higher pedigree in one's son-in-law, a great fortune made the inequality in rank much easier to stomach!"

"Oh, I can believe it, Papa, and do you know, I'd rather be envied than pitied? I don't want it known that I was forced into this marriage because our family had a—a money problem. Let everyone think that Jared and I made a bargain, his fortune for my social position."

Some of the strain lifted from the duke's face. "Oh, my darling, what have I been telling you? You should have been the oldest son in this family. You're a true Amberly." He cleared his throat. "Well, then, shall we go? We can't keep the groom waiting for his aristocratic bride, can we?"

Diana hesitated. "There's one thing . . . do you really insist on giving me away? You won't ask Miles to substitute for you?"

"No. If you can bring yourself to marry this man, the least I can do is to walk down the aisle with you."

It was a bright warm day at the beginning of June, but Diana began to feel chilled during the short ride from Amberly House to Hanover Square. The chill had nothing to do with the temperature. Time was running out, and in a short while she would be irrevocably bound to a relationship from which she could never extricate herself. She and her father rode in complete silence.

The carriage stopped in front of the huge portico of St. George's. Diana and the duke stepped under the six tall Corinthian columns, and as they entered the vestibule of the church a curate and Diana's young attendant, Dolly Armstrong, were waiting for them. The curate greeted them in a low voice. "You're in good time, Your Grace, my lady. Mr. Amberly and his groomsman are also present. With your leave, I'll notify the organist that the bridal party is here."

As soon as the organist began playing Diana nodded to Dolly Armstrong, who started slowly down the aisle.

Every seat in the church was taken, and the galleries were full. In Diana's increasing nervousness the faces of the guests were only a blur to her until she and the duke reached the front pews, where, on the right, in a place obviously reserved for him, sat a large, imposing figure in an impossibly tight coat. Diana drew an incredulous breath. As Jared had instructed her, she had sent a wedding invitation to the Prince Regent. She had never expected him to come.

At the railing of the chancel Jared stood waiting for her, all dark, graceful elegance. But he held himself with a tension that wasn't normally evident in him, and his fingers when he clasped her hand, and later, when he put the ring on her finger, felt as cold as her own hands.

The brief ceremony was over before Diana quite grasped the truth that she was now a married woman, and the signing of the register in the vestry took only a few minutes.

Before the wedding party left the church, the Regent put an unmistakable stamp of approval on the marriage. He clapped Jared on the shoulder, saying jovially, "I see you're lucky in love as well as in many other things, my boy. Congratulations. Lady Diana, my best wishes for your happiness."

Diana caught a glimpse of her father's face as His Royal Highness was speaking. The duke's expression seemed torn between an understandable pride that the Regent had honored him by attending his daughter's wedding and an urge to plant a dagger in his royal guest's heart for behaving in such a friendly fashion to Jared.

The ballroom of Amberly House was the scene of a lavish wedding breakfast, with the guests sitting at small tables arranged around the room. Diana and Jared sat at the principal table with the duke, Miles, Dolly Armstrong, and Kamal.

Mrs. Armstrong, who had seen little of Diana in recent years and who was apparently oblivious to any currents of conflict or emotion, kept up a sprightly chatter.

The clerk, Kamal, was obviously uncomfortable to be sitting in the company of his employer and his ducal host, though he tried to keep his face impassive. He spoke as little as possible.

Suddenly Diana wondered if the Indian woman—Rana, was that what Jared called her?—had been at the church. Probably not. She would have been very visible in her exotic garments. Diana wasn't sure she believed Jared's statement that the woman wasn't his mistress. She told herself she didn't care. However, she was glad that Jared hadn't roiled the waters of convention by inviting the woman to his wedding.

During the breakfast the duke and Miles were studiously uncommunicative, pecking at their food, keeping their eyes averted from Jared and Kamal.

On the other hand, his mask of imperturbability once more in place, Jared chatted easily, exchanging comments with Dolly Armstrong on the church and the wedding ceremony and the guests. At one point he said to Diana, "I haven't told you how much I like your gown. The necklace goes well with it, I'm happy to see. Don't you agree, Duke?"

The duke raised his eyes. "Yes. It's a handsome piece." That was his sole contribution to the conversation.

Then it was time to toast the newly married couple. The duke rose with his usual inimitable grace. Not a tinge of his real feelings showed as he lifted his glass to say, "Let us drink to the bride and groom. May they enjoy a long and fruitful life together."

Jared glanced inquiringly at Diana, and she nodded. They rose, and walked hand in hand from table to table, thanking their guests for coming to the wedding.

They stopped at the table where Aubrey Dalton sat. Diana had been surprised to see him at the church. He'd been avoiding any contact with her since the engagement announcement. She supposed he'd become reconciled to her marriage, however unwillingly. This morning he looked tired and haggard, as if he hadn't slept for days. He congratulated Jared with a wooden lack of enthusiasm. To Diana he said, his heart in his eyes, "I pray you'll be happy."

As they moved away, Jared murmured, "Dalton may have wished you happy, my love, but he seemed rather dubious that you would be."

Without speaking, Diana shot him a repressive look. He shrugged, smiling faintly.

They paused at the Lyons' table. Lord Lyon was effusive, his wife even more so. "The wedding of the year, the wedding of any year, my dear Lady Windham," she gushed. "Oh, I beg your pardon. I must call you Lady Diana now, I believe."

"Indeed, Lady Lyon," said Jared politely. "By an odd twist of fate, my wife has resumed her girlhood name. She's become Lady Diana Amberly again." He looked at Charlotte. "I understand your marriage to Lord Brentford will be the next wedding in the Amberly family, Miss Lyon. I look forward to celebrating the event."

Charlotte turned pink with pleasure. "Thank you, Mr. Amberly. I look forward to seeing you at my wedding." Her eyes sought Miles at another table, and he raised his glass in salute.

Well, at least one member of the Amberly family will be making a happy marriage, Diana reflected. And then an odd thought struck her. Charlotte's wealthy parents wanted a higher social standing for their daughter, and had arranged for her to marry Miles, the son of a duke, who needed money. On the other hand, it could be said that Diana, who also needed money, had married Jared for his fortune, thereby enabling him to share in her exalted rank. On the surface, at least, many people might consider the marriages of brother and sister to be very similar. Except that Miles and Charlotte loved each other, Diana thought savagely, and no one had forced or blackmailed either of them into the marriage.

As they completed the circuit of the ballroom, Jared murmured, "I think we should leave now. We have a long day's driving ahead of us. Unless you would rather spend the night here, and leave for Abbottsleigh early tomorrow morning?"

"No. Let's go now," Diana replied, and instantly regretted the note of urgency in her voice. She wouldn't have admitted it to Jared, nor did she fully understand her feelings, but the mere thought of spending her wedding night here under the same roof with her father appalled her.

She slipped away to her bedchamber, where Rose waited to help her out of the exquisite blue-violet gown and dress her in a white jaconet carriage dress sprigged in green with a matching green pelisse and a straw Gipsy bonnet trimmed with green ribbon.

"That will be all, Rose, thank you. Are you all ready to go?"

"Yes, my lady, and all your luggage, too."

"Good. I'll see you tonight, then, at Abbottsleigh." Rose would be traveling with the luggage in a second carriage.

Diana went down the back stairs of the house to the mews, where Jared stood waiting beside a traveling carriage. Silently he extended his hand to help her up the steps and climbed in after her. A groom put up the steps and closed the door and the carriage started up.

"You changed very quickly," Jared observed. "I hope that's a good omen. I dislike waiting on someone to join me."

"Then you'll be pleased to know that promptness is one virtue I can honestly claim," said Diana dryly.

"You mustn't be so modest. I'm sure you have many virtues."

Diana couldn't decide whether a satirical note lurked in Jared's voice.

The carriage proceeded out of Hill Street to Park Lane and Hyde Park Corner, the start of the journey Diana had made so often since her childhood that she was familiar with virtually every turn in the road.

Jared said suddenly, "So we've actually done it. We're married. Somehow, I never really thought it would happen. Do you feel different? For instance, will you dislike hearing us introduced as Mr. Amberly and Lady Diana Amberly?"

Diana gave him a level look. "Not at all. No matter what I'm called, I'll always be myself, I trust. An Amberly of Abbottsleigh. The daughter of the Duke of Edgehill."

"Oh, I have no doubt of that. You're a very consistent woman, Diana."

This time there was no doubting the tinge of irony in Jared's voice. He lapsed into silence, gazing abstractedly out of the window as they neared the first stop at Southall. Diana wondered bleakly if they would make the entire seventy-five mile journey without speaking. But then, what did they have to talk about? They both already knew the motives that had brought the other into this marriage. There was no point in further discussion. She sat as far away from him as she could, pressed against the lefthand door of the carriage, and he made no move to narrow the distance between them.

They changed horses again in Uxbridge. As the carriage moved out of the courtyard of the posting house Diana's nerves began to tighten. A few miles farther on she drew an involuntary sharp breath as they entered the hamlet of Litchfield and passed the unprepossessing gates of the Royal Arms Inn, where she and Jared had taken refuge from that winter storm.

Stirring slightly, Jared turned his head to look at her. "Memories, Diana?" he asked softly.

She pressed her lips firmly together. After a moment she said, "Yes, I have memories. Unpleasant ones."

"Really? My memories of our stay at the Royal Arms are quite pleasant, all in all. It was such a relief to escape from the blizzard into warmth and reasonable comfort, for one thing. And we became—shall I say friendly?—at the inn, as you'll recall, and as a result we became even more friendly later during my visit to Abbottsleigh."

Diana tried to swallow the lump in her throat. He was baiting her, using the word "friendly" to describe that brief idyll when she had fallen headlong in love with him.

"If we were 'friendly' it was because you were conducting yourself under false premises," she said sharply.

His eyes narrowed. "In what way? I told you who I was. That is, I told you my name after you finally gave me permission to do so. I told you about my banking business. I told you I was a distant connection of your family."

"You never told me you had Indian blood. You never mentioned you were illegitimate. . . ." She broke off, biting her lip.

"I didn't mention it because it wasn't true. I'm not illegitimate, remember? You've seen my birth certificate, and my father's birth certificate. I and my immediate ancestors are legitimate back to the fourth Duke of Edgehill." He stared at her. "Why can't you be honest, Diana? You disapproved of me—you turned against me—when you learned that I was part Indian. I didn't come to you under false pretenses. The only thing about myself I didn't tell you was that my maternal grandmother was an Indian. I thought that was self-evident. My skin is darker than yours. You didn't seem to mind the color of my skin when you showed me around Abbottsleigh, the home of your ancestors—and mine."

Averting her eyes from him, Diana muttered, "You don't understand, you've never understood, the importance my family attaches to remaining true to our traditions."

Jared's voice turned to ice. "You're wrong. If I didn't understand before, I understand now. Preserving the purity of the Amberly blood is more important to you than love or loyalty or personal happiness."

He bit off his words, as if he regretted speaking, and settled back on his side of the coach. Stealing a sideways glance at him, Diana noted that his face had turned grim and somber. He seemed more like the frightening dark stranger she had first met. He said very little during the remainder of the long journey, except to ask her politely if she required refreshment during the various post stops.

It wasn't like her first wedding trip, Diana thought, shivering with distaste as she remembered how Windham had hugged and kissed her and made it plain that he could hardly wait for their arrival at his country estate so that he could possess her utterly. Jared didn't touch her. Even when he helped her in and out of the carriage, he dropped her hand so quickly that it might have been a burning coal. Shivering again, Diana knew that, regardless of the seeming indifference of Jared's behavior now, this second wedding journey would end in the same way as the first.

Dusk had fallen when the carriage reached Burford, near the Gloucestershire border. Diana roused herself to say, "We're only a few miles from Abbottsleigh. I'm glad. I feel very tired. I daresay you're fatigued, also."

"Yes. It might have been more sensible to break the journey in midpoint and continue on in the morning. However, I assumed you wanted to spend your wedding night at Abbottsleigh."

Diana was glad the darkness in the carriage concealed the sudden hot flush in her cheeks.

The remaining few miles of the trip seemed interminable, fraught with a sort of electric tension. At last the carriage drew up in front of the medieval gatehouse that was the main entrance of Abbottsleigh. An alert footman appeared out of the gatehouse to bow deeply as Diana and Jared descended from the carriage, and when they stepped into the inner courtyard the butler and the housekeeper and their staffs were already assembled before the door opposite the gatehouse.

The butler said with stately dignity, "Welcome home, my lady. With your permission, all of us at Abbottsleigh would like to wish you and Mr. Amberly great happiness in your wedded life."

"Thank you, Stowe. What Mr. Amberly and I require first of all is food. We haven't had a meal since our wedding breakfast."

"At once, my lady, or as soon as you and Mr. Amberly are ready. Your abigail, I might add, arrived a few minutes ago." The butler lifted an inquiring eyebrow at Jared. "Your valet is not with you, sir. Shall I send one of the footmen to assist you?"

"No. I don't require a valet."

Diana found that Rose had already begun to unpack her belongings in the bedchamber that she had occupied at Abbottsleigh since her girlhood.

"The butler has put Mr. Amberly into Lord Brentford's old rooms, as you instructed, my lady," said the abigail without a trace of expression. It suddenly occurred to Diana that Rose knew, or at least suspected, a good many details about her mistress's marriage to Jared.

Changing quickly into a gown of pale primrose silk, and placing a coquettish wisp of lace on her head, Diana made a hasty toilet and went down to the vast dining room, where Jared was already waiting. He wore severe black evening clothes with an exquisitely embroidered white satin waistcoat and an intricately tied cravat. She wondered if he was aware of how perfectly his expertly tailored clothes complemented his tall graceful figure. She wondered, too, why he hadn't brought a valet to Abbottsleigh. Surely he must have one.

Jared pulled out her chair for her at one end of the long table and retreated to a seat at the other end. Servants began serving the meal. Diana and Jared ate in silence, barely exchanging a word. With a curiously hurtful pang, Diana thought of those other meals during Jared's last visit to Abbottsleigh when they had talked continually, interrupting each other as they discussed with absorbed excitement their activities during the day and what they intended to do on the following day.

The footman served the dessert course. To Diana the caramelized apple tart tasted like sawdust, though ordinarily it was her favorite sweet. She guessed, too, that Cook, well aware of her partiality, had made a special effort to provide the tart, as well as several other desserts that were Diana's favorites.

Pushing the plate with the uneaten apple tart aside, Diana rose from the table. "I'll leave you to your port," she told Jared. "I don't care for coffee. I believe I'll go up to my bedchamber."

Jared stood up, waiting politely while she walked to the door. Diana hurried to her bedchamber, where Rose expertly divested her of her gown, slipped a lacy muslin nightdress over her head and helped her into a peignoir of sheer green silk.

"Thank you, Rose. I won't need you anymore."

Rose dipped a curtsy and hurried out of the room, but not before Diana had glimpsed a flicker of excited, avid curiosity in the girl's face.

Clinging to a precarious calm, Diana walked to the window, where she stood looking over the gardens, the pride of Abbottsleigh, now bathed in the silvery light of a full moon.

She turned away from the window at the sound of a door opening. Jared entered the room and closed the door behind him. He was wearing a dressing gown of dark red and gold brocade that reminded Diana of the exotic costume he had worn at the Pantheon ball on the night they met. In one hand he carried a champagne bottle and in the other two glasses.

"You didn't drink much wine at dinner, Diana. I thought you might like a glass of champagne."

"Yes, thank you, I would." Perhaps the wine would calm her racing pulse.

Jared set the glasses down on a small table and poured wine into them. He handed one to Diana and raised the other, saying, "Shall we drink a toast? To us?"

"To us," she murmured with a dry mouth. She took a sip of the wine.

Jared was standing very close to her, so close that she could see the beginnings of a beard on his dark face, and smell the faint scent of a freshly bathed masculine body. He stared at her as he slowly drained his glass. "Diana, I must know," he said abruptly. "At Litchfield, during the storm, you talked about your first husband. I gathered he was old and clumsy and perhaps he was impotent as well. Did he consummate the marriage?"

Diana's fingers tightened convulsively on the stem of her glass, causing some of the wine to spill on her peignoir. She choked, "How could you . . . ?"

Jared pried her glass from her fingers and set both glasses on the table. Turning back to her, he said, "How could I ask you that? How could I not? Before we—I must know if you're a virgin."

"No, I'm not! Now are you satisfied?" Diana glared at him in mingled rage and disgust.

"Diana . . ." Jared stepped toward her and caught her by the shoulders. "Why are you so angry? I didn't mean to insult you, or embarrass you. I didn't want to hurt you, that's all. Because if you were a virgin I—"

"You needn't say any more. You've been quite crude enough."

His fingers tightened on her shoulders. "That's what you think of me, isn't it? That I'm a crude savage?"

"What does it matter what I think of you? You've won. You have what you want. You've revenged yourself for whatever slights you think the Amberly family has inflicted on you."

Releasing her, he stepped back, his dark face a mask. The brilliant blue eyes had turned almost black. "Yes, I've won. I'm glad you acknowledge that. Do you also acknowledge that you must submit to me in every way, as a good wife should?"

"Yes," said Diana. She could hardly form the word between stiff lips.

"You agree that I have a right to make love to you at any time, as often as I like?"

"Yes."

"And that you will do your best to respond with a suitable enthusiasm, in order to bolster my male ego, even though you consider me crude and ungentlemanly?"

"Yes . . ." Diana stared uncertainly at Jared.

"Good. Then I understand you. Now please understand me. I have no wish to make love to a woman who is merely submitting to me out of duty. That's why I don't patronize whores. To satisfy me, the sexual act should include elements of mutual passion and desire, which are decidedly lacking in our case. Therefore, I'll forgo exercising my marital rights tonight. Later, if I should decide I want children, I'll dispense with the passion and settle for the mechanical. Until then, Diana, you can remain the chaste widow you were when I met you."

Before Diana realized what he was doing he pulled the peignoir away from her body and tossed it onto a chair. Then he shrugged out of his dressing gown and kicked off his slippers. He was wearing only a pair of thin linen drawers.

He said curtly, "Go to bed, Diana." At her look of mingled bewilderment and apprehension he added, "I'll be your platonic bed partner. I have no intention of allowing your servants, and through them the public, to realize that I haven't consummated this marriage." He added, with a touch of grim humor, "Fortunately, since you've already had a husband, there'll be no need to worry about the lack of bloodstains on the connubial sheets."

* * *

Diana awoke with a nervous start. She had lain awake for hours after she and Jared had settled into the bed in which she had slept during her entire life, except for the few brief years of her marriage to the Earl of Windham. She hadn't been able to sleep, conscious of the powerful male figure in the bed with her. Jared had apparently suffered no such inhibitions. He'd fallen into a deep sleep immediately.

She felt a slight movement beside her and turned her head to find Jared awake and looking down at her, his head braced on his hand. A flame sparked in the blue eyes, and he shifted his body closer to her. She felt a sudden hard swelling against her leg.

"You're not like most women, Diana," he said huskily. "You look as beautiful first thing in the morning as you do at night."

A soft knock sounded at the door. Jared inhaled a deep breath and swung his legs out of the bed. "One moment," he called, as he pulled his dressing gown around him. He walked to the door and opened it. "Good morning, Rose. You'll find her ladyship most anxious for her tea." He walked past the abigail and disappeared down the corridor.

Twelve

Diana tied the ribbons of her bonnet and took one last glance into the mirror before leaving her bedchamber to begin her journey back to London. She paused at the window to look out into the gardens, where the flower beds, which she preferred to the stiff formal plantings, were a riot of bright colors. Ordinarily she would have grieved to leave Abbottsleigh before her mother's glorious rose garden came into full bloom, but today she felt more relief than regret to be returning to London. These past two weeks of her "honeymoon" had been enormously stressful.

She had tried not to dwell on her wedding night. The memories made her feel too uncomfortable. She'd been so apprehensive that Jared would consummate the marriage roughly, triumphantly, as the crowning proof of his victory over the Amberly family. He hadn't done so. He'd claimed he didn't want an unwilling partner, but was that his real reason? Surely he couldn't have expected tenderness or passion from her, but merely an involuntary submission, after he had forced her into this marriage.

Occasionally she had qualms of guilt. She'd promised to be Jared's wife, in return for her family's financial salvation. Had she lived up to her bargain? She remembered her angry, wounding reply when he asked her if she was still a virgin. Had her words put him off, could they actually have hurt him, so that he hesitated to reveal any part of himself or his feelings in the physical act of love? And was this arid, unnatural relationship to endure for the rest of their lives?

The experience of her wedding night hadn't been repeated. She hadn't been forced to share a bed with her husband again, but Jared had found another way to create the illusion that theirs was a consummated marriage. Each night he came to her bedchamber while Rose was preparing her for bed, so that there was no possibility that the household would fail to note his visit. On each occasion he stayed for several hours, sometimes talking desultorily, sometimes actually reading a book or dealing with a business paper, before saying a curt goodnight.

Last night, for example . . . Diana's cheeks flamed. Jared, clad as usual in his dressing gown, had come to the bedchamber while Rose was still brushing out Diana's hair. After he had stood quietly for a few moments, watching the abigail at her task, he said, "Here, Rose, let me do that."

Diana felt a quicksilver shiver of sensual excitement as Jared lifted a strand of her hair in one hand and slowly glided the brush down its length with the other. His eyes met hers in the mirror, and she was convinced he was fully aware of her shaken feelings. Suddenly he bent his head and buried his face in the waving mass. "It looks like amber satin and smells like roses," he murmured, and then straightened with a self-conscious smile, saying, "Rose, you may go. I can do whatever her ladyship wishes."

He moved away from the dressing table as soon as Rose left the room and sat down in his customary chair. Diana jumped up to face him, saying resentfully, "You did that on purpose. You wanted Rose to think you couldn't touch me without—without being carried away by your emotions."

He shrugged. "I thought it was a way to suggest to Rose, without expending an undue amount of effort, that I was, indeed, subject to irresistible carnal urges. The servants' hall will love it."

Diana glared at him. "Do you mean to keep on with this playacting?"

"As long as it suits my purpose, yes."

"Well, it doesn't suit my purpose," she burst out. "It's driving me to distraction. I'd almost rather you would make love to me once and for all, and get it over with."

He straightened in his chair, lowering the book he had just picked up from the table next to him. "Are you saying you've succumbed to a passion for my body?"

"No—no. I meant . . . oh, you know what I meant."

"I do, yes. And I'll tell you again that I have no taste for passive partners. At any time in the future, however, if you should feel the stirrings of that passion I mentioned, I'll be happy to oblige you. I'm not fussy. I don't demand affection, just a little honest physical desire."

Gritting her teeth, Diana knew she had just made a fool of herself. Jared could twist anything she said to sound ridiculous. She thought he enjoyed doing it. "Is this the way we're to go on after we return to London tomorrow? You'll come to my bedchamber every night and read your books and consult your business papers?"

He considered the question with a grave thoughtfulness that made Diana want to throw something at him. "Perhaps not," he said at last. "At that point, some two weeks after our marriage, my servants might be expected to suspect that my husbandly appetites had been slaked. So I'll probably make fewer visits to your boudoir. Then, too, you must remember that I'll have less free time in London. I have a business to run."

"Good," Diana retorted. "You can turn your attention to matters that concern you, instead of meddling in other people's affairs."

A frown furrowing his forehead, Jared said, "What do you mean?"

"I mean you've been riding around Abbottsleigh as if you were the lord of the manor, poking your nose into every nook and cranny, making suggestions to our estate agent about improving the administration of the estate. Several days ago, for example, Roberts, the agent, told me that, at your instigation, he'd persuaded the tenant of my home farm to adopt the Small's swing plough and to plant Swedish turnips."

"Which is precisely what you once told me you wanted your agent to do to improve estate farming methods."

Diana glared at him. "Yes, but I would have preferred that Roberts had taken my suggestion, rather than yours." She paused, knowing she sounded rather childish, and then plunged on, "Another thing. Roberts also said you told him that he should ask for a percentage of whatever profits the home farm might make as a result of adopting these new practices."

"What's wrong with that? I've found that it increases efficiency if I reward my employees for a profitable suggestion."

"Do as you like with your own business," Diana fumed. "You have no right to dictate how the Amberly family should administer Abbottsleigh."

Jared's expression hardened. "I'll remind you, Diana, that I have a strong interest in Abbottsleigh. I would own the property today, if I hadn't refrained from calling in the promissory notes signed by your father and your brother, to the amount of fifty thousand pounds, in return for the privilege of marrying you. I'll abide by my promise, but only so long as your father and Lord Brentford continue to make their interest payments. Meanwhile, you must excuse my efforts to make the estate more profitable. Who knows? At some time in the future I may own the property."

Diana walked across the great inner quadrangle of Abbottsleigh and through the portals of the gatehouse to the courtyard where the carriage was waiting. Jared paced impatiently beside the carriage. "I'm sorry," she said, a little breathlessly. "I didn't mean to keep you waiting. I was—I was taking one last look at the gardens. They're so beautiful at this time of year."

He nodded without speaking, holding out his hand to help her up the steps. In a few moments the carriage was rolling along the winding driveway through the Abbottsleigh parkland. Diana gazed wistfully out the window. When would she return? Her father and Miles could barely bring themselves to speak civilly to Jared, and she doubted the duke would invite his new son-in-law to stay at Abbottsleigh while he himself was in residence. Or that Jared would be willing to accept such an invitation, if offered.

The journey to London went swiftly and smoothly. At Hyde

Park Corner Jared glanced at his watch, "We've been on the road just under nine hours. Very good time. We'll be at my house—excuse me, Diana, *our* house—in ten minutes."

Diana had vaguely expected that Jared's household in Chesterfield Street would include many Indian servants. In this she was wrong. Jared had a proper English household staff, which included butler, footmen, and maids. She followed a footman up the stairs to a large sunny room overlooking the gardens of Chesterfield House. The room was luxuriously furnished in the latest mode, with delicate satinwood furniture and a muted jewel-like carpet that echoed the soft rose and blue and green hues of the bed hangings and the draperies. She wondered who had decorated Jared's house. Or had he simply bought the furnishings along with the house?

A footman brought a tea tray. "The housekeeper says as how dinner will be served in an hour, my lady, if that is agreeable."

"Yes, of course."

Her abigail arrived while Diana was sipping her tea, and began unpacking.

"Do you think you'll be happy here, Rose?"

"Oh, yes, my lady. I have a very nice room ter myself on the third floor. The—the housekeeper seems very kind." The abigail paused, looking faintly embarrassed. "She's a foreign lady, ye know. Wears very strange clothes. I never saw the like. Silks, and bright colors. Her skin is dark, too."

Diana gave Rose an intent look. Had the abigail heard rumors about Jared's Indian mistress? Very probably. Servants seemed to know everything about their employers' lives.

Diana changed her gown and went down to the dining room, and took her place opposite Jared at the far end of the table. The dining room was as well-furnished as her bedchamber. An imposing display of silver plate filled the sideboard. Jared had certainly spared no expense in the furnishing of his house.

A little later she said to Jared, who had had little to say during the meal, "This is an excellent dinner. You have a very good cook."

He took a sip of wine and put his glass down. "Rana wouldn't stand for anything but excellence. Sometimes she prepares Indian dishes for me. Would you object to that?"

"Not at all. I like to try new dishes." Diana stiffened slightly at Jared's mention of the Indian woman. Would he have talked of this Rana on Diana's very first night in the house, especially in such a casual fashion, if the relationship was illicit?

After the dessert course Diana rose from the table. "I believe I'll go to my bedchamber now, Jared. I'm a little tired from the journey."

He stood up, bowing politely.

Diana dismissed the abigail after Rose had helped her into nightdress and peignoir and straightened the bedchamber. "Goodnight, Rose." She restlessly paced the room for a few moments before settling into a chair with a book. Would Jared come to her tonight?

A soft knock sounded at the door. Diana released a sigh of resignation. "Come."

The Indian woman entered the room. She was even lovelier close up than from a distance in her brilliant red sari. She bowed low gracefully three times. "Good evening, mistress. I am Rana, the Sahib Amberly's housekeeper."

"Yes, I've heard of you, Rana." Diana hoped she had kept a note of chilly reserve out of her voice.

"I came to inquire if you find your rooms satisfactory," said Rana, glancing about her. "There is another room down the corridor which has a larger dressing room, but it does not face on the gardens."

"This room is quite satisfactory, Rana. Thank you."

"Then I will say goodnight, mistress. Please to send word to me if there is anything you require." Rana bowed three times again and left the room.

Jared slipped his arms into the dressing gown that Rana was holding for him and tied the sash. He smiled, saying, "I missed your services while I was gone, Rana. I cut myself shaving several times. The servants at Abbottsleigh thought it was very odd that I didn't bring a valet with me."

"It would not have been seemly for me to accompany you, Sahib."

"No, perhaps not." He sat down in his usual chair by the fireplace and reached for a sheaf of papers on the table next to him. "Thank you, Rana. You can go now."

She lingered, watching him with grave, troubled eyes. "You are not going to your bride tonight, Sahib?"

Jared made a slight, involuntary movement that he controlled immediately. "No. Lady Diana is weary from our long journey."

"The lady is very beautiful."

"Yes. Very beautiful."

"You are happy?"

"Of course. I've married the most eligible woman in England. Why wouldn't I be happy?"

Rana waited.

Jared sighed. "You know, don't you?"

"I know when you are unhappy, Sahib. I see it in your eyes. I hear it in your voice."

Resting his elbow on the arm of the chair, Jared placed his hand over his eyes. "She despises me, Rana," he muttered.

"She will not let you love her?"

"Oh, yes. She's quite ready to do her duty. But I want more than compliance from her."

"You want her love."

"Yes." Jared removed his hand from his eyes and gazed bleakly at Rana. "I'm not likely ever to have Diana's love, so . . ." He shrugged. "So I'll concentrate on remaining the wealthiest man in England. Or the second wealthiest. I think my friend Nathan Rothschild has caught up to me."

Diana tried to be suitably gracious to Lady Lyon, but found it very hard going. The lady was beginning to grate on her nerves. Miles had brought Charlotte and his future mother-in-law to pay a wedding call, and, unlike her reception of most of the other callers who had deluged her with cards, to whom she could be "not at home," she had felt obliged to welcome the Lyons personally.

"This seems a very elegant house, Lady Diana," said Lady Lyon. "But perhaps a tiny bit too small, compared to Amberly House, for example. Have you considered moving to a larger establishment? In Grosvenor Square, perhaps? You and dear Mr. Amberly will doubtless be entertaining very considerably."

"Mama, we must allow Lady Diana and Mr. Amberly to decide on the size of their house," said Charlotte with a nervous smile.

"Oh, indeed, my dear. But I'm most pleased that you and Lord Brentford have decided to make your London residence with the duke. Amberly House is such an ideal place in which to make one's social mark."

Diana looked at Miles's impassive face, and wondered if his affection for Charlotte would totally compensate for Lady Lyon's gaucheries.

"Mama, we mustn't stay too long. Miles wishes to have a private word with Lady Diana."

Miles escorted Lady Lyon and Charlotte to their carriage and returned to the drawing room. In an irritated voice he said, "I can't wait to have Charlotte to myself, without that dreadful woman interfering in every moment of our lives. How did such a family produce a warm, delightful person like Charlotte? You'd think from the way Lady Lyon talks that the only reason Charlotte is marrying me is to become a great society hostess."

"Many people would say that there's nothing wrong in marrying for social position. But in your case, Miles, it's quite obvious that Charlotte is very much in love with you."

Looking self-consciously pleased, Miles said, "Yes, I think Charlotte does love me. And Lord knows, Diana, that I love her. It's Lord and Lady Lyon that I don't love."

Diana smiled sympathetically. "Don't forget that, after you're married, you'll still be obliged to associate with Lord and Lady Lyon. They're Charlotte's parents, after all."

He grimaced. "I know. Papa and I are in much the same quandary with that husband of yours. Sorry. I know you don't like me to say things like that. Er—how is it going? Is Amberly being decent to you?"

"Oh, yes. Jared is being most generous, actually." Diana

doubted that Miles had remained behind for this *tête-à-tête* merely to inquire if Jared was treating her well, a situation about which he could have done nothing even if her reply had been in the negative. And she knew her brother very well. Miles tended to avoid the unpleasant if he possibly could. No, he had some personal reason for wanting to talk to her.

"Jared has a more active social life than I had imagined," she went on to fill in the pauses when Miles didn't seem disposed to introduce the subject that was on his mind. "Tonight, for example, we're giving a dinner for some of his banking associates."

"Good God," Miles exclaimed. "You'll be overwhelmed by the odor of Cits and trade!" He fidgeted with his watch fob, avoiding her eyes. At last he said abruptly, "Diana, I want you to speak to your husband. I'd approach Amberly myself," he added hastily, "except that I don't think he'd pay any heed to me. He might listen to you."

Diana frowned. "Speak to Jared about what?"

Miles's anger slipped its leash. "Do you know what that bounder has done? He's warned every cent-per-center in the city not to extend a loan to me in any amount, and they're acting accordingly."

Apprehensively Diana said, "But Miles, why do you need to borrow from the moneylenders? Have you been gambling again? And losing?"

He flushed a dark red. "I've been doing a spot of gambling, yes. Oh, I know I promised to reform my ways when I became engaged to Charlotte, but dash it, what's a man to do when he goes to his clubs? A certain amount of play is expected of you, and I'm plain unlucky. But that's neither here nor there. Amberly has no right to interfere in my private affairs, and I'd like you to tell him so."

"How much do you owe, over and above the promissory notes that Jared holds against you? I presume these are 'debts of honor' we're talking about."

Flinching at Diana's barbed emphasis on "debts of honor," Miles mumbled, "They're gambling debts, yes. No great sum. Well, five thousand. Will you speak to Amberly?"

"Yes," said Diana reluctantly. "Mind, I can't promise to change Jared's mind."

After Miles had left, Diana thought about Jared's intervention in her brother's financial affairs, and found herself resenting the interference as much as Miles did. Then a comment her father had once made slipped into her mind. "Perhaps Miles can't help himself," the duke had said. "Perhaps he can't stop gambling." Was it possible that Miles was, well, addicted to gambling in the same sense that the poet Coleridge was reputed to be addicted to opium? In that case, would it be a good or a bad thing to prevent him from having access to funds with which to pay the debts caused by his "addiction?"

She was still thinking about Miles's problems as she dressed for dinner in a gown of gossamer net over an apricot-colored slip, trimmed with deep flounces of lace and tiny knots of cream-colored roses.

"It's a lovely gown, my lady. Will this dinner be an important affair?"

"Oh—quite important, Rose, I daresay. Mr. Amberly's business associates will be the guests."

The abigail's question drove Miles out of Diana's mind as she began feeling nervous about the dinner. It would be the first time she would act as hostess to Jared's friends in his house. Would she be completely out of her depth with people with whom she had nothing in common?

"You look charming," said Jared, giving her a close look as they stood in the drawing room awaiting their guests. "The pearls go very well with the gown."

"Thank you. The pearls belonged to my mother." But despite Jared's compliment Diana felt a little resentful that his careful scrutiny had been more in the nature of an inspection, as if she were a product he was about to offer to the consuming public. His attitude did nothing to make her feel more at ease.

The butler soon announced "Mr. and Mrs. Simmons," who were followed in quick succession by—Diana knew the dining table seated thirty-six guests—sixteen other couples.

Diana pasted a bright smile on her lips and attempted to be gracious and charming to Jared's guests. However, as the evening progressed, she discovered to her surprise that these people she had considered so alien to her were not so very much different from her own circle of friends.

The bankers and their wives were dressed as fashionably as anyone in the *ton*. More so, perhaps. After all, they had more money to spend on their appearance than a number of her acquaintances who were perpetually in low water.

Jared's friends were also well-spoken; indeed, their understanding of politics and the war against Napoleon was in some respects superior to that of anyone she knew, with the possible exception of her father. But then, of course, their livelihoods often depended on their accurate perception of what the government might do to prosecute the war.

One of the bankers, a Mr. Fairbanks, a middle-aged man with shrewd gray eyes, remarked to her, "I've often wished that I had had the opportunity to congratulate your father personally on his speech about the Bullion Report. It was masterly."

Diana smiled. "Thank you. But apparently Papa wasn't very persuasive. Parliament negatived the Report overwhelmingly."

"Yes, to the misfortune of all of us." Mr. Fairbanks added abruptly, "Do you know, I've often thought that brilliant men among the nobility, like the Duke of Edgehill, are cutting their own throats when they refuse to be associated with trade. Only income from land is truly respectable to them. They don't seem to realize that, at roughly two percent a year, land isn't even as good an investment as Consols." He cleared his throat, looking suddenly embarrassed. "I beg your pardon, Lady Diana. I shouldn't be speaking to you in that fashion."

"Not at all, Mr. Fairbanks. You must feel free to express your opinions."

Diana's reply had been merely polite, but for the first time in her life it crossed her mind to wonder *why* trade was so distasteful. Money was money, wasn't it? And why should it come only from land? Her eyes met Jared's, and she colored faintly. He'd obviously overheard her conversation. Was he now reading her mind?

The bankers' wives, she discovered, were no more vapid than many of the women in her circle. One of them, a beautiful

Italian girl who had married an English banker, was delighted to hear that Diana shared her enthusiasm for Canaletto's paintings. "My husband and I have a Canaletto landscape you might wish to see, my lady," the girl said shyly. "It's our proudest possession, a view of the Grand Canal in Venice."

Diana was about to invite the girl to view her own Canalettos, but stopped short when she remembered that her father and her brother didn't yet know that Jared had restored the precious paintings to the Amberly family.

Standing together at the door of the drawing room at the end of the evening, Jared and Diana bade farewell to their guests. As the last couple left the room, Jared murmured, "A most successful evening, I think. Most of our guests were quite impressed to be dining with the daughter of a duke. Thank you, Diana, for not letting your prejudices show. I'll say goodnight to you. I have business to take care of in the library."

As she went up the stairs to her bedchamber, Diana felt slightly ruffled, thinking of Jared's phrase, "not letting your prejudices show." The words implied she was a snob, unable or unwilling to appreciate the good qualities of those who didn't belong to her class. Was she a snob, merely because she was proud of her family and the contributions they had made to their country? Didn't standards and traditions matter?

A little later, ready for bed in peignoir and nightdress, Diana sat staring at the clock in her bedchamber. Eleven o'clock. Was Jared coming to her tonight? He hadn't made an appearance in her bedchamber in the week following their return from Abbottsleigh. Perhaps he had tired of the sport of discomfiting her, or he was indifferent to what his servants thought of his activities in the boudoir. Diana stirred restlessly. She'd promised Miles to speak to Jared, and she'd had no opportunity during the evening to do so.

Taking a quick decision, she walked down the corridor to Jared's rooms and tapped softly on the door.

"Yes?"

"May I come in, Jared?"

"Of course."

Diana took several steps into the bedchamber and froze. Jared stood near the fireplace, tying—or was it more accurate to say untying?—the sash of his dressing gown. Rana was folding back the coverlets of the bed. She turned, bowing deeply to Diana, and walked past her to the door, where she paused to say, "Goodnight, Sahib, Lady Diana," before leaving the room.

"I beg your pardon for interrupting you at an awkward time," Diana said stiffly.

"Awkward?" Jared looked mildly surprised. Then he smiled sardonically. "You've jumped to the wrong conclusion, Diana. Rana wasn't in my bedchamber tonight to serve as my bed partner. I told you she wasn't my mistress. She's my—my valet, for want of a better word. She's been taking care of my personal needs since I was a small boy. Didn't you notice I didn't bring a valet with me to Abbottsleigh? Rana didn't come with me in her usual capacity, because I hesitated to raise eyebrows in your ancestral home."

"I see. I'm sorry," said Diana even more stiffly. She wasn't sure she believed Jared. But what did he have to gain by telling such a preposterous story if it wasn't true? She could certainly understand, however, why the London rumor mill believed that Jared kept an Indian mistress.

He came close to her as she stood in the middle of the floor. "Why did you come here, Diana?" The sardonic smile curved his mouth again. "Could it be that you were stirred by those feelings of irresistible passion that we once discussed? If so, I'm quite ready to reciprocate."

He slipped his arms around Diana in a swift, fluid motion and kissed her. The touch of his lips, gentle but seeking, sent Diana's senses reeling. Suddenly her whole body felt alive, aching to be in closer contact with him. Her mouth drank in his kisses greedily. He tightened his embrace, and his kiss became deeper, more demanding. "Is this what you really want, Diana?" he murmured, his lips fluttering against her mouth.

Something, insidiously enticing, urged her to say, "Yes. Yes, I want this, Jared, I want you." Something else, a remnant of her fierce pride, impelled her to say breathlessly, "It's your right. You're my husband. I won't deny you."

Instantly he released her and stepped back. A mask closed

down over his face, making it expressionless. He said coolly, "Of course you won't deny me, Diana. You're an intelligent, conscientious woman, well aware of your marital obligations. At the moment, however, I'm not disposed to make any husbandly demands." He shrugged his shoulders. "Now, then, I seem to have misinterpreted the reason for your visit to my bedchamber tonight. You wished to speak to me?"

A mixture of emotions warred in Diana's mind. She felt gauche, guilty, and yes, if she was being truthful to herself, disappointed, unfulfilled. "I do, yes. Or, rather, Miles asked me to speak to you."

"Oh? Lord Brentford didn't feel that he should bring the matter, whatever it is, to my attention personally?"

"I—" Diana floundered. "You see, you and Miles aren't very congenial, so . . ."

"So he prefers to send a message through you. Well, what is the message?"

"Miles says you've persuaded the London moneylenders not to extend loans to him. He feels this is an unwarranted intrusion into his affairs, and I agree with him."

"On the contrary, it's a self-protective measure. If Lord Brentford goes deeper into debt he won't be able to pay the interest he owes me on his promissory notes."

"Then you have a recourse. Miles's notes have become notes on demand. You can call them in."

"And after that? If Miles is unable to pay the principal, do I then give your father a choice between raising the money and breaking the entail on the Abbottsleigh estates?"

"But—you promised," Diana stammered.

"Exactly. I promised not to call in your father's notes and your brother's, provided regular interest payments were made, in exchange for your hand in marriage. You've married me. Your father will doubtless continue to pay his interest on time. As long as he does so, would it be fair to penalize him for his son's faults? I think not. Do give me credit for a little elemental justice, Diana."

Jared continued in a patient tone, as if he were explaining the alphabet to a not very bright pupil, "Therefore, to enable

Lord Brentford to continue paying me what he owes, by making it impossible for him to contract any new debts, I've notified all the London moneylenders about the fifty thousand pounds the Amberly family owes me. They all know now that, if they loan Lord Brentford any money, he's likely to default, in which case there's no possibility of obtaining the money from the estate, and certainly not from me. The moneylenders' only recourse would be to clap Lord Brentford into debtors' prison, a highly unsatisfactory proceeding, because they would wait for years, or forever, for their money."

"So you're really doing Miles a favor by this interference, saving him from debtors' prison," said Diana, a rising note of anger in her voice. "Naturally, you have no intention of annoying him, or humiliating him."

"Oh, I don't mind raising his hackles. I'm a good hater, Diana." He raised an eyebrow. "I'm a little surprised by your attitude. Do you really want to see your brother gambling his life away, falling deeper and deeper into the hands of the cents-per-centers?"

"Of course not. But Jared—I don't think he can help himself. He can't stop gambling." To her horror, Diana heard a sound of appeal in her voice.

Jared's face turned somber. "Then God help him. No one else can. Not you. Not me. Was there anything else you wanted to discuss? If not, will you excuse me? I have a busy day tomorrow."

Feeling very much like an errant pupil dismissed by her headmistress, Diana returned to her bedchamber. She couldn't understand Jared. For those few moments in his arms she'd craved physical union with him, and he knew it. He'd wanted her, too. But still he'd refused to make love to her, for some unfathomable reason of his own.

Several days later Diana drove to Amberly House in what had become a part of her daily routine since her return from her honeymoon, a visit to her father. The duke had quietly but firmly refused to enter Jared's house in Chesterfield Street, and Diana had made no attempt to change his mind.

She found the duke in the drawing room instead of in his bedchamber, where he spent most of his days. He was reading a letter, and there was a deep frown between his eyes.

"Look at this, my dear," he said, handing Diana the letter. "What do you make of it? I've read the confounded thing several times, and I can't make head nor tale of it."

The letter, or rather, note, read tersely, "Your Grace: I propose to call on you on Wednesday afternoon to discuss an important matter. With respect, Lyon of Radnor."

"What the devil does Miles's future papa-in-law want with me?" the duke inquired querulously. "I had to see quite enough of him, thank you, in the days when Miles was courting his daughter. I'd hoped not to encounter him again until the wedding."

"Papa, hush," said Diana, as a footman appeared in the doorway to announce, "Lord Lyon, Your Grace."

Charlotte's father didn't appear his usual ingratiating self, Diana noted immediately. He was obviously suffering from some sort of nervous strain.

"Lady Diana, Duke." Lord Lyon looked at Diana with narrowed eyes. "I had hoped to see you alone, Duke."

"I have no secrets from my daughter. You may speak freely in front of her. Will you sit down?"

Lord Lyon shifted uneasily in his chair. "I've heard some very disturbing rumors, Duke. I'd be obliged if you would either confirm them or deny them."

"Yes?"

"Well . . . I've heard that Lady Diana's husband, Jared Amberly, bought up promissory notes signed by you and your son to the amount of many thousands of pounds. His intent supposedly was to obtain control of the Amberly estates through the device of breaking the entail. Further rumor hints that Amberly was bribed by the promise of marriage to Lady Diana to desist from his demands."

Diana's heart sank. Perhaps it had been too much to expect that the circumstances of her marriage would remain secret.

Gossip of which she was unaware had undoubtedly been circulating. Some people had obviously talked—the moneylenders, the bankers, perhaps even Jared's colleagues—enough to produce a garbled version of the facts.

The duke's expression was glacial. "There may be a certain amount of fact in your account, Lord Lyon. What I should like to know is how our personal family affairs concern you."

"Good God, Duke," Lord Lyon exploded. "How can you ask? My daughter is about to marry your son. You must tell me this: is it within Jared Amberly's power to force you to bar the entail on your estates?"

"Theoretically, yes," replied the duke after a moment of cold silence.

"Jared won't make such a demand," said Diana quickly.

"How can you be sure of that, Lady Diana? It's quite well-known that your husband dislikes your brother. There was even a duel some time back, I believe, though the details were quickly hushed up."

"A duel between Miles and Amberly? That's a lie," snapped the duke.

"Papa—there was a duel," faltered Diana. "We didn't tell you about it because you were so ill. Neither Miles nor Jared was seriously hurt."

The duke opened his mouth to speak and shut it again, his lips clamped firmly together. After a moment he said, obviously attempting to subdue his anger, "I've told you everything I care to say on this matter, Lord Lyon. Was there anything else?"

"Yes." Lyon's body seemed to swell, making him appear remarkably like a pouter pigeon. "I wish to inform you, Duke, that I hereby revoke my consent to the marriage of my daughter to your son."

"On what grounds, may I ask?" inquired the duke, tight-lipped.

"I believed that on her marriage Charlotte would enjoy an eminent and secure position in society as the wife of a future duke. Now it appears she could become Duchess of Edgehill without also becoming mistress of Abbottsleigh, an empty honor indeed! I want more than a meaningless title for my daughter."

Shocked, Diana exclaimed, "Surely you can't have considered the scandal . . ."

"There will be a certain amount of gossip, I grant you, when Charlotte cries off from this engagement," replied Lord Lyon stiffly. "I consider this a small price to pay for saving my daughter from a disastrous marriage."

"But it won't be disastrous. Only yesterday my husband repeated his promise that he would never require Papa to bar the entail. In due time Charlotte will become Duchess of Edgehill and mistress of Abbottsleigh as my mother was before her."

"I don't have the same confidence in your husband's word that you do, unfortunately. In any case, I can't in conscience entrust my daughter's future to the promise of a man who's sometimes been described as a financial adventurer. Good day, Duke, Lady Diana."

Thirteen

When she left Amberly House that afternoon, shortly after Lord Lyon's shocking announcement, Diana went to the Albany instead of returning to Chesterfield Street.

"I won't be long, Rose," she told her abigail as she left the carriage at the entrance to the Albany. She found Miles in his rooms in the company of Aubrey Dalton.

"Welcome to my bachelor quarters, sister mine, such as they are," Miles said with a grin. "Aubrey and I were about to set forth for White's, but I daresay Aubrey would be happy to delay our departure in order to have a cup of tea or a glass of wine with you."

Ignoring Miles's teasing, Aubrey said, staring at Diana with his heart in his eyes, "How are you? It seems so long since I've seen you."

"I'm very well, thank you." Diana felt uncomfortable under Aubrey's intent scrutiny. He reminded her of a man dying of thirst who has suddenly approached a life-giving spring.

After Miles had ordered his man to prepare tea, he said to Diana, "Did you talk to Amberly about his interference with the moneylenders? Aubrey knows all about it," he added as Diana flicked a quick glance at his friend.

"Yes, and I think it's monstrously ungentlemanly of Amberly to meddle in Miles's affairs," declared Aubrey. "But then, of course, the man is no gentleman." He turned a bright red. "Sorry, Diana. The fellow *is* your husband."

Miles looked expectantly at Diana. "Well?"

"Yes, I talked to Jared. He feels justified in warning off the moneylenders because he wants to make sure that you won't fall behind in your interest payments to him."

Miles uttered an incoherent oath.

Aubrey said hotly, "It's not to be borne. There must be some way we can stop this—this persecution."

Diana stopped herself from saying what she was thinking, that Miles could avoid future interference from Jared by living within his income. Instead she said, "I didn't come to talk about Jared and the moneylenders, Miles, but in a sense he's concerned in another matter that's far more important. Charlotte's father came to see Papa today. I daresay Lord Lyon will be calling on you or writing to you shortly."

"Oh? What about?" Miles's voice expressed only a mild interest.

"Lord Lyon informed Papa that he was withdrawing his consent to your marriage with Charlotte, on the grounds that Jared could at any time force Papa to bar the entail, thereby making Charlotte's marriage to you less desirable in her parents' estimation."

Turning a pasty white, Miles exclaimed, "That devil Amberly! This is all his fault. I'll kill him. I'll call him out again."

"Hold on, Miles," begged Aubrey. "You still can't shoot. This time Amberly would surely kill you."

"But what can I do? I can't lose Charlotte." Miles appeared utterly dazed.

On an impulse, Diana said, "I'll go see Charlotte. I know she loves you, Miles."

"What good would that do? She won't go against her parents' wishes."

"No, perhaps not, but she might be able to persuade them to change their minds. They want her to be happy, you know."

A note of hope crept into Miles's voice. "Then do it. Go see Charlotte right away."

"I will. One thing I'm very sure of. Charlotte loves you, and love can sometimes work miracles." Diana patted Miles's shoulder and left his rooms, feeling rather less confident than she probably sounded.

At the Lyons' house in Cavendish Square she presented her

card to the footman and requested to see Charlotte. The footman returned shortly with the message that Miss Lyon was not at home.

"Then I'll wait until she returns," said Diana briskly, stepping past the astonished footman into the foyer.

"Er—as ye wish, my lady, I'm sure. Will ye come with me ter the drawing room?"

Five minutes later, as Diana sat in the drawing room, impatiently tapping her foot, Lady Lyon swept into the room, followed by Charlotte.

"My dear Lady Diana, you must forgive me," said Lady Lyon with a sugary, unconvincing smile. "My stupid footman—he completely misunderstood my instructions about callers. Of course, we are always pleased to receive you."

"Pray don't apologize," Diana replied. "I quite understand." And she did. Lady Lyon had no wish to see Diana, in view of the decision the Lyons had made to terminate Charlotte's engagement, but Lady Lyon could hardly ignore a duke's daughter who refused to budge from her drawing room, short of having her unwelcome caller forcibly removed by the servants.

Diana addressed Charlotte directly. "My father and I and Miles were so distressed to hear from Lord Lyon that he and your mother had withdrawn their consent to your marriage. I've come to ask you if you really wish to cry off from your engagement."

"Lady Diana," said Lady Lyon sharply. "This is most unseemly. You surely won't deny that a young female should be guided by her parents."

"No, indeed. And I know that Charlotte is a most filial daughter. However, I also believe she should have some voice in her future." Diana turned to Charlotte, who looked pale and wretched. "Your parents believe you should break your engagement because of the possibility that my husband will obtain control of the Edgehill estates. I assure you—I would stake my very life on it—that Jared will never attempt to do such a thing. Charlotte, do you love Miles? Do you still wish to marry him?"

"Lady Diana!" Lady Lyon exclaimed in outrage.

Charlotte faltered, "I—oh, yes, I love Miles, but . . ."

"But you trust your loving papa's judgment about your welfare," interjected Lady Lyon, fixing Charlotte with a mesmerizing stare.

"Yes . . . yes . . ." Charlotte appeared close to tears. She couldn't take her eyes from her mother.

"I think, Lady Diana, that you had best leave us," said Lady Lyon coldly. "My daughter is unwell."

Diana took one last look at Charlotte's woebegone face and realized that nothing she could say would give the girl the courage to resist her parents. She rose, saying, "Goodbye, Lady Lyon. Charlotte, I'm truly sorry that we won't be welcoming you into our family."

Diana returned home to Chesterfield Street, where the first thing she did was to write a note to Miles telling him of the failure of her mission.

That evening, one of the few for which Diana and Jared had no outside engagement, they ate a quiet dinner at home. As usual, they spoke desultorily and impersonally, rather, Diana thought, like a husband and wife who had been married for many years and had exhausted, not only all topics of conversation, but also any real interest in each other. Only, in their case, they had never been husband and wife at all.

"Do you like this dumpoked fowl that Rana prepared for us?" Jared inquired politely.

Diana tasted the chicken, which had apparently been boiled in butter and stuffed with raisins and almonds. "Why, yes. It's different, but delicious."

"Good. She'll be happy to know that. However, if in the future you don't care for a dish that Rana has prepared, you have only to tell her so. Did you have a pleasant day today?"

"Yes. I went to see Papa."

"He's well?"

"Yes, or as well as can be expected. How about you? How was your day?"

Jared shrugged. "Much as always. Gold is up again."

"I presume you're pleased." Diana hesitated. Jared would learn sooner or later about Miles's broken engagement. Why not tell him now? She said, "Lord Lyon came to see Papa today.

The Lyons have withdrawn their consent to Charlotte's marriage."

"Really? Why did they do that?"

There was a decided edge in Diana's voice as she said, "Somehow they learned some of the details of your scheme to obtain control of Abbottsleigh. Papa conceded there was a remote possibility that at some time you could force him to bar the entail. The Lyons concluded that a future shadowed by such a possibility wasn't good enough for Charlotte."

Jared flicked her a quick, intent look. "I told you the other night I had no intention of forcing your father to bar the entail."

"Yes, and so I informed Lord Lyon. He didn't believe me."

Jared took a sip of wine. "Frankly, from a practical point of view, I think the Lyons were wise to cry off from the engagement. Aside from the fact that your brother can make Charlotte a duchess one day, he's not a good financial risk. Doubtless the Lyons would have found themselves in the position of pouring money down an endless rat hole for the entire period of Charlotte's married life."

"How can you be so heartless?" Diana demanded. "Miles and Charlotte *love* each other."

Raising an eyebrow, Jared said, "So? I understand that in your circle of society romantic love isn't the most important factor in marriage, or even a necessary one. Are you asking me to believe that your brother and Miss Lyon would have become engaged if he wasn't the son of a duke and she wasn't a wealthy heiress?"

"Oh, you make it sound so mercenary," Diana burst out. "And I daresay you're glad Miles's engagement is broken off. You've never liked him. For that matter, how did the details of your precious little plot become public? Did you spread rumors, hoping they would reach Lord Lyon's ears and cause him to withdraw his consent to Charlotte's marriage?"

The blue eyes darkened almost to black. "I did not, and I resent the implication. Use your head, Diana. Do you think I'd want it known that I had to blackmail my wife into marrying me?"

"Which is exactly what you did—" Diana broke off as a

footman entered the dining room. In an agony of embarrassment she realized she had almost committed the cardinal sin of discussing her personal affairs in front of a servant.

"A message for you, my lady." The footman brought Diana a note on a tray.

Diana read the note and stood up so abruptly that her outstretched hand grazed her wine glass and caused it to overturn.

"What's the matter?" Jared asked quickly.

"It's Papa. Miles says he's been taken ill. I must go to him." Jared rang the bell. "I'll order the carriage immediately."

In the carriage during the short drive to Berkeley Square Diana sat ramrod straight, refusing to lean back against the squabs. Jared, who had insisted on accompanying her, sat in silence beside her.

When Diana entered the foyer of Amberly House, she found Miles waiting for her, his face creased with anxiety. He gave Jared a bare nod.

"How is Papa?" Diana asked, giving her brother a fervent hug.

Miles gulped. "Very bad, I'm afraid. Dr. Phelps is here. He says it's apoplexy. I saw it coming on, but I didn't recognize the signs. I came to see Papa after I received your note saying you hadn't been able to change Charlotte's mind about the engagement. While Papa and I were talking I noticed he seemed confused at times, forgetful of what he'd already said, losing the thread of a sentence. Then, suddenly, he collapsed."

"Can I see him?"

"Yes. You can go right up to his bedchamber. But Diana, I must warn you . . . Papa isn't himself."

Racked with fear, Diana hurried upstairs to her father's bedchamber. A footman standing outside the door silently opened the door for her. She walked slowly into the room. Dr. Phelps turned as she entered, motioning her to approach the bed.

Diana gasped at her first glimpse of her father. His left eye was unfocused, unseeing, and the left side of his mouth was slack and drooling.

"His Grace has a paralysis on the left side of his body," the doctor murmured. "He can't move his left hand and leg. Nor can he speak."

Diana leaned over her father, pressing his right hand. "Papa, can you hear me?" She felt a faint squeeze on her fingers and the duke opened his mouth slightly, but he didn't speak. In a moment his eyes closed.

The doctor beckoned Diana to come away from the bed. "I'm so sorry it's come to this, my lady," he said in a low voice. "I've been most apprehensive about His Grace. His heart condition was very precarious. I confess that I'm not surprised about this latest attack."

"Doctor, will he—will he be all right?"

The doctor gave her an infinitely pitying look. "I don't believe so, my lady. You mustn't raise your hopes. This was a very severe attack. I suspect His Grace will sink into a coma, from which he won't recover."

"Oh, God," Diana whispered.

The doctor clasped her hand. "Think, my lady. Do you think His Grace would care to live paralyzed and speechless? What kind of a life would that be?"

"No kind of a life at all. Papa would hate it."

"Then death might be a blessing, something His Grace would welcome."

"Yes." Diana shut her eyes against a sting of acrid tears. "Doctor, how long . . . ?"

"I can't say, my lady. It could happen at any time, or His Grace could linger for several days, or even longer."

"I want to stay with him."

"Well . . . perhaps you could sit beside him for a little while."

Diana took a chair by her father's bedside. His eyes were closed. He seemed to be sleeping. After an interval his eyes opened. A faint smile grotesquely lifted the right side of his mouth. She was sure the duke recognized her. Then his eyes closed again. The minutes and the half hours and the hours slipped away. The doctor approached the bed to take the duke's pulse and to lift his eyelids. The patient didn't stir.

"I'm sorry to tell you this, my lady," the doctor murmured. "His Grace has lapsed into a coma."

"You mean . . . ?"

"I don't believe it will be very long. On the other hand, he may linger. I think you should leave him now. You can't help him while he's in this condition. I'll come to you if there is any change."

"Yes. Very well, doctor." Reluctantly Diana walked to the door and into the corridor. Miles and Jared were standing against the wall, considerably apart from each other, obviously not speaking.

"Papa is in a coma, Miles," Diana said in a low voice. "Doctor Phelps doesn't think he has long to live."

"Oh, God . . ."

Jared took her arm. "Come along, Diana. I've ordered the servants to bring tea to the morning room."

"Oh, no. I want to stay here, near Papa."

"It may be hours before—before the crisis. You must preserve your strength. Come." Jared's slender powerful fingers tugged at her arm, and Diana gave in.

In the morning room Jared poured a cup of tea, stirred in milk and sugar and silently handed it to her. She leaned back in her chair, suddenly conscious of a dragging fatigue, and sipped the hot sweet tea slowly.

"If the duke is in a coma he's not suffering, you know," Jared observed after a moment.

"He's *dying,* Jared!"

"Yes, but he's not suffering. That should be of some comfort."

Miles came into the room and sank into a chair, burying his face in his hands. "It's my fault, all my fault," he mumbled.

"That's nonsense," Diana exclaimed. "How could Papa's illness be your fault? He's had a weak heart for a long time."

Miles looked up, saying, "Oh, I know his heart wasn't strong. I suppose he couldn't have gone on much longer. But this evening he became very overset when I stormed in to him, imploring him—no, ordering him—to intervene with Charlotte's father about the engagement. He said he couldn't, and wouldn't, approach Lord Lyon, and I kept badgering him, and then—then he collapsed."

Diana went to Miles, placing a comforting arm around his shoulders. "Of course you shouldn't have distressed Papa so, but you were distressed yourself, and you certainly didn't mean him any harm. Don't blame yourself."

"Lady Diana, Lord Brentford."

Doctor Phelps stood in the doorway. Diana and Miles rose slowly, staring at him with a strained intensity.

"I am so sorry to tell you this," said the doctor. "His Grace has passed away. It was a peaceful death. He slipped from life between one breath and the next."

"Papa—I must go to him. I never said goodbye." Diana ran out of the room and up the stairs to the duke's bedchamber. She stood by the bed looking down at her father's face, which in its cold unresponsiveness seemed almost unrecognizable to her. The hot tears began to stream down her face. "Papa, why have you left me? It's too soon, I still need you so much. . . ."

A pair of strong arms encircled her. Jared's voice said, "Diana, you must come away now. There are things that must be done to prepare your father. . . . Come home with me. The doctor can give you something to make you sleep. . . ."

Tearing herself away, Diana cried, out of control from grief and anger, "Home? Your house isn't my home. This is my home." She gestured to the still figure on the bed. "That's your doing. Miles didn't kill Papa, you did. You plotted against him, and drove him to distraction, and almost succeeded in robbing my brother of his inheritance and finally forced me into a marriage I loathed. And now this, Miles's broken engagement. It's no wonder Papa's heart gave out. He couldn't bear the humiliation, and the disgrace."

Jared stepped back, his dark face stony. "Do you mean that, Diana? You blame me for your father's death?"

"Yes, I do. Oh, go away. Leave me to my dead."

Dressed in a gown of black bombazine, Diana sat in the morning room of Abbottsleigh, following in her mind's eye every step of her father's funeral cortege from the village church to the graveyard where all the previous Dukes of Edgehill, and before them, the Earls of Brentford, had been laid to rest during the past centuries. A prayer book lay on the table next to her chair. She had already read the lines of the funeral service. She longed to be with her father on his last earthly journey, but she hadn't cared to flout the conventions that dictated that a lady's sensibilities were too tender to be subjected to the strain of attending a public funeral. Nor would the duke, with his delicate perceptions of what was proper behavior, have approved.

She felt unutterably weary. It was only a scant week since her father had died, but it seemed so much longer. At Amberly House she and Miles had endured several days during which they had received an interminable number of friends and acquaintances making condolence calls, and then had followed the slow progression to Oxfordshire, where the duke had lain in state in the village church, and now the funeral.

Diana felt at peace. Much as she would miss her father, who had been the adored center of her existence from her babyhood, she was content to let him go. He would have so hated dragging out the last weeks or months of his life in a less than human condition, paralyzed, unable to speak. Death had come as a mercy to him.

Miles entered the morning room. His handsome, engaging face seemed strained and years older. "It's all over, Diana. The last mourner has left Abbottsleigh. Everyone in the county came to the funeral. The church was packed. I never quite realized before how much Papa was loved."

Miles turned, his expression darkening, as Jared walked into the room.

"I've come to take you home, Diana," Jared said coolly.

Rising, Diana faced her husband. She had barely spoken to him since she had driven him out of the room where her father had died with the accusation that he was responsible for the duke's death. She hadn't returned to the house in Chesterfield Street. Instead, she'd stayed at Amberly House until it was time for her and Miles to accompany their father's coffin to Oxfordshire. She had been vaguely aware that Jared had arrived at

Abbottsleigh for the funeral. He hadn't intruded on her in any way.

Miles said angrily, "Can't you leave Diana be, Amberly? She's still in mourning for our father."

"She's also my wife, *Your Grace*," Jared replied, making an exaggerated reference to Miles's new status as Duke of Edgehill. "I require her presence in London."

"You require," Miles repeated scathingly. "You order, you mean. Diana, you needn't go with him. You can stay here at Abbottsleigh for as long as you like."

"You forget, *Duke*," said Jared, again sardonically emphasizing Miles's new title, "that I'm Diana's lawful husband, and as such I may require her to do anything I like."

Miles opened his mouth to expostulate, but Diana said quietly, "It's all right, Miles. Jared is well within his rights." To Jared she said, "I'll be ready to leave in half an hour, if that's satisfactory."

He bowed. "Quite."

In the carriage Jared sat in silence as they drove through the parkland of Abbottsleigh. As they neared Burford, their first posting stop, however, he spoke for the first time. "Diana, whether or not you really believe that I'm responsible for your father's death is your affair."

"Actually . . ." Diana hesitated. Several times during the past week she'd felt vaguely ashamed of her outburst against Jared on the night of her father's death. "Actually, I shouldn't have accused you of causing Papa's death. He had a weak heart. Doctor Phelps has told me Papa wouldn't have survived for too much longer, even if he hadn't been subjected to severe stress."

Jared went on as if he hadn't heard her remark. "As I was saying, you can believe what you like, but you are not to breathe a word of your suspicions in public. Is that clear?"

"Yes," said Diana between stiff lips. Jared's face was quite frightening in its grim implacability.

"I'm sincerely sorry, for your sake, that the duke is dead," Jared went on. "You may also believe that or not, as you choose." He shrugged. "What matters to me, whatever our personal feelings may be, is that you resume your duties as the mistress of my establishment. I intend to do a great deal of entertaining between now and the end of the Season, and I will require you to act as my hostess."

"Require," said Diana, her lips curling. "That seems to be a favorite word of yours."

"It may be. It expresses my feelings exactly."

"Aren't you forgetting that I will be in mourning for my father for a full year?"

He gave her a level look. "That need not prevent you from fulfilling your social, and marital, obligations. I understand that modistes derive a goodly portion of their incomes from sewing mourning costumes for their clients. Titled ladies lose a husband, or a father or a brother, and many still carry on socially once the modiste has produced for them a suitable mourning wardrobe. You look especially charming in black, my dear. I prophecy you'll be the toast of the *ton*."

Fourteen

"I'll be away from London for two days, beginning next Wednesday," Jared informed Diana as they sat at dinner one evening a week after their return from the duke's funeral at Abbottsleigh. "Doubtless you'll wish to cancel any invitations for those two days. Or perhaps you could ask your brother to escort you."

His tone, and even his words, reminded Diana of the times when she'd overheard her father giving instructions to his secretary. Jared sounded impersonal, authoritative, and, above all, nonexplanatory. He didn't deign to give her any indication about where he was going, he seemed indifferent as to whether she attended social functions without him.

What satisfaction, Diana wondered, did Jared derive from this arid marriage? He'd long since achieved his goal of revenging himself on her and her family. Apparently he didn't want, or expect, physical relations with her. They lived as virtual strangers, seeing each other only at dinner, or at the social engagements they attended together. Was it merely that Jared was loath to admit publicly that their marriage was a mistake?

A footman brought Diana a note on a salver. She looked up, saying, "Miles would like to speak to us."

"Of course." Jared spoke to the footman. "Ask the duke to join us here in the dining room."

Miles strode into the room, saying stiffly, "I'm sorry to disturb your dinner."

"Not at all," Jared replied. "Please sit down. A glass of wine?"

"Thank you." Miles sat hunched over his glass for a few moments, staring down into the wine. He seemed tired and strained. The black band on his arm was a mute symbol of his loss.

Diana broke the silence. "Miles, is something amiss?"

"No more than usual." Miles glanced from Diana to Jared. "I went to visit Charlotte today. Lady Lyon wouldn't allow me to see her. So I begged Lady Lyon, and through her, her husband, to reconsider the engagement. Matters are different now, I told Lady Lyon. I'm the Duke of Edgehill. I could make Charlotte a duchess immediately."

Diana inquired, "What did Lady Lyon say?"

"She told me that, so far as she and her husband were concerned, the situation was unchanged. They still did not consider me a suitable husband for Charlotte."

"I'm sorry," said Diana. "I must confess, though, that I'm not surprised by Lady Lyon's attitude."

"Nor I," said Jared.

"We were always aware that Lord and Lady Lyon are extremely ambitious for Charlotte," Diana went on. "In fact . . ." She paused, biting her lip.

"What?" Miles demanded.

"Oh—at a soirée the other evening I overheard a silly woman saying that the Lyons have their eye on another great catch for Charlotte. The Marquess of Darlington."

"Silly Willy?" Miles exclaimed. "He's years older than Charlotte. She told me once that he was the most boring man she'd ever met."

"He's also one of the biggest landowners in England," Jared murmured.

Miles shot him an angry glance. "You—" Miles cut himself short, obviously curbing his temper. After a moment he said, "I've come to ask a favor, Amberly."

"Yes?"

Forcing the words out, as if he could barely restrain his repugnance in discussing his personal affairs with Jared, Miles said, "I presume you're familiar with the rules of entail. Under the terms of the deed of settlement I signed, the Edgehill properties on my death will go to my firstborn son, or, failing a male heir, to the nearest male heir in a collateral branch of the family."

"Who happens to be me."

Miles shot Jared a look of active dislike. "Yes. The point I'm trying to make, however, is that, even though I've succeeded my father, I'm still bound by the laws of entail. And because my debt situation is the same, I'm in the same position in regards to you as my father was. So I want you to intercede with Lord Lyon on my behalf. I want you to give him your word of honor that you will never call in any debts incurred by either me or my father in order to force me to bar the entail to allow you to obtain control of the Edgehill estates. I believe that, if Lord Lyon were absolutely confident that Charlotte would become not only Duchess of Edgehill but also mistress of Abbottsleigh, he might be inclined to relent. Will you do that for me, Amberly? Will you go see Lord Lyon in my behalf?"

"No."

"Jared!" Diana exclaimed.

"May I ask why, with no explanation, you've refused my request?" Miles asked resentfully. "Diana told me that you promised not to make any further attempt to force our family to bar the entail." His mouth twisted. "Are you now going back on your word?"

"I made that promise in regard to your father. I made no such promise in regard to you. You're a bad financial risk, my lord duke. When you go under, as you assuredly will, because you're incurably addicted to gambling, I want to be able to take advantage of the situation to become the owner of Abbottsleigh."

Pushing himself away from the table, Miles rose, his face black with rage. "I won't forget this, Amberly. I'll hate you to my dying day. I wish to God I'd put a bullet into you during that duel. Then Papa and I and Diana would have been spared all the grief you've caused our family." He stormed out of the room without a backward glance.

"Jared, how could you have been so cruel?" Diana said, her voice trembling. "How could it have hurt you to go to Lord Lyon?"

Jared gave her a level look. "Business is business. As I told him, your brother is a poor risk. For that matter, I was being a good citizen. I wouldn't accept a man like your brother as a husband for my daughter, if I were ever fortunate to have one. Why should I try to persuade Lord Lyon to make such a mistake in the case of *his* daughter?"

Miles sat with Aubrey Dalton in the dining room of White's, staring into space between gulps of Madeira.

"You're not eating, old boy," remonstrated Aubrey. "This is quite a tasty shoulder of lamb."

"I can't eat. Food tastes like gall and wormwood. Aubrey, is there nothing I can do to prevent this fellow Amberly from ruining my family?"

"He holds all the cards, Miles."

"There must be something . . ." Miles said savagely, "If I could find someone to kill Amberly, quietly, secretly, I'd hire him. The fellow doesn't deserve to live."

"Oh, I agree with you. He belongs on the gallows, even if the law hasn't seen fit to brand him as a felon. Pity we can't ship him across to the Frenchies, who seem to know how to take care of such vermin. But look at it this way, old boy. If you hire a thug to dispose of Amberly you run the risk of being caught up in a capital charge."

"I daresay." Miles drew a dispirited sigh. "So I have no recourse. I'll have this fellow hanging like a shadow over my life until I die. And if I don't find a bride who will give me an heir, Amberly will succeed me."

"Perish the thought," Aubrey said in horror. His expression grew pensive. "There might be a solution. . . . I heard a very interesting bit of information today from an acquaintance in the banking community." He lowered his voice and leaned across the table. As Aubrey talked to him Miles's face brightened.

Jared glanced sideways at Kamal, who occupied the seat beside him in the carriage. "Are you growing weary of these journeys to Folkestone, Kamal?"

Shrugging, Kamal replied, "Not as long as they're profitable to the bank, sir."

Jared smiled. "Spoken like a true businessman. Anything for a profit, eh?"

"Yes, sir. Or practically anything."

Jared lapsed into silence as the carriage headed toward the first posting stop at Eltham. For his part, he was glad to be leaving London. The atmosphere at the house in Chesterfield Street was becoming intolerable. From the beginning Diana had so bitterly resented their forced marriage that she had barely managed to speak civilly to him. Now, despite the faint disclaimer she'd made on their journey returning from the duke's funeral, she blamed him both for her father's death and the breakup of her brother's engagement to Charlotte Lyon.

He longed to possess her with every fiber of his being. He lay awake at night with an aching fire in his loins. He knew he could make love to Diana at any time he chose, and she wouldn't deny him. According to her aristocratic code of honor she had made a bargain with him, and that bargain included submitting to his physical demands.

But he didn't want submission. He didn't want just her body. He wanted all of Diana, including her spirit and her love. Which he would never have, and his own fierce pride revolted from the thought of allowing Diana to know what he really wanted from her. Meanwhile he had to live in the same house with her, where every sight of her, every sound of her voice, only intensified the raging hunger in his blood.

The long journey ended in late afternoon at the Royal George in Folkestone, where Jared sent his usual message to Captain Appleton at his cottage.

To while away the interval until it was dark enough to take their cargo to the docks, Jared and Kamal ate a leisurely dinner in a private dining parlor. They chatted desultorily, with Jared doing most of the talking. He knew Kamal still felt slightly self-conscious to be dining with his employer.

"Do you fancy me as a prophet, Kamal?"

The head clerk smiled faintly. "As near as makes no difference, sir. Why do you ask?"

"Why, only to tell you that by midsummer the price of gold will be up again, perhaps sharply. I've just heard reports that this year's harvests will be poor."

"The experts can gauge the quality of the harvest this early?"

"They can make an intelligent guess."

At another point Jared said idly, "You make a good salary, and you can expect to do better. Have you thought of marrying?" At Kamal's quick flush Jared added, "I apologize. I had no right to query you about your personal plans."

"Please don't apologize, sir. Actually, I had thought of marrying, but . . ." Kamal shrugged.

"But your choice of brides in London is limited. I understand. There's a considerable Indian community here, however. Has no one caught your eye?"

"I—no."

Jared looked up from his cutlet. "You don't sound exactly certain."

Clearing his throat, Kamal said, "I should have said that yes, someone did catch my eyes, but the interest wasn't—er—mutual."

"Good God, Kamal, how can that be? You're a catch! Oh . . . is the lady already married?"

"No. However, she has—she has other loyalties."

Jared eyed his head clerk fixedly. "Kamal, are you talking about Rana?"

"Yes," Kamal answered, almost inaudibly. He turned a fiery red.

"Have you asked her to marry you?"

"No. I've never mentioned marriage to her. What would be the use? She's cared for you since you were a boy. She will never leave you."

"You might give her the opportunity to tell you that in person," Jared retorted. He glanced out the window of the dining parlor. "It's full dark. Shall we go?"

In the courtyard of the inn they found that the horses were already harnessed to the carriage. The two footmen-clerks and the coachman had been guarding the two heavy valises in the boot since the arrival of the party at the inn. Jared and Kamal took their places in the carriage and it moved out of the court-yard.

A short distance from the inn the carriage entered a narrow street that was so heavily shaded by overhanging trees that the faint light of the rising moon was completely obscured. The vehicle came to a grinding halt as the coachman reined in his team abruptly. Shots sounded, and a chorus of startled, angry voices. Jared and Kamal pulled out their pistols and piled out of the carriage, to find their coachman and guards desperately trying to fend off a group of shadowy attackers.

It was almost too dark under the trees to see their opponents clearly, but Jared took as careful an aim as possible and was rewarded by a shriek of pain. With no time to reload he seized the pistol by the barrel and waded into the nearest thugs, using the pistol as a club. Beside him Kamal, having also fired his weapon, was fighting with a grim ferocity with fist and clubbed pistol. In a matter of moments the struggle was over and the attackers had fled, save for one still body on the roadway.

"Well, that was close," Jared said, wiping his forehead on his sleeve. "Good work, lads, there'll be a little bonus for you—" He heard the crack of a shot and felt an instantaneous fiery pain in his shoulder. Kamal caught him in supporting arms before he could fall to the ground.

Diana sat in her bedchamber, trying to concentrate on her book. It seemed to be a sensible book—in fact, the author had titled it *Sense and Sensibility*—and it was about ordinary, understandable people rather than hideous villains and abducted heiresses shut up in haunted castles, but Diana couldn't keep her mind on the troubles of the two sisters, Elinor and Marianne.

Instead, Diana was thinking about Jared. She knew she ought to be relieved to be free of his presence these past several days. However, she couldn't prevent herself from wondering about his mysterious absences from London. This was the second time in her experience of him that he had left town for an unknown destination. Where did he go? And why did she care?

She looked up from her book at the knock on her door. Had Jared returned? "Come in."

Rana entered the room, bowing her usual three low bows. "Forgive me if I intrude, my lady."

"Not at all." Diana gazed curiously at the lovely dark creature. She still wasn't sure in her mind what Rana's status really was. At the least, Jared hadn't taken his "housekeeper" on his mysterious journey. "What did you wish to see me about, Rana?"

The Indian woman's face was serene, but her fingers nervously crinkled the gossamer silk of her sari. "It was just . . we've talked, a number of times, since you returned from your father's funeral, my lady, but I never found the opportunity to express my condolences about your parent's death. Will you allow me to do so now?"

"Yes, of course. Thank you, Rana."

"It is a very great sorrow to lose one's father, especially a well-loved father."

"Yes." Diana's eyes filled. "I was fortunate. I loved my father dearly, and he loved me."

"You were indeed fortunate, my lady."

"Yes, I was." Diana paused. She suspected that Rana hadn't come to the bedchamber merely to express her condolences. The housekeeper had another purpose in mind, and Diana wondered what it was.

About to speak, Rana turned, startled, at a peremptory knock at the door. Kamal, travel-stained and weary-looking, strode into the room. He addressed Diana. "My lady, I've brought the master home. He's badly wounded."

"Wounded?" Diana and Rana exclaimed, almost in unison.

"I'll explain later. My lady, who is your doctor? Phelps, is that his name? Rana, send a message to this Doctor Phelps immediately. Say that it's a matter of life and death." Kamal turned to go, pausing to say to Diana, "I've ordered the servants to bring the master to his bedchamber."

Diana followed Kamal down the corridor to Jared's rooms. Two footmen had removed his soiled and bedraggled clothing as he lay on the bed and had pulled up the covers under his

rms. There was a bandage around his right shoulder, heavily
loodstained. Jared's eyes were closed and his face was a
eathly white.

"What happened? How did Jared get hurt?" Diana asked
Kamal.

He hesitated. "The master and I were attacked. We were in
Folkestone on—er—business. Doubtless the attackers thought
ve were carrying valuables. Mr. Amberly killed one of the
hugs, and others in our party fought off the rest of them. Just
s we thought the incident was over, a stray shot struck Mr.
Amberly. A local doctor treated him, assuring us it was a clean
vound, unlikely to result in complications. So we completed
ur business in Folkestone and began the return trip to London.
Midway through the journey, Mr. Amberly began to bleed. It
vas all I could do to stop the hemorrhaging. He became un-
onscious as we approached London."

Jared opened his eyes. They were unfocused at first, then
ecame clear. "Diana," he whispered weakly. "What are you
loing . . . ? Where am I?"

Kamal spoke up. "You're in London, Mr. Amberly, at your
nouse in Chesterfield Street. Do you remember being ambushed
nd wounded in Folkestone?"

"Yes. My shoulder hurts infernally." Jared made a slight
novement and instantly the bandage on his shoulder became
tained a deeper red.

Diana gasped, clutching in panic at Kamal, who reached
lown to hold his hand firmly against the bandage. "Bring me
loths of some kind, toweling, anything," he ordered Diana.
'The master's hemorrhaging again."

Before Diana could move Rana entered the room, grasped
he situation immediately and dashed out the door, to return
noments later with an armful of linen. She and Diana stood
welplessly by, watching as Kamal attempted to staunch the flow
of blood by applying pad after pad to the wound.

"There, I think that's done it," Kamal muttered after a nerve-
ackingly tense period that seemed to go on for hours but which
actually was a matter of minutes. He rose from his kneeling
osition, flexing his arm and hand. Jared's blood stained his

hands and his sleeves. Jared himself was unconscious, his face the color of parchment.

"You called the doctor?" Kamal asked Rana.

"Yes. He should be here soon. He lives not far from here."

As if on cue, Doctor Phelps bustled into the room. Mumbling a perfunctory "Good evening, my lady," he went straight to Jared. "Gunshot wound?" he inquired as he began removing the blood-soaked bandaging.

Kamal stepped forward. "Yes, Doctor. Mr. Amberly was attacked by thieves."

Glancing over his shoulder, the doctor said to Kamal, "You, sir, stay with me. I may need help. Ladies, will you wait outside?"

In the corridor Rana said to Diana, "Perhaps you should go to your bedchamber, my lady. I will come to you if you are needed."

Diana felt a pang of anger. It seemed to her that Rana was, doubtless unconsciously, assuming the responsibility that rightfully belonged to the mistress of the house. "Thank you, Rana. I prefer to stay here."

Rana bowed her head. The two women stood side by side in silence, occasionally gazing in strained attention at the closed door of Jared's bedchamber. At length Doctor Phelps came out of the room, followed by Kamal.

"How is he, Doctor?" Diana inquired.

The doctor smiled. "I'm happy to tell you, my lady, that I think Mr. Amberly will recover nicely. It was a clean wound, and doubtless would have mended without incident, if your husband hadn't elected to return to London today. Nine hours of jolting travel in a carriage caused his wound to reopen, and he lost a great deal of blood. Far too much. He's very weak. However, with careful nursing, and if he observes a strict bed rest, I fancy Mr. Amberly will be himself in a short time."

"Thank God," Diana said. She turned to Kamal. "We have your presence of mind to thank for this. But for you my husband might have bled to death."

"I did what anyone would have done, my lady. And now please excuse me to get some sleep. Since Mr. Amberly won't be at his desk for a time, I must be ready to assume his duties."

The doctor bowed. "I'll be going too, Lady Diana. I'll look in on the patient tomorrow. Don't hesitate to call if you need me."

After Kamal and the doctor had left Rana said to Diana, "I will be happy to sit with the sahib tonight, my lady, unless you would rather do so yourself."

Rana spoke quietly and respectfully, with nothing in her manner to suggest that she was attempting to impinge on her mistress's authority, but Diana could detect an underlying note of pleading.

"Yes, very well, Rana. Stay with Mr. Amberly tonight. I'll sit with him tomorrow."

Diana went to her bedchamber and prepared for bed, more relieved than she would have considered possible to learn that Jared wasn't seriously hurt. The thought did cross her mind that if he were to die she would again be a widow, and free. Somehow, to her faint surprise, the notion had not the slightest degree of attraction to her. She would rather not achieve her freedom at the price of Jared's death.

She came into Jared's bedchamber early the next morning to find Rana sitting tensely upright in her chair beside Jared's bed, clasping his hand in one of hers, while with the fingers of her other hand she felt for his pulse.

"Is something wrong?" Diana said quietly.

Rana lowered Jared's hand to the bed. "The sahib's pulse is tumultuous, my lady. He has a fever."

Apprehensively Diana looked at Jared. He had a high fever. He was tossing restlessly, muttering disjointed phrases, and though his eyes were open he obviously wasn't aware of his surroundings.

"I'll send for Doctor Phelps," Diana said. She went to her room to instruct her abigail to send the message, and returned a few minutes later with a bowl of cool water and some clean cloths. "I think he might feel better if we sponge his face," she told Rana.

"Oh, yes, I'm sure the sahib will be more comfortable."

"I'll do it, Rana. You go get some rest. You look exhausted."

"Begging your pardon, my lady, I cannot leave the sahib. I any event, I could not sleep, knowing he was in danger."

Diana shrugged. She couldn't increase the Indian woman evident anguish for Jared by sending her away. But once mor she found herself wondering what the exact relations betwee the two really were.

Doctor Phelps, when he arrived, merely confirmed the obvi ous. "I'd hoped this wouldn't happen," he told Diana. "M Amberly's wound was a clean one, and he received immediat medical attention. However, as I'm all too aware, gunshc wounds often result in fever under the best of conditions."

"Will he live, Doctor?" Diana asked in a low voice.

"If he can throw off the fever, yes. Otherwise . . ." The docto shrugged. "Continue to sponge him off, Lady Diana. Keep hir as cool as possible. And try to persuade him to drink liquids."

Throughout a long day Diana and Rana sat beside Jared' bed. The Indian woman adamantly refused to leave the room and Diana ceased to urge her.

Caught in the grip of a raging fever, Jared alternated betwee quiescent periods, when he lay quietly, breathing heavily, an bouts of restlessness, when he threshed his limbs and mutteree in delirium, sometimes in words that sounded like gibberish t Diana. At other times he spoke in phrases that were clea enough, but which she didn't understand.

At one point he exclaimed, "Father, I'm your son, too. Wh can't you love me?"

Rana drew a sharp breath. Diana looked at her questioningly "Rana, what does Jared mean? Did he quarrel with his father And I wasn't aware that he had a brother."

Rana hesitated, tears streaming down her cheeks. Then, as i she couldn't help herself, she told Diana about Richard Am berly's marriage to Jared's mother.

Horrified, Diana exclaimed, "You mean that Jared's fathe denied his legitimate wife and son and entered into a bigamou marriage with another lady, because the so-called second wif was of pure English blood and Jared's mother was a Eurasian?'

"That was his only reason, my lady. Mr. Amberly didn't re

veal the truth until his son by the English lady died, and he had no other heirs except my sahib."

Diana stared unseeingly into space. For the first time she understood Jared's bitterness at his treatment by her father and Miles and yes, herself. Her family had denied dignity and recognition to Jared largely on the grounds of his native blood. He must have felt that he was being repudiated a second time, by the same class of people—indeed, by the same family, in a sense—to which his father belonged.

Later during that interminable day Jared began muttering her name. "Diana, my darling, my beautiful one . . . I want you, I need you. . . . Don't turn away from me. . . . Come to me, let me love you. . . ."

Overwhelmed by embarrassment, Diana glanced sideways at Rana, who sat as still as a statue, her dark features frozen in a mask of pain. Something impelled Diana to say defensively, "I never denied him. Jared is my husband. How could I deny him?"

At last Rana turned her head to look directly into Diana's eyes. "The sahib does not want duty from you, my lady. That is not why he married you. He does not want sex, either. That he could obtain from anyone, at any time he cared to have it."

"From you, perhaps?" The moment the words left her lips, Diana felt a burning sense of shame.

Rana flinched, as if Diana had physically struck her. "No, not from me, my lady. I took his mother's place, at a time when no one else would offer him love and comfort." Rana pushed her chair back and jumped up, rushing out of the room.

Diana followed her into the corridor, where Rana, her slender shoulders shaken by sobs, stood wrapped in Kamal's protective arms. He was murmuring soothing phrases in a language Diana didn't understand.

As soon as he saw Diana Kamal gently disengaged himself. "I came to inquire about Mr. Amberly after I closed the bank premises for the day, my lady. Rana tells me he is very ill."

"Yes, he has a high fever." Diana's mind was alive with conjecture. It was obvious that Kamal and Rana were more to each other than mere fellow servants. Were they romantically involved?

"May I see Mr. Amberly, my lady?"

"Yes, of course."

Diana followed Kamal into the bedchamber. The clerk's dark face expressed an apprehensive concern as he looked at Jared. It struck Diana that both Kamal and Rana felt a deep affection for Jared that went far beyond a master-servant relationship.

Kamal turned away from the bed. "You'll notify me if Mr. Amberly's condition worsens, my lady?" At Diana's nod he added hesitantly, "If I might make a suggestion . . . I think Rana should go to bed. She looks exhausted."

"She hasn't slept for well over twenty-four hours. I've suggested to her several times that she get some rest. She insists on staying with Jared."

"Then you must order her to leave," blurted Kamal. He looked momentarily aghast at his temerity. "I beg your pardon, my lady. I—er—would you wish me to instruct Rana in your name to go to her room?"

"Yes, do that, Kamal. It's for her own good."

He bowed and left the room.

Diana resumed her seat beside Jared's bed. He was restless again, burning with fever. His face as she sponged it with cool water was hot to her touch. He muttered disjointed phrases, sometimes in English, sometimes in the musical language she had heard Rana and Kamal using. Bengali, is that what the language was called? She heard her own name several times. She caught words like "gold" and "interest" and "repayment." Then, at one point, a clearly enunciated sentence: "Mama, is Papa never coming home again?" Diana's eyes welled with tears. The voice was Jared's, but the tone was that of a very young boy.

The hours wore on. Dr. Phelps looked in. Soft-footed servants came and went, with tea and food for Diana and bowls of cool water and fresh cloths with which to sponge Jared's burning face. Jared alternated between a comalike lethargy and bouts of restlessness. The fever continued to ravage him.

It was almost midnight when the change came, when Diana

was nearing the limits of her vitality. Suddenly she noticed that Jared's forehead was beaded with perspiration. Hardly daring to hope, she touched his hand. It felt cool. A moment later his eyes opened. For the first time in many hours they were lucid.

"Diana?" he whispered. A thread of a sound.

"Yes, Jared."

"Have I been ill?"

"Very ill. But you'll be all right now. Your fever has broken."

"I remember now . . . some thieves were after the gold. They shot me. Kamal?"

"Kamal is fine. He wasn't hurt."

Jared's eyes closed again, and Diana had a moment of panic. Then he said, "Diana, have you been with me since I took ill?"

"Mostly. Since early this morning."

"Why? Why did you . . . ?"

"Because I wanted to be with you." Diana knew with a sudden dazed certainty that it was true.

Jared smiled faintly, and this time, when he closed his eyes, Diana didn't panic. He was sleeping naturally.

Fifteen

Diana awoke the next morning with a feeling of urgency. Jared! How had he passed the night? Rana had come to Jared's bedchamber last night shortly after the fever had broken, and, after bursting into a storm of happy tears, she had firmly announced that she would sit with Jared until the morning. Almost too weary to move her legs, Diana had given in to Rana's insistence without argument, and had stumbled down the corridor to her own rooms, where she had fallen into an exhausted slumber. Now, fully awake, she pushed back the coverlets, swung her legs over the edge of the bed and hurried over to the wardrobe.

"My lady, whatever are you doing?" inquired her abigail, who had just entered the room with a tea tray.

"Selecting a dress," Diana said impatiently. "I must go to my husband."

"But the Indian lady, that Rana, is with him. And when I went down to the kitchens jist minutes ago ter fetch yer tea, the servants were saying that Mr. Amberly was much better this morn. So do drink yer tea and have a bit of toast, my lady, afore ye goes ter Mr. Amberly."

Resignedly Diana drank her tea and swallowed several bites of toast and then allowed Rose to help her into a figured muslin round gown. She rebelled, however, when Rose attempted to dress her hair in its usual elaborate curls. "Just comb my hair, Rose, and arrange it in a chignon," Diana ordered. She perched a lacy little cap over her hair and rose from the dressing table.

When she opened the door of Jared's bedchamber a few moments later she paused in horror on the threshold. Jared was lying half propped up on pillows, his eyes closed, while Rana shaved him.

"Stop this nonsense immediately," Diana exclaimed as she advanced into the room. "Rana, I'm surprised at you. My husband has barely passed the crisis of his illness. A shave is the last thing he needs."

Momentarily Rana's slender fingers ceased their delicate manipulation of the razor. Jared's eyes opened. In a faint but perfectly clear voice he said, "I told Rana to shave me. I don't care to appear like a hedgehog, thank you."

"Oh." Feeling mildly foolish, Diana walked to the bed. Jared looked drained and pale, but the intensely blue eyes had regained their old vibrancy. "How are you feeling this morning?"

"Very well." He smiled faintly. "That's a lie, of course. I'm certainly not prepared to conquer the Stock Exchange, or even to sit behind my desk at the bank, but compared to yesterday, I'm well enough. Doctor Phelps has already paid me a visit this morning. He's pleased with my progress. He says I can actually have some food today. Gruel."

"Gruel!" Diana had a sudden memory of childhood illnesses, and made a face.

"Exactly," said Jared.

"Gruel is good for you," said Diana firmly. "It will help you get well."

"That's what Rana says. I'm at the mercy of two female dictators."

"And a good thing, too," Diana retorted. "Men don't know how to take care of themselves."

Jared rolled his eyes, and both Diana and Rana fell into a fit of giggling. After a moment Jared said, "Rana tells me you sat with me from dawn to midnight yesterday. Thank you."

"Rana took much greater care of you than I did," Diana said quickly.

"Nevertheless, I thank you. What's more, I want both you and Rana to stay away from my so-called sickroom today and get a proper rest. There are certainly enough servants in this large household to take care of my needs for a few hours."

"But . . ." chorused Diana and Rana in unison.

"No buts. Those are my orders. Be off with you, both of you. Send in one of the footmen to see to me. Young Edmonds, perhaps. He has a cheerful face."

Diana and Rana stood in the corridor outside Jared's room, looking at each other in silence. A slow smile appeared on Rana's lips. "He's much better, my lady. He's out of danger."

"So he is. He's becoming tyrannical again," Diana retorted, and then, as she noticed the amused twinkle in the house-keeper's eyes, she began to laugh.

"It's a small price to pay, my lady," murmured Rana.

"I daresay." Diana laughed again. "Much better than to see him dead. Well, Rana, you may do as you like, but I intend to obey my lord and master and go back to bed. I'm weary to my bones."

Before Diana could return to her bedchamber, however, a footman brought her a message that His Grace the Duke of Edgehill and Mr. Aubrey Dalton wished to see her.

Sighing in frustration, Diana went down to the drawing room. Miles and Aubrey rose as she entered.

"Good for you, Diana," said Miles cheerfully. "There's no need for you to have a face as long as a fiddle, at least not with Aubrey and me, and I'm glad you're not playing the hypocrite."

"What on earth are you talking about, Miles?"

"Why, about your dear departed husband, of course." Miles grinned. "Sorry, that was a slip of the tongue. I meant your dear *departing* husband."

"Yes, the latest *on dit* has it that Amberly isn't long for this world," said Aubrey with a chuckle. "Or is the fellow already dead, Diana? No, that couldn't be. I didn't see any crape on your door as we came in. But is it the next best thing? Is Amberly indeed at death's door?"

Diana stared at Miles and Aubrey in disbelief. They suddenly seemed like strangers to her. Or rather, for the first time in her life, she had the sensation that her brother and his oldest friend were on the opposite side of a great divide from her.

"I think you must both be out of your minds," she said in a trembling voice. "That, or you've become monsters."

"By Jove, Diana, that's coming it too strong," protested Miles. "What have Aubrey and I done, pray? Surely you didn't expect *us* to be hypocrites, pretending to feel grief for Amberly's passing. No should you, my dear pea-goose. Good God, don't you realize you'll soon be free of the fellow? And you'll be a wealthy widow, to boot, if I remember correctly what Papa told me about your marriage settlements."

"Just a moment, Miles," said Aubrey, gazing intently at Diana. "Perhaps we've pulled the wrong pig by the ear. Perhaps Diana doesn't fancy being a widow. Perhaps she's grown fond of Amberly and regrets that he's about to kick the bucket."

"Don't talk fustian," Miles snapped. "Diana fond of Amberly? All my eye and Betty Martin."

"I must ask you not to be vulgar," Diana said coldly. "And I'm sorry you and Aubrey think so little of my integrity that you can imagine me gloating at the prospect of becoming wealthy at the price of another human being's life. What's more, you're laboring under a false assumption. Jared is *not* dying. He's making a rapid recovery."

Miles exclaimed incredulously, "But it's all over town that Amberly's servants brought him back to London in a dying condition after he was attacked somewhere on the Channel coast. I heard he barely survived the journey."

"The prattle-boxes, as usual, were mistaken. And now, if the pair of you came here only to mount a death watch on my husband, I suggest you go. Jared is very much alive, and intends to stay that way."

Miles reddened with anger. "I never thought to see the day when I'd be unwelcome in my sister's house. Come along, Aubrey."

"In good time. Diana, when I suggested you might be averse to being a widow you didn't express any denial. *Are* you becoming fond of Amberly?"

Diana said angrily, "Another question like that, Aubrey, and I'll begin to question why I ever thought you were a gentleman." She broke off to say impatiently, "Yes, what is it, Baxter?" A young footman had entered the room to stand at her elbow, his eyes popping with excitement. "Speak up, man."

"Oh, my lady, it's—it's the Prince," spluttered the footman. "See?" Diana's gaze followed his pointing finger to the large, imposing figure who swept into the drawing room, followed by a uniformed aide.

"Your Royal Highness," she gasped, sinking into a deep curtsy.

"How do you do, Lady Diana?" said the Regent with an affable smile. He acknowledged the low bows of Miles and Aubrey. "It's Edgehill, isn't it, and—?"

"Aubrey Dalton, sir."

Both Miles and Aubrey seemed to be so petrified with astonishment that they could scarcely utter a syllable.

"Oh, yes, Mr. Dalton. I fancy we've met." The Regent turned to Diana. "Forgive me if I intrude, but when I heard that your husband had suffered an accident I had to come by to inquire how he was. The corporal works of mercy and all that, you know. How is Mr. Amberly, Lady Diana? We heard some horrifying reports."

"My husband is well on the road to recovery, thank you, sir."

"Capital. Is the patient up to receiving visitors?"

"If that visitor is you, sir, certainly. Please come with me."

As Diana went up the stairway she heard the sound of hard breathing behind her and felt a qualm. The Regent was now so obese that he probably found climbing stairs a trial. She heard another sound, too, a faint clicking noise. Was it true, she wondered, that her royal guest never ventured out these days without being trussed into heavy stays to conceal his weight?

Jared was dozing when Diana ushered the Regent into the bedchamber. He opened his eyes at the sound of footsteps and came to a startled attention, making an instinctive move to sit up.

"Jared, lie still. You'll reopen your wound," Diana cautioned.

"Indeed, my boy. You mustn't strain yourself." The Regent glanced about him and sank gratefully into the chair that his aide pushed into position. "I was desolated to hear about your injury, Mr. Amberly. We can't afford to lose a prominent citizen like yourself. But Lady Diana assures me you are recovering."

"Thanks to good nursing, sir, yes."

"Splendid. I'm sure Lady Diana is an excellent nurse."

"Indeed, sir. The best." Jared flicked a glance at Diana.

The Regent stayed for a few minutes, chatting pleasantly on a number of topics. Seeing him close up, Diana could appreciate the legendary charm that had led so many people to forgive His Royal Highness for his many faults and mistakes.

At one point his gaze fastened on the sandalwood chest that stood beside Jared's bed, serving as a table. "This is beautiful work, Mr. Amberly," said the Regent, examining closely the intricately carved foliage, fruit and flowers that covered every inch of the cabinet. "Eastern craftsmanship, I daresay?"

"Yes, sir. The table came from southern India. It belonged to my mother."

"I thought so. More and more I find myself fascinated by the art of the East. Have you seen the new stables at my Pavilion in Brighton? No? You might be interested. They are in the Hindustani style. Well, now, Mr. Amberly, I mustn't tire you and outwear my welcome! I'm pleased to see you looking so robust. Pray keep me informed about your progress."

Rising from his chair with considerable difficulty, the Regent inclined his head graciously to Jared and Diana. "Goodbye. Don't bother to see me out, Lady Diana," he begged. "Save your energies for your good husband."

After the royal visitor and his aide had departed, Diana looked bemusedly at Jared, murmuring, "That was most gracious of His Royal Highness. Of course, I understand he does occasionally visit the sick if they—" She stopped short, biting her lip. "I mean . . ."

"You mean the Regent sometimes visits the sick if the invalids are of sufficient rank," finished Jared. He smiled crookedly. "I presume the Regent doesn't often visit the sickbeds of bankers. On the other hand he has a very real appreciation of money. That, Diana, doubtless explains the honor we received today. His Royal Highness owes me a great deal of money."

"I daresay." Diana wasn't sure if Jared was angry at her near faux pas, or merely amused.

A footman came into the room just then with a tray containing a steaming bowl of unappetizing-looking gruel. Jared waved Diana away. "I won't subject you to the torture of helping me eat this dreadful stuff. Edmonds will take very good care of me."

During the following days Jared slowly began to recover his strength. The footman, Edmonds, continued to care for Jared's more mundane needs, his bathing and his shaving, while Rana insisted on sitting with him through the night. Diana developed a routine, looking in on him briefly every morning and every evening, and spending a block of time with him during the afternoons. Sometimes she read to him from the newspapers. Mostly, in the first few days, she simply sat beside his bed while he dozed or lay with his eyes closed.

She felt an odd constraint whenever she was with him. They had crossed some kind of a boundary in their relationship, but what it entailed she couldn't fathom. All she knew was that she now saw Jared as a person in a different light, not as a money-making machine bent on revenge but as a man of infinitely more complicated emotions.

One afternoon when Diana was sitting with him, some ten days into his recovery, he woke with a start, his face twisted with pain.

"Here, have this," she said, reaching for a glass containing a mixture of laudanum.

"No," he muttered. "I don't like the stuff. It clouds the mind. You need a clear head for business."

"Oh, and I suppose you're in prime twig at the moment to do business?"

A grimace, composed equally of discomfort and amusement, crossed his face. "I'm *always* prepared to do business. What's that?" he asked as Diana picked up a piece of paper from the stand beside the bed.

"Well, since you're *always* prepared to do business, I have a letter here that Kamal left this morning with instructions that you were to read it if you felt up to the effort."

Extending his right hand for the letter, Jared drew a sharp breath at the discomfort caused by the movement to his injured shoulder and lowered his arm. "You read it."

It was a letter from a Mr. Ashby, a proprietor of the East India Company, proposing to sell Jared a large block of shares. "I offer you the first opportunity to buy my shares, my dear Mr. Amberly, because I believe that the future of John Company will be more secure in your hands than in those of any other Director of the Court."

"Quite a compliment," commented Diana when she finished reading the letter. "Mr. Ashby has a great deal of confidence in your abilities."

"Mr. Ashby overestimates the amount of power or influence I have. A director of the Company, unless he also happens to be a member of the Secret Committee, is somewhat of a fig-urehead." A faint frown appeared between Jared's eyebrows as he considered the matter. "Yes," he decided after a moment, "tell Kamal to buy the shares."

Diana smiled. "Because you think the purchase might help you to become a member of this Secret Committee?"

"It can't hurt," said Jared coolly. He paused, looking thought-fully at her. "Why are you continuing to play the ministering angel, Diana?" he inquired. "You must have better things to occupy your time, and Rana and the servants between them can take care of my needs very adequately."

Diana felt a stab of hurt, which she instantly tried to suppress. "You don't wish me to share in your care?"

"I didn't say that. I just—I wondered why you felt obliged to be my nurse. *Noblesse oblige*, perhaps? A dutiful observance of your marriage vows? If the latter, I assure you that I don't expect you to exert yourself in any way that might—that might seem oppressive to you."

"I don't feel oppressed, Jared," Diana said quietly. She picked up a newspaper. "Now, would you like me to read you the news? It seems there's been a hard-fought battle in the Peninsula, at a place called Albuera. The newspaper reports heavy casualties on both sides."

Diana left Jared's bedchamber that afternoon plagued by

Lois Stewart

doubts and uncertainties. Jared had asked her why she felt obligated to share in his nursing. She didn't know why. She hadn't really thought about it. It had seemed right and natural to do everything she could to assist in Jared's recovery. But his question was forcing her to think. Why *hadn't* she left Jared's care to Rana and the servants after the initial crisis had passed?

She spent several hours wrestling with the problem. She had dinner on a tray in her room, as she had been accustomed to doing since Jared's injury; it had seemed ridiculous to sit alone at a long formal table in the cavernous dining room, waited on in silence by an entourage of servants. She allowed her abigail to help her into nightdress and robe and brush out her hair, and she sat for a while trying to immerse herself in *Sense and Sensibility*. At last, making up her mind, she left her room and went down the hall to Jared's bedchamber.

In an agony of uncertainty she stood for a moment outside the door before she knocked once, rather timidly. No answer. She knocked again. Again no answer. Perhaps Jared was asleep. Then she heard a murmur of voices from inside the room. Rana must be with him, having assumed her duties earlier than usual. Diana opened the door and stepped inside. She drew an appalled, humiliated breath.

Jared was sitting in his favorite chair beside the fireplace. During the past few days he had felt well enough to leave his bed for several hours at a time. Rana knelt in front of Jared, her head buried in his chest, her arms clutching him tightly. Jared's hand caressed her dark hair.

As Diana turned to flee, Jared looked up, saying sharply, "Diana, wait."

Rana jumped up from her kneeling position and rushed across the room, past Diana at the door and out into the corridor. The Indian woman's face was wet with tears.

"Close the door, Diana."

Diana shut the door and stood stiffly beside it. Every instinct told her to leave the room before her pent-up emotions exploded.

"That little scene wasn't what you thought, Diana."

"No? How do you know what I thought?" Diana managed to say with a gritty calm.

"You thought Rana and I were enjoying a romantic tryst. Am I wrong?"

"I—What do you take me for, Jared, an idiot? I *saw* you!"

"You saw me comforting a grieving woman. Rana had just told me she was leaving me, and her heart was bursting with grief."

"Leaving you? I don't understand," Diana stammered. "Hasn't she been with you since you were a boy? Where will she go?"

"She came to me twenty—no, twenty-one years ago, the year before my mother died. She was little more than a child herself at the time. Where will she go? To Kamal. He proposed marriage to her last evening. She thought about it during the night and into today, and finally decided to accept his offer. But she was devastated by the necessity of making such a decision. She felt torn with guilt at the thought of leaving me, as if she were betraying a sacred trust."

Jared paused. "You see, at the time of my mother's death she and my father were—were living apart, for reasons I won't go into," he said, choosing his words carefully. "I was very young, and my mother wanted to be sure I would be cared for properly when she died. Rana promised she would stay with me always. She's kept that promise—until now."

"I know, Jared. Rana told me."

Jared frowned. "She told you? What did she tell you? When?"

"When you were ill. You were consumed by the fever, and both of us thought you were dying. You called out for your father in your delirium, begging him to come back to you and your mother. Rana broke down. I think she felt that your senseless death at the hands of those thieves was the final unjust blow in a lifetime of tragedy. The words poured out of her, as if she had to share her grief with someone. She told me that your father had repudiated you and your mother and married another woman bigamously, and how he refused to acknowledge you until his son by his second wife had died."

Jared muttered, "She shouldn't have told you all that. It's in the past, and it should stay in the past. I'm sure it didn't interest you." He cleared his throat. "In any case I didn't die, and I think Rana took my recovery as a sign that her stewardship was over. She told me I didn't need her anymore, since I was grown-up and prosperous and I had a wife. But of course, she still felt guilty. She's been putting my comfort and happiness ahead of her own for so many years that she found it hard to break the habit."

"I see. Thank you for explaining. I'm sorry I misinterpreted the situation."

Jared looked at Diana's clinging robe of pale green silk. A flame ignited in the blue eyes. "Why did you come here tonight?"

Diana wondered if she looked as uncomfortable as she felt. "I—I thought you should know that my opinion of you has—has changed."

"Oh? In what respect, may I ask?"

"Well . . . now that I know about the mistreatment you received in your childhood I can understand why you felt so outraged by the Amberly family's behavior toward you. Your father was an Amberly, and it must have seemed to you that history was repeating itself. I don't condone my family's behavior, or my own. We were insufferably rude and arrogant to you. Nor do I condone your actions. Revenge is never pretty. You had no right to threaten Papa and to force me into an unwanted marriage. But I think it's time to put all the bitterness behind us and get on with our lives."

Jared became very still. "Us? You mean you and me?"

"Yes. You and I." Diana swallowed. "Papa is gone, and I can't answer for Miles."

"And how do you propose that we—as you put it—'get on' with our lives?"

Diana looked straight into Jared's eyes. "Since we're married, for whatever the reason, bargain or no, and since that marriage can't be undone short of scandal, I propose that we make the most of our bargain and begin living together as man and wife. I presume you want an heir. I've always wanted children."

Jared rose from his chair, wincing slightly as the exertion put a strain on his injured shoulder. He came up to her, his arms remaining by his sides. "Kiss me, Diana."

Slowly, hesitantly, she put her hands on his chest and raised her head to press her lips to his mouth. Instantly a quicksilver shiver of delight stirred in her loins, and her lips clung to Jared's in a deepening kiss.

A shudder ran through his body. His uninjured arm caught her close to him. Looking into her eyes, he murmured huskily, "We talked of passion once. Is that what you feel? Do you want me, Diana? God knows, I want you."

"Yes," Diana whispered. "I want you."

His mouth crushed her lips in a devouring, possessive kiss while his arm locked their bodies together in a fierce embrace that told Diana he was fully aroused. He broke the kiss, his breathing fast and uneven. "Are you sure, Diana? I can stop now if you . . ."

"Don't stop . . ."

Both his arms swept around her and immediately loosened as Jared uttered a smothered exclamation of pain.

"Your shoulder," Diana gasped.

He stepped back, his face a study in frustration. "My God, I'm a useless lover," he said in disgust. "I can't disrobe you, I can't carry you to my bed, I can't even take off my dressing gown without going through the motions of a contortionist."

"The problem isn't unsolvable," Diana said breathlessly. Slowly she untied the ribbons at her throat and shrugged out of her robe, allowing it to fall in shimmering folds at her feet. Clad only in a wisp of a nightdress she went to Jared, untying the sash of his dressing gown. She slipped the dressing gown from his left arm and gently eased the garment from his injured shoulder.

He glanced down at his thin cotton drawers. "Finish the job," he urged her in a voice slurred with passion. "I can't wait any longer, Diana."

"Nor can I," she whispered, as her fingers drifted to the buttons of his waistband.

Sixteen

Rana and Kamal were married in mid-July in a little church in Holborn. There were only a few people in the church, including a number of Kamal's acquaintances from the Indian community in London, and several clerks from Jared's bank and brokerage house and their wives. Rather to Diana's surprise the pair were married in an Anglican ceremony. Kamal had been educated in a church-sponsored charity school in Calcutta for the children, legitimate or otherwise, of English soldiers stationed in India, and had become at least a nominal Anglican. Rana, according to Jared, had never displayed any strong interest in religion.

Save for his dark skin, Kamal looked the typical English bridegroom in his tailored coat, elaborate cravat, and pantaloons. Rana, on the other hand, drifted into the church on Jared's arm like an exotic butterfly, in a brilliant green sari interwoven with gold thread. On her slender neck and arms she wore a glittering array of gold chains and necklaces and bracelets.

Diana glanced sideways at Jared, sitting beside her in the pew while the clergyman conducted the service. Had he presented this fortune in gold jewelry to Rana? Where else could she have obtained it? Diana had learned from Jared that the dowries of Indian brides often consisted in large part of jewelry.

The ceremony over, Rana and Kamal started back down the aisle. As she came abreast of Jared Rana dropped Kamal's arm and sank into the familiar three low bows. Her dark eyes were brimming with tears. Tears of sorrow or of joy, Diana wondered? Or a little of both?

The thoroughly conventional wedding breakfast—save for a number of Indian dishes—took place in the small house Kamal had bought for his bride in the vicinity of Lincoln's Inn Fields, fairly close to Jared's banking offices in Lombard Street.

"Rana doesn't consider London houses proper dwellings," Kamal remarked to Diana with a faint smile at the breakfast. "But I believe she's reconciled to a house without a colonnade or verandas or acres of gardens."

"I think she must be very pleased with this house, Kamal," Diana remarked. However, as she gazed around her the thought crossed her mind that the house, small but substantial, must represent a very large purchase to a man who worked as a clerk, even though she knew that Kamal was Jared's most trusted employee.

"Yes, I think Rana does like the house," Kamal commented. "The real question is, I suppose, will she be happy here?" His gaze shifted to his wife, who stood talking to Jared.

"May I be frank, Kamal? I think Rana will miss Jared. I believe she's cared for him for more than twenty years. But I also think she will be very happy with you. She chose to marry you, remember."

The slight look of strain left Kamal's face. Diana was glad she had spoken.

A little later she discovered that Rana had secret doubts of her own. She took Diana aside to say a little anxiously, "Is it permitted that I return to Chesterfield Street to visit you occasionally? Oh, not a formal call. I would not presume to place myself on an equal status with your friends. But could I come see you to talk about—about the sahib?"

"Yes, of course, Rana. You've been a part of Jared's life for so long. You've been almost like a mother to him. You'll want to know if he's happy."

"Yes. Thank you for understanding, Lady Diana." Rana glanced at Jared on the other side of the room. "The sahib looks happy now."

Jared stood talking to one of his clerks. Tall, magnetically handsome, assured, superbly dressed, he seemed much as usual. He also looked the picture of health. His shoulder was now completely healed. But Diana knew what Rana meant. There was a subtle added dimension about Jared these days. Was it an aura of happiness? Or was it simply an added self-confidence? Diana really didn't know.

Jared waited until he and Diana were about to leave the wedding breakfast before he presented the newlyweds with a gift.

Gazing curiously at the sealed document Jared had given him, Kamal handed it to Rana. "You open it."

Rana broke the seal and looked at the document. "I do not understand, Kamal."

Kamal took the document and examined it. "It's the mortgage to this house, Rana," he said in a wondering voice. "It's marked paid in full."

"Oh, Sahib," Rana murmured. The ready tears came to the liquid brown eyes.

Gently flicking her cheek, Jared smiled, saying, "Diana and I couldn't let you and Kamal start your married life in a house that wasn't completely yours."

Later, as she and Jared left Holborn in their carriage, Diana observed, "That was a very generous wedding present you gave Rana and Kamal."

"We, Diana. It was a joint gift."

Diana smiled. "Oh, come, that was a euphemism if I ever heard one. Legally, I own nothing. That is, except for the pin money you insisted on giving me. As soon as we were married you became the undisputed master of our financial assets."

Jared's brows drew together. "I don't want you ever to feel that you must come to me hat in hand for anything you require. What I own is yours."

"Thank you. That's a very pretty sentiment," Diana said lightly. She knew, of course, what the outcome would be if she came to him, "hat in hand," asking for a large sum of money to tow her brother Miles out of the River Tick.

That night, after Diana's abigail had prepared her for bed, Jared came to her bedchamber. He came almost every night now. Tonight, as always, he said casually, "Am I disturbing you?"

"No, not at all," Diana replied, also as always, and closed her book, putting it on the table beside her.

"Good." Jared came over to her chair and pulled her to her feet. Placing one hand under her chin he kissed her thoroughly and satisfyingly, while with his other hand he caressed the soft skin at the back of her neck. Gradually his lips shifted to her throat, nuzzling the robe off her shoulders. "Did you take my suggestion?" he murmured.

"Yes."

Skillfully his slender fingers untied the ribbons at her throat and removed her robe, leaving her naked. "There, what did I tell you? You don't need a nightdress, at least until the weather turns cold."

"How about you?" Daringly Diana reached out to untie the belt of his dressing gown. Jared shrugged out of the garment. Diana drew a sharp involuntary breath. His naked male body was beautiful.

"Diana, oh Diana . . ." Jared swept her up in his arms and deposited her on the bed.

Later, much later, Diana lay beside Jared, listening to his regular breathing. She was physically sated. Never, during the years she had been courted by various men, including Aubrey, and during her first marriage, had she imagined she would enjoy the enticing sensual delights she shared with Jared. He was a perfect lover, patient, considerate, passionate, satisfying her every need and desire.

But there was something missing. In the darkness of the room her face flamed as she admitted to herself that both she and Jared could have found physical fulfillment elsewhere. Jared in the arms of a skilled courtesan. She with one or another of the practiced rakes of the *ton*. Her heart protested. She didn't want another lover. She wanted . . . she wanted something she couldn't have. Not once in the delirious hours she'd spent in Jared's arms had the word "love" been mentioned.

"Rana came to see me today," Diana remarked a few nights later as she and Jared sat at dinner.

He looked up from his roast lamb. "Is she happy?"

"I think so. She seems to enjoy organizing her own household."

"Kamal goes around these days looking happily abstracted. He even misquoted the price of gold to me today."

"Rana wanted to know if you had hired a valet. She says you don't know how to shave yourself properly."

Jared touched his chin, which displayed a faint cut, and said ruefully, "Rana is quite right. Will you find a valet for me, Diana? Perhaps you could contact the labor exchange."

"Yes, I'll see to it." It struck Diana with a sense of unreality how completely prosaic this conversation sounded. These days she and Jared could be taken for a long-married couple who had settled into a comfortable domestic routine. They behaved toward each other in a natural, easy manner, without a trace of the stiffness and veiled hostility that had previously marked their relationship. It was also a curiously divided relationship. Their casual, friendly behavior to each other outside the bedchamber bore no resemblance to the silent wild passion of their nights together.

Diana shook herself out of her thoughts as Jared said with a hint of amusement, "You look very serious. Is there a problem?"

"No, not really. Actually, I was just thinking that the Season is almost over."

"Thank goodness. I'm growing weary of balls and routs and dinners every night."

"Had you thought of leaving London at the end of the Season?"

Putting down his glass of wine, Jared said, "No, I hadn't. I have a business to run. Banks and stock brokerages don't shut up shop during the summers."

"You don't wish to go down to the country, then?"

"To Abbottsleigh, you mean? Diana, you must know I'd be as welcome there as a leper on the streets of Jerusalem. Your brother is the Duke of Edgehill now. What makes you think he'd tolerate me among the guests at his ancestral home?"

"It's my ancestral home, too, remember. I presume Miles

won't object to my going there, especially since I'm still supervising the running of the estate from long distance. I've spent every summer there since I was born, except for . . ." She bit her lip.

"Except for the years of your marriage to Lord Windham." Jared knit his brow. "You really want to go to Abbottsleigh for the summer, don't you, Diana? Go, then. You don't need me there."

"But what would people say? Your friends, my friends, your business acquaintances? There might be gossip, a suspicion that we were estranged."

"Does that concern you so much?"

"Well . . . yes. I don't like gossip."

"Then I'll come down when I can. Now and then, for a few days. I warn you, though, that your brother won't be pleased to see me."

"I don't think you run too much danger of seeing Miles. He's very proud of being the *owner* of Abbottsleigh, but he doesn't much care for country pursuits. Papa was used to host a large house party every August, but Miles often didn't bother to attend. He usually comes down for the cubbing in September and the opening of the partridge season, and in November for the fox hunting, if he hasn't been invited elsewhere."

"You reassure me. Very well, I'll arrange my schedule to allow for short visits in August and September." The familiar blue flame kindled in Jared's eyes. "Perhaps my visits will be rather longer than shorter," he added, smiling faintly. "I'll miss—I'll miss your company, Diana." There was the slightest hesitation when he said the word "company." Diana knew exactly what he meant.

In the latter part of July a splendid *fête* at Carlton House, in honor of the inauguration of the Regency, was the last great event of the Season. Soon thereafter Diana began packing for her return to Oxfordshire.

One afternoon as she sat in the morning room writing instructions for the new housekeeper—whom she had hired to replace Rana—for the management of the house during her absence, a footman brought her a calling card with a brief note scribbled on it: "I should like so much to talk to you."

Diana examined the card thoughtfully. "Is Miss Lyon unaccompanied?" she asked the footman.

"Yes, my lady. Well, except fer her abigail, awaiting fer her in the carriage."

"Ask her to come in." Diana was perplexed. Unmarried females of good family customarily didn't pay calls without being chaperoned by a parent or an older friend. She had never before encountered Charlotte Lyon except in the company of her redoubtable mother.

"Good afternoon, Charlotte. I'm pleased to see you," Diana said as the footman ushered her guest into the morning room. "Won't you sit down?"

Charlotte was plainly nervous. Her fingers played with the little beads embroidered on her reticule, and she seemed unable to begin a conversation.

Trying to put her at ease, Diana remarked, "I hope your mother isn't ill. Usually Lady Lyon goes everywhere with you."

Charlotte flushed a deep red. "Mama is quite well. She doesn't know I came to visit you. She thinks I'm at the modiste's, having a fitting."

"I see. I gather you wanted to see me alone?"

"Yes, Lady Diana. I need advice. I don't know anyone else to turn to, and you've always been so kind."

"Oh . . . I don't know that I'm really qualified to give you advice."

"I think you are," said Charlotte eagerly. "You're a woman of the world, and you're happily married. If anyone can tell me what to do, you can."

"I'll try. I'll listen, at least. At a guess, I'd say your problem has to do with marriage?"

"Yes. You see, my parents are pressing me to accept an offer of marriage from—it doesn't matter what his name is. I'll call him Lord X. He's a very fine man, wealthy, from an old family, very personable. A little older than I am. Well, quite a bit older, in fact. He's in his forties. Mama says he's a great catch, as great a catch as—" Charlotte broke off, looking hideously embarrassed.

"As great a catch as your parents were used to consider my brother. I understand. So. Your parents are urging you to accept Lord X's offer, and you don't wish to do so. Is that correct?"

"Yes." Charlotte sighed. "Perhaps there's something wrong with me. Lord Carring—Lord X is such a nice man. So kind and considerate. He's told me he'll spend the rest of his life making me happy."

"But . . . ?"

"Yes, but. Lord X isn't interesting. In fact, he's *dull*. I can almost tell what he's going to say before he says it. I don't feel the slightest spark of any emotion toward him except friendship and respect. I don't want to marry him, and yet . . . Lady Diana, do you think I must always obey my parents?"

Into Diana's mind flashed the memory of Miles's remark when he heard the rumor that Lord and Lady Lyon were attempting to fix the interest of the Marquess of Carrington in their daughter. "Silly Willy?" Miles had exploded. "Charlotte says he's the most boring man she ever met."

"I've always considered that a young female should be guided by her parents," Diana said cautiously. "However, marriage is for a lifetime, and I personally believe it should involve a certain degree of—of affection. If you truly can't abide this Lord X, I don't think you should marry him."

An expression of pure relief crossed Charlotte's face. "Oh, thank you, Lady Diana. You can't know how much it means to me to hear you say that." She rose to take her leave, saying, "And I promise I won't mention your name when I tell Papa and Mama my decision. I'll let them think I came to it entirely on my own."

Diana watched Charlotte leave the room with mixed emotions. In one part of her mind she felt appalled that she had actually advised a well-bred young girl to defy her parents' wishes. She knew it was advice she couldn't have given short months ago, when family duty and honor had seemed the most important things in the world to her, more important than personal happiness. Twice she'd been in Charlotte's shoes, and twice she'd married to oblige her family. But the second time was different, a still small voice whispered to her. She hadn't loved Lord Windham. She'd abhorred his every touch. And she hadn't loved Jared, but his touch made her dizzy with longing.

Still half asleep, Diana put out her arm, groping for a familiar hard-muscled body. The space next to her in the bed was empty. She jerked upright, her face flaming. She had been at Abbottsleigh for only two weeks. How could she possibly miss Jared's physical presence so much already?

Her abigail came in with her breakfast tray and Diana quickly consumed her tea and toast and dressed for the day, eager to resume her ramblings about the estate.

She had already visited the home farm and a number of the other tenants, and she had received, and returned, calls from her neighbors. She had spent many hours conferring with Roberts, the elderly Abbottsleigh estate agent, who surprised her with his eager inquiries about Jared.

"I'm right sorry, my lady, that Mr. Amberly didn't come down with you. I was quite looking forward to talking with him."

"Really? Why is that?"

"Why, because he seems to have such advanced ideas about farming. I believe he said that in his lands in India the margin of profit was one third of the gross produce. Now, if we could apply Mr. Amberly's methods here at Abbottsleigh, think of the increased income to the estate."

Diana frowned in perplexity. "I'm quite sure my husband doesn't own any farming land in India. His family were engaged in commercial and banking activities."

Scratching his head, Roberts said, "I allow as how I might have been mistaken, my lady. Somehow, though, the word 'zari,' or 'zandari' seems to stick in my mind. Mr. Amberly was one o' them, as I recall, and he told me they realized thirty-three percent on their farming investment."

Diana let the matter drop. Old Roberts, as she knew from her own experience, was loath to relinquish his convictions.

As if she had never been away, Diana fell into the routine she had followed since her childhood at Abbottsleigh. She rode every day, she puttered happily in the flower gardens, she conferred with the housekeeper about needed replacements of furniture or household supplies, she reread all her favorite books in the estate library. She tried not to admit that there was a missing element in her days. Or, rather, her nights.

"Are ye still wishful ter keep this in yer dressing room, my lady?"

Diana glanced away from the cheval glass to look at the bulky parcel the abigail was holding up for her examination.

"The Canalettos," Diana murmured. "I'd almost forgotten about them." Immediately she was struck by the irony of her remark. Only short months ago the forced sale of the Canaletto paintings to raise money to pay for Miles's debts had represented one of the great tragedies of her life. So much had happened since then.

"Unwrap the paintings, Rose," she told the abigail. "I'd like to see them again."

Rose propped the paintings against the wall, and Diana stood looking at them in bemused admiration. They were as luminously fresh and beautiful as on the day they had gone on sale at Christie's Auction Rooms. The day Jared had bought them. When he haughtily returned them to her she had hidden them away at Abbottsleigh so that she wouldn't have to explain their embarrassing reappearance to her father.

"They *are* lovely, aren't they, Rose?" she said dreamily. "I think we should rehang them."

"I'm surprised you didn't rehang them long ago. What stopped you?"

Spinning around, Diana gasped, "Jared! You didn't tell me you were coming."

He walked into the room, followed by a footman carrying a portmanteau. With a nod he dismissed Rose and the footman, and firmly closed the door behind them.

"I came on the spur of the moment. Kamal can carry on without me for a few days." Jared looked at his portmanteau. "I told the footman to bring my luggage to your bedchamber. Or am I to be relegated to the cavernous guest bedroom I occupied during my first visit to Abbottsleigh?"

"Not if you don't wish it," Diana said composedly.

"I emphatically don't wish it."

"However, your new valet might be inconvenienced if we don't occupy separate bedchambers."

"I didn't bring the fellow. I fancy I can manage to scrape the whiskers off my face single-handedly for a brief interval." Jared stripped off his coat and waistcoat and pulled at his cravat.

Men, Diana thought with a resigned sigh. She picked up the discarded garments and took them to the dressing room. Returning, she knelt beside the portmanteau and opened it, saying, as she began to lift out articles of clothing, "What do you wish to wear for dinner?"

"I'll decide that later. Dinner can wait."

Somewhat annoyed, Diana turned her head to look at Jared. He had already stripped off his shirt and had seated himself to pull off his boots. As she watched him he stood up and unfastened the waistband of his breeches.

"Jared," she began apprehensively, "I'm already dressed for dinner. It will be served in half an hour."

"It will be served when you and I arrive in the dining room," he said coolly, and stepped out of his drawers. "My God, Diana, I'm not hungry for food. I'm hungry for you. It's been two weeks."

Rather to Diana's surprise, Jared slipped easily into the routine of Abbottsleigh, almost as if he had been accustomed all his life to spend his summers at an English country estate. It was a complete reversal of their "honeymoon," when every day had produced several awkward, hostile moments to remind them of the forced nature of their marriage.

Jared spent hours chatting with the agent, much to the old man's gratification. He rode with Diana the length and breadth of the estate, dismounting frequently to talk to the farmers in the fields.

"The Abbottsleigh harvest looks promising," Jared remarked after one such stop at a farm. "I've heard rumors of poor harvests in other parts of the country. Perhaps it's your soil here. Seems to be a nice, friable loam."

"I didn't realize you knew so much about farming," Diana observed.

"I don't, you know. I just ask questions. In the end, farming is a business, too."

"Which reminds me," Diana said suddenly. "Where did Roberts get the impression that you were a landowner in India? He says you told him you were a—" She knit her brow. "Roberts claims you were a 'zari' or 'zandar' or some such thing, and made a profit every year of thirty-three percent."

Jared laughed. "He misunderstood. I was telling him about the *zamindars* in Bengal. The term means 'landowners,' but they're really simply tax collectors for the government. They customarily take one-third of each farmer's produce."

"So much for Roberts's dreams of untold wealth for Abbottsleigh," Diana said dryly.

On another occasion she drove Jared in a phaeton to Burford, the nearest town of any size, on an errand to purchase sundries requested by the housekeeper.

Jared didn't seem uncomfortable to be driven by a woman, unlike some gentlemen of Diana's acquaintance. "You handle the ribbons very well," he said approvingly. "Have you ever considered driving a phaeton in London?"

"Oh, no."

"Why not?"

"I don't wish to appear fast, that's why not."

"Lady Diana Amberly fast? Perish the thought! With your style and dignity and grace you can do anything you like. Other women will flock to imitate you."

Flushing, Diana said, "What flummery."

"I never say flattering things unless I mean them. No, I insist you drive a phaeton in town. I'll buy you a new one." Jared frowned. "Not a High Flyer, I think."

"Good heavens, no! I'd look a perfect guy. And I might break my neck."

"Can't have that. No, we'll buy you a proper phaeton. What color would you like?"

"Red?" Diana smiled at the thought of herself driving a brilliant red phaeton in Hyde Park.

"No. A bit overpowering, don't you think?" Jared looked at her appraisingly. "I vote for green, to match your eyes."

Once again Diana was startled by a strong sense of unreality. Never in her wildest dreams could she have imagined a lighthearted conversation like this with Jared until a few short weeks ago.

During another of their leisurely excursions they rode through the Abbottsleigh park, dismounting to stroll through the grounds of the ruined abbey. A light breeze was blowing, and the sun cast dappled patterns through the swaying branches of the trees that ringed the enclosure. Wild flowers grew profusely among the grasses—bluebells and daisies, forget-me-nots and poppies—and the intoxicating sweet scent of the dog roses permeated the air.

"You told me once that this was your favorite corner of Abbottsleigh," Jared remarked.

"Yes." Diana took a deep breath of the fragrant air. "I always feel so peaceful in this spot, as if none of my troubles could reach me here."

"You also said that no one ever comes here." In a swift, fluid motion Jared drew Diana down beside him on a blanket of yielding grass beneath a broken arch of the cloister.

"Jared! What if somebody should come?" Diana gasped when she could wrench her mouth from the pressure of his hungry lips.

"You *said* nobody ever came here," he murmured. His fingers paused in their task of unfastening the tiny buttons of her riding habit. "Don't you want me, Diana?"

"Yes . . . yes." Her heart was pounding, and she ached for the touch of Jared's knowing, sensitive hands on her bare flesh. "But we can't . . . not here . . . if someone should see us . . ."

"No one will see us."

Diana lay with her head cradled on Jared's bare shoulder, dreamily watching through half-closed eyes the shifting play of

sunlight through the foliage and listening to the rippling murmur of the little river as it ran beside the abbey ruins on its way
to join the Windrush.

"Diana," said Jared suddenly. "I can't go on like this."

Diana raised herself on an elbow, staring down at his somber
face. "What do you mean?"

"I mean I can't go on pretending that all I want from you is
your body. I want your love, and if I can't have that, I'd rather
settle for nothing."

An explosion of wild, wondering delight spread through Diana's body. "Jared . . . you love me?"

"I've loved you since the first moment I saw you in that
upper room of the Pantheon."

"But . . . I killed your love when I refused to marry you after
Papa told me about your ancestry. You told me so. Then you
retaliated by forcing me into this marriage. You married me for
revenge, not for love."

Jared's lips tightened. "That's what I wanted you to think. I
couldn't come groveling, begging for a scrap of love from a
woman who despised me, who thought she'd married beneath
her. I have some pride."

Reaching out her hand, Diana gently traced her fingers across
Jared's face. "And I have pride too, enough for both of us, far
too much of it. I almost let my pride destroy my love for the
one man in the world who could make me happy. Almost. Thank
God, I came to my senses in time."

Jared grasped Diana's hand and stared at her with a strained,
painful intensity. "Diana, my only love, do you mean it? Do
you really mean it?"

For answer, Diana bent her head to kiss him, and when he
pulled her against him so that their naked bodies fused in an
electric flame she didn't give a thought to the possibility that
Peeping Toms might come upon them.

"I'm a disgraceful sight," said Diana ruefully as she and
Jared rode away from the abbey ruins. She had tried to push
her tousled hair beneath her riding hat, but elusive strands kept

escaping. No amount of shaking and brushing with her hands had rid her riding habit of the stray wisps of grass and other vegetation that clung to it.

"You look entrancingly lovely."

"Jared, be sensible. What will the servants think when they see me returning in such a state?"

"I don't care a damn what the servants think, and you shouldn't, either. You should care only about what *I* think."

"And what's that?" inquired Diana with a sideways smile.

"That you're the most beautiful, accomplished, perfect woman in the world, and I adore you."

Diana burst out laughing, and suddenly she didn't care a fig what the servants might think of her disheveled appearance. She swept into the house from the stable entrance with only a polite nod to the footman who opened the door for her.

"My lady—"

Pausing in mid-stride, Diana said, "Yes, Freel?"

"The butler thought you would wish to know, my lady, that His Grace has arrived at Abbottsleigh. And his friend, Mr Aubrey Dalton."

"Miles is here?" Diana asked in surprise.

"Yes, my lady. His Grace arrived several hours ago."

"Thank you, Freel." As she and Jared went up the stairs to their bedchamber Diana muttered, "I wonder why Miles didn't send word that he was coming? And why has he come at all? He's always hated Abbottsleigh in high summer. He prefers to go to the shore."

Jared shrugged. "Doubtless he has his reasons. Do you want me to leave? It might be awkward for you, having us both here."

"Of course I don't want you to leave! I'd rather ask Miles to leave!"

Jared paused on the first landing of the stairs, doubled over with laughter.

"What, pray, is so amusing?"

Straightening, Jared flicked the moisture from his eyes with a forefinger. "My darling ninnyhammer, have you forgotten that Abbottsleigh belongs to your brother? You can't order him out of his own house."

"Well, you're my guest—you're my *husband*—and if Miles can't act civilly toward you, you and I will both leave."

When Diana and Jared came down to the drawing room a little later they found Aubrey alone in the room. He and Jared exchanged curt bows.

"Miles will be down shortly," Aubrey informed Diana. "Er—could I have a word with you? Privately?"

"Do you want me to go, Diana?" Jared inquired.

"No." Diana's eyes shot sparks. "Aubrey, can this matter wait?"

"I'm sorry. I really need to talk to you."

"Then we'll talk in the library. Jared, I won't be long."

Diana closed the door of the library behind them and turned to face Aubrey. "Well? What did you wish to talk to me about?"

Looking harassed, Aubrey said, "It's Miles, of course. Since Miss Lyon jilted him he's been going to pieces. Doesn't sleep, doesn't eat. Mostly he drinks, far more than is good for him. And he's taken to gambling again. He seldom leaves White's until the small hours of the morning. He usually loses. I've been at my wits' end about him, I don't mind telling you. So when he told me he was of a mind to go down to Abbottsleigh on a bit of a repairing lease, and asked me to keep him company, I jumped at the opportunity, naturally. I thought I'd take you aside and ask you to talk some sense into that brother of yours."

Frowning, Diana said, "I had no idea he was wearing the willow for Charlotte Lyon to this extent."

"Oh, he was very fond of Miss Lyon, but I don't think he's suffering from unrequited love. When she cried off from their engagement it was more a blow to Miles's pride than anything else. It *was* a blow, you know. From being the most eligible bachelor in all of England he went to being a puppet dangling from his brother-in-law's purse strings. It rankled."

"I know that. But the situation is different now. Miles is the Duke of Edgehill in his own right. He has full control of the family estate."

Aubrey shrugged. "All I know is that Miles is going straight to the devil. Talk to him, Diana."

By the time Diana and Aubrey returned to the drawing room,

Miles had also come down from his rooms. He and Jared sat in widely separated chairs, not speaking. Diana greeted Miles warmly, trying not to show her dismay at his appearance. His skin had an unhealthy pallor, and there were dark circles under his eyes. He was also much thinner.

She asked, "How long will you be staying, Miles?"

"Not long," he replied curtly. He shot a malevolent look at Jared but said nothing more.

Dinner was an uncomfortable affair. Diana tried to make conversation with Aubrey and Jared, and Aubrey made a few remarks to her, but Miles sat like a brooding specter at the head of the table, drinking glass after glass of wine and making little pretense at eating. Diana was glad to escape to the drawing room, leaving the men to their port.

She sat uncomfortably over her coffee, wondering how Jared was coping with the strained atmosphere of the dining room. Then, from across the corridor, she heard the sound of angry voices, followed by the tinkling crash of glass. She jumped up from her chair and raced to the dining room. The occupants of the room were momentarily motionless, frozen in time, as if they were actors taking part in a tableau.

Jared stood beside the table, staring down at the shards of glass and spilled wine that littered the carpet. Several wide-eyed servants huddled near the door leading to the kitchens. Aubrey and Miles were also standing. Aubrey's expression was torn between anger and disbelief. Miles's rigid face was a mask of hate.

"What in God's name is happening here?" Diana demanded. Her words seemed to break a spell, releasing the participants in the scene from their immobility.

"Your brother threw a decanter of wine at me," Jared said coolly. "He missed."

"I won't miss this time," Miles growled, launching himself at Jared with wildly flailing arms.

Nimbly sidestepping, Jared seized Miles's arms and twisted them behind his back.

"Let go of me, you damned half-caste," Miles shouted, struggling frantically to release himself. "We're going to have this out."

Darting around Jared, Diana faced her brother, saying urgently, "Miles, I won't have you disgracing this house by fighting with my husband in front of me and the servants." Out of the corner of her eye Diana noticed the little knot of interested servants hurriedly exit from the dining room.

Some of the wild light faded from Miles's eyes. He ceased struggling. "Yes, all right," he muttered after a moment. "You can let me go, Amberly. I won't try to mill you down again."

Releasing Miles's arms, Jared stepped back quickly, keeping a wary eye on his brother-in-law.

"Now then, Miles, tell me what this was all about," said Diana.

Still tense as a bowstring, Miles glared at Jared, saying bitterly, "I'll tell you what it was about. To put it simply, your husband is scheming to take control of the Edgehill estate, and I don't intend to stand by and let him do it. I'll see him dead and in hell first."

"Miles, for heaven's sake, what's put such a harebrained notion into your head?"

"You won't consider the notion so harebrained when you hear what this half-caste has done. I wrote to old Roberts a week ago, telling him to send me—well, it makes no matter how much rhino I told him to send me. It's my money, I think you'll agree. Back came a reply from Roberts, saying politely he couldn't extend me *any* amount. So down I came to Abbottsleigh to confront Roberts, and do you know what I discovered? *Your husband* had instructed *my* agent not to give me any of my own money."

Turning to Jared, Diana said in bewilderment, "Is this true? Did you really give Roberts such orders?"

Jared's face had become still, unreadable. "I did."

"But *why,* Jared? You have no right—"

"I have the right to protect my investment, Diana." Jared looked directly at Miles. "You've been gambling like a madman for weeks, Edgehill. You always lose. You owe enormous sums. Oh, you haven't gone to the moneylenders. You know they wouldn't advance you a shilling. Your losses are 'debts of honor' to your friends and fellow club members. But debts of honor must be settled at some time, and quarter day is approaching. Do I understand the situation correctly?"

"Yes, damn you! What's it to you? Now, see here. you'll countermand your instructions to Roberts, or I'll dismiss the slippery old devil, I don't care which. And in future, Amberly, you'll keep your nose out of my affairs."

"You'd better rehire Roberts," said Jared. "The poor fellow was doing his best to protect you, you know. I told him that if he advanced you any more than the normal income your father had been receiving from the estate I would call in all your notes for immediate payment. And you'd land in debtors' prison."

Miles's skin color faded to a ghastly white tinged with green. He staggered and put out his hand to the table for support.

"Miles—" Diana took an instinctive step toward him.

Aubrey was there before her, slipping his arm around Miles's shoulder. "He's drunk as a wheelbarrow, Diana," Aubrey muttered. "He doesn't know what he's doing. And if I'm not mistaken, he's about to shoot the cat. You won't want to see that. Let me take him to his rooms."

Diana waited until Aubrey had helped Miles stumble from the room. Then she turned to Jared. "Will you come up to our bedchamber, please. We need to talk."

Seventeen

As soon as the door of the bedchamber closed behind them, Diana burst out, barely able to control her anger, "Jared, how could you do such a thing? Oh, I know that you've never forgiven Miles for the arrogant way he treated you, any more than you ever really forgave Papa. But you had no right to forbid Roberts to withhold money from him."

A muscle twitched in Jared's cheek. "I admit I've no love for your brother. But I didn't do what I did for revenge, Diana. I did it for you."

"Me!"

"Yes. Think about it. You know in your heart of hearts that your brother is an addicted gambler. Left unchecked he could pilfer the estate, leaving Roberts, or any other agent, without sufficient operating income to administer it properly. Do you agree that could happen?"

"Yes, possibly. But—"

"And is that the kind of future you want for Abbottsleigh?"

"No. Certainly not. But it's not for me to say. Miles *is* the Duke of Edgehill. He can do whatever he likes with Abbottsleigh."

"Even if what he does jeopardizes the estate?"

Diana bit her lip. "He has the absolute right. Abbottsleigh belongs to him."

Throwing up his hands, Jared exclaimed, "Good God, Diana, ever since I've known you, you've made it clear that the Amberly name and heritage is the most precious thing in the world to you. Time and again you've sacrificed your personal interests for the good of the family. You've even made two loveless marriages to keep your father and your brother afloat financially. You dutifully followed your father's wishes to the point of denying your love for me. Yet now you're furious with me for attempting to prevent Miles from destroying the estate."

Diana lapsed into silence, as her thoughts drifted back to the past. "All my life I've accepted the premise that the head of the house of Amberly has the unquestioned authority to make decisions about the family and the estate," she said at last. "Legally that's so, but morally? Can I stand by, watching Miles destroy the Amberly heritage, and not lift a finger to stop him?" She stared at Jared. "What are you smiling about?"

"Because, my darling, for the first time in your life you've put logic above blind family loyalty."

Diana stiffened for a moment in instinctive resentment. Then, seeing the twinkle in Jared's eyes, she relaxed. "Must you always be right?" she inquired, only half crossly. "Seriously, Jared, what *can* we do about Miles? You meant well, telling Roberts not to advance Miles any money, but what's the practical effect? Miles has simply dismissed Roberts as his agent. He can hire another agent, or manage the estate himself, and in either case he can take as much money as he likes out of the estate. Who's to stop him?"

"I can stop him. I can make good my threat to call in his notes and put him into debtors' prison."

"Jared, no. An Amberly in prison? It doesn't bear thinking about. In any case, what good would it do? You couldn't leave him in Newgate forever, and when he came out he'd just go back to his old habits."

"He might be chastened enough by the experience to change his habits."

Diana shivered. "I don't even want to consider it." She thought for a few moments. "I'll talk to Miles tomorrow, after he's sober and has had a chance to reflect on the situation. The threat of debtors' prison may have brought him to his senses. Perhaps I can persuade him to stop gambling. If so, a one-time levy on the estate would clear his immediate debts . . ." She faltered as she observed Jared's expression. "You don't believe in a word I'm saying, do you?"

"I think your brother has a very serious problem," Jared said gently. "But by all means talk to him. If anyone can reach him, you can."

"Oh, Jared."

He drew her into his arms, holding her closely, comforting her without words.

"A message for you, Mr. Amberly," said the abigail, Rose, the next morning when she brought the tea tray.

"That's Miles's handwriting," said Diana apprehensively.

Jared read the note quickly and passed it to Diana.

"Amberly," it began curtly. "We must talk. This situation has gotten out of hand. Meet me at ten o'clock at the old abbey. Diana will tell you where it is. We'll be undisturbed there. Edgehill."

Diana's eyes glowed. "Jared, this is wonderful! It's what I thought might happen. The very threat of debtors' prison has forced Miles to see reason. He realizes that you have the upper hand and he knows he must compromise."

"I hope you're right." Jared sounded dubious.

"I know I'm right. Jared, you'll—you'll go easily with Miles, won't you? He can be very prickly at times."

"For your sake, I'll turn the other cheek," Jared promised.

After Jared had left to go to the stables en route to his meeting with Miles, Diana felt too restless to write letters or to attend to household tasks. She went to the gardens, where she could hold her thoughts at bay by snipping off wilting flower heads and picking bouquets for the drawing room. Aubrey joined her there, inquiring idly, "Have you seen old Miles?"

"No, not since dinner last night."

"Wonder where he can be? He's not in his rooms, and one of the footman told me he had breakfast quite early. I thought I'd challenge him to a game of billiards, don't you know? Get his mind off his troubles, so to speak."

"I haven't seen him."

Aubrey's glance grew sharper as he studied Diana's face. "You're hiding something, aren't you? And you're worried."

"Oh, don't talk fustian, Aubrey." Diana hesitated. "I'm a trifle concerned, perhaps. Miles sent a message to Jared this morning, arranging a meeting at the abbey ruins. I can't wait to learn whether they've composed their differences. It isn't pleasant, having your husband and your brother at odds."

"No, I daresay it isn't. I only hope—" Aubrey broke off.

"You hope what?" said Diana quickly.

"Well . . . oh, hang it, Diana, it's just that I don't trust Miles's temper. It's hair trigger at best, as you very well know. And he was so angry last night. Not that I blame him. That husband of yours had no right to interfere in his affairs. You say Miles and Amberly are meeting this morning to compose their differences? A nigh impossible task under the best of conditions, if you ask me. After what happened between them last night at dinner, I'm afraid Miles will explode with rage again. Oh, well, at least he's probably sober this morning. If it comes to a fight with Amberly he'll give a better account of himself with his fives than he did last night."

A feeling of apprehension that had been lurking at the back of Diana's mind came to the fore. "I won't have the pair of them fighting again," she exclaimed, starting to walk to the stables. "I'm going after them."

"Now, wait, Diana," said Aubrey, coming along behind her. "Miles—and your husband, too, I expect—won't take kindly to a female interrupting their quarrel. If there is a quarrel, that is."

"Men!" sniffed Diana. "They'd be a great deal better off if they allowed females to manage their affairs. You come with me, Aubrey. I may need help if Miles and Jared are actually engaged in a mill."

"Oh, I say, I'm not sure if I should—"

"I'm sure. Come along, Aubrey."

At the stables the grooms quickly saddled their horses and Diana and Aubrey were off on the short ride to the abbey ruins. Diana didn't give a thought to the odd picture she must present, dressed as she was, not in a riding habit, but in a morning gown with a saucy little black lace cap perched on her head.

Two horses were tethered to trees outside the abbey enclosure. One was Miles's favorite mount. The other was a bay gelding, not the horse Jared usually rode.

As she and Aubrey started off down the winding path leading to the cloisters Diana began to feel easier in her mind. There was no sound of angry voices or scuffling bodies. There was, in fact, no sound at all except for the singing of birds and the sighing whisper of the wind through the trees.

The silence continued until Diana and Aubrey entered the cloister and paused at the sight of Jared bending over Miles's still body.

"Jared!" Diana screamed. "What's happened to Miles?"

His movements stiff and jerky as a puppet's, Jared slowly turned to face her. His face was blank, his blue eyes dulled.

"Miles is dead, Diana."

"Dead! No. No." Diana threw herself on her knees beside her brother's body. Miles lay on his back in the grass. His unseeing eyes stared skyward in his slack-jawed face, and his white waistcoat was sodden with blood.

"Diana, come away." Aubrey's strong arms lifted her up. Still supporting her, Aubrey turned to Jared. "What happened?"

"I don't know." Jared's voice sounded curiously lifeless. "I just arrived here. Miles had asked me to meet him. I was late—my horse stumbled in a rabbit hole and went lame, so I had to walk it back to the stables and get another mount. I was afraid Miles might have grown tired of waiting for me, but then I saw his horse, and I knew he must still be here. However, he was nowhere in sight when I entered the abbey grounds. Then I walked into the clearing inside the cloister, and there he was. I don't think he's been dead for very long."

"But—my God, man! Who killed him?"

Jared shook his head. "I don't know. There was no one else in the clearing when I got here. The only thing I could think of was that a poacher may have shot Miles accidentally. Then, when the poacher realized what he'd done, he panicked and ran away, hoping no one would ever connect him with the crime."

"Well . . . I suppose a poacher might have done the shooting . . ."

"What difference does it make who shot Miles?" Diana cried "He's dead, it doesn't matter how he died." The tears began pouring down her cheeks. Jared's face lost its blank, shocked expression, and he gathered Diana into his arms, holding her close while the heavy sobs racked her body.

"See here, Amberly, I'll ride to Abbottsleigh and bring back a cart," said Aubrey. "We can't leave Miles's body here a moment longer than necessary."

"Yes, do that Dalton. I'll come with Diana as soon as she' recovered a little."

For the first few hours after the discovery of Miles's body Diana was in a daze. Images of Miles's dead face kept flashing into her mind, interspersed with fleeting memories of him at various ages. As a boy, the teasing older brother who rescued her from pranks during the long summers at Abbottsleigh. A a rakish young man about town whose faults were all too easy to forgive.

"My lady, ye're shivering with the cold. Ye'd best go ter bed."

Diana clutched a shawl more closely around her as she sat huddled in a chair in her bedchamber. "I'm not really cold Rose. I'm suffering from shock. I can't go to bed. I have too many things to attend to. My brother . . ."

"But surely, my lady, ye can rest easy. Mr. Amberly will take charge of the—the arrangements."

Of course, thought Diana with a soaring sense of relief. For the first time in her adult life there was no need for her to assume either full or partial responsibility for the latest catastrophe in the Amberly family.

When he brought her back to Abbottsleigh from the deadly glade at the abbey ruins Jared had told her, "There are many things that must be done to prepare for the funeral, Diana. Do you want me to start making the arrangements?"

"Oh, yes, Jared. Thank you."

"Just tell me what you want me to do."

Diana had tried to pull her chaotic thoughts together. "Let me see. . . . Miles should lie in state in the village church for a full day, as Papa did. That will give all our tenants and our neighbors the opportunity to see him. Send notices to the London newspapers so that our friends in the rest of the country will be informed about Miles's death. And I think you should send personal letters to the closest of our relatives. There aren't many."

Jared gave her a quick hug. "I'll begin immediately. Don't worry your head about it. Try to get some rest."

By late afternoon, after several pots of strong tea and a glass of brandy that Rose had insisted she drink, Diana had begun to recover her equilibrium. When the agent, Roberts, sent up a message that he wished to see her, she dressed and went down to the morning room. The macabre thought passed through her mind as she descended the stairs that she would not have to buy a new wardrobe because of Miles's death. She was still in mourning for her father.

The agent rose as she entered the morning room. "Thank you for seeing me, my lady," said the old man. "I had to come and tell you of my sorrow on hearing of the duke's death."

"Thank you, Roberts. We've all suffered a great loss."

"But you see, my lady, I feel more than loss. I feel guilt. The last time I saw the duke, we quarreled bitterly, so much so that he dismissed me."

"You shouldn't feel guilty. You did what you thought was your duty."

"I did, yes. Still, I wish we had parted more amicably. But who could have thought that His Grace would die so soon? I still can't believe he was *murdered*. They're saying he was probably killed by a stray shot from a poacher." Roberts was silent for a few moments, his old face worn and anxious. Finally he shook himself out of his thoughts, saying, "Mr. Amberly has asked me to resume my duties as agent." There was a hint of question in his voice.

"Yes, I agree."

"I quite understand the appointment will probably be very temporary. The new duke will wish to employ his own agent."

"The new duke?"

"Why, yes, Mr. George Amberly that was. I hope he'll be

able to arrive in time for the funeral. However, it's a very long journey indeed from Northumberland."

"But—" Diana's mind was racing. Why hadn't the truth dawned on her before now? "George Amberly isn't the new duke, Roberts. My husband is now the Duke of Edgehill."

The old man's eyes fairly bulged with astonishment. "I don't understand, my lady," he stammered. "I knew Mr. Amberly was distantly related to the family, of course, but since my arrival at Abbottsleigh it has been accepted that Mr. George Amberly was the next heir in succession after your father and your brother."

"I believed that to be the case, too, until recently. Then I discovered that Jared—my husband—is descended from the fifth son of the fourth duke, and thus is closer in succession to my brother than George Amberly. The family never considered that this newfound relationship was very important, and certainly never publicized it. Naturally, we expected my brother to marry and have offspring."

The agent shook his head. "Begging your pardon, my lady—I mean Your Grace—the news will come as a great shock to a good many people, I daresay."

Diana frowned. "Yes. Should anyone, including George Amberly, question my husband's status, Jared has all the documentation necessary to prove his claim to the Edgehill title to the Crown Office of the House of Lords."

"I trust such proof won't be required. May I say, Your Grace, how happy I am that you and His Grace will be the new occupants of Abbottsleigh? The estate will be in good hands."

As Roberts took his leave, still appearing rather stunned by the new development, Diana knew that the agent would swiftly pass the word that Abbottsleigh had a new and unexpected master.

Jared joined her in her bedchamber a little later, followed by several footmen carrying trays. "I thought you might prefer to have dinner up here tonight." He grimaced. "The Lord knows I'd as lief not dine with Aubrey Dalton."

Diana gave him a grateful look. "I'd much prefer to dine alone with you."

He drew up a small table and set out the dishes, scolding

Diana when she took only token amounts of food. "You must eat, Diana. The next several days will be very difficult for you. You'll need your strength."

"I know. I'll try." She put a tasteless piece of meat in her mouth and chewed away at it. Swallowing hard, she said, "Jared, I think I could bear Miles's death more easily if it weren't so senseless. Who would ever have thought he'd be cut down in the prime of life by a stray poacher's bullet?" Diana shuddered. "I hate to think he may have died, even by accident, at the hands of someone on the estate, someone I know, a person I may actually have talked to within the past few days . . ."

Reaching across the table to press her hand, Jared said gently, "Don't you think it's better not to know who fired the shot? Would it comfort you to learn definitely that one of your own tenants killed your brother? Try not to think about it. And eat your dinner."

While Diana obediently put another forkful of food into her mouth, Jared helped himself to a piece of ham and some asparagus. Between bites, he said, "I've made all the arrangements with the vicar. Miles will lie in state on Thursday, and the funeral will be on Friday. And I've sent the notices to the newspaper and notified the relatives. The condolence calls by the local gentry have already begun, by the way."

Putting down her fork, Diana said, trying to smile, "Thank you, Jared. I don't think I could have gotten through this dreadful day without you."

Jared returned her smile. "Yes, you could. You're the strongest woman I know. I'm only glad I was here to help." He put a glass of wine to his lips, then set it down. "It's the oddest thing," he said thoughtfully. "Suddenly the servants have taken to calling me 'Your Grace.' "

"Roberts has spread the word. I knew he would."

"Yes, but Diana—"

She smiled at the oddly ambivalent look on his normally confident face. "You *are* the Duke of Edgehill."

"I know. That is, I know it in one part of my mind, but I can't seem to accept it as true in the rest of my mind." He stared bleakly at Diana. "Look at me. Can you imagine me taking your father's place? Now, there was a man who really knew how to be a duke."

Diana burst out laughing. Some of the accumulated burden of the long difficult day seemed to lift from her shoulders. "That's what your oldest son is going to say about you: 'Papa really knew how to be a duke.' "

For a moment Jared looked utterly dumfounded. Then he threw back his head and laughed until he choked.

For Diana the lightening of the strain and tension lasted for only a brief time. Later that night the mourning tears inevitably returned. Cradling Diana in his arms, Jared waited patiently while she worked through her grief.

Jared strode into the bedchamber, where Diana was pulling down over her face the mourning veil attached to her black bonnet. "It's time to start for the church," he said. "Are you really sure you want to go with me?"

"Yes. I think I *must* go. I didn't attend Papa's funeral, and I always felt that I'd failed him in some way, not accompanying him to the grave."

"But this English custom you've told me about, that females don't attend funerals . . ."

Diana set her chin. "It's a foolish custom. It implies that women are too weak to bear the strain of seeing their loved ones buried. These same women probably nursed the deceased in their last agonies, while the men of the household stayed away from the sickroom! I have no patience with such idiocy."

A smile curved Jared's mouth. He pressed Diana's hand to his lips. "I find some new reason to love you every day. Come along, then."

In the carriage as they drove to the village Diana said, "I thought of something this morning, Jared. Tell me if I'm being utterly unfeeling. If Miles had lived, he would have faced an uncertain future. I understand at last that he probably couldn't have stopped gambling. He would have gone on, sinking deeper into debt, growing more bitterly unhappy. Now he's at peace."

"You're not being unfeeling, Diana. I agree with you. I've always been convinced that Miles couldn't conquer his gambling habit. He was a true addict."

"And now he doesn't have to struggle anymore," Diana murmured. "It helps, a little."

The village church was packed with mourners. Many of the more humble folk had been unable to find places in the church, and stood in silent groups outside. As she walked down the aisle with Jared to the front pew Diana could feel, rather than hear, the astonishment of the congregation at her presence.

She sat through the short service in the church, holding tight to Jared's hand as she fought to keep her composure. She walked to the open grave in the churchyard, where, after the vicar had read the final prayers, she was the first to scatter ashes on the coffin. Slowly, clinging to Jared's arm, she left the churchyard, feeling some measure of comfort in knowing that she had followed Miles to his last rest.

As she and Jared reached the gates of the churchyard, a burly, middle-aged man accosted them. After bowing deeply to Diana, he addressed Jared. "Your Grace, I'm John Danforth, the coroner of this county. I regret intruding on you and the duchess at this sad time. However, as you may know, I am obliged to investigate every case of violent or suspicious death that occurs in my jurisdiction. Accordingly, I am now formally requesting that you and the duchess attend an inquest I have scheduled for tomorrow in the church hall of the village of Westbridge at nine in the morning."

"Yes, of course," said Jared after a brief pause. "My wife and I will be there." As the coroner, after a second deep bow, moved away, Jared murmured to Diana, "I'm sorry, darling. I'd completely forgotten that a coroner's inquest was necessary in cases of violent death."

Diana braced her shoulders. "The inquest won't last long. It will be just a formality, in any case. And then, as soon as it's over, I'd like to go back to London. If we stayed on at Abbottsleigh I'd be seeing Miles's ghost around every corner."

* * *

The inquest took place the next morning in the church hall, where normally the most important event of the year was the annual parish harvest festival. A table had been set up at one end of the room, with chairs beside it for the members of the jury. Spectators filled the chairs in the body of the hall.

The inquest began prosaically enough. Jared was the first witness called. He testified that he had come upon the body of Miles Philip Amberly, Earl of Brentford and Duke of Edgehill, in the ruins of the ancient abbey situated in the park of Abbottsleigh. The duke had died of a gunshot wound to the chest.

The coroner inquired, "How was it that you went to the abbey ruins that morning, Your Grace?"

"I had agreed to meet my brother-in-law there on a matter of—of family business."

"I see. No one else was present when you discovered the duke's body?"

"I saw no one. I presumed—and still believe—that the duke was accidentally shot by a poacher, who then escaped."

"Very well. Thank you, Your Grace. You are excused."

The coroner next called Diana, who related briefly how she and Aubrey had found Jared with Miles's body.

"Would it be correct, Your Grace, to say that you and Mr. Dalton followed your husband to his appointment with your brother?"

"Why—yes."

"May I ask why you did so?"

Diana hesitated, feeling suddenly uncomfortable. "I—I was concerned that my husband and my brother might have a disagreement."

"Ah. And what gave you the impression that such might be the case?"

Diana cleared her throat. "That, Mr. Danforth, is surely a very personal question?"

"Very possibly, Your Grace. A question, however, that requires an answer. I will remind you that you are under oath. I must also tell you that under the law you are not required to testify to anything that might be detrimental to your husband."

A cold chill ran down Diana's spine. "Detrimental? What do you mean?"

"I think my remark was sufficiently clear, Your Grace."

Casting a quick look at Jared, whose dark face remained inscrutable, Diana said crisply, "For your information, Mr. Danforth, I know of *nothing* that might be detrimental to my husband. To answer your question, he and my brother had quarreled the night before. I went to the abbey ruins in the hope of preventing another possible quarrel."

"Thank you, Your Grace. I have no further questions."

Returning to her seat, Diana said under her breath to Jared, "What on earth is going on?"

He shook his head slightly. "Listen."

The coroner next called Aubrey. "You accompanied the Duchess of Edgehill to the old abbey, where you found the present duke standing over the body of his predecessor?"

"Yes."

"And why did you do that?"

"The duchess asked me to do so. She told me she was afraid her husband and her brother might renew their quarrel of the night before. I had the same concern. There has been bad blood between the two men for many years."

"Will you explain your last statement?"

"Certainly. I was a fellow student at Eton with Miles—the last duke, who was then Earl of Brentford—and the present duke, who I knew as Jared Amberly. I knew them both very well. Jared Amberly was deeply envious of Lord Brentford, and bitterly resented the fact that he was not invited into the social circle of the Duke of Edgehill. More than once he came to blows with Lord Brentford. After he finished his schooling Jared Amberly returned to India for some years. He returned to England recently and promptly began what I can only call a vendetta against Lord Brentford, so much so that Miles challenged Amberly to a duel."

A collective gasp rose from the audience assembled in the hall.

"And what was the outcome of that duel, Mr. Dalton?"

"Lord Brentford was wounded slightly."

"Now, coming to the present. Do you have any knowledge

of a quarrel that took place between the late duke and the then Mr. Amberly on the night before the duke's death?"

"I do. I was present. Jared Amberly had been maliciously interfering again in the duke's affairs, and Miles came down to Abbottsleigh to have the matter out. He and Amberly had a violent quarrel. They actually came to fisticuffs. So the next morning when Diana—the duchess, that is—told me that her husband was meeting with the duke at the old abbey I was naturally concerned. Like her, I feared there might be another quarrel."

"And was there a quarrel, to your knowledge?"

"I have no idea. All I do know is that the duchess and I came upon her husband in the abbey clearing, standing over the body of the late duke."

Pausing for a dramatic moment, the coroner said softly, "Mr. Dalton, do you believe the late duke was killed by a poacher's bullet?"

"I do not."

The silence in the hall was so complete that the slightest sound, such as a hastily suppressed cough, seemed to reverberate.

"What, then, Mr. Dalton, do you believe really happened in that deserted glade in the abbey ruins?"

"I believe that the present Duke of Edgehill—or so he calls himself; *I* have never seen any proof of his claim, nor has anyone else, to knowledge—I believe that the man who now calls himself the Duke of Edgehill shot and killed my dear friend Miles. I'm convinced that Jared Amberly has been scheming for years to acquire control of the Abbottsleigh estate and the title that accompanies it."

Diana gasped and started to leap from her chair. Jared's iron grasp held her down.

The coroner went on, "That is a very serious accusation, Mr. Dalton. Do you have any proof to support your allegation?"

"I don't, no," Aubrey replied coolly. "However, I believe *you* possess that proof, Mr. Danforth, as a result of a call I paid two days ago on the justice of the peace."

"Please explain, sir."

"I pointed out to Squire Bringhurst, the justice of the peace, that it was highly unlikely that a poacher had killed the duke.

Poachers normally don't operate in the daylight hours. Also, I had seen the duke's body while he was being laid out for burial, and I was of the opinion that the wound was smaller than one would expect to find inflicted by a twenty-bore musket. I also pointed out to the justice that Jared Amberly had ample motive and opportunity to kill the duke, and had indeed been discovered alone with the body. Finally, I suggested to the justice that I had reason to believe Jared Amberly customarily carried a pistol, and that it might be profitable to search his belongings for such a weapon."

"Thank you, Mr. Dalton. You are excused. I next call Constable Henry Mason."

The village constable was a gangly, stolid-faced individual who carefully avoided looking at Jared as he settled into the witness chair.

The coroner asked, "Henry Mason, were you recently ordered by the justice of the peace to make a search of the Duke of Edgehill's apartments at the estate known as Abbottsleigh?"

"Yes, sir."

"And what, if anything, did you find?"

"I found a pistol in the pocket o' one o' the duke's coats. It had been fired, an' not long before, neither. Ye could smell the burned gunpowder. It weren't cleaned."

A ripple of sound swept through the hall, quelled instantly by a stern glance from the coroner.

"And where, Constable, is this pistol at the present time?"

"I believe ye has it, sir. The justice, he told me as I was ter give it ter ye."

The coroner turned to a table behind him and picked up an object wrapped in a cloth. Removing the cloth, he showed the object to the constable. "Is this the pistol you found in the duke's coat pocket?"

"Yes, sir." The constable pointed to the tag that was tied to the handle of the pistol. "Them's my initials, right and tight."

"Thank you, Constable. That will be all."

The coroner approached the members of the jury, talking to them in a low tone. The jurors said very little, in most cases simply nodding in answer to a point that the coroner was making. After a few minutes of the one-sided conversation the coroner left the jury to give a brief order to the constable.

Picking up his staff of office, the constable walked over to Jared, pausing in front of him. "Will ye please ter rise, Yer Grace?"

His face a grim mask, Jared slowly stood erect.

The constable said in a shrill voice, "Jared Richard Amberly, Earl of Brentford, Duke of Edgehill, I arrest you in the King's name for the murder of Miles Philip Amberly, Earl of Brentford, Duke of Edgehill, on the twenty-sixth of August, in the year of our Lord eighteen hundred and eleven, on the premises of the estate known as Abbottsleigh."

Following close behind the constable, the coroner said stiffly, "Your Grace, as a peer of the realm you can be tried only by a jury of your peers in the House of Lords. I am therefore sending you immediately under armed guard of the local militia to London to await your trial."

Diana jumped to her feet, saying desperately, "No—no. You can't do this. . . ."

Turning to her, Jared grasped her hands in a hard grip. "Steady," he murmured. "Don't make a scene. It will be all right, I promise you." His eyes expressed the love he wouldn't allow himself to declare in public. "Be my brave girl."

Diana stood in frozen horror, watching the constable lead Jared away.

Aubrey came up to her. "Diana, I must talk to you."

Recoiling, her voice throbbing with hurt and anger, she exclaimed, "I never want to speak you as long as I live." She turned her back on him and walked rapidly out of the hall to her waiting carriage.

Eighteen

Diana rushed into her bedchamber at Abbottsleigh, calling for her abigail. Rose appeared in the door of the dressing room.

"Is something wrong, Yer Grace?"

"Yes, horribly wrong. Rose, I'm returning to London immediately."

"But . . . I thought ye'd planned ter go back ter London ter-morrow. I'm not finished wi' yer packing yet."

"Hang the packing. The servants can send on anything you don't have time to pack. I've ordered the traveling carriage. We leave in ten minutes."

Trailed by her puzzled abigail and several footmen laden with luggage, Diana came down the staircase just under ten minutes later. Her butler and the housekeeper waited for her in the foyer. Glancing at their wooden faces, Diana realized that they had already learned, by some mysterious grapevine, the verdict of the inquest.

"Carry on as usual," she told them. "You can apply to Mr. Roberts for advice about any problems, or you can write to me in Chesterfield Street."

Nodding, she walked out of the foyer into the quadrangle separating the main house from the old gatehouse. Aubrey came hurrying to meet her from the gatehouse. "I must speak to you, Diana."

"I've already told you I have nothing to say to you. And I want you to leave Abbottsleigh at once. You're no longer welcome as a guest here."

Putting his hand on her arm he said under his breath, "I know you won't wish to make a scene in front of the servants."

She stared at him distastefully. "Very well. Come to the morning room. I'll give you five—no, three—minutes."

In the morning room Diana shut the door and remained standing. "Well, Aubrey? Are you proud of playing the Judas? Where will you collect your thirty pieces of silver?"

Aubrey said hotly, "Damnation, you can't think I enjoyed what I did. I had to do it. Jared Amberly killed Miles, and I had to bring the killer to justice."

Her voice trembling, Diana said, "Stop. Don't say another word. My husband is not a killer."

"Will you just listen to the facts, Diana? Everyone admits that the theory that a poacher shot Miles won't hold water. Then who could have committed the crime? Some secret enemy who traveled down from London? You know as well as I do that Miles had no enemies. Except one. Jared Amberly has hated Miles from the first moment they met at Eton."

Aubrey's voice rose in intensity. "Think. Since he came back to England your husband has been making a systematic effort to take over the Amberly estates. Oh, he temporarily desisted from his plan to force your father to bar the entail when you agreed to marry him, but he's never wavered from his original purpose. Since your marriage he's cast the financial net tighter and tighter around Miles, with the ultimate aim of forcing him to liquidate Abbottsleigh in order to pay his debts. Only the night before Miles's murder Amberly threatened again to call in his notes and throw Miles into debtors' prison."

Aubrey spread his hands. "Can't you see the pattern, Diana? Amberly's been eaten up with anger and jealousy against your family for all of his adult life. He knew his ultimate revenge would be to take control of the Amberly estates. Then, a few days ago, when he saw an opportunity to kill Miles and have the murder blamed on some person unknown, he took that opportunity in order to gain possession, not only of the Amberly estates, but the title of Duke of Edgehill as well."

Between stiff lips Diana said, "Are you quite finished, Aubrey?"

"Yes, but . . ."

"Then I'll say goodbye. I'm returning to London immediately. And I meant what I said: you are no longer welcome as a guest at Abbottsleigh."

The carriage stopped in front of the monumental stone facade of Newgate Prison on the east side of Old Bailey Street. A footman opened the door of the carriage and let down the steps. The tall, distinguished silver-haired man sitting next to Diana in the carriage climbed down the steps and turned to extend his hand to her.

Diana paused to look at the forbidding structure, with its two gaunt windowless wings separated by a three-story building with many windows and entrance lodges to left and right.

"Do you feel up to going inside, Duchess?" inquired Diana's companion gently. "Perhaps you would prefer to wait in the carriage while I see your husband."

"Thank you, Mr. Bannerman. I think I should go with you, to introduce you to my husband, and also to see if he has any commissions for me."

"Very well. Come with me, then."

The gentleman walked with Diana to the lefthand lodge, where a clerk looked at them inquiringly at their entrance.

"My name is Bannerman, and this is the Duchess of Edgehill," said the silver-haired man in a voice of clear authority. "We've come to see the Duke of Edgehill, who I believed is lodged in the Keeper's House, rather than in the prison proper."

"Oh, yes, indeed, sir, His Grace has the finest room in the house." The clerk rang a bell. Soon a turnkey appeared. "Take the lady and the gentleman to the Duke of Edgehill's quarters," the clerk ordered.

"The room had jolly well ought to be the finest in the house," muttered Bannerman, as he and Diana followed the turnkey. "They're charging the duke thirty guineas a week for his accommodations. Not that the Keeper's House isn't a vast improvement over the rest of the prison, including the State Side," he added hastily. "As I understand it, the duke is allowed to have his valet with him, and to order meals brought in from the outside."

The turnkey knocked on a door and opened it, standing aside to allow Diana and Bannerman to enter a large room, clean and well-furnished, with a comfortable bed, chairs, a wardrobe, and a desk. The room was nothing like any prison cell that Diana might have imagined. His face brightening, Jared rose from a chair by the window. "Diana! You came straight to London."

"Yes, I arrived last evening. Jared, this is Serjeant-at-Law Wilfred Bannerman. The Edgehill solicitors recommended Mr. Bannerman to represent you at your trial."

The serjeant bowed. "Your servant, Duke."

"How do you do, Mr. Bannerman." Jared smiled crookedly. "I daresay you don't often represent peers indicted on a capital charge."

"No, indeed, Duke. You will be my first such client. May we sit down and review the salient facts of the case as they have developed to date? The duchess has, of course, spoken to me. I should like to discuss your impressions."

At the end of half an hour, the serjeant leaned back in his chair, pressing his fingertips together. "I may take it, then, Duke, that the principal evidence against you will be Mr. Aubrey Dalton's testimony that you and the late duke had an enmity of many years standing, the fact that you were discovered with the dead body, and the discovery of a discharged pistol among your belongings."

Jared nodded.

"And one further development, Duke. The Edgehill solicitors have informed me that they have received a letter from a certain George Amberly, challenging your right to succeed the late duke. Do you have documentation to prove your claim to be Duke of Edgehill? Birth certificates, marriage lines, that sort of thing? Because, if you cannot produce such documentation, you would no longer be a peer, and your case would be tried in King's Bench rather than in the House of Lords."

"Yes, I have the documentation." Jared spoke to Diana. "Kamal has all my family papers locked in a safe in my offices.

Ask him to make the documents available to Serjeant Bannerman."

Bannerman rose, saying, "That is all the information I require at the moment, Duke. I will, of course, be conferring with you in the near future."

"Thank you for coming, Mr. Bannerman. If you'll excuse us, I'd like to have a private word with my wife."

"Certainly." Bannerman bowed. "I will wait for you in the corridor outside, Duchess."

As soon as the door closed behind the serjeant, Jared took an eager step toward Diana, his arms outstretched. "Darling, I've missed you so much in just two days—" He broke off, staring at Diana as she evaded his embrace. "What is it?" he said slowly.

She looked away, shaking her head. There was a hard lump in her throat, preventing her from speaking.

"Diana, surely you don't—you *can't*—think I had a hand in your brother's death?"

She looked at him then, her eyes wet with unshed tears. "Jared, I don't know what to think," she faltered. "You hated Miles. You've never made any secret of it. So you had the motive, and you certainly had the opportunity. There's no other suspect. And the constable did find that pistol in your coat, recently fired. Was it your gun?"

"Yes. However, I didn't fire it. If I had, I assure you I would never have dropped it into my coat pocket, uncleaned."

Diana continued to look at Jared in silent, helpless misery. Finally, swallowing hard, she said, "I'm sorry I can't help how I feel. . . . Publicly I'll support you in every way I can. I know how important it is that you receive a fair, impartial trial, so I promise I won't breathe a word of my—my doubts to anyone. And I understand that as your wife I can't be forced to testify against you."

"Testify to what?" exclaimed Jared savagely. "Testify to what isn't true, that I killed your brother?" He turned away from her, saying over his shoulder, "Please go, Diana. You've made your position perfectly clear."

"Jared—"

"Just go, Diana."

Blinking back her tears, Diana joined Mr. Bannerman in th corridor. Tactfully forbearing to ask any questions, the Serjeant at-Law offered her his arm and escorted her down the stairs t the Keeper's office.

Diana managed to preserve her composure until the carriag arrived in Chesterfield Street and she reached the safety of he bedchamber. There she tore off her bonnet and collapsed on th bed in a flood of tears.

The interview with Jared had torn her heart in two. She ache to believe in his innocence. In fact, she had never doubted for an instant until Aubrey had forced her to listen to the cas against him. During the long drive from Abbottsleigh yesterday Aubrey's accusations had done their deadly work. Repeatedly as the hours and the miles had slipped by on her way to Londor she had gone over in her mind the damning litany of facts.

Jared *had* hated the entire Amberly family. He *had* scheme to revenge himself by taking possession of the Amberly estates And, though he had at least implicitly promised, if Diana agree to marry him, that he would not make any further effort t obtain control of Abbottsleigh, provided the interest on hi promissory notes was paid, he had again threatened Miles wit debtors' prison on the evening before her brother's death. Sh had found Jared standing over Miles's body. Who else coul have killed her brother? And however hard she tried to maintai her belief in Jared's innocence, she always came back to tha recently discharged pistol, which Jared had admitted to be his Why had he fired the weapon, if not to pump a bullet int Miles's body?

"Yer Grace, what's amiss? Do ye have bad news o' the duke?"

Diana sat up on the bed, brushing away her tears with th back of her hand. "No, Rose. The news is no worse than it was I'm feeling a trifle blue-deviled, that's all."

"And no wonder, Yer Grace." Rose hesitated. "That Ran and her husband are downstairs, wishing ter see ye. Shall I sen them away?"

"Yes—no. Take them to the morning room and tell them I'll be down shortly."

As she rinsed her tear-stained face and tidied her hair, Diana rebelled against the thought of talking to Rana and Kamal, though her sense of fair play would not allow her, in this crisis, to ignore the two people who loved Jared the most.

When she walked into the morning room, Rana and Kamal jumped to their feet, staring at her anxiously. Rana was the first to speak. "Is it true, my lady, what we read in the newspapers?" she faltered. "The sahib has been arrested for your brother's murder?"

"I fear he has, Rana."

Rana shrank back, as if she had received a physical blow.

Kamal said quietly, "My lady—excuse me, it's 'Your Grace' now, isn't it? Your Grace, could you tell us a little about what happened? The newspapers gave few details."

Diana quickly summarized the facts about the discovery of Miles's body and the verdict of the inquest.

Kamal listened in silence. When Diana finished he remarked, "The case against Mr. Amb—the case against the duke seems flimsy to me."

"The prosecutors for the Crown apparently don't agree with you," Diana blurted.

His tone sharpening, Kamal said, "And you? Your Grace, surely you don't have any doubts about Mr. Amberly's innocence?"

"Of course my lady has no doubts," exclaimed Rana. "How could she? The sahib could never do such a monstrous thing."

"Hush, Rana." Kamal stared accusingly at Diana. "You do have doubts."

"Oh, stop, Kamal," Diana cried in anguish. "Don't you think I want to believe in Jared? Can't you see it's tearing me apart?"

Kamal said urgently, "Listen to me, Your Grace. Mr. Amberly did dislike your brother, but he could never have killed him in cold blood. That's not in Mr. Amberly's character. Now, I admit that if, during a quarrel, the former duke had drawn a weapon on him, Mr. Amberly might well have fired back to defend himself. His natural reaction would then have been to inform the authorities of the incident. Probably there would have been no prosecution, because the physical evidence would have revealed that there were two pistols at the scene, both of them fired. You'll note, however, that no second pistol was discovered."

Diana stared at Kamal with a dawning hope.

"To any reasonable mind," Kamal continued, "the case against Mr. Amberly has to appear suspicious. Motive? If he had really wanted to kill your brother, remember, he could have done so during their earlier duel. Instead, Mr. Amberly chose to delope, to fire at your brother's feet. The pistol that was found in his pocket? Mr. Amberly is a very intelligent man. If he had killed your brother, he would have gotten rid of the pistol. At the very least he would have cleaned it! Do you know what I think? Some other person killed your brother and tried to make Mr. Amberly the scapegoat by planting that pistol in his pocket."

"But who . . . ?"

Her dark eyes blazing, Rana cried, "It doesn't matter who! The sahib is no murderer. He is the most honorable man I have ever met. Kill your brother? He would have given his own life to defend your brother from harm, in order to save you from unhappiness. Don't you realize yet that your husband adores you, that he would rather die himself than cause you pain?"

"Hush, Rana," Kamal said again.

But Diana wasn't listening. She was suddenly consumed with shame. Kamal's cool arguments and Rana's impassioned plea had brought her to her senses. No matter how overwhelming the evidence against Jared, her love and loyalty should have been strong enough to make her incapable of doubting his innocence even for a moment. An enormous weight lifted from her heart.

Kamal noticed the change in her expression. "Everything is all right now?"

"Yes." Diana smiled at him mistily. Then, her tone abruptly changing, she snapped, "No, of course everything isn't all right. Jared is in Newgate, facing trial on a capital charge."

"He has legal counsel?"

"According to my solicitors, he has the best counsel in London. A Serjeant-at-Law Bannerman."

"And what does this Bannerman think of the case?"

Shaking her head, Diana said, "I don't know. He's only had the commission for a few hours."

"We must do everything in our power to assist this Bannerman." Kamal thought deeply for a few moments. "Your Grace, do you have a small likeness of your late brother?"

"I have a miniature painted on Miles's twenty-first birthday. Why do you ask?"

Kamal shrugged. "I have an idea. . . . Will you loan me the miniature for a few days?"

"Certainly. Kamal, do you think you can help Jared?"

"I don't know. I told you, I have an idea. Let me look into it."

After Kamal and Rana had left, Diana ordered a carriage. Five minutes later she was on her way with her abigail to Newgate. The clerk in the Keeper's lodge was obviously surprised to see her again so soon, but made no objection to her visit.

The turnkey led her and Rose up the stairs, opened the door of Jared's room and stood aside for them to enter.

"Wait in the corridor, Rose," Diana said, and walked into the room.

Jared's valet, engaged in placing linen in the wardrobe, discreetly disappeared at Jared's slight nod.

Standing near the window, Jared said curtly, "Well, Diana? Why have you come? I thought we'd settled matters between us." He made no move to approach her.

Her hands clenched tightly together, Diana said in a low voice, "I've come to ask you to forgive me."

"Oh? For suspecting I killed your brother? You've changed your mind about my guilt?"

"Yes. I know you didn't kill Miles. You *couldn't* have killed him. You're not capable of murder. I must have been temporarily deranged to doubt you for one second."

Diana stood as if rooted to the floor, looking pleadingly at Jared. For several moments he stared back at her, his face an unreadable mask. Then the mask slipped, and he held out his arms to her. She rushed to throw herself into his embrace.

"Darling, my darling," Jared muttered, "I thought I'd lost you, and I didn't much care if I'd lost everything else, too."

His eager lips sought hers and his hard body crushed her tender flesh, and as the familiar fire engulfed them he swept her up and deposited her on the bed. He untied the ribbons of her bonnet and tossed it to the floor, and his unsteady fingers tore at the buttons of her pelisse. Suddenly he paused. "My God, Diana," he said huskily, "I can't make love to you here. The damned turnkey could come in at any moment."

Drowning in a wave of desire, Diana whispered, "Hang the turnkey. Your valet and Rose will keep him out, and if they don't, who cares? I want you, Jared."

Diana sat at her desk in the morning room, staring at the wall. She was ostensibly doing the household accounts, but all she could think of was Jared. It was almost a week since he had been brought to London and imprisoned at Newgate. During that time Serjeant-at-Law Bannerman had visited his client twice. On these occasions Bannerman had seemed encouraging, even confident, but both Jared and Diana had sensed the counsel's belief that the circumstantial case against Jared was very strong.

Diana came out of her brown study as the footman announced, "Mr. Mukherjee is here, Yer Grace. Will you see him?"

"Oh, yes. Send him in."

Kamal swept into the room, carrying with him an unmistakable air of excitement.

Diana jumped up saying eagerly, "You've done something discovered something, that will help Jared?"

Kamal hesitated. Some of his excitement evaporated. "First I should explain the situation, Your Grace. You recall that Mr Amberly was wounded on a business trip to the Channel coast some weeks ago?"

"I certainly do. Jared almost died."

"Well . . . Mr. Amberly won't like my telling you this. . . . You see, that business trip was illegal. Mr. Amberly and I were transporting gold to the coast for the purpose of smuggling it across the Channel to France."

"Oh." Diana's eyes widened. "That's the reason for Jared's mysterious trips."

"Yes, Your Grace. We send gold to the Continent to take advantage of higher exchange rates. I might add that many reputable bankers and merchants engage in the practice, including the Rothschild family, of whom you may have heard. The fact remains, however, that the trade is illegal. During our last gold run to the coast, Mr. Amberly and I were attacked by thieves. We beat them off, though Mr. Amberly was seriously wounded. One of the thieves died in the attack. He turned out to be, not a local man, but a London resident. Since then I've been investigating the incident."

"But why?" Diana asked, her expression puzzled.

"Mr. Amberly considered that the participation of a Londoner in the attack was suspicious. It seemed to indicate an outside interest in our activities. He was quite correct. Yesterday I tracked down the widow—or, I should probably say, the leman—of the dead thief. She's a sot, and almost certainly a slut. Her neighbors say that until recently she was spending money freely."

"I don't understand, Kamal. What does this woman have to do with Jared's arrest and trial?"

Kamal said patiently, "Mr. Amberly and I suspected that this attack on him was aimed, not merely at the theft of our gold, but at Mr. Amberly's death."

Diana gasped. "But why. . . . ? Who . . . ?"

"Mr. Amberly's tremendous success in London financial circles, in so short a time, has been unprecedented. He may well have made enemies, who preferred to have him out of the way. At any rate, when Mr. Amberly was arrested for murder, I naturally wondered if this was another attempt to get rid of him by making him the scapegoat for a murder he didn't commit."

"And you think this woman—the widow of the dead thief—might help you prove that?"

"I'd been hopeful, yes. Unfortunately, when I went to see her yesterday, she wouldn't talk to me. I think she distrusted the color of my skin, or my accent—something about me that was different. However, I'm convinced she knows something."

"So what can we do?"

Kamal cleared his throat. "I think this woman—her name is Peg Sands—might talk to you, rather than to a foreigner like me. Doubtless she'd be impressed to meet a real live English duchess. I must warn you, though, that this Peg lives in Whitechapel, in one of the worst criminal 'rookeries' in London. You could be in real danger if you went there."

"Jared is in real danger of going to the gallows," Diana retorted. "Just let me get my bonnet and pelisse, and—did you come in a carriage?"

"I came here in a hackney, but I took the liberty of ordering Mr. Amberly's town carriage. I rather thought you would decide to visit Peg Sands."

Diana gave him a grim smile. "You know me quite well. I'll be with you in five minutes."

"Good. Oh, and Your Grace, I realize you're in mourning, and wearing day dress, but could you wear an expensive piece of jewelry? Diamonds, perhaps. It might catch the eye of Peg Sands."

When Diana walked out to the carriage drawn up in front of the house she paused, looking intently at the two footmen waiting on the pavement. "I don't recognize these men," she said to Kamal, raising an inquiring eyebrow.

He nodded. "They're clerks from the bank, Your Grace, and they're armed." He patted his pocket. "As I am."

Her eyes widening, Diana made no further comment. She sat quietly beside Kamal in the carriage as it proceeded along Oxford Street into Holborn and Cheapside and Fenchurch Streets to Whitechapel High Street. Diana had rarely ventured into this part of London, and she marveled at the sheer volume of traffic on the High Street. Coaches arriving or departing from the many coaching inns that lined the street jostled for position with farm carts and haywains and flocks of cattle and sheep.

Away from the busy commercial activity of the High Street

he area disintegrated into a maze of mean streets, strewn with
efuse and populated by vacant-eyed, poorly dressed men,
nearly naked children and tired-looking women, many of them
clearly suffering from the effects of cheap gin.

Kamal stopped the carriage at the entrance to a narrow, winding alley, barely wide enough for two people to pass abreast.
He helped Diana down the steps and nodded to the two footmen,
who dismounted from their perch and stood beside the carriage,
gazing around them with watchful eyes.

"In here," Kamal murmured, taking Diana's arm. He guided
her into the alley, around piles of garbage and pools of odorous
liquid that she refused to attempt to identify, to a small court
ringed by ramshackle houses that seemed in imminent danger
of collapsing. Kamal knocked on the door of one of the houses.
There was no answer, but Diana and Kamal could hear the
sound of steps inside. Kamal knocked again.

A thin woman with disheveled hair, wearing a soiled cotton
dress, opened the door. She reeked of spirits. Diana couldn't
determine how old the woman was. She might have been
younger than her beaten-down appearance indicated. The moment she saw Kamal, she snapped, "I ain't got nuffing ter say
ter ye," and started to close the door.

Kamal put his foot in it. "If you won't talk to me, Peg, perhaps you'd care to talk to this lady. She's the Duchess of Edgehill, and she might be willing to make the conversation worth
your while."

The woman's eyes fastened on the flash of diamonds at Diana's throat. "A duchess? A real duchess in this place?" She
stepped back. "Come in, then."

The small room shocked Diana. It was filthy beyond imag-
ining, and contained practically no furniture except for a table
and several rickety chairs. A flight of stairs led up to what was
presumably a bedroom. The table was littered with soiled,
grease-congealed dishes and several empty bottles. Another
empty bottle lay on its side on the floor.

"Well?" said Peg truculently. "Wot did ye wish ter talk aboot,
my fine lady?"

Diana nodded to Kamal, who began the conversation. "You

are Peg Sands, the widow of one Joseph Sands, who died re cently in Folkestone while attempting a robbery?"

Tossing her head, Peg replied, "So wot if I be? Ain't no crim ter being a widder woman, as I knows of."

"No, of course not. The duchess and I have no wish to mak trouble for you, I assure you. However, we have reason to be lieve that your husband had information that might be usefu to us."

"Oh? And wot might that be, may I ask?"

"We think your husband was hired, together with a numbe of other men, to go down to Folkestone to attack and rob certain well-known London banker."

From the woman's involuntary intake of breath and chang of expression, Diana knew that Kamal's words had struck home However, Peg shook her head, declaring, "I don't know nuffin aboot sich fings."

Diana said quickly, "We know you had nothing to do wit any—any criminal acts, Mrs. Sands. We merely want informa tion about the man who hired your husband and his friends t injure the banker. We're prepared to pay handsomely for sucl information."

Peg Sands gave Diana a long, calculating look. "How hand somely?"

"That depends on how much the information is worth to us," Kamal intervened. "Now, I've heard—never mind how chanced to hear—that several men came to your house to enlis your husband in their scheme, and that you were present at th interview."

"An' if I was? I *told* Joe not ter git mixed up in somefin that were agin the law."

"I'm sure you did," said Kamal hastily. "You're a law-abidin woman. Your husband ignored your very sound advice. Th question is, can you tell us anything about these men that migh help us to identify them?"

"Weel . . ."

"For, say, fifty pounds?" The woman hesitated, and Kama added, "We could go as high as seventy-five pounds, perhaps if the information was helpful."

"Yes, all right. There was two fellers who came here one night. Gentry-coves, both on 'em. They told Joe as how this other gent had done somefing terrible, raped a respectable lady or somefing o' the sort, an' there was no way the law could reach the cove, so these two fellers was out ter see the man got what was coming ter 'im. Weel, Joe agreed as how he'd take on the job, and the two gents said fine an' they'd be sending word aboot the time an' place fer the job ter be done. Which they done, aboot two weeks later."

"What did these men look like?"

"As I was saying, they was both gentry-coves, dressed ter the nines—"

"Is this the likeness of one of them?" asked Kamal, taking an object from his pocket. Diana stiffened at the sight of the miniature of her brother that she had loaned to Kamal.

Peg Sands's eyes widened. "That's one o' 'em, sure enough."

"What did the other man look like?"

"He were tall an' slim, an' 'e 'ad gray eyes an' light 'air, not dark like t'other one."

"How did the men send word about when they wanted the 'job' done? Did they send a messenger?"

"Yes. One o' the young 'uns who live around these parts, wi' a note. Joe could read, he could."

Kamal's interest quickened. "Do you still have that note?"

"Oh, I dunno. Mebbe, mebbe not." Peg went to the table and pawed through its unappetizing-looking litter. " 'Ere it is." She handed Kamal a piece of paper that was stained by some unidentifiable substance.

Kamal tucked the note and the miniature back in his pocket. "Thank you, Mrs. Sands. You've been most helpful." He took out his purse and counted a number of bank notes into Peg's outstretched hand.

She thrust the money into her bodice. "Ye're sure I won't git inter trouble wi' the law?"

"I swear it. Goodbye. Come, Your Grace."

Diana retained her silence and her composure until she and Kamal had negotiated the noisome alley and reached the carriage. Kamal handed her up the steps, the two "footmen" jumped up on their perch and the carriage moved off.

Only then did Diana vent her feelings. "I don't believe that woman," she said in a choked voice. "She must be mistaken. My brother had his faults, but he was no assassin. He couldn't have plotted to kill Jared. Why would he do such a thing?"

"Your brother might have felt that Mr. Amberly was crowding him to the wall financially, and I believe he blamed Mr. Amberly for his broken engagement," said Kamal quietly. "And what about the other man? Didn't Peg Sands's description remind you of someone you know?"

"Aubrey Dalton," replied Diana between stiff lips. "That could be sheer coincidence. Many men resemble Aubrey."

Kamal handed her the grimy, stained note, which read, "Be ready to act on Friday next at the Royal George Hotel in Folkestone. You will receive your pay when you complete the assignment."

"Do you recognize the handwriting, Your Grace?"

Diana whispered, "Yes. Aubrey wrote the note."

Nineteen

Jared and Serjeant-at-Law Bannerman rose hastily from their chairs beside the table serving as a desk when Diana rushed into Jared's room in the Keeper's quarters at Newgate.

"Diana, darling, what's the matter?" Jared exclaimed in dismay. "Are you ill? You're shaking like a leaf."

In a cracked voice, barely recognizable as her own, Diana said, "Kamal and I have just learned that Miles and Aubrey paid members of a London gang to kill you in Folkestone. There's no doubt. We have proof."

"Oh, my God. My love, I'm so sorry." Jared pulled Diana into his arms in a brief, comforting embrace.

To Bannerman, who was standing by, polite but puzzled, Jared explained, "Kamal is my head clerk. I was attacked in Folkestone not long ago on a—a business trip. At first I thought the motive for the attack was robbery. Then I learned that one of the attackers, who died in the incident, was a London man. I began to suspect that someone among my acquaintances in London wanted me not only poorer, but very dead. Now it turns out that the 'someone' was my own brother-in-law."

His lean, intelligent face creased in intense thought, Bannerman said slowly, "And you think your present predicament is the result of another attempt to get rid of you, this time by sending you to the gallows on a false murder charge."

Swallowing hard against the painful lump in her throat, Diana cried, "But that's ridiculous, if you mean that Miles and Aubrey conspired to have Jared arrested for murder. Oh, don't mistake me, I believe my brother and Aubrey were capable of almost anything," she added in a trembling voice. "I found out this morning how violent they could be. But in this case, how could they gain? Miles is *dead!*"

Bannerman gave her a keen look. "Let's examine the facts. The duke and I have just been reviewing the possible evidence against him, particularly in respect to Mr. Dalton's testimony. The duke tells me that Mr. Dalton feels almost as great a hostility toward him as did your brother. Do you agree?"

"Yes," said Diana after a moment's thought. "Aubrey was my brother's closest friend for many years. He would always have taken Miles's side in any dispute. He was convinced that Jared was maliciously persecuting Miles. And Aubrey had his own reasons for disliking Jared. He was furious when Jared beat him out for the seat on the Court of Directors of the East India Company."

"And don't forget, Diana, that Dalton has been madly in love with you for many years," put in Jared.

"Ah," said Bannerman with a look of quick comprehension. "In view of all these facts you don't consider it possible, Duchess, that Mr. Dalton might have killed your brother and then decided to blame the duke for the crime?"

"No," said Diana. Her shoulders slumped. "Not for a second. Haven't you been listening to me? Aubrey *adored* Miles. He wouldn't have hurt a hair on Miles's head."

"But supposing Mr. Dalton and your brother quarreled. Supposing, in the heat of the moment, Mr. Dalton produced a pistol and fired it, killing the duke. And then, aghast at what he had done, he decided, both to avoid punishment himself and to take revenge on a man he hated, to attempt to ensure that your husband would be indicted for the crime."

"Wait a moment, Mr. Bannerman," Jared interjected, frowning. "I just remembered something from the inquest. Diana, think back. Don't you recall that Dalton testified he told the justice of the peace 'he had reason to believe' I customarily carried a pistol? He couldn't have known that if he hadn't already learned from the thugs he and Miles hired to kill me in Folkestone that I did indeed carry a pistol as protection on my business trips. And one more bit of corroboration . . ."

He went to the door, giving a brief order to the turnkey who stood outside in the corridor. Soon Jared's valet entered the room. "Yes, Your Grace?"

"Moxon, think back to the time of the late duke's death at Abbottsleigh. Do you recall seeing anyone in or around my rooms, other than the servants? Anyone at all who had no reason to be in my apartments?"

Wrinkling his brow, the valet stood silent for a few moments. At last he said, "I remember seeing Mr. Dalton coming out of your bedchamber on one occasion."

"And was it after that the constable discovered the discharged pistol in my coat pocket?"

"Yes, yes it was." An injured expression flitted across the valet's face. "And I must tell you, Your Grace, that, while I didn't care to disturb you about such a small matter in your time of great loss, I'd like you to know that I do *not* neglect my duties. I always brush and clean your garments after each wearing, and I never fail to check your pockets. The constable discovered that pistol in the pocket of a coat you had worn the previous day, a coat whose pockets I had checked immediately after you removed the garment."

Jared smiled faintly. "Thank you, Moxon. You may go." Jared turned to Bannerman. The eyes of the two men met in perfect understanding.

"I don't understand," Diana said uncertainly. "Are you saying that Aubrey searched your luggage, Jared, found your pistol, took it somewhere to fire it, and then placed it in your pocket?"

"I fear so, love."

"I still don't understand. . . . The only explanation I can think of is that someone—an enemy we don't know about, a passing stranger—killed Miles for whatever reason, and Aubrey, coming on the scene, took advantage of the opportunity to incriminate you. But how will you ever prove that?"

Bannerman said quietly, "Unfortunately, Duchess, we don't yet know all the facts surrounding your brother's murder. I fancy the truth will only come out on the witness stand."

"And you think you can elicit the truth, Mr. Bannerman, by examining the witnesses?"

"I have some small skills in such matters," replied the serjeant, trying to appear modest and failing abysmally.

It was eight-thirty on the morning of Jared's trial for murder before the House of Lords. Diana stood with Rana and Kamal behind the Bar of the House among a crowd of perhaps a hundred and fifty spectators.

Diana had never previously appreciated the comparatively small size of the chamber occupied by the Lords. It was a rectangular room, perhaps eighty feet by forty feet, and on normal occasions was quite large enough to accommodate the rather small number of peers who attended the sessions. On this occasion, however, the Gentleman Usher of the Black Rod, in charge of the proceedings, had anticipated so much interest among the peers in this trial of one of their own accused of murdering a fellow member that he had ordered temporary stands erected above the benches lining both sides of the chamber.

Black Rod, also anticipating a great public interest in the trial, had allotted each peer a single daily ticket for spectators, the barons receiving tickets on one day, the remaining orders on alternate days. Diana had ruthlessly extracted tickets for herself and Rana and Kamal from her wide circle of acquaintances among the peerage.

The trial hadn't yet started. Immediately ahead of the Bar the various Counsels had already gathered, in robes and full wigs, Serjeant-at-Law Bannerman prominent among them, wearing his coif, a round piece of black silk perched on the top of his wig. He turned, catching sight of Diana, and gave her a confident smile. Behind the Counsels were seats for the witnesses, and, off to the side, a small table reserved for representatives from the newspapers.

"Look," Kamal whispered. "They're coming."

Into the chamber paraded slowly a line of peers, judges, and officers of the court, shepherded by the Garter King of Arms in his splendid tabard of red, blue, and gold. The Lord Chancellor of England in full wig and black robe took his place on the woolsack, an oblong box covered with red cloth, situated in front of the vacant throne.

With three low bows, the Clerk of the Crown in Chancery presented to the Chancellor a Commission under the Great Seal, appointing him to the position of Lord High Steward for the duration of the trial. The Lord High Steward handed the lengthy document back to the clerk to be read aloud, after which the Serjeant-at-Arms exclaimed "God save the King," and Garter King of Arms and Black Rod knelt to present to the Lord High Steward his staff of office.

The small crowd noises—the coughs, whispering, and murmured conversations—died away as the Gentleman Usher of the Black Rod, distinctive in his black frock coat with the white satin bows on his shoulders and carrying his ebony stick surmounted by a golden lion, escorted Jared into the chamber.

Diana looked at Jared with her heart in her eyes. She saw him for a moment, not as her lover, but as others saw him, tall, lithe, darkly handsome, faultlessly groomed, supremely poised. She remembered the moments last night in Jared's cell at Newgate, when she had clung to him, reluctant to leave.

"I'm so afraid of this trial, Jared," she'd whispered.

"Darling, don't be," he'd said, cradling her closer. "We know I didn't kill your brother."

"But we don't know who did kill Miles, and I don't see how Mr. Bannerman can solve the case in court. Jared, if anything were to happen to you I couldn't go on. You're all I have in the world now."

"You're not going to lose me, I swear it. We'll be together until we're ancient and hobbling, still loving each other so much that the rest of the world can't touch us."

And with that Diana had had to leave Newgate, only faintly comforted.

She watched now as Jared knelt respectfully at the Bar of the House, according to protocol, until the Lord Chancellor told him to rise.

In a hushed silence the Clerk of the Parliaments read the arraignment: "Jared Richard Amberly, Earl of Brentford, Duke of Edgehill, a peer of the United Kingdom of Great Britain and

Ireland, you are accused of murdering and killing one Miles Philip Amberly, Earl of Brentford, Duke of Edgehill, a peer of the United Kingdom of Great Britain and Ireland, on the twenty-sixth day of July in the year of Our Lord one thousand eight hundred and eleven in the parish of Westbridge in the county of Oxfordshire. How say you, my lord Duke, are you guilty of the felony with which you are charged, or not guilty?"

Jared said in a low, clear voice, "Not guilty."

"How will you be tried?"

"By God and my peers."

The clerk replied, "God send your lordship a good deliverance," after which the Chancellor directed Jared to a stool within the Bar of the House.

Both Counsels made brief opening statements. The Attorney-General asserted he would prove that the defendant had both motive and opportunity to kill the deceased. Serjeant Bannerman declared that his client was innocent of the crime of which he was accused, and the juror-peers would soon be convinced of his innocence.

The first—and chief—witness for the prosecution was Aubrey Dalton, looking subdued and serious, and giving the impression that he was very conscious of performing his civic duty.

"Mr. Dalton, you were acquainted with the victim in this case, the late Duke of Edgehill?"

"I was, indeed. I was on intimate terms of friendship with Miles—who was then the Earl of Brentford—for many years. Our friendship began when we were students at Eton."

"Are you acquainted with the defendant?"

"I am. He—I knew him as Jared Amberly—was also a student at Eton."

"Let us, for purposes of clarity, refer for the time being to the victim as Lord Brentford and to the defendant as Mr. Jared Amberly. Now, then, Lord Brentford and Mr. Amberly also knew each other?"

"Oh, yes."

"How would you describe their relationship at that time?"

"I would say they were very unfriendly."

"Please explain."

Aubrey described a number of rancorous incidents that had taken place between Miles and Jared in their student days, culminating with the incident in which Jared had been ignominiously ejected from a ball at Amberly House.

"Mr. Dalton, what was your impression of the defendant's attitude toward Lord Brentford during their years at Eton?"

"Jared Amberly bitterly resented Lord Brentford's refusal to become friends with him. He particularly resented his exclusion from the Amberly family circle."

"Tell me, Mr. Dalton, did you continue to have contact with Mr. Amberly after your school days?"

"No. I believe he returned to India for some years. I learned about a year ago that he was back in England."

"Did he then renew his acquaintance with you and Lord Brentford?"

Aubrey's mouth twisted. "You could say so, after a fashion. Amberly proceeded to conduct a vendetta against Lord Brentford. He bought up all of Lord Brentford's debts, with the object of forcing Miles's father, the Duke of Edgehill, to bar the entail to the Amberly estates so that he, Amberly, could acquire possession of them."

Serjeant-at-Law Bannerman rose with a graceful languor. "I must protest, my lord, against the witness's remarks. Pure hearsay."

The Chancellor cast an inquiring eye on the Attorney-General, who waved a piece of paper, saying, "I have here a letter from the victim to Mr. Dalton, confirming the latter's testimony, which I ask permission for Mr. Dalton to read aloud."

The Chancellor nodded, and Aubrey read the short letter: "Aubrey, old fellow, with your Treasury experience, can you help me to a source of some ready rhino? That fiend, Jared Amberly, has bought up all my promissory notes, and he's trying to force Papa to bar the entail so he can lay his dirty fingers on the Amberly estates."

The Chancellor said mildly, "This letter is demonstrably in the late Duke of Edgehill's handwriting?"

Bannerman rose to say, "My lord, we will stipulate that the late duke wrote the letter."

The Attorney-General went on, "What happened next, Mr. Dalton?"

"Miles—Lord Brentford—fought a duel with Jared Amberly. Miles was painfully, but not seriously wounded."

"We come now to the period immediately preceding the victim's death." The Attorney-General guided Aubrey through an account of Miles's quarrel with Jared on the evening before Miles died. "Tell us what you remember of the events of the next day."

"Well, the next morning I slept a trifle late, had breakfast, and joined the Duchess of Edgehill in the gardens. She informed me that her husband had gone off to a meeting with Miles, and that she felt somewhat alarmed about the outcome of the meeting, in view of the intensity of the quarrel between the two men on the previous evening. I shared her alarm, so when she asked me to accompany her to the place of the meeting, I gladly agreed."

"And?"

"We found the defendant—the present duke—standing over the dead body of the victim, who had been shot in the chest."

"Did you see a weapon?"

"No, but—"

"That will be all, Mr. Dalton," said the Attorney-General hastily. "I have no further questions for you."

"Do you care to cross-examine the witness, Mr. Bannerman?" inquired the Chancellor.

"Briefly, yes, my lord." Bannerman addressed Aubrey in a calm, almost disinterested tone. "Mr. Dalton, I wish to be sure I thoroughly understand your testimony. You have told us that the victim resented and disliked my client. What were your own feelings toward Mr. Amberly, as he then was?"

"I shared Miles's resentment. Amberly was persecuting my friend."

"But you had no personal reason to dislike Mr. Amberly?"

"He wasn't the type of person I would choose to be friendly with, but no, I had no personal reason to dislike him."

"You felt no animosity toward Mr. Amberly when he defeated you for a post on the Court of Directors of the East India Company?"

Aubrey reddened. "I certainly thought I was more qualified for the position than he was."

"I see. Let us proceed to the day of the murder. You had no contact with the late duke that morning until the actual moment when you and the duchess discovered the body?"

"That is correct."

"Thank you, Mr. Dalton." To the Chancellor, Bannerman added, "My lord, I reserve the right to question this witness more fully later."

The Chancellor bowed his head, and the Attorney-General called his next witness, a Doctor Lucius Penrod. After being sworn, Dr. Penrod testified that he had been the attending doctor at the duel in which the Earl of Brentford had fought Jared Amberly.

"What was the outcome of that duel, Doctor?"

"Lord Brentford was wounded before he could fire a shot."

"What was the nature of Lord Brentford's wound?"

"A bullet struck the ground immediately in front of Lord Brentford's foot, producing agonizing and immobilizing pain."

"Would you say the shot demonstrated expert marksmanship?"

The doctor smiled thinly. "I would not. It was a very poor shot—and a very lucky one."

"Thank you, Doctor. You are excused."

Bannerman rose to cross-examine the witness. "Please tell us, Doctor, who issued the challenge in this duel."

"I believe Mr. Amberly was the challenger."

"Even so, let us suppose that Mr. Amberly took part in the duel merely to satisfy his honor. In your opinion, could he have fired his pistol in such a way as to put Lord Brentford out of action, but not to wound him seriously?"

"I do not," snapped the doctor. "It's my belief that Mr. Amberly had every intention of wounding his man."

Bannerman shrugged, and sat down.

The next witness, scruffy and obviously uncomfortable with his surroundings, took the oath.

"You are Henry Mason, presently employed as a constable in the village of Westbridge in Oxfordshire?"

"Yes, sir—my lord."

"Sir Robert will be quite sufficient," said the Attorney-General dryly. "Now, then, on the day following the murder of the Duke of Edgehill, were you instructed by the justice of the peace to perform certain duties at the estate of Abbottsleigh?"

"Yes, sir. The justice, he told me to search the apartments o' the Duke o' Edgehill. That would be the new duke, the one ye've been calling Mr. Amberly."

"And what did you find, if anything?"

"I found a pistol that had recently been fired in the pocket o' one o' the duke's coats."

"Thank you, Constable."

Serjeant Bannerman then addressed the constable. "Did the justice of the peace tell you why he wanted the duke's apartments searched?"

"Well, yes, he did, sir. The justice, he told me that a gentleman named Dalton had informed him that the duke usually carried a pistol."

After the constable was dismissed, the Attorney-General turned to the Chancellor. "That is the case for the Crown, my lord."

The Chancellor consulted his watch. "It is now a quarter past noon. I will adjourn the proceedings for one hour. Upon our return, Mr. Bannerman, will you be prepared to act for the defense?"

"I will, indeed, my lord."

Diana felt tired and cramped from so many hours of standing among a close press of people. She was glad to walk with Kamal and Rana to her carriage, which they had left on a side street near the Abbey. There they sat down in comfort to eat the lunch that Diana had brought with her.

"The sahib knows you are present at his trial, my lady," Rana observed shyly. "I saw him looking at you. He must have felt comforted to know you were near."

"I hope so, Rana. Kamal, how do you think the trial is going?"

"About as Mr. Bannerman expected it to go, I think. He warned us that the prosecution would present His Grace in the worst light."

Diana said, frowning slightly, "I thought Mr. Bannerman was overly gentle with Aubrey."

Kamal shrugged. "We can only trust the Serjeant. Wait until he recalls Mr. Dalton for questioning."

But, after the adjournment, the first witness Bannerman called was a complete stranger to Diana, a man named Thomas Montague.

"Mr. Montague, you know my client, the Duke of Edgehill, who is on trial here today?"

"We're actually casual acquaintances. We see each other at Manton's Shooting Galleries."

"You have shot against the duke?"

"I have. He's a crack shot. I've seen him split the edge of a playing card."

"Do you consider him capable of aiming a bullet into the ground at the very tip of a man's boot?"

"Definitely. The duke is the best marksman I know."

"So if you knew that the duke, engaged in a duel, had fired such a shot, what would be your impression?"

Mr. Montague replied promptly, "I would conclude that the duke, reluctant to inflict serious injury on his opponent, had, in effect, deloped."

"Thank you, Mr. Montague."

"No questions," said the Attorney-General.

The next witness was Jeb Rice. Diana tensed at the sight of him.

Mr. Bannerman said genially, "You are Jeb Rice, and you are employed in the stables of the Duke of Edgehill's estate of Abbottsleigh?"

"Yes, sir."

"On the morning of the late duke's death, were you working in the stables?"

"Yes, sir."

"You saw the duke that morning?"

"Yes. He come ter the stables aboot nine or a bit before. I saddled a horse fer him, and he rode off."

"Was he alone?"

"No, sir. his friend, Mr. Dalton was wi' him. They rode off tergether. Mr. Dalton, he come back by hisself aboot an hour later."

"Thank you. Your witness, Sir Robert."

Diana stole a look at Aubrey, sitting among the witnesses. He had suddenly tensed.

Frowning, the Attorney-General spoke sternly to the stable-hand. "Are you positive, Jeb Rice, that the late duke and Mr. Dalton were together on that particular morning? After all, I understand that Mr. Dalton was a frequent guest at Abbottsleigh. You may have confused the times."

"No, sir, I didn't. Y'see, I'm not likely ter fergit anything that happened the day the master died."

The Attorney-General gave it up, and Bannerman called John Moxon.

"Mr. Moxon, you are employed by the defendant, the Duke of Edgehill, as his valet?"

"I am."

"Please describe in general detail how you care for your employer's clothing."

"After each wearing, I brush and clean the duke's garments and check that the pockets are empty."

"Have you ever found a pistol in the duke's pockets?"

"No, sir."

"Now, then, on the day following the murder of the late duke, were you pursuing your usual duties?"

"Yes, sir."

"Did anything out of the ordinary occur that day?"

"Yes, sir. I was returning to my duties after eating my lunch, and as I came down one corridor I saw Mr. Aubrey Dalton coming out of the duke's apartments."

"Was this before or after Constable Rice discovered a pistol in a pocket of the duke's coat?"

"Several hours before."

Kamal nudged Diana. She glanced at Aubrey. His face looked pinched, and his skin had turned ashen.

On his cross-examination, the Attorney-General said sharply to the valet, "Do you know why Mr. Dalton visited your master's rooms?"

"No, sir."

"Mr. Dalton may simply have been searching for the duke, perhaps to discuss the family funeral arrangements?"

"I daresay, sir."

"That will be all."

The presence of Peg Sands in the witness box caused a minor stir in the chamber. She was wearing a clean gown, and she had made an attempt to arrange her hair neatly, but her general appearance was still disreputable. Diana looked at Aubrey. He was in shock. He might have been staring at a ghost.

Bannerman handled his witness gently. "Mrs. Sands, I believe you are the widow of one Joseph Sands. When did your husband die, and in what circumstances?"

Peg muttered an incoherent phrase, and Bannerman prompted her. "You must speak up, Mrs. Sands."

"My husband died in Folkestone a few months back. The authorities, they said Joe was killed while he was trying ter rob a gent by the name o' Amberly."

"Do you believe your husband was indeed engaged in such a crime?"

"Yes," Peg replied sullenly.

"Why do you believe that?"

" 'Cause two gents come ter my house not long before ter talk ter Joe. They said as how they wanted somebody killed—a banker name o' Amberly—and they wanted the killing ter look like a robbery. They offered Joe a hundred pound ter collect a few o' his friends ter do away wi' this Amberly."

"And your husband agreed?"

"Yes. Mind, I *told* 'im not ter git mixed up wi' the law."

"I'm sure you did. Did you know the identity of the two men who proposed this crime to your husband?"

"No. Never saw 'em before nor since."

The Serjeant took an object out of his pocket. "I have here

a miniature painting." He handed it to Peg. "Do you recognize this man?"

Looking at the miniature carefully, Peg said, "Yes, he was one o' the two men who hired my husband ter kill that Amberly feller."

The Chancellor intervened. "Mr. Bannerman, may I see the miniature?" After a long look, the Chancellor said in a bemused voice, "Bless my soul. Unless I'm mistaken, Mr. Bannerman, this is a likeness of the late Duke of Edgehill, the victim in this case."

"Yes, my lord. So I believe."

A low murmur of shocked surprise swept through the chamber.

Returning the miniature, the Chancellor said, "Please continue, Mr. Bannerman."

"Thank you, my lord. Mrs. Sands, can you describe the second of the two men who visited your husband?"

"I kin do better'n that. I kin show 'im ter ye." Peg pointed dramatically. "There he be, asitting wi' the witnesses."

"To whom are you pointing, Mrs. Sands?"

"At that yeller-haired gent in the first row. Name o' Dalton."

Aubrey leaped to his feet, shouting, "The slut's lying in her teeth."

The Chancellor said calmly, "You're out of order, Dalton. Please sit down. Mr. Bannerman, do you have any further questions for this witness?"

"No, my lord."

"Sir Robert, do you care to cross-examine?"

Obviously shaken, the Attorney-General said to Peg, "My good woman, you have made some very serious accusations against two men, one of whom is dead and cannot defend himself. The other is a highly respected member of society. I submit that someone paid you to make these accusations."

Peg tossed her head. "I'm an law-abiding woman, I am. Ain't nobody paid me ter tell lies. I seen what I seen."

His jaw clenched, the Attorney-General turned away.

Bannerman said in a ringing voice, "My lord, I recall Mr. Aubrey Dalton to the stand."

Aubrey was clearly in a state of nervous shock. he stumbled like an old man as he made his way to the witness box. He stared at Bannerman, saying shrilly, "I want it on the record that I categorically deny the lies that woman told. The slut is trying to ruin my good name."

"As to that, Mr. Dalton, the jurors may choose to believe or disbelieve Mrs. Sands's story. I should like to review your earlier testimony. You said you did not have any contact with the late duke on the morning of his death. And yet the stableman has informed us that you rode out with the duke at about nine o'clock that morning, and that you returned alone about an hour later. How do you account for this discrepancy?"

"The stableman is lying, too," Aubrey said sullenly. "Probably Jared Amberly bribed him to make that statement. After all, the man works for Amberly now, and he'd do anything to curry favor with his new employer."

"Let us go on to another subject. My client's valet has testified that he saw you coming out of the duke's rooms a short time before the village constable found a recently discharged pistol in one of the duke's pockets. I suggest to you that you placed that pistol in the duke's pocket for the purpose of incriminating him in the murder of his predecessor."

"I did no such thing. I admit I came to Amberly's rooms to talk to him, as you yourself suggested, about the funeral arrangements for Miles. Amberly wasn't there, so I came away. Why in God's name would I wish to plant a false clue against the present duke?"

"Ah, that's the crux of the matter, is it not, Mr. Dalton? Let me put to you what I believe the jurors will consider a plausible solution to this case. According to the testimony of Mrs. Sands, you and the duke had tried once to have Jared Amberly killed, and you had failed. You yourself told the court that the late duke believed that his brother-in-law was continuing to press him financially. I put it to you that the duke enlisted your help to get rid of Mr. Amberly once and for all. The duke arranged a meeting with Mr. Amberly at the ruined abbey in the Abbottsleigh park, on the pretense of making up their quarrel. You, Mr. Dalton, were to be in hiding, ready to shoot Mr. Amberly when he appeared. The duke's story would then be that Mr. Amberly became angry and threatened the duke with a pistol, at which point the duke had no recourse but to shoot Mr. Amberly in self-defense."

Bannerman paused, staring intently at Aubrey, who seemed mesmerized by the Serjeant-at-Law's statements, almost like a cobra listening to the piping of a snake charmer. "But something went very wrong with the scheme, didn't it, Mr. Dalton? You and the duke quarreled, you pulled pistols on each other, and you killed the duke. You then left the scene, taking both pistols with you, and returned to the house. Subsequently, in order to hide your own guilt, you did your best to incriminate Mr. Amberly as the killer."

Suddenly Aubrey broke. "That isn't the way it happened," he screamed. "I never wanted to kill Miles. He was the best friend I had in the world. There was only one pistol. At the last minute Miles decided he wanted to fire the shot that killed Amberly, and he snatched the gun from me. I tried to get it away from him, because he was the world's worst shot, and I knew he'd bungle the job. The pistol went off, and the next thing I knew Miles was lying on the ground dead—"

Aubrey stopped short, his mouth working. He stared wildly around him.

"My lord, the defense rests," said Bannerman.

Stonily avoiding looking at Aubrey, the Lord Chancellor asked the Attorney-General, "Do you wish to make a summation, Sir Robert?"

"Under the circumstances, no, my lord."

"Mr. Bannerman?"

"No, my lord."

"Then, Clerk of the Parliaments, please call the roll."

The Clerk called on every peer in turn, beginning with the most junior of the barons, asking each of them, "Do you find Jared Amberly, Duke of Edgehill, Earl of Brentford, guilty or not guilty of the crime of murder?"

Several hundred peers rose, one by one, to say, "Not guilty upon my honor."

Pandemonium erupted in the chamber. Diana, ignoring attempts by court officials to stop her, burst past the Bar of the House to throw herself into Jared's arms.

"Darling, darling, you're safe," she said tearfully. "I've prayed so hard—I'll never ask God for anything else as long as I live."

"And as long as I have you, I'll never need to ask Him for a favor," Jared said huskily.

ZEBRA REGENCIES
ARE
THE TALK OF THE TON!

A REFORMED RAKE   (4499, $3.99)
by Jeanne Savery

After governess Harriet Cole helped her young charge flee to
France—and the designs of a despicable suitor, more trouble soon
arrived in the person of a London rake. Sir Frederick Carrington
insisted on providing safe escort back to England. Harriet
deemed Carrington more dangerous than any band of brigands,
but secretly relished matching wits with him. But after being
taken in his arms for a tender kiss, she found herself wondering—
could a lady find love with an irresistible rogue?

A SCANDALOUS PROPOSAL   (4504, $4.99)
by Teresa DesJardien

After only two weeks into the London season, Lady Pamela
Premington has already received her first offer of marriage. If
only it hadn't come from the *ton's* most notorious rake, Lord
Marchmont. Pamela had already set her sights on the distinguished Lieutenant Penford, who had the heroism and honor that
made him the ideal match. Now she had to keep from falling
under the spell of the seductive Lord so she could pursue the man
more worthy of her love. Or was he?

A LADY'S CHAMPION   (4535, $3.99)
by Janice Bennett

Miss Daphne, art mistress of the Selwood Academy for Young
Ladies, greeted the notion of ghosts haunting the academy with
skepticism. However, to avoid rumors frightening off students,
she found herself turning to Mr. Adrian Carstairs, sent by her
uncle to be her "protector" against the "ghosts." Although,
Daphne would accept no interference in her life, she *would* accept
aid in exposing any spectral spirits. What she never expected was
for Adrian to expose the secret wishes of her hidden heart . . .

CHARITY'S GAMBIT   (4537, $3.99)
by Marcy Stewart

Charity Abercrombie reluctantly embarks on a London season in
hopes of making a suitable match. However she cannot forget the
mysterious Dominic Castille—and the kiss they shared—when he
fell from a tree as she strolled through the woods. Charity does
not know that the dark and dashing captain harbors a dangerous
secret that will ensnare them both in its web—leaving Charity to
risk certain ruin and losing the man she so passionately loves . . .

*Available wherever paperbacks are sold, or order direct from the
Publisher. Send cover price plus 50¢ per copy for mailing and
handling to Penguin USA, P.O. Box 999, c/o Dept. 17109,
Bergenfield, NJ 07621. Residents of New York and Tennessee
must include sales tax. DO NOT SEND CASH.*